Tim Dickinson is first and foremost a Yorkshire man. He studied art and worked as an advertising creative in London before living in the Middle East.

He wrote campaigns for the biggest international brands and worked alongside the richest men in the world. His life experience is vast, and he humbly admits "it's a jungle out there". After 50 years of being involved in the 'ad game', he is now retired and lives in the beautiful English Lake District. "The peace is a delight," he says. Tim is very much a family man, father of two sons and a very proud grandfather.

To Elizabeth and Lewis
Enjoy

Other Book by the Author

Tim Dickinson

Top Girl

The Ad Man

AUSTIN MACAULEY PUBLISHERS™

LONDON • CAMBRIDGE • NEW YORK • SHARJAH

A CIP catalogue record for this title is available from the British Library.

ISBN 9781528931458 (Paperback)
ISBN 9781528966689 (ePub e-book)

www.austinmacauley.com

First Published (2019)
Austin Macauley Publishers Ltd
25 Canada Square
Canary Wharf
London
E14 5LQ

Help

Her heart is pounding, like a steam engine. She wraps her arms around me and buries her face into my neck, 'terrified' is not a strong enough word to describe her. I lay on top of her in silence, not daring to move, my ears are straining to decipher what is going on only feet away. We are both praying the gang of drunken youths will stop chasing us and go home, but it doesn't seem likely. This rowing boat is by no means the ideal place in which to hide, but it was the only place we could think of. I managed to pull the boat's canvas tarpaulin over us, just before they rounded the corner, but they don't need a greyhound to find us.

I met this girl only 30 minutes ago; and here I am, laid on top of her in the bottom of a rowing boat, might I add in fear of my life. I can't even remember her name, she was just about to tell me when we had to run for our lives. She must be in her teens; I could get arrested for this. "Don't move, for God's sake, don't move," she whispers, "if they find me, they will rip me apart, they are animals." I am too scared to move even if I wanted to.

We can hear their footsteps pounding up and down the quay; they have reached the corner where we managed to lose them, they are angry and screaming abuse.

"Where the hell has she gone? I really fancy her, she must be here somewhere, she can't just disappear," one of them shouts.

"You're a randy pig, Michael, but I must admit she is sexy, and she owes us fifty quid," shouts another.

I despair at their behaviour; I can't understand why the young men of today get themselves into such a state. When I was their age, I didn't have enough money to drink till drunk. I didn't even want to, nor have I ever been on a pub-crawl or experienced an 18-30 holiday. My thoughts are racing through my head. I too am angry; and in my fright, I find myself laughing. I have never lain on top of a pretty girl in the bottom of a boat before; mmm! Maybe I have been missing out?

We can hear the boys snapping open more beer cans as they search the quay, if they walk another 20 yards, they will surely see us, and then what will I do?

"Hey look, there's a boat tied up over there, she might be hiding in it."

She whimpers, "Please help me, you have to help me." We can hear one of them climbing down the ladder onto the wooden pier to which we are tied. It's only a matter of seconds before he finds us.

How did I get myself into this ridiculous situation?

Earlier this evening, I was attending the mother of boring business dinners. I didn't want to go and knew it would be a big bore, yet it was my job to represent my company, and I recognised it as an opportunity to progress my career. Our biggest clients would be there, and my MD needed my support. He depended on me to know their names, which I would whisper in his ear if he started stammering. I saved him from embarrassment tonight. I stopped him referring to Lord James's wife as 'your secretary'. She was his secretary six months ago, but his wife caught him screwing her on his desk at the Christmas party and divorced him, so he promoted his secretary to Lady James Brown, or whatever the title is for the latest wife of a lord. Another reason for my being there tonight was to meet the marketing director of British Chemicals. Tomorrow morning, I am leading our agency presentation to his senior management team, in the hope of winning the British Chemicals advertising and marketing account. It is a piece of business we desperately need, its advertising budget alone is 20 million pounds. My boss' final instruction as we entered the hall was, "Gain this guy's trust, promise him the best service in the world. If that fails, buy him a villa overlooking the Arabian Gulf. Do what you have to do, Tim, to get his signature on the contract."

Anyway, I survived. I said 'hi' to the people who needed a 'hi', and I shook the hands of the people who needed their hands shaking. It was 11:30 when I escaped through the French windows into the garden, and that was when an uninspiring evening turned into a disastrous evening. As I rounded the corner where my car was parked, it raced passed me; driven by two men, dressed in ballerclarvers. It was my pride and joy: a 6 series BMW drop-top, I only took delivery of it three weeks ago. The salesman told me it had more security devices on it than a Hatton's Street Jewellers; yet someone had managed to nick it, probably by using an android key, which I believe can be purchased on the internet. The car will be on a ship to Eastern Europe by now. It took the police two hours to arrive, and then they spent 15 minutes checking my road tax and insurance details before putting out an all-car search, to their credit, they offered to drive me home.

"This is the work of a professional gang," the police officer told me. I had worked that out for myself, I didn't spend £63,000 on a new car for a kid to steal. I just hope they drive it carefully and don't scratch it.

"What are the chances of you finding it?" I asked him.

"None, sir, it will be on its way to Moscow within an hour."

I knew that as well. I refused their offer of a lift home, preferring to walk. I needed to clear my head; and as the night air was calm and refreshing, I hoped a walk across the millennium footbridge and around the marina would do just that.

As I step off the bridge, I hear the voice of a young woman. "Hello, sir, would you like a good time?" I look around in her direction, but there is no one.

"Hello, sir, you look as if you are in need of a good time. I can make you very happy. I'll do whatever you want; just don't hurt me." There are several people on the quay. One guy is swaying from side to side, much the worse for drink, I doubt he will make it home. There is also a young couple with their arms wrapped around each other, they stop to kiss every ten paces; sometimes it is only eight when the urge to fondle each other becomes too much to bear. I watch them enviously; right now, I could do with some affection. I search for the girl, but there is no one to be seen. For a moment, I doubt if I have heard the voice at all, maybe it is the sea breeze playing a game with me. It has been said that pirates and mermaids haunt the quay.

The marina is especially beautiful at this time of night. It poses a typical Victorian postcard scene, the cobblestones are glistening, like black pearls, reflecting the flickering flames from the mock antique gas lamps, which line the waterfront. The lights were erected last year and rightly won an environmental design award, the recent renovation of the marina is a triumph. The 18th century warehouses have been converted into luxury apartments and reported to be very desirable. They are occupied by a new generation of homeowner, young, confident, business go-getters. The architectural detail of the buildings is truly stunning, the circular windows of the old crane tower are a work of art, and the refurbished crane hoist, protruding from the roof, is a sculpture worthy of any museum of remembrance. Other features from times gone by are still evident, like the old crane tracks embedded in the road surface, and the cast iron chains and anchors hanging from the walls. This is truly a place of character and charm.

From the shadow of a doorway, a pair of bright red, high-heeled shoes, strapped to a pair of beautiful, slim, ankles step out into the light.

"Hello, sir, would you like a good time?" I turn towards her.

"Are you talking to me?" I ask.

"I can cheer you up." I hadn't realised I was so obviously depressed.

"What are you doing here all on your own, you should be at home at this time of night."

"Are you going to take me home, sir?"

"Not tonight, my dear… but you are quite right, I am not in a good mood." I turn to leave her.

"Don't go, sir. I can make you happy, sir, please let me make you happy."

Maybe I feel sorry for her, or am I feeling sorry for myself, but before I know it, I am walking back to her. In the light, she looks amazing. She is as appealing as she is persuasive; a pretty girl in her late teens; slim and sexy with long, black hair dangling down her back. A tight knitted jersey dress is gripping her body, stopping short of baring her essentials.

"Please stay and talk with me. I too am suffering a bad night. Please, sir, stay and talk with me."

It is really too cold to sit and talk. There is a chill in the breeze. This girl must be frozen, I offer her my scarf, which she accepts and hurriedly twists it around her neck.

"Let's sit over there." She points to a cast iron bench that faces out across the water. It backs onto a statue of Ludlow Leeming: a local lad, who single-handedly, saved the lives of 40 people on a freighter, on 19 November 1897. A ferocious gale was blowing in from the channel, and the 'Osprey' was desperately trying to reach safety. The delicate gas flame in the harbour beacon had been blown out; so young Ludlow Leeming set fire to a dilapidated wooden shack on the cliff, guiding the ship away from the danger of the jagged rocks and into the safety of the port. He was an instant hero, and the shipping company thought he should be remembered for his fast thinking and heroic action, so they made a statue of him. Engraved on the plinth, on which he stands, is a description of his deed. That's how I know what happened. Once again, he is doing a good deed by shielding us from the wind. As we huddle closer, a cat scurries out from between his feet and screeches down the quay. The girl grabs my arm tightly. "Stupid cat! It scared the living day-lights out of me," she screams.

"Me too." We laugh as our adrenalin slowly returns to something resembling normality.

"Where have you been tonight, sir?" She presses her body against me for warmth, I can feel her shaking. She smells divine, and her big green eyes send a tingle of excitement through my body. I tell her about my boring meeting and my misfortune with the car.

"So now I understand why you are walking across the marina at this late hour. I thought I hadn't seen you before. If I had seen you, sir, I would have remembered."

"Thank you, that is nice to know, what is your name?"

It isn't long before I am totally absorbed by her story, and my feeling sorry for her turns to admiration.

She tells me her name is Angela, and she is 20 years old, homeless, cold and fed up."

I find it difficult to totally believe her. She is too buoyant and obviously too intelligent for someone in such a desperate predicament.

"So where do you sleep, where will you sleep tonight?" I ask her.

"Sir, I wake up in a different place every morning. Sometimes, if I don't find a bed, I go to the hostel down the High Street. I know the janitor, he is a kind old man. He says he has a granddaughter my age and takes pity on me."

"Do you sleep with him?"

"Of course not, he must be 70 years old." Her laugh is magical.

"How long have you been living like this?" She puts her fingers to her mouth and thinks for a minute.

"Six months, yes, it was April, the days were warming up, I found it exciting at first. I got a job working at McDonald's but couldn't get the smell of burger and fries out of my hair, so I moved onto Marks & Spencer, but that only lasted a month, my line leader was a bitch and absolutely useless at her job. One day, I told her so and suggested she got another job, she hated me after that, and we argued every day. I lost, of course, one day, I called her a rude name, insulted her parents and threatened to slap her. I got the sack, and they wouldn't give me a testimonial."

"Why should they give you a testimonial when you were so disruptive?"

"Because I was right, she was useless." She took a deep breath. "Have you any idea how much unemployment benefit I get? I have to search the bins for food and steal skirts and blouses from the market."

Her shivering increases, it is time to move on. The air is much colder, and her little dress gives her no protection. If I was a gentleman, I should offer her my coat, but I am no Ludlow Leeming, but I unbutton it and wrap it around her shoulders. She cuddles into me.

"Is Angela your real name?" She pulls away from me.

"What is my name to you?" She is indignant and rightly so; I have no right to know.

"Sorry, I shouldn't have asked."

"It's okay, don't I look like an Angela?" I laugh; she is fun.

"You are more refined than any Angela I know. Your make-up has been artistically applied, and your hair is in perfect condition and your perfume… well, your perfume is exquisite, you have good taste."

"You are very observant and right, my full name is Angela Grace Rebecca Louise Baldwin."

"Goodness, couldn't your parents make up their mind." Her laugh is absolutely infectious.

"I never knew my real parents. I was adopted at the age of two. I suppose I am lucky, my stepfather is rich, he has a job in the government, but don't ask me what he does." My mind scans the ministers I have heard of.

"The only Baldwin I can recall is the Right Honourable George Baldwin: the secretary of state for works and pensions."

"That could be him, his name is George. Does he live in Yorkshire?"

I admit that this is true. "Yes, he owns a stately home in Yorkshire, I don't know its name. Come to think of it; you have a hint of a Yorkshire accent."

"That's because I too am from Yorkshire. This guy is probably my stepfather, we live at Haringey Hall."

"So what the hell are you doing here? Does he know you are living on the streets?"

We are interrupted by a group of drunken louts, staggering down the marina. Their singing, shouting and swearing is disgraceful. Angela jumps to her feet.

"Sir, I have to go. These guys made a pass at me, last night. They are not nice, they pushed a fifty-pound note down my blouse and started pulling me about. One of them, who they called Michael, tried to get up my skirt; and when I stopped him, he slapped me. I managed to break free and get away from them. They were too drunk to run after me." She grabs my hand and pulls me into the shadows. "Come on, we must go."

"Hey, that's the whore from last night," I hear one of them shout. "She owes us 50 quid, let's have our money's worth." He runs after us, but as luck will have it, he stumbles on the cobbles and rolls over squealing, like an injured pig.

I have to help her. In this drunken state, they are capable of doing anything. Maybe I could get the better of two of them but all five, I have no chance. She kicks off her shoes, and we run for our lives around the corner of the quay where we lose sight of them for a couple of seconds. I spot a boat tied to the end of the pier, it has a tarpaulin over it. If we can squeeze under it, maybe we can hide from them.

"Angela, this way, the little boat, can you see it?" She immediately understands my intention.

"Yes, let's hide in the boat, I am right behind you." We race down the boardwalk and scramble under the cover.

And that is how I find myself in this ridiculous situation.

A Close Shave

A look of terror crosses Angela's face; her grip is so tight I have to stop myself from yelling out. One of the guys jumps down onto the floating walkway and screams as he falls backwards into the water, a string of spluttering swear words are followed by an almighty splash.

"Bloody hell, Michael has fallen in, what an idiot." His mates laugh at his stupidity. "Well, I'm not pulling him out. He'll probably pull me in with him."

"I'm not getting wet to save him either," agrees another. "Come on, let's go home." We peer out through a gap in the tarpaulin and watch, one of them eventually comes back for him. They are only feet away from us. His thrashing of the water is rocking our boat. I don't know why he is creating such a fuss; the water is only three feet deep. We wrap our arms around each other in fear of the boat rolling over.

"Hey, help me, I can't swim."

"Michael, you really are an idiot, no wonder your father won't give you a seat on the board of the company."

"Shut up, and give me your coat." He makes a pitiful sight as he is dragged onto the wooden quay, his clothes sopping wet, and his trousers halfway down his legs. Thank goodness, he has lost his sexual urge and forgotten all about Angela.

"Wait for me, you bastards. I am soaking. Has someone got a coat, I will catch my death of cold." They all ignore him.

Goodness, one of these days, these guys could be running our country; I hope it's later rather than sooner. We lay in silence and watch him stagger after the others, towards the car park. After an argument as to who is sitting in the back with him, they drive off in a silver Volkswagen Golf.

"They shouldn't be driving, they are quite incapable," Angela whispers in my ear.

"Do we care?"

"Have they gone?"

"Yes, you are safe."

"Am I?" she asks, with a hint of a smile on her face.

"Of course you are."

"I am enjoying being with you, let's take this boat for a sail."

"Absolutely not."

She pulls back the cover, takes hold of the outboard motor and yanks at the engine chord. The motor bursts into life; and with a screech of the propeller, we rocket out into the channel.

"You are crazy, what do you think you are doing?"

"Having fun."

"Do you know how to drive a boat?"

"I have been watching these boats for the last four weeks; and anyway, we have a yacht in Nice." She turns up the power, raising the bow out of the water and screams with delight as I roll about in the bottom of the hull for a second time.

"Where do you live?" she shouts, trying to be heard over the screaming propeller.

"In the next marina," I shout back. "I have an apartment next to the old clock tower."

"I know it, let's go home." And with that, I am thrown into the bottom of the boat for a third time as she spins it around and heads towards the clock tower.

"Should we tie the boat to the quay?" I ask as I clamber out.

"I threw the rope away, let's go home; I need a pee."

Just Doing My Job

"Hurry up in the bathroom, will you, I need to use it."
It has been a year since I shared an apartment with a woman; I have forgotten the first rule of male survival: 'If you both need the loo at the same time, go first.'

My phone gives out a lion's roar; I have a different call for each friend; which represents them in some way or another. I know this call is from my boss, a call from my ex-wife is an 'air-raid warning'. If she had known that, we would have been divorced many years earlier. I take the phone from my pocket, and the screen confirms the call is from my boss.

"Tim, it's Isaiah, I hope I haven't woken you."

"Not at all, sir. I was just putting the finishing touches to the 'British Chemicals' presentation." I am pretty good at lying when needs must. "I just wanted to add a few facts after speaking with John Daley at the conference, this evening."

"Oh! Is that his name? I couldn't remember it. Is he their marketing director?"

"Yes, sir."

"I remember him now, a nice guy. He likes you a lot, Tim. I don't know what you were telling him, but he was very impressed with you. He says we are only competing against the incumbent agency, and their biggest failure is a lack of ideas on development and expansion. Apparently, they only answer the brief, which they do very well, but they never innovate or contribute to the marketing plans. I told him that would not be the case if they were to work with you, as you are full of ideas. He was pleased; in fact, he was excited; he said he hopes you will be on the team."

"Well, sir! I wanted to speak with you about that. I don't mind leading the presentation, but I don't want to work on the account, should we win it. The thought of selling chemicals bores me silly. I would much rather be working on a consumer brand than with a business-to-business client."

"Nonsense, Tim. This will be a big opportunity for you, with a ten million pound account on your arm. You will be running this agency next year, your future is bright."

"We will see, sir, but bare it in mind. Did he say anything else about the incumbent agency?"

"Nothing of importance… only."

"Only what?"

"Only his CEO is screwing the agency's PR girl."

"What can I do about that?"

"I don't know, Tim. Employ her if you have to. You will think of something. Anyway, well done tonight, see you in the office in the morning. Good night, Tim."

"Good night, sir." My attention is drawn back to the matter in hand.

"Have you finished in there, whatever you are doing?"

"I'm having a bath, your bathroom is beautiful."

"Having a bath! Oh my God."

I survive the wait, and as she climbs into bed next to me, I find it very difficult to concentrate on tomorrow's presentation.

"Do you want to make love to me?" she whispers.

"No!"

"No! Why not?"

"I don't know you."

"What has that got to do with it?"

"I need to know who you are." I pause for a second. "Okay, you have ten minutes to tell me who you are."

Mid-Life Crisis

Louise Buchanan pulls her legs up to her stomach and rolls over, but sleep is a distant objective, she is tossing and turning nervously. Her head aches as she tries to make sense of her life. She has everything a woman in her mid-40s could dream of. More money than she knows what to do with, a beautiful daughter aged 20, a son at university, a beautiful car, an amazing home and freedom which enables her to take regular shopping trips to Cannes, Milan, New York and Paris. Sometimes, she goes alone; sometimes, she takes her younger sister. There is only five years between them; but at 45, Louise is jealous of her younger sister, who is taller, slimmer and prettier. Yes, there is no denying it; she is beautiful. This is proven by the attention she receives from men much younger than herself, they come on to her in every coffee house and wine bar they visit. Collette could pass for 30. When the two of them stop over in a hotel, she will arrive for breakfast, accompanied by a young hulk; she has been known to arrive with two. They will have a broad smile on their faces, and so they should, she is quite a catch.

Louise is also beautiful, but she thinks she is past her sell-by date, which isn't the case. The years have been good to her, her figure is slim, her face almost creaseless, her energy and enthusiasm... well, in comparison with her sister, it is waning slightly. Going out with her sister isn't doing Louis' confidence any good. If only her husband came home more often to give her the attention she deserves, but he is a busy man. He has an important job in the chemical industry and is also a member of parliament. This means he spends most nights away, usually in the city, which is why Louise is in her silk, sheeted circular bed all alone. She can't remember the last time he made love to her. When he is home, he is too exhausted to fire her passion. He tells her he loves her, and she believes him, but words are no longer enough.

Her days are full. She runs several charities, including 'Homes for Battered Mothers', 'Poverty in Asia'; and the campaign to renovate the leaning steeple of the parish church, which includes coffee mornings, raffles, bazaars, and bring and buy sales. She is chairwoman of the local WI and has even spoken at the European Parliament on 'The place of the women in modern society'. For relaxation, she goes horse riding and takes her favourite horse Jollaper for a canter, across the common, as often as she can. Jollaper is actually her daughter's horse. They gave it to her as a graduation gift, but at the moment, she is backpacking around the world, doing what rich girls do during their gap years; this month, she is in Cambodia. Louise cherishes the relationship she has with her daughter and feels closer to her when she is riding Jollaper.

Her mobile beeps with an incoming text. "Just got back to the Savoy... this is the third evening in a row that I have had to attend late discussions in the house. Enjoying a nightcap with George... then off to bed... hope you had a good day... love you, XXX."

Kiss, kiss, kiss! You should be here kissing me, not sipping brandy with that stupid George. She rolls over and pulls the sheets up tight around her chin. *That is... if you are sipping brandy with George, you could be bedding any one of your many long-legged secretaries for all I know.* He contacts her every evening, and she takes consolation from the fact that he is at least thinking of her.

She texts back, "Wish you were here darling, take care and don't work too hard, kiss."

Lesley Buchanan takes his job with British Chemicals very seriously; he is the CEO and very proud of his rise to the top: his promotion was fast and popular with both staff and shareholders. He doesn't really have time to be an MP, but it serves a purpose. He is well informed, and his contact list is second to none, so most evenings are spent representing the people of Kilnsey and Kettlewell in North Yorkshire. This is the second time they have voted him their MP, so if he isn't spending the night in a sumptuous London hotel, he can be found in the Shepherd's Arms: a typical white-painted country pub, nestling between the valleys of the Yorkshire Moors.

The sun eventually rises, and Louise is planning a day at the races with Collette. She considers asking Jones to drive them in the Bentley, but decides against it, the sports car will be more fun. She hates the image of being a rich, frumpy lady and much prefers being a rebel. When she is feeling down, her sports car saves her sanity, and this is one of those mornings. She loves speeding around the country roads and stirring up the dust in the villages. As she passes, the locals give her a wave, most of them in admiration; they know her as the lady of the manor and have a lot of respect for her. As for the car, she hasn't a clue what type of car it is. She thought it was a Mercedes, but the other day, someone asked her if she still had the Ferrari, so maybe it's a Ferrari. She doesn't care, it doesn't interest her.

Jones drives her 1985 Mercedes 350 SL convertible around to the front of the manor and is polishing his fingerprints off the wing mirror as Louise steps out.

"Have you filled it with petrol, Jones? You know how I hate calling at that dirty garage."

"I have, ma'am, all you have to do is drive with care and look after your beautiful self."

"You are a charmer, Jones, that is why I love you so much." He wishes she did love him.

"Why don't you take the day off, Jones. It will be late when I get back. I might even stop over at Collette's cottage. So take yourself off to Brighton in the Beemer, go visit your mother, you haven't seen her for ages."

"She has been ill, ma'am, but that is a nice idea. I might do just that." He starts up the Mercedes and re-adjusts the position of the driving seat for her; he knows the settings of the seat, although today, she is wearing high heels. "You shouldn't be driving in those shoes, ma'am. I have told you before."

"I want to feel girly today, Jones... because I feel naughty."

"Yes, ma'am!" And with that she slams the car door shut, massages the gearshift into drive and leaves him wanting at the front door.

Spoilt Something Rotten

"Recounting my childhood is going to take longer than ten minutes and will probably bore you?"

"Please continue; let me decide." Angela sits up in bed and strokes my brow; I am already totally infatuated with her.

"I hated my childhood. I had to be so proper, always saying 'yes sir and no sir' all the time, and 'I hope you are well, ma'am'. My parents spent a fortune on my education. They sent me to Marlborough School for Girls, a boarding school 50 miles from where we lived, and I always thought they resented spending their money on me; anyway, I was out of sight and out of mind. School was not all bad; every Friday evening after dinner, we were given a free period in which we could follow an activity or hobby. Instead of playing records, writing to boys back home, sewing or writing poetry, like the other girls in the school, I used to climb out of the dormitory window with Doreen, Beverly and Hilary Jenkins and sneak down to the village pub. There we would drink ourselves stupid, dance and tease the local boys; and one evening, we stayed out all night. I got caught climbing over the school wall at 6:00 in the morning. My father was sent for, and I was packed off to finishing school in Switzerland."

"You must have enjoyed your time there. Switzerland is a great place to live."

"You are right, I did enjoy it, but I felt I had been thrown out, got rid of, do you understand?"

"Could you have been mistaken?"

"My foster parents never had time for me. When I did come home during the school holidays, I never saw them. They were always working or socialising, so I just sat around on my own. After completing my final year, I came back to the house but ran away after two months. You know the rest."

She snuggles down into the bed and cuddles up close; I kiss her.

"Are you going to screw me? I'll give you a special deal, £50 for whatever you want."

"No! I am not going to screw you; I might put you over my knee and give you a spanking, because that is what you deserve. Now go to sleep, I have a presentation in the morning, and I must be in top form."

"I have never been spanked." She giggles.

"Your father should have spanked you when you were a girl, and then you might have made a success of your life."

"I like my life, I am a success."

"Go to sleep, I will decide what to do with you in the morning."

"Yes, sir!"

Men

Lesley Buchanan drains his brandy glass and wishes George Baldwin a good night. He rises to his feet and unsteadily makes his way across the dimly lit hotel lounge. The bartender jumps to attention as he staggers towards the elevator and wishes him a peaceful night; relieved he is leaving and confident he will soon close the bar and go to his own bed. The rules of the hotel states he has to remain on duty until the last guest leaves. He has spent the past hour twiddling his thumbs and wondering what these two guys have to talk about so late into the night. He looks towards George and prays he is sober enough to get himself to bed. Last night, the old dodderer fell asleep in the chair; and it was four o'clock before he could lock up. Maybe a little encouragement will do the trick.

"Have you had a busy day, sir? Can I help you to your room?" George is only just on the brink of sanity, he shuffles down into his chair.

"Extremely busy, young man. So many bloody problems to solve when you have a country to run, it's not an easy job." He belches as his last swig of brandy burps back into his mouth. "Ups! Excuse me, I should go to bed before I embarrass myself."

It is far too late to save him from embarrassment; the bar tender helps him to his feet and directs him towards the elevator. Unfortunately, his miniscule push of encouragement proves to be too strong, and George's tottering legs fold under him. He falls into the trolley of dirty glasses, the pile of soiled wine glasses crash to the floor around him.

"Are you alright, sir? Do you need the nurse?"

"Of course not, I just tripped, doing it all the bloody time these days."

"Very good, sir, let me summon the elevator for you." He helps him to his feet and holds him vertical until the elevator arrives. "Is it floor five, sir?"

"I haven't a bloody clue, I have my room key somewhere." George searches through his pockets and eventually pulls out his door card. The tag confirms he is in room 501 on the fifth floor and first door on the right of the elevator.

"Floor five it is, sir." And with that, he props George up in the corner of the lift and presses button five, quickly stepping out to avoid the closing doors. The last thing he wants is to be sealed in the lift with this disgusting wreck of a man. He looks at the remnants of the broken glasses scattered all over the floor and wonders how a stinking rich government minister can let himself get into such a mess. *Stinking rich,* he thinks to himself, putting the emphasis purposefully on the stinking.

Lesley Buchanan is also behaving ungentlemanly. Stephanie waited up for him until she could stay awake no longer. She is awake now, he over-balances whilst removing his pants and falls on top of her. She pulls the bed sheets tighter to her shoulders and hopes he won't want her, but luck is not on her side. She has a job to do, to deliver the British Chemicals account safely into the hands of her agency; and to do this, she has been Lesley's mistress for four years. She has done her job well. It would be a shame to fail with him tonight, only hours before the presentation. The relationship has not been all one-sided, she has been well rewarded for her work. He bought her an apartment in Woolwich, overlooking the river; and a Mazda sports car, which was the car of the year, four years ago, but now she has sights on a BMW Z4 Roadster. It's only a matter of time before she gets one. She is good at her job, so much so that Lesley has fallen in love with her. Apart from these exorbitant gifts, she has a luxurious lifestyle; she spends thousands of pounds on designer dresses, dines at four-star Michelin restaurants, travels first class and visits a West End theatre or night club at least once a week. She is a dedicated clubber.

Unknown to Lesley, he isn't the only client she services, but he is her most important and in her own way, she loves him too. She will submit to him if he demands her, she will stare at the ceiling and dream of her next vacation, visiting the most exotic Mediterranean ports aboard the company yacht. What girl wouldn't work hard for a dream holiday, aboard a yacht in the South of France, with her own BMW sports car parked on the quay?

Lesley is convinced she is deeply in love with him, and during moments of intense passion, he has asked her to marry him. "Ask me again when you have divorced Louise." Stephanie would whisper seductively into his ear, knowing he would never have the courage. Tonight is not one of his better performances; his breath smells of sherry and olives, and as for making love, nothing seems to be happening. Stephanie digs her nails into his back and claws them down to his buttocks in an attempt to stimulate him, but to no avail. He collapses with his arms wrapped around her and apologises over and over again for his failure. He blames his impotence on the presentation in the morning, and his mind being on his future with the company.

"I hope your agency gives a good presentation tomorrow, my love. My new executive team is complaining about the service we get from your creative department." Stephanie wipes away his spittle from his mouth.

"Go to sleep, darling. Don't you worry about the presentation, just concentrate on my love for you. You are the envy of every man having me in your bed." And with that she does what a girl on a mission has to do, saving his embarrassment... and to keep his account.

Playing with Fire

I never sleep well the night before a presentation, and tonight is no exception, facts and figures are spinning around in my head. I have twice changed the structure of the presentation, and still I am not happy with it. I have to emphasise it is our intention to be their business partner and not their service agency. I have to demonstrate our ability to have lots of new ideas, not only in the creative department but also in marketing and product development. I have to prove we understand their products, their clients, their markets and the importance of meeting their targets. I have spent many nights surfing the web for facts and information, and I am confident I can win this account on our professional ability, but the one thing that concerns me is the CEO's affair with the incumbent agency's PR girl. I once lost a pitch because I wasn't aware of the competing agency's horizontal marketing skills. I do not intend losing this one, especially as I have prior knowledge of it.

The CEO is Lesley Buchanan; his profile states he has a wife and two children, a daughter aged 20 and a son at university. His wife is Louise Buchanan, an attractive 45 year old who spends most of her time working for charities. She is a typical mother, possibly frustrated, probably feeling unloved and forgotten. I know nothing of the PR girl. Goodness, how did I let that slip through my net? I jump out of bed and activate my laptop. Within seconds, I am scanning the directors of the incumbent agency. There she is. Public relations director; Miss Stephanie Stirling.

Title:	Miss
Name:	Stephanie Stirling
Age:	35
Marital Status:	Single
Education:	Exeter University (1998-2001)
Qualifications:	BA (Hons) Public Relations

Her profile is impressive; she has previously worked for two leading advertising agencies and been with her present agency five years. Stephanie is well travelled and has spent two years working in Eastern

Europe and three years in the States. Her profile picture is not a recent one, she looks about 30, but that does not distract from the fact that she is very attractive. Amongst the pictures in her image gallery, she is modelling swimwear, city suites and summer dresses, apparently in her teens, she accepted modelling jobs to pay her way through university. I guess she will be a few pounds heavier by now but wow! She is hot. No wonder Lesley is playing away from home.

Angela utters a little groan and turns in her sleep. She is so sweet laid there; I wonder what her comparative profile would say.

Title:	A cheeky girl
Name:	Angela Grace Rebecca Louise Baldwin.
Age:	Too young
Marital Status:	Available
Education:	Streetwise
Qualifications:	Good in bed

I laugh at the profile I have just written for her, but Angela has far more to offer than this. Educated in Switzerland, brought up by the aristocracy, well connected with the UK government, great personality, charming, has a great understanding of humanity and social behaviour, can wrap men around her little finger and is very pretty. The down side to that is, she knows it. I have to admire her free spirit and admit she always gets her own way. I laugh again to myself, not a typical profile I know, but the profile of an exceptional girl.

My plan might just work. If anyone could break up Lesley and Stephanie, Angela could. I don't usually play dirty, but this trick could also be fun. I will let Angela sleep until 8 o'clock, then explain my plan. I'm sure she will do it. It's just the price we will disagree on. In the meantime, I will check out Louise Buchanan. I need to know why Lesley is playing behind her back. Why is their relationship failing, does she know about Stephanie? Does she also have a lover? I type her name into my computer, which reveals her life, her friends and her interests.

Louise Buchanan

Her picture gallery is vast and impressive, she is attending bazaars, performing shop openings, giving speeches, attending civic functions, but most of the pictures are of her riding horses. She is a very confident woman, elegant, sophisticated and refined. Maybe she is so full of herself, she has driven Lesley away, or is she keeping herself busy because she feels abandoned? At first, I fail to notice her similarity to Stephanie, and I am not the first to do that. One of the pictures is captioned, 'Lesley Buchanan leaving a West End night club with his wife Louise.' The woman is not Louise but Stephanie. So I can assume that Louise knows of his infidelity and is bringing up their children alone, her over-active lifestyle will be an attempt to stay sane. My respect for Lesley Buchanan is diminishing rapidly; to be honest, I have no respect for him at all.

The Plan

"Angela, wake up, we have a busy day ahead of us." I shake her but get no response. "Okay you have asked for it." I pull the duvet off her. Wow, she looks amazing all curled up.

"What the hell are you doing, leave me alone," she screams at me and covers herself.

"You have ten minutes to get up, shower and make it to the breakfast table where your porridge will be waiting, or I will throw you out just as you are."

"Porridge! I was five years old when I last ate porridge. I hope you have some golden syrup, I can't eat it without syrup."

"Eight minutes."

"OK, OK." I flip through the pages of Lesley's Facebook profile. His snapshots clearly reveal his preference for tall, blond women, not only do Stephanie and Louise both have cascades of long, blond locks, but his secretary and many members of his badminton team too. I wonder if I am asking too much of my small, dark-haired girl.

"Hurry, breakfast is ready."

"Bloody hell, what is the rush, most men go to work and leave me in bed?"

"I am not going to work, you are. Sit down and listen, would you like more milk on your porridge?"

"No, it's horrible, give me more syrup."

"Say please."

She reluctantly answers, "Please."

I explain my predicament and ask if she is up for the job. She laughs.

"You want me to come on to him, so he will break up with his mistress, who he has been with for four years, you must be joking?"

"You can do it. You might even fall in love with him and earn yourself an apartment and a sports car."

"I don't need either of those. Anyway, I can have both whenever I want. How long have I got to make this happen?"

"Four hours."

"Four hours!"

"Yes, the presentation is in four hours."

A First-Time Hit

Lesley Buchanan has worked hard to earn the title of CEO of the British Chemical Company. He joined the company 20 years ago as a Junior Sales Executive. Granted, his father was a senior director at this time. He had previously owned a company called Chemstream; a company specialising in aero fuels, which was swallowed up by BCC two years prior. It is said that Lesley had an easy ride up the promotion ladder, but Lesley does not agree. The pressure not to fail his father was immense and because of this, he sacrificed his family for his career. Now his wife brings up their children practically on her own as he never has time to spend with them and play with his kids. Lesley has become a workaholic and would have been an easy lay for an ex-model, like Stephanie Stirling.

BCC is expanding rapidly, and Lesley is highly respected; but during the last three years, the stress has started to show. The company has created a new management incentive with the intention of promoting its most dynamic, forward-thinking men into management positions. These men are hard-hitting and hungry for success. They are demanding change, and their less than enthusiastic advertising agency is taking the blame. Lesley knows his relationship with Stephanie is at risk. They have done their best to keep their infidelity a secret and never speak of it, but it is common knowledge and seen amongst his peers as a company joke, the time for him to choose between his job and his mistress is rapidly approaching.

Angela is ranting on and on. "Four hours! All I can do in four hours is ask him if he wants a fuck, and I doubt he will be up for that this morning."

"I agree, you must be far more subtle. My suggestion is you meet him around 10:30, just before the presentation. Come on to him, excite him and let him know that Stephanie isn't the only girl in the world. If he thinks he can have you, he might not be so possessive towards her."

"Do I introduce myself as a street girl?"

"No, you are who you are, a rich, beautiful debutant. You can even come clean and tell him you are George Baldwin's daughter, he will be impressed."

31

"And what should I look like? He prefers tall, blonde women. Do I buy a wig?"

"No silly, let's hope he is tired of blonds and fancies someone different, be sophisticated, be eloquent and act intelligent. Make a date to meet him for lunch or for a drink. Tell him you would like to see the latest show in town. It's a musical called *Lucky;* it's getting great reviews. Goodness, Angela, do I have to tell you how to pick up a guy?"

"Of course not, but I need some new clothes; your credit card please." She holds out her hand and laughs at the horrified look on my face.

"And the pin number please?" I can tell she is enjoying this.

"9753, remember 9, the last of the single numbers; then come down the odd numbers to 7, then 5 then 3, can you remember that?"

"Of course I can. Where will this guy be at 10:30?"

"That I don't know. The presentation is being held in the Savoy Hotel. He might be in the lounge, he might be taking a late breakfast. God, Angela, use your brain and search for him, we will code name this little task 'dunkirk'. Let me know how you are getting on, my mobile number is 0 78 34 56 78 91."

"Will Stephanie be with him?"

"I doubt it. They won't want to be seen together before a presentation."

"OK, I'm on my way… Hey! Why dunkirk?"

"You're going to bring the guy home."

"Oh!" She's too young to understand the connection.

"Now please go."

"Hey! What do I get out of this?"

"A new apartment and a sports car if you play your cards right."

"Ha, ha."

Phew! As the door closes, I collapse onto the sofa, my brain is already hurting. I still have to complete my presentation.

Dunkirk

Angela knows which shops sell the prettiest dresses. She loves the '20s and '30s' fashions, so a buttoned-up top with a collar, belt and a flowing pleated skirt, down to her knees, is her choice. She chooses a beige dress, with white polka dots; she really wanted the bright red one but thought beige would be more suitable. Seamed stockings, heeled court shoes, red lips, a bit of glitter around her neck and wrists, and she can have any guy in town; *Stephanie Stirling, your time is up.*

It is already 10:00 a.m. She hails a taxi and instructs the driver to take her to the Savoy. She would have preferred a chauffeur-driven limo, but due to the time, a street cab will have to do. The driver is enchanted with her; he has been driving American tourists around London all morning, cringing at their geeing and wowing, which they are so painfully good at. He has been to the Palace twice and crossed Tower Bridge three times; lucky for him, he was on his way back from the heliport when Angela hailed him. To have a pretty English girl in his cab is a refreshing change and a cheery start to his day.

Angela waits for the Savoy concierge to open the taxi door and hands her driver a £20 note; he refuses it.

"Have this ride on me, luv, you have cheered me up this morning." It has been a long time since she has been complimented for bringing joy. She feels good, and she steps into the hotel full of confidence.

"I have a parcel for Mr Lesley Buchanan, which room is he in?" The receptionist runs her finger down the list of guests.

"721, ma'am! His room is on the seventh floor. Can I call him or deliver it for you?"

"No, thank you, I need to deliver it personally. Is he still in his suite, or is he in the lounge?"

"I haven't seen him this morning. I guess he must be in his room."

Angela is amazed how easy that was, she didn't even know he was staying at the Savoy; it was just one lucky bluff after another. She stands outside room 721 and listens to the voices inside if only she could think of an excuse for knocking on the door and announcing herself, but she can't. She needs to bump into him accidentally. The elevator would be an ideal place to meet, especially if he is alone. She lingers at the end of the corridor and leans against the tall, stained-glass window and massages her foot. Her shoes are killing her, and the belt around her skirt is far too tight, *what a woman has to endure to look amazing*. It is 10:25, Lesley will be leaving for the conference hall within the next couple of minutes… well, she hopes so.

Door 721 opens, and she jumps to her feet. A man steps out into the corridor and struggles to close the door whilst holding on to a large, black leather briefcase. He hurries down the corridor away from her and presses the elevator button. Angela runs after him as fast as her shoes will allow. Shit! The elevator arrives immediately, and she is still only halfway down the corridor.

"Wait! Wait for me please," she can see the porter inside and tries to attract his attention by waving her arms wildly in the air. Lesley spots her and places his foot between the closing doors.

"Thank you, thank you so much." She grabs his arm to steady herself whilst removing a shoe and giving her toe a quick rub. "My shoes are killing me."

"Mi, you are in a hurry this morning. I am pleased to be of service."

Angela smiles and looks up at him. He is a good-looking guy and so tall, she stares directly into his eyes and holds his gaze for several seconds.

"Aren't you Lesley Buchanan, the MP for Kilnsey and Kettlewell?"

"Yes, have we met before?" He steps back in surprise.

"My father knows you, George Baldwin, you must have met him in the House?"

"Goodness! Old George, I had a drink with him only last night. He didn't tell me he had such a beautiful daughter."

"I bet you say that to all the girls."

"Only when it's true." Angela lets go of his arm and places both her feet back on the floor.

"I am going to scald old George for keeping you a secret, we must meet for a drink." She grabs his hand and shakes it.

"A drink would be very nice. I would like that a lot. When?"

"I am busy until 2:00 p.m. Let's say 2:30; then, we can grab a spot for lunch together."

"2:30 it is. I will be in the circular bar, don't be late." She gives him a teasing look.

The porter announces their arrival at the conference hall, and Lesley picks up his brief case.

"Nice to meet you."

Nice meetings, like this, don't happen to Lesley. She has cheered him up immensely; he is very pleased with himself. As the elevator door closes, Angela gives him a little quirky wave.

"See you at 2:30."

"Where to, ma'am?" inquires the porter.

"Oh, anywhere."

"Yes, ma'am."

Job done, wow, I am better at this than I thought. She calls me to confirm her successful but brief encounter.

"I am having lunch with Lesley at 2:30, he was easy." She boasts, then, she starts describing every detail of her morning's shopping adventure.

"Angela, stop. Tell me about it later. I have work to do."

"Spoil sport, I am working hard for you."

"I know you are, you are great, but I have to go." I end the call. I bet she is throwing a tantrum right now. She won't forgive me for putting the phone down on her. She will probably give me a hard time and make me grovel and make me want her even more. This girl is a master at man-ipulation.

Yes or No?

The presentation is going well; I am encouraged, I sense a ten million pound account coming my way. My team has definitely done their homework. They recite the list of products that the British Chemical Company has, and it is vast; it ranges from agricultural pesticides and animal growth supplements to missile fuels and even household paints. My marketing department has researched all these products and has a recommendation for every single one. Our understanding of their sales targets and growth aspirations are appreciated. To restore a lively, upbeat vibe, I play a ten-minute film of our creative work. This includes award-winning TV commercials, our latest digital communication techniques and examples of our worldwide marketing achievements, they have to be impressed. I deliberately focus my gaze on the new executives; they are easily identified by their age and enthusiasm. Lesley Buchanan is sitting in the centre of the BCC board of directors, he appears to be relaxed, but the rest of them are sitting stony-faced and giving nothing away. I can't even guess what is going through their minds.

I want to keep the presentation down to one hour. Clients start shuffling in their seats and leaving for the loo after that, so I bring the presentation to a conclusion by introducing the agency team that has been designated to service the account should we win the business. Then, as a stroke of luck, Angela appears in the doorway. She has simply entered the wrong room but at the right time. I grab her intrusion with both hands.

"And may I introduce Angela Rebecca Louise Baldwin." She hasn't a clue what is happening but goes along with the charade. "Angela is the newest addition to our team. Should we be successful in winning your account, Angela will be... well, in my day, her title would be 'girl friday'; but in today's fast digital world, let's give her the title of human router."

They all laugh.

"She will be the express link between you and the agency. She will direct you to the relevant agency departments, and in return, link us with you. Her task will be to guarantee fast and efficient communication between us. Her office can be at the agency or at your head office, or even in both places."

Several of the younger executives are suddenly resuscitated at the introduction of a hint of glamour; the lucky ones on the front row are treated to a whiff of her perfume, which for my liking is far too strong. Lesley sits upright, recognising the girl he has just previously met in the elevator. For the first time, he smiles. I usher my team out of the room and thank him and his directors for the opportunity to present.

They applaud. That is always a good sign of appreciation. If our competitors in the adjacent room, waiting to present next, can hear this response, they will know they have a fight on their hands.

"What was that all about, parading me in front of a group of brooding businessmen? They were looking me up and down as if I were a window manikin."

"A very sexy window manikin, may I add. Forget the young guys, your task is to attract Lesley away from Stephanie. We don't have time to mess about. They have to announce which agency they are signing by the end of the week, now go and get him, he looked interested."

"He must be 48, he is far too old for me." We are forced to step aside, as a group of people head down the corridor towards us.

"I think this is the competing agency on their way to the presentation lounge, let's see if we can spot Stephanie."

It isn't difficult to recognise her; there is only one woman in the group. I must admit she is a very imposing woman. Dressed in a smart-skirted blue suit, a pale blue blouse with too many buttons hanging loose and a golden heart around her neck. I guess a gift from Lesley.

Angela turns and slaps my chest. "I can't compete with her, she is beautiful. What have you got me into?"

"Of course you can compete, use your head as well as your body. Don't give him everything at once, tease him, make him want you." Angela turns and watches Stephanie lead the group through the double doors into the boardroom. "Look! She has been screwing him for four years. He must be fed up of her by now; and compared to you, she is an old woman, and not only that, she is a dead ringer of his wife. Every time he gets into bed with her, he must be reminded of his wife."

"I am not the type of woman he likes. I am not blonde, not tall and definitely not a substitute for his wife."

"Trust me, I am a man, and I want you." She looks up at me and glares into my eyes. I realise the mistake I have made.

"Are you saying you want me? You could have had me last night, why didn't you take me last night." I laugh, and after making sure nobody is watching, I kiss her forehead. "Just teasing you, my pretty.

Play your cards right, and you can have me when you have grown up a bit."

"Stuff you, I wouldn't sleep with you if you gave me a thousand pounds."

"That's my girl, think big. Now focus on your task. Get him to believe he can sleep with you whenever he wants if he takes the bait; keep him dangling until we have his signature on the account, because once he announces we have won the business, Stephanie will make his life a misery. Now, if he asks what your job will be, tell him it is to ease communication between his company and the agency. It is a common practice these days to link this gap, and both his company and the agency will share your expenses, including your salary. Avoid the details by saying they have not yet been defined, in fact, he can dictate what you do, and where you will be based."

"How much will I get paid?" Ups! I suddenly realise she is taking this seriously.

"Name your price… because it will never happen. Remember, this is a sting."

"OK! What if I fall in love with him?"

"Ha! Then you are an idiot, he has a wife and two children and a very proud ex-mistress. If you want to get involved in that triangle, then you really are an idiot. I have to go, find yourself a mirror and practice those innocent girlie expressions. Pout your lips, drop your eyes, lick your lips and flutter those eyelashes, there is more to sex than taking your knickers off. Did you learn nothing in Switzerland?"

"I could have had every boy in town, when I was at school."

"And so could every other pretty girl in the school. We are not talking about sex here, we are talking control."

I turn to walk away. She jumps up and kisses me again. "You could have me for a thousand pounds." She giggles.

"Darling, I can have you for free." She throws me a punch but misses… on purpose, I hope.

07837247800

I deliberately walk past the lounge bar at 2:30. Angela is sitting in the corner, playing on her mobile. She looks stunning; any man in his right mind will want her. What are the chances of Lesley standing her up; now he believes she is working for the competing advertising agency, maybe he is already being screwed by Stephanie in her final attempt to secure the account, or has he just been delayed, so many maybes, all we can do is hope and wait.

The same thoughts are going through Angela's mind, she has convinced herself there is no pressure to succeed; her mindset is simply to enjoy the encounter. It is 3:10 when Lesley steps into the bar; thankfully he is alone, Angela feared he might bring Stephanie with him. That would have put her into panic mode.

"I am so sorry, please excuse my lateness, I had to chair a company directors meeting to review the presentation. May I get you a drink?" He appears to be sincerely sorry. She smiles and allows him to take her hand. She could down a beer if she was to be honest. Her throat is dry with anxiety, but she manages to ask for a medium white wine, a drink she feels is more in keeping for a woman with a £120,000 a year job… plus sports car, pension and riverside apartment. She has a little giggle to herself at her dream.

She directs Lesley to sit on the soft, cushioned sofa positioned at a right angle to her. From here he can see all of her, so she can use her legs and her body to full effect. He calls the waiter.

"I didn't know you were working with the ad agency."

"I didn't know you were working with British Chemicals," they both laugh. "How long have you been working with…" They both recite together and burst out laughing again.

Lesley breaks the formality. "I had dinner with your father last night, he is a great man."

"Unfortunately, I do not know much about him. When I was a girl, he was too busy to spend time with me. I attended finishing school in Switzerland. He is not my real father, did you know that he is my step father?" Lesley is fascinated as she unravels her story; he has a lot of respect for George and wonders why he has never admitted having a daughter.

All the time, Angela is using her body skills to attract him, crossing her legs and then uncrossing them, fingering her mouth and picking at the buttons of her blouse. She is slowly inching closer to him, she is already in his space. He should be able to smell her perfume by now; and before she has exhausted her family history, she is touching him, wiping a drop of spilt wine off his tie with a tissue from her handbag. "You need looking after, Mister Lesley, you need a good woman in your life." She wants him to admit his relationship with Stephanie, but there is no mention of her nor that of his wife.

"No one has ever called me Mister Lesley before, I like it. It is both friendly and respectful at the same time," she smiles, job accomplished.

"Like your father, I also have to work away from home most of the time… I mean your stepfather," he corrects himself. "I work long hours." He describes his job and his responsibilities and explains the pressures and the stresses he has to endure. Angela is starting to wilt; her wine is taking its toll. *Is this the third or the fourth glass I have had. Oh dear, I have lost count.* He tells her about his dreams for the future, and his ambition for his company. There is one thing he doesn't talk about; there is no mention of Stephanie.

"Will you excuse me, I have to go to the ladies room." He stands to acknowledge her departure.

"In fact, I have to go also, I have so much to do. Thank you for such an interesting afternoon. I hope I haven't bored you with my work."

"Not at all." He takes her hand and leans over to kiss her. She pulls back but does not let go of his hand. "Can I look forward to meeting you again, I would like that."

She softens her stance and touches his cheek, "You are a good man, I do hope so."

"No one has ever described me as a good man before. Goodness Angela, you are coming out with a whole string of firsts. Would you really like to meet me again?" His manner is meek and longing.

"I would like that very much, but only if you agree not to talk business." She is very pleased with this remark; she has immediately put the relationship onto a social footing, maybe even onto a sexual one.

"I agree." And with that she takes out a pen, pulls back the cuff of his shirt and writes her mobile number on his arm. "You will have to remember it or transfer it to your diary today because it will have faded by tomorrow, and I will be gone. I hope you won't let that happen."

"I won't."

Congratulations

Lesley packs his bag, places a £50 note on the pillow of the bed and checks out of the Savoy. He always leaves a tip for room service. He believes in rewarding the staff directly, adding a gratuity to the bill never seems quite right to him, convinced the management keep it for themselves. His Bentley is already parked at the hotel door, and the concierge opens the boot and places his brown leather over-night bag carefully between his golf clubs and squash rackets. Lesley's head is in turmoil. To save his credibility at work, he has to sack his advertising agency, to continue his relationship with Stephanie, he has to renew their contract. His heart sinks when he looks in the rear view mirror of the car and sees Stephanie sitting seductively in the rear seat. She is the last person he wants to encounter right now.

"I hope you have persuaded those stupid directors of yours to make the correct decision, darling. Let's go to my apartment and celebrate, you deserve a reward."

It is 6:30 p.m. when my phone rings. "Tim, it's Isaiah, have you heard?"

"Heard what?"

"We won the business, they had a meeting straight after the presentation, and we have been awarded the account."

"Wow! So soon. I didn't think we would get a decision until the end of the week."

"Forget the end of the week, Tim. I have already instructed the solicitors to draw up the contracts; and we are to meet them at British Chemical's head office tomorrow evening, at 7:30."

"I will be there."

"Let us go in the same car. I will pick you up at 6:00, this will give us time to get our act together."

"Okay! Did they say anything about our presentation?"

"Apparently, their meeting this afternoon got quite heated. Lesley argued in favour of the other agency, but his new directors beat him down. I believe several threatened to quit if he didn't change direction, so he is not a happy guy. I hope you have this covered, Tim, we don't want to be working with a guy who is going to be difficult. We will need all the help we can get."

"I have it covered, sir. I will tell you what I have done tomorrow when we meet."

"Good man, have a great evening and… Oh Tim!"

"What?"

"Well done."

I shake Angela who has been asleep on the sofa, for nearly an hour; her brain must be processing the day's activity because she keeps making those little squeaky noises that I love so much. She is so cute, laid there in her Audrey Hepburn dress, twitching and squeaking. Her shoes have fallen off, and her big toe has come through her tights. All the same, she is very, very pretty.

"Congratulations Angela, we won the account. I don't know what you said, and I definitely don't want to know what you had to do, but whatever it was, it worked."

"I did nothing." She grunts, "I just rabbited on about my life. I thought he was falling asleep at one point."

"So what did you think of him?"

"He is a nice guy, I feel sorry for him; he is a slave to his work."

"And a slave to Stephanie I would guess."

"He never mentioned Stephanie, but he did mention his wife, just once, Louise, I think, her name is. He feels guilty that she is bringing up his children without him."

"Does he love her?" I ask.

"I don't think love is a part of his life, but there IS a desperate, passionate man in there, trying to get out. I can tell by the way he looks at me."

"How did you leave it?"

"I wrote my mobile number on his arm, and he promised to call."

"Well, let's hope we sign the contracts before he washes it off."

"Hey! I like the guy, and I fancy a new apartment."

We are interrupted by Angela's mobile ringing.

"It's an unknown number. I don't answer calls that don't leave a number. I will ignore it, get me a drink."

"It might be Lesley." Angela sits up and smartens her dress as if she can be seen.

"Hi! Who is that?"

"Wise girl, never give your name away to an unknown caller."

"Angela, it's Lesley Buchanan, you remember we had a drink this afternoon."

"Of course, I remember you. Have you decided which agency you are employing?"

"Hey! I thought we agreed not to talk shop."

"Sorry, I wasn't thinking."

"I did enjoy our meeting. I was hoping we could have dinner tomorrow evening."

"That would be nice."

"What is your favourite meal?"

"Err... I don't have a favourite dish. I suppose I eat more fish and chips than anything else."

Goodness! What image is this she is giving out? I dance up and down in front of her like a demented baboon, trying to catch her attention. "Raise the bar, you are representing my agency, be upmarket."

"I think we can do better than that, Angela. I will pick you up at 8:00, text me your address."

"OK, see you tomorrow at 8:00." She puts down the phone and beams all over her face. "Job done. What are you jumping up and down for?"

"Be posh! Stephanie is high class."

"He just might appreciate a touch of naïve innocence. Leave Lesley to me." I have to admit Angela has not put a foot wrong, maybe I should trust her.

My TV flashes into life. I have it programmed to come on every evening at 8 o'clock, so I can catch up with the evening news. Tonight, they are reporting the same old stuff. Interest rates up, unemployment figures up, crime figures up. The prime minister is on his way to Berlin for yet another bullying from Angela Merkel; and Dick Jones, the famous film star of the 1950s, has died at the age of 93, after fighting cancer for ten years. The biggest news is the date of the general election. It is to be in nine months on Thursday, 20 January. There is a last minute breaking news bulletin. The newsreader scans the note handed to her.

"We are receiving news of a shooting in Chelsea. A body has been found in an apartment in this prestigious area of London. Two hours ago, the police were called to 14 Park Terrace, after gunshots were reported. The police have just announced the body is that of Stephanie Stirling, a model and high-profile city executive. Lesley Buchanan, Member of Parliament for Kilnsey and Kettlewell and CEO of British Chemicals, owns the apartment and is helping police with their enquiries."

Angela downs her gin and tonic in one gulp.

"What the hell have you got me into? He blows his mistress away, then calls me for a date?"

The Rt Hon. George Baldwin

The Rt Hon. George Baldwin, government minister and secretary of state for works and pensions, wakes up with his usual hangover. He reaches over to his bedside table for the remains of his nightcap. He believes a slurp before breakfast energises him for the day ahead. This morning, his shaking hand fails to grip the cut-glass brandy tumbler, and it crashes onto the hardwood parquet floor, shattering into a thousand shards of glass. He utters an oath, without his morning hit; it will take him hours to become completely compos mentis, which is why he arranges his meetings late in the day.

It is nine months to the general election, and his increased workload is getting through to him. He has to improve the countries appalling unemployment figures and, at the same time, increase the job opportunities for this year's university leavers. If that isn't enough, he has to pacify the 20 million men and women living on a pension; inflation is eating away at their standard of living. So in all, George is responsible for the old age pensioners (33% of the population), students (21% of the population) and the unemployed (10% of the population). This is a staggering 64% of the UK population; and if his party fails to win the election, the finger of blame will point to him. He used to be the people's favourite, the most trusted and respected member of the cabinet; but this was at a time when buses had conductors, when tube trains had drivers, and people shopped in the high street. But with the introduction of automation, driverless trains and online shopping, he has lost the desire to save the country. How can the prime minister expect him to increase the number of jobs when the government's policy is to automate everything? He gropes his bedside cabinet, searching for his brandy glass. He remembers filling it before climbing into bed, it should be on his bedside table. His memory is failing, but he refuses to admit it. As he steps out of bed in frustration, he receives a painful reminder of where it is.

Today is going to be extra busy; he hasn't been to Westminster this week, and his excessive expenses claim will be questioned if he fails to make an appearance, his attendance is a priority. He also has to pick up the latest copy of the party manifesto; it is re-written every two weeks as the election committee twist and turn to appease the latest poll figures. He has been through so many elections, he finds it difficult to take it seriously. It will promise the earth, not commit to anything and give instruction on how to avoid difficult questions; and most important, it will advise on what to avoid and what not to say. Then tonight, he has to vote on the immigration bill, which clashes with the European football final on TV. He laughs to himself, he should have chosen a different career with regular hours. At least, he would be at home in the evening, watching what all men watch, but that would have meant having a proper job, and work is not an activity that ever appealed to him.

It's 9:30 when room service arrives with his breakfast, a cafetiere of black coffee and a pair of poached kippers. On the tray is also a copy of *The Times* and *The Daily Mail*. He scans through the city headlines to see if anything applies to him. Today's news is bleak: Banks are in the doghouse, his shares have dropped another 2%, and another 2,000 soldiers are being sent to defend our interests in the Middle East. He turns to the *Daily Mail* for refreshment, but the people's news is just as bad. Rail fares are increasing for the third time in six months; the bus strike organised for next Friday is still on. Only one item of news catches his attention: Alina Zolnerowich; a Russian ballerina has been arrested at Heathrow in possession of drugs. A shame that; she is a brilliant dancer. He has been enchanted by her performances many times and has tickets to see her next week at the Royal Opera House.

The smell of kippers penetrates through his thickening sinuses. His heavy drinking is taking its toll, his blood pressure is sky high, his cholesterol is 8.3, and he has added three stone in weight during the last 18 months. He knows he should cut back on the alcohol and take more care of what he eats, but to be honest, he is passed caring.

His room phone tingles.

"Your car has arrived, Sir George, can you come immediately? There has been an accident in the street, a truck has knocked down a cyclist, and the police will not allow your chauffeur to wait outside the hotel." He puts down the phone without even responding and shuffles over to the door, knocking the skeleton of his kippers off the plate. *Bloody kippers, who left them there, and who cares a toss about those bloody policemen.*

This is not a good start to his day.

Mr Funny Guy

Before George sits at his desk, his secretary interrupts.

"Good morning, sir, you have been summoned to the exchequer's office," she smiles at him, knowing the request will annoy him intensely.

"What now!" he growls.

"Immediately you arrive, sir, so I suppose that means now."

"Make me a coffee, the bastard can wait."

The office phone rings. His secretary picks it up, looks at George and points anxiously at it.

"OK! OK, tell him I am on my way."

"He will be with you immediately, Lord Chancellor." With that, the phone is replaced onto its hanger, and George reluctantly heads off towards the main building, mumbling expletives all the way.

"Good morning, George. I trust you are exceedingly well?"

"Do you mean like a Kipling fruit pie, Lord Chancellor?"

"I don't understand. Is that another of your jokes, George? You know I don't do jokes."

"It is, Lord Chancellor, it means I am exceedingly good. Just like the Kipling's fruit pies advertised on TV."

"I don't have time to watch TV, you are a lucky man, George, if you have the time."

"I listen to the news bulletins, sir. Now what can I do for you?"

The chancellor lowers his voice.

"George, I want you to hear this first from me." *Here we go again*, George sits opposite the Chancellor. This man's oversized ego and zero sense of humour positions him in the lower echelons of humanity. George sits in expectation of his words of wisdom.

"We are cutting council budgets by 30%, the prime minister will announce it to the press in half an hour. We have to save 20 billion pounds, so we will let the councils squeeze their people for more money. This way, we keep the party's image squeaky clean." The chancellor laughs at his own remark. "Ha, you see, George, I can tell a joke."

"Very funny, Lord Chancellor, what has this got to do with me?"

"The first thing the councils will do is sack their manual workers. They will cut back on waste collection and disposal schedules, road repairs, libraries and social care. Unemployment is going to rocket, so you have to put your thinking cap on, or else, you and your increasing unemployment figures are going to be splashed all over the papers."

"Don't worry, sir. I will save your face."

"What do you say, George. I missed that."

"I said, don't worry, Your Grace. I will save the day. How is your good lady these days?"

"She is very well, George. I saw her only last week." With that, he indicates George's time is up, and it is time for him to go.

George shuffles out. *What a disgustingly big office, what a pathetic man; what an enormous desk, I hope he suffocates in his pile of self-importance; poor bastard.*

George is still uttering disgust as he reaches the sanctuary of his own office. *Stupid man. Doesn't he know when people are out of work, not only do they stop paying taxes, they have to be given social benefits, which costs more than the money he is trying to save. I hope his old lady is still screwing her butcher's son; she deserves all the fun she can get.*

"Everything okay, sir?" his secretary enquires.

"Everything is hunky-dory, everything is just as it always is and always will be."

A Date with a Killer

Angela has been standing at the window, watching the road since 7:30 p.m.

"Do you think he will come for me? The police might have detained him. He might be locked up in a police cell and can't get a message to me. He might have a gun. Tim, I am frightened."

"Angela, please stop chattering. If he comes, it's because the police have nothing to charge him with, so he must be innocent."

"And if he doesn't come?"

"Then I will buy you a fish and chip supper."

"I rather fancy fish and chips with you, Tim, can I have mushy peas as well." She puts her arms around my neck.

"Get down, Shep! (A joke from my Blue Peter days.) You and I have a working relationship, not a sexual one."

"What about a romantic one?" she asks all angelic like. A car rattles up the cobbles and pulls up beneath the window.

"Bloody hell, have you seen his car?"

Lesley is sitting behind the wheel of a beautiful pale blue Bentley convertible. She rushes to the door, "Don't wait up."

"Don't let him shoot you," I shout after her.

"Tim, in that car, he can do whatever he likes to me." With that, she is gone. I am concerned, but more than that, I am jealous.

"I didn't expect to see you today, whatever are they doing to you?"

Lesley smiles but looks pale and tired.

"So you have heard about Stephanie. I am living a nightmare."

"Her murder is all over the newspapers."

"I have been at the police station all day, so let's have a fun evening; and I will tell you all about it. I have reserved a table at Carravagio. I hope you like Italian."

"I do. Wow, Carravagio, that is the most exotic pizza house in town. Am I okay in my little summer dress, do you think I am underdressed for such an impressive restaurant?"

"You look great, Angela. I will be honoured to take you there tonight." The car door closes automatically; he slips the shift into 'drive' and glide out of the mews.

The food is amazing, and the venue spectacular, they eat mostly in silence… Angela not wanting to appear too nosey, and Lesley is obviously exhausted. He takes hold of her hand.

"I would like to show you something, it's a favourite place of mine, you will love it. Are you up for a short drive?"

"With the top down?"

"If you like."

"I like."

The heated leather seats wrap around her; and with warm air blowing up her dress, she is in heaven. Even with the top down, there is no sound of the engine, the only noise is the rush of air blowing over the windscreen rustling her hair.

"How fast are we going?" Lesley glances at the row of figures reflecting up the windscreen, directly in front of him.

"One hundred and ten."

"Wow, isn't that against the law?"

"Are you complaining? The police don't stop people in Bentleys, they know we are either famous or important. Anyway, I don't care, I am sick of the police." As they race down the A47 towards Kent, Angela gets a shiver of concern. Lesley has lost his friendly, easy-going attitude, his face is stern, and his teeth clenched tight together.

"I think you should slow down, Lesley, this is insane." He not only ignores her request but presses on the pedal even harder.

"We are nearly there, did you enjoy that?"

He pulls the car off the main road and steers the bulbous Bentley down a tree-lined cart track. She can see rabbits fleeing for their lives in the headlights, a hedgehog curls up as they pass, and birds and bats scatter, shrieking angrily into the intricate, interlocking branches above them.

"Where are you taking me? I must warn you, I can take care of myself, and my mobile is giving out my location all the time. My boyfriend knows exactly where I am." This isn't true, but she is frightened. She has suddenly realised she is totally vulnerable, helpless, in fact, visions of him holding Stephanie by the throat and pushing a gun into her face flash through her head. She is scared.

"You are quite safe, my love, you will love it."

"Love what; what are you going to do to me?" He bursts out laughing.

"Do to you? I'm not going to do anything to you, except show you something which you will find delightful. Angela is not convinced and shuffles as far away from him as possible, watching his face all the time as he steers the car through the trees and then out into a clearing. In front of them is the most spectacular view of the city. Lesley brings the car to a standstill at the edge of the escarpment, turns off the engine and kills the lights. "Listen," he whispers to her.

"Listen to what, I can't hear anything."

"Exactly, listen to the silence, isn't it beautiful?" She curls up on the seat and pushes herself tighter against the door. He smiles at her. "You are silly; look, over there you can see the Olympic Stadium in Stratford, in the centre of the city is Canary Wharf, Tower Bridge and the London Eye; and over here to the west is Richmond. Can you see the planes leaving Heathrow?"

It is indeed a beautiful place. He has relaxed and lost his aggressive nature. Maybe she was wrong; maybe he is the nice guy everyone claims he is. She uncurls her legs from beneath her and sits in the centre of the seat; it's warmth still penetrating through her flimsy dress. A four-engine Emirates plane rises into the sky and heads towards them. They watch as it approaches and then banks left, over their heads, before disappearing over the trees.

"This is my favourite place, Angela. I want to share it with you. I come here to think, to clear my mind of problems and to appreciate what I have. I sit here and dream."

"Dream? You are so rich, you can buy anything you want, you don't have to dream."

"Life isn't like that, Angela. As you grow older, you will realise there are many important things we desperately need that cannot be bought. One is happiness and the other is peace of mind; and of course, there is love. I am in love with my wife, but my career has driven us apart. I was in love with Stephanie, but she wasn't in love with me; I didn't know it, but I was just her sugar daddy. After the presentation yesterday, I was on my way home to Louise, but Stephanie was sitting in the car, waiting for me, so we went back to my London apartment. She was fun and buoyant at first, but when I told her I was moving the account, she went berserk. I could not believe the disgusting things that came out of her mouth. She insulted me, Louise, my job, my work for over an hour. I must have been stupid, thinking she loved me for what I am."

Angela listens; she can feel her blood pumping around her body as her anxiety rises again; she is convinced he is about to admit to killing Stephanie; and if he does, what will he do to her?

"And then, she saw your phone number written on my arm, did you really have to sign it? She trashed the apartment and threatened to kill herself. I had to physically restrain her from throwing herself off the balcony. She eventually calmed down and told me our relationship was over, and she was going back to live with her mother. She said she wanted nothing from me and wanted nothing to do with me. I left her ranting and raving and sat in the car to wait for her to leave, but she didn't. I sat for an hour until I realised she had no intention of leaving, so I booked in at the Park Crescent Hotel; and that's where the police found me this morning. That was when I learned she was dead."

"You left her in the apartment?"

"Yes!"

"That was a silly thing to do."

"I agree!"

"You shot her?"

"No… I didn't shoot her. I left her ranting and raving, she was going to go back to her mother."

"So she shot herself."

"I don't know, the police have not found a gun."

"Do you have a gun?"

"Yes."

"Where is it?"

"I keep it in the drawer next to my bed."

"When did you last see it?"

"Oh, it must be six months ago, when I was searching the drawer for a tie or something."

Angela feels a tiny bit sorry for him, she wants to believe him. Even if he did kill her, she deserved it; she was a bitch. She runs her fingers through his hair and pulls his face towards her, he is crying. His arms wrap around her, and he slides down her body until his head comes to rest on her lap. His tears seeping through her dress. She caresses his head and senses him pressuring up. Her heart goes out to him. He is a nice guy, he deserves a little comfort, and she is in the mood to give it, she allows him to use her.

It is four o'clock when they drive off the escarpment.

"I will take you home."

"I don't have a home to go to," she admits. "I was staying with a friend. I can't go back there at this time."

"You can't go to my apartment; the police are still searching it, nor can I take you home. My wife would not appreciate that. I do know of an apartment which is vacant." He reaches into his brief case and pulls out a set of keys. "It's Stephanie's apartment. Well, it's mine really, I pay for it, so you can sleep there, you will like it." And with that, he manoeuvres the car back through the trees, and 30 minutes later, drops her at the front door of Priestley House; a prestigious apartment block located on the river at Battersea.

"I don't have time to show you around, I have to get home; but make yourself comfortable." He kisses her, runs his hands down the front of her body before triggering the door release. "Thank you for being here for me. I am sure we can work together."

As he drives away leaving her on the pavement, she peers into the reception area of the impressive apartment block. The concierge raises his head from a book and smiles at her. She smiles back at him; *I can't stay in Stephanie's apartment, it just isn't right.* She steps back into the street; cold, tired, scared and used, but she feels she has done a good turn and doesn't regret it. The street is deserted; the chance of a street cab passing is remote, to say the least. She fingers through the contacts on her mobile. 'AL Taxis', she used to call them many times, she just hopes she still has an account.

"We will have a car with you within five minutes," promises the girl on the response line. Angela waits and shivers, relieved when she hears the drone of a taxi's diesel engine.

Cheeky and Spicy Hot

Even at the races, surrounded by the rich, famous and the most beautiful, Louise Buchanan and her sister Collette stand out from the crowd. They giggle their way down today's running sheet and flutter their eyelids at the touts. Louise puts £50 on Bukfastleigh for the 2:30 and Catchthewind in the three o'clock. Her big bet of the day is £100 on Merry-go-round: a stable mate of Jollaper. A 100-1 outsider, but what the heck, it's only £100, and he is a beautiful horse. She has run her hands over his flanks many times while waiting for Andrea to saddle 'Jollaper'.

Collette as usual is proving to be a firm favourite; she is surrounded by highly desirable men prying for her attention. Louise is used to playing second fiddle to Collette. Unable to compete with her energy, she watches as Collette works her body and exercises her charms. There is a party tonight at Raffles, a new club opening in Chelsea. She will leave it to Collette to get an invite or better still; get them invited to a party in Monaco and taken there by private jet, of course. You might laugh, but that's what happened last year; and neither of them knew the name of the guy whose party it was, but his villa was amazing. It looked down onto the casino; and beyond that, the harbour and palace which dominated the skyline. Louise pauses to recall those four crazy days of passion, the deep husky voice of that yacht captain, whose name also has slipped her mind, melted her resistance; and his touch… well, his touch was something else, when he stroked her shoulder and slid his hands down her arms to pull her in tight. Oh, she still tingles at the memory, but family commitments and a busy diary stopped the magic. Nice memories though! Louise is surprised to hear her name being called through the crowd. She turns to see Jones, her chauffer, gopher and handyman pushing a wheelchair towards her. In the chair is an elderly; delicate lady who she assumes is his mother.

"Have you won anything yet, ma'am? I saw you placing a bet, and my mother wanted to meet you."

"Pleased to meet you. I believe you have been ill, are you feeling better?" Louise bows and takes hold of the old lady's hand.

"Oh yes, a lot better, thank you, and I believe it was your idea that Thomas should bring me to the races today."

Louise's brain is racing, "Err… I do believe it was my suggestion that Thomas visit you. I work him so hard, he deserved a break." Louise is suddenly aware that she never knew Jones' first name. He has been her chauffeur for over five years, and she only ever refers to him as Jones, she could not have recited his name to anyone. She stares at him and sees a slightly different man to the one who drives her car and cleans the silver. He is still rough on the edges, his accent still grates especially when he drops his h's and t's. He is the only person she knows who says 'O' instead of 'hot', how can anyone drop two characters from a three letter word? He has broad shoulders and thick arms, she has never noticed his muscles before. He is always wearing a jacket; but today, in his short-sleeved shirt, she sees someone quite macho and quite appealing. Add this to his tanned, smiling face and a gentle nature, something else she hasn't appreciated before, he is very desirable. Louise is quite taken with him and proud he is working for her.

"No, I haven't won anything yet, Thomas," Jones quivers on hearing her call him Thomas. "I have backed three horses, which will run later in the day. I don't expect to win, but it adds to the excitement of the day, can I treat you to a drink in the VIP enclosure?" Thomas' mother is quite excited at the offer, but he declines.

"We must go, ma'am, there is a lot I want to show mum before her energy wanes. Oh, ma'am," he pauses and turns towards her. "The police called just after you left this morning, they were looking for Mr Buchanan. I told them he hadn't been home for several days as he worked in the city. I hope that was right?"

"Of course, that is quite correct, he works such long hours. Did they say why they wanted to speak with him?"

"They asked that we contact them as soon as he came home."

"Whatever has he been doing now? I will ask him this evening when he calls me." With that, Jones swings his mother's chair around, and they disappear into the crowd.

Girl Power

It is 5:15; I peer at the bedside clock in disbelief.

"What is the idea of coming back at this time, did he throw you out?" I do not take lightly to being awakened at this ridiculous time; and as Angela thinks it funny, I am not well pleased.

"It was your idea that I accept this date, where did you expect me to sleep?"

"You usually find a place."

"Well, I did find a place, but I didn't fancy it." She dangles a bunch of keys in front of me. "See! These are the keys to my new apartment. It's Stephanie's apartment on the river, and as she doesn't need it any more, he says I can have it."

"Bloody hell, I didn't think you would earn an apartment that quickly."

"It was easy. I just gave him a blow, and he gave me the keys."

"So why aren't you sleeping with him right now?"

"He's gone home to his wife. He was at the police station all day and thought it better if he went home."

"So the police have not arrested him?"

"Not yet, but they will. He says he didn't kill her, but he could have. They were arguing, he told her he was moving his account, and she went berserk. She admitted she was using him and that hurt him, he had fallen in love with her, so he told her to move out of his apartment and find herself another place to live and left her packing her bag. He then booked into the Park Crescent Hotel, and that's where the police found him this morning and took him in for questioning."

"Whoa, slow down, take a breath, I didn't understand half of that. So why have you come back here?"

"I didn't think it right that I move in whilst her bed is still warm, but I will tomorrow. It's a beautiful apartment, it has a…"

"Hey… Are you going to rabbit on, like an estate agent, all night? I have work to do in the morning."

"You old misery; put your arms around me. I'm frozen." I don't need telling twice, she straddles me and pins me to the bed, snuggles her nose into my neck and strokes my face. *What a girl! The power this girl has is unbelievable. She has won me a ten million pound account, made a guy fall in love with her, then kill his mistress, been given a luxury apartment on the river and got me pinned down in my own bed. Amazing!*

Arrested

Lesley steers the Bentley up the tree-lined drive of his home. His head is spinning, anxious to explain to Louise what has happened, the problem of how to tell her has preoccupied his thoughts all the way. He knows he has been stupid, he knows he loves her like crazy, and the last thing he wants is to upset her. Oh why couldn't he see through Stephanie's game, why did he have to work away from home, why couldn't he have an ordinary job and be there for his children? He tries to console himself, it will be okay, Louise loves him, she will understand that Stephanie means nothing to him, and know he didn't shoot her. As he feeds the steering wheel through his hands, only just missing the flowerbeds, he sees the police cars parked at the front of the house. Several still have their amber emergency lights flashing, his house door is fully open, and the light from the hallway cascades down the stone steps illuminating the gravel. He recognises the family doctor running into the house; his doctor's bag in his hand. A police constable closes the door behind him and stands on duty at the top of the steps.

Louise is laid on the divan, wrapped in a blanket; she is as white as a sheet, and her breathing erratic, she is in shock, and her nervous system is in tatters. Jones is sitting next to her, mopping the sweat from her brow; the doctor is forcing a concoction of tablets into her mouth, which he promises will calm her.

Lesley has no idea what Louise has been told. She will know of Stephanie's death by now, and this alone could be enough to destroy his marriage. If she believes he has shot her, goodness he has to talk with her and explain. The police are not sympathetic, they read him his rites and slip handcuffs around his wrists and drag him protesting to the waiting police cars. There is nothing he can do.

Louise has been heavily sedated, and Jones is gently stroking the back of her hand. As her butler he knows he shouldn't be touching her like this, but he is concerned; and yes, he does love her. He has always loved her; from the first moment he set eyes on her, he wanted her. He remembers the day she interviewed him and ordered him to stand in front of her, maybe it was the way she looked him up and down, maybe it was her dominant nature that he found so exciting. Anyway, he was hooked and wanted her. Now she is subdued and helpless, his natural instincts are kicking in. He resists the urge to whisper words of love into her ear, but the desire to caress her pale delicate face is too great to resist. The doctor checks her blood pressure for the third time, then her temperature and, finally, her heart rate.

"I have given her quite a strong sedative, she needs constant observation tonight." Jones listens intently to his instructions. "Can you stay with her tonight?" Jones nods, of course, he can. "And call me if her temperature rises?" He runs his finger across her brow and pulls her hair away from her eyes. Her face is white and expressionless. Even her lips, always full and temptuous, are pale and dry. His heart goes out to her, he hasn't served her for five years to let anything happen to her now, so he gathers her gently in his arms and carries her up the majestic staircase to her bedroom. It is going to be a long night, but one he will willingly endure. He pulls up a chair and sits next to her, watching her constantly until he too finally submits to fatigue and falls asleep, still clasping her hand.

Ups!

Angela is like a dog with two tails. She was out of bed before the morning paper arrived. Her bowl of porridge was devoured rather than eaten, and that was without syrup. Today is to be the biggest day of her life; she is taking possession of her first home.

It was only ten o'clock when she inserted the key into the front door of Stephanie's impressive apartment. The door swung open; and in her haste to see inside, she walked straight into the arms of a police officer standing guard. You have to feel sorry for the guy, he was only obeying instructions, which was to stop anyone entering the apartment until the forensic team had searched for fingerprints, but maybe he shouldn't have grabbed her where he did. He grabbed her shoulders, spun her around and pinned her up against the wall, screaming at her to identify herself. She did what any young girl would have done being taken by surprise; she retaliated by scratching his face and trying to twist his nose off. She was hysterical, it took three police officers to pull her off him; but that was only after her fingernails had criss-crossed his face, drawing blood down his cheek. At eleven o'clock, she was read her rites at Borough Police Station for attacking a police officer and resisting arrest.

It is now three o'clock. I am reading all about the incident on the front page of the national newspaper. The accompanying picture is not very complimentary; she is being marched out of the apartment, fighting and obviously shouting obscenities at two police officers holding her arms. Behind her, a young police cadet is stood in the doorway of the apartment, wiping his bloodstained face.

The description is dramatic and untrue.

'Street hooker arrested in Chelsea socialite murder case... Today at 11:00 a.m., a young woman was arrested as she tried to gain entry into the apartment of Stephanie Sterling, who was found shot dead late yesterday. A police spokesman said, the unknown girl had keys for the apartment and told them that Lesley Buchanan, owner of the said place, had given her the apartment for a trick she did for him. There will be a police press report within an hour.'

A member of parliament killing his long-standing mistress for a new girl on the block; has the making of a very exciting, moneymaking story.

Not only; is Lesley Buchanan an MP, but he is also CEO of the largest company in the country, this is a high-profile murder case, inter-woven with sex and jealously and is worth millions to any newspaper that can gain the right to publish it. Plus, we have an election in eight months; press editors are already anticipating government resignations, shattered careers and broken marriages amongst the high society. This could bring the government down, all they have to do is ask embarrassing questions, with the intention of stirring up trouble: questions, such as, did the prime minister know what was happening? How many more MPs are spending taxpayer money on call girls? Then, we will have the spin-off stories, such as, who gives the best value: a top class call girl or a street hooker?

Angela calls me from the police station. She is in tears and tries to explain her situation between sobs and sniffles. I have to admit I find her day rather amusing, but by the time she arrives home, I am feeling sympathetic. The police have put her through a very traumatic interrogation and made her repeat her story over and over again.

"They didn't believe me when I told them Lesley gave me the apartment. They said, no girl is given an apartment on her first date."

"It is difficult to believe."

"They practically accused me of being Stephanie's killer." Her desperate tale is interrupted when her mobile rings; she hands it to me. "You take it, I can't concentrate."

"Hi, my name is Bowden Leaver from the *Daily Spectator*. Can I speak with Angela?"

"I'm sorry, Angela is resting right now. Can I give her a message?"

"Hey man, tell her I called. My editor is willing to pay big bucks for her story, I'll call again in one hour," I tell her about the call.

"Wow! Big Bucks, maybe I wasn't in the wrong place after all."

Her phone rings continuously, I leave the calls to her answering machine. The first is a CIA detective, wanting clarification of her name, the next is another reporter, seeking an interview. One call is from the prime minister's office, requesting she makes an appointment; and the second is from Louise Buchanan. I play the recording.

"Good evening, my name is Louise Buchanan. I believe you know my husband. I need to speak with you as soon as possible. Could you please call me back on 0 89 31 24 26 25." There is desperation in her voice.

Angela screams in excitement and points at the TV monitor.

"Look, look I am on TV." She jumps to her feet, pointing at the screen. Sure enough, Angela is the main story on the early evening news. She sits and watches herself in disbelief.

"I'm famous," she bursts out laughing, "Look, I am on the tele."

I have written press campaigns and made many TV commercials in my career, but I have never witnessed a story spreading as quickly as this. The emphasis has changed slightly from being a minister's mistress to a street girl who can earn herself an apartment overlooking the Thames, after only one trick. Her phone rings again, she grabs it from my hand, her enthusiasm regained.

"Who...? When...? Why...? Really... Of course... tomorrow at 10:00, I will be there." She puts the phone down and burst out laughing.

"Well, who was that?" I ask, smiling at her excitement.

"You won't believe this." I wait for her to calm down until I can wait no longer.

"Well! Who was it?"

"That was the editor of Vogue magazine, she wants me to write a feature, I can't believe it... a feature on what a girl should wear if she wants a new apartment, then they want me to judge a competition on what a girl should wear on a blind date and the winner... Guess what?"

"What?"

"Wins an apartment." We both roll about the apartment in hysterics. "This is outrageous, what a stupid world we live in."

"Absolutely stupid, nice isn't it?"

The Campaign

"I am famous," she screams and skips around the lounge like an eight-year-old. "How easy was that? WOW! Am I clever or what?"

"You are very clever and lucky. It just shows how a story at the right time is all you need to become popular."

"I can do anything, I can make anything happen, I can have anything I want." She jumps onto the sofa, "Now let me think, what do I want next?" She screams with delight, "I know! I want a Bentley motor car, and a villa in... let me see, yes, a villa in Switzerland. Switzerland is a nice place to live, and then I want..."

"Hey, come down, you mustn't take your success for granted."

"You are an ad man, you can make it happen. Make me rich, make me famous, come on, you can do it, let's have some fun."

I find the challenge quite fascinating; it will definitely be more fun than selling pharmaceutical products for British Chemicals. She bounces off the sofa and jumps onto my knee, kissing my face like a pet poodle.

"So what are you going to do with me; tell me what I have to do next; who are you going to introduce me to; just make sure he is stinking rich."

I try to pull her off my face. She wriggles with excitement until we topple over onto the floor, only by applying all my weight do I manage to pin her down by her shoulders and hold her still.

"Listen, I have an idea, this is what we are going to do."

She breaks loose and tries to bite my nose. "Tell me what we are going to do."

"Ouch! You little bitch, I'm not going to tell you for that."

"No, no, tell me now. I am sorry, I am so excited."

"OK, are you listening?"

"Yes, I am listening, tell me, tell me."

"Then lay still and stay calm." I can feel her body relaxing. This is the first time I have presented a marketing and advertising campaign whilst laying on top of a beautiful girl who has her legs wrapped around me. "We are going to..." She tightens her grip.

"Yes?"

"We are going to get you elected to the position of..."

"Of what?"

"Of prime minister."

"Prime minister, you must be joking. I can't be prime minister; I am a woman."

"OK, prime mistress then." She releases me from her leg grip and falls to my side.

"You are not joking, are you?"

"No, I am not joking. I believe we can do it, are you up for the job?"

"You bet I'm up for the job, we will make living in this country happy and fun for everybody."

"Ouch!" she tightens her legs again, and I am forced to submit to her enthusiasm.

Meeting George

George is refilling his brandy glass, and it's only 9:30. He actually arrived at his office early but has achieved absolutely nothing. The news of Lesley's arrest is totally occupying his mind. He is convinced Lesley is incapable of killing anyone; he has known him for over ten years and worked closely with him on several government incentives. He feels it is his duty to ring Louise and offer her his sympathies, but all she does is cry. George sees himself as her uncle, but in reality, he is not related. He is a close friend of her father, and his heart goes out to her. Of course he knew Lesley was screwing Stephanie, or more to the point, Stephanie was screwing Lesley, but doesn't a man working under as much pressure as Lesley need some TLC from time to time? He lied to Louise and told her he knew nothing of his infidelity, but surely she must have known or at least been suspicious. He is surprised she is taking it so badly.

He reads the newspaper report for a second time; there is a photograph of Lesley sitting with a girl in the Savoy lounge, whom he doesn't recognise. He would have expected him to be with Louise or even Stephanie, he needs to identify this girl, maybe she can throw some light on the shooting. He calls the editor, and with a little persuasion, talks him into releasing her name.

I wonder what his relationship is with this girl, is she a work colleague; is she his latest mistress or is she a simple street girl who got lucky? He dials the number he was given but only gets a recorded message, promising to call him back.

His desk phone rings.

"George," he splutters into the mouthpiece. "What can I do for you?"

"Hello, my name is Angela, you just rang me. I am returning your call."

George sits up, coughs and clears his throat. "Angela, thank you for calling back. I am a friend of Lesley Buchanan, and I believe he is a friend of yours. Are you aware he has been arrested for the murder of Stephanie Stirling?"

"Yes, but this has nothing to do with me."

"Well, I was hoping you could clarify some points, as I don't believe for one minute he killed Stephanie. I think he has been set up. Could we meet so I can ask you a few questions, maybe you can help me?"

"I don't know what I can tell you. I met him only two days ago, but if you think I can help, yes, he is a nice guy, I would like to help him."

George scratches his head, thinking where they can meet.

"Look! My name is George Baldwin. I work at the Palace of Westminster. If I send a car for you, could we meet here?"

"I suppose so."

"Have you ever been inside the houses of parliament?"

"No, that would be exciting."

"I am so pleased you think so, is twelve o'clock okay? I will order a spot of lunch. Is salmon and a bottle of rose acceptable?"

"That would be cool." She jumps up and rushes into the bedroom.

"I'm lunching at Westminster today with my stepfather, who I haven't seen since I went to Switzerland, now what should I wear?" she mocks me jokingly, obviously enjoying every minute of her new-found fame.

"Does he know you are his stepdaughter?"

"No, and he won't even recognise me, now come on clever dick, what should I wear?"

"I think you should wear a clown's circus suit; that would cause a stir at Westminster." My joke is not appreciated; I get a slap.

"Look silly, this is serious, it must be a business suit, pencil skirt, dark court shoes, white, open neck blouse and cheap smelly." She pulls on another skirt and poses in front of the mirror. "Credit card, darling. I will need your credit card."

"Why cheap smelly?"

"It smells naughtier. I haven't got where I am today by smelling rich." She laughs out loud.

It isn't easy having a serious discussion with a girl whilst she admires herself in a full-length mirror.

"If you are serious about becoming prime minister, I will spend the day constructing your election campaign."

"Prime mistress," she corrects me, trying on yet another blouse.

"Okay, prime mistress! Are you listening?"

"Yes."

"Step one, we must create a PR campaign."

"What is a PR campaign?"

"Public relations, we must make sure the public know of you."

"Oh!"

"Can't you hurry up and decide which blouse to wear, you have to concentrate and understand what we have to do."

"I can hear you, carry on."

"Step one," I repeat. "Everyone must know you…

Step two: Everyone must like you; no… they must love you. Step three: Everyone must trust you and…

Step four: Everyone must believe in you."

She eventually stands still and twists left then right. "All the men love me already."

"Everybody must love you, not only the men."

"Sounds exciting! I've never had a woman love me before."

"My God, what am I going to do with you?"

"This blouse, sweetie?" She unfastens the top button, then the second and then the third. "Do you approve?"

"Of course, I approve."

Right or Wrong?

Louise pulls her silk sheets up around her shoulders, she can't remember going to bed. In fact, she can't remember much about last night at all, except that Lesley has been arrested, and Jones gave her a cocktail of tablets which she vaguely recollects drinking with a glass of water, or was it white wine? Maybe this is the reason the chandelier above her head is spinning so rapidly.

Jones appears at her bedroom door, looking tired and dishevelled. His shirt is crumpled, and his tie hanging limply over his shoulder. She has never seen him looking this rugged before.

"Good morning, mi lady. I hope you are feeling better. What can I get you for breakfast?"

"What are you doing, Jones, you should not be in my bedroom?"

"You were very sick last night, mi lady. We were all worried about you, and the doctor asked me to take care of you."

Louise pulls the bedsheets even higher to protect her vulnerability and realises she is dressed in her finest Victoria Secret skimpy night dress, the one she bought for her most intimate evenings and never worn.

"Who put me to bed?" she holds her head as a pain flashes across her brow.

"I did, mi lady. I couldn't leave you on the lounge sofa, it was too cold."

"And who undressed me and put me in my night dress?"

"I did, mi lady. I found it hanging in your wardrobe." She is lost for words.

"How dare you go through my wardrobe. I am your boss, the lady of the manor, and you are only my houseman. You are not allowed to go through my underwear." She is quite upset at the thought of him seeing her naked. She wonders whether she should sack him, but thinks better of it, instead, she just lies there, looking him up and down.

He looks creased and exhausted; she finds his masculinity attractive, even with him leaning against the door to steady himself. She can't help but be sympathetic; and as she catches sight of his feet, she is amused to see his toes turn up. She continues her visual exploration of his body, and the intensity of her passion increases. His face is heavily creased and in need of some care. His morning stubble needs removing, yet she must admit, it does makes him look rather distinguished; it's whiter than she expected but enhances his blue eyes. Oh my God, his eyes, she is totally captivated by his bright blue eyes. His stare is messing with her inner senses; she is losing control.

He is indeed a very physically imposing man, in great shape for his age, with a hint of a five pack showing through his shirt. She wasn't aware that he visited a gym, but he obviously works out. He stands in front of her, aware she is exploring his body, just as she did the first time they met, that was the day she interviewed him for the job of chauffer. He straightens up and shuffles a little, helpless to avoid her gaze. He wants her so bad, and his body hides no secrets, he too is out of control, and there is nothing he can do about it.

She quivers as she realises his secret. Lesley never had this effect on her. She loved Lesley for all the right reasons, but the affect this man is having on her is pure animal lust. This man is different to any man she has met before. His masculinity and domination over her is extraordinary, his need for her is sparking needs she didn't know she had, she is finding him difficult to resist. She struggles to sit up. Her gown slips off her shoulders and hangs precariously on her breasts; she doesn't try to save her nakedness. Quite the opposite, she is willing to submit to him. She runs her tongue around her lips and swallows heavily as her throat tightens. In a moment of coy innocence, she drops her head and raises her eyes to him.

"Come here, Thomas."

He childishly obeys, his need for her has maxed out, and he is unable to hide his want. She reaches up to unbutton his shirt, starting at the top, she fumbles her way down his chest, one button at a time until she reaches his breeches and unzips him. He is magnificent. For him, her touch is a dream come true; and as she strokes his body, he reacts in violent pulses of approval. His passion and love for her is overwhelming. He leans over her and searches for a kiss, any place will do, but she guides him down on her. Her smell, her sighs, the rising of her breasts is pure joy. He knows he can have her, and her open body is his for the taking.

"I will care for you," he whispers. "You will be safe with me, mi Lady." She puts her fingers to his lips.

"Shhh, there is nothing to say, Thomas," and with that, they surrender to the right or the wrong of a chauffeur-lady relationship.

Yes Minister

Angela slips her little flowered summer dress over her head and steps into a pair of beige, high-heeled shoes, increasing her height by three inches. She hasn't yet dried her hair and it looks as if she has been dragged through a hedge backwards.

"Are you not going to dry your hair before you go?" I thought this was quite an innocent remark and only wanted to demonstrate my interest, but I wish I hadn't.

"No silly, I want it to look wild and exciting. If I went to a hair-stylist, it would cost a hundred pounds to make it look like this, and you would have to pay, anyway, I need a new dress." Why do I get the distinct impression she is taking advantage of my generosity?

"There is nothing wrong with the dress you have on. I love the way you swish around the apartment in it, you look amazing."

"You might be right, Tim, I do like this little dress. It will wake up those boring, starched civil servants."

"I take it you don't have a very high opinion of our members of parliament?"

"It depends how rich they are, sweetie." She gives me a peck on the cheek. "Nothing else matters, and your credit card is safe today, except for a little lose change for the things your girl might need during a trip to the city."

I empty my wallet and count £300 into her outstretched hand; she looks at it with disdain, pauses, then stuffs it into her little, glittery clutch bag.

"Have you any instructions for me before I go."

"Yes, of course I have."

"Do I have to sit down and listen intently?"

"Yes!"

She pushes me down onto the sofa and straddles my lap."

"Okay, I am listening."

"Ouch, you are sitting on my…"

"Talking of which, when are you going to make love to me?"

"When you are prime minister."

"I can't wait that long."

"You will have to, now listen..." I shift her weight to ease my discomfort as she wraps her arms around my neck.

"I am listening, come on, give me what you've got."

Focusing on her lunchtime meeting with George is not easy.

"You have to be seen... you have to introduce yourself to as many people as possible. I don't mean you go up to them and say, 'Good morning my name is Angela.' I mean you have to be vibrant and full of fun, so they ask who you are."

"I know that, why do you think I am wearing a short flowery dress?"

"If you see a film crew, make sure you get in the picture. If they interview you, have something controversial to say. Disagree with the norm, be cheeky, be positive, always smile, be bouncy and be happy. Any publicity good or bad at this stage of our campaign is good. Do you think you can do that?"

"Easy peasy; what time is it?"

"Ten to twelve."

"George's car will be here. Should I flash my knickers when I get in and out of it?"

"Always."

"You are bad, I love you." And with that, she plops a big red lip mark on my cheek.

"I love you too." Oh wow!

The chauffeur opens the door of the big black Jaguar; and as she clambers inside, he watches her every move. He is well rewarded; up-flips the hem of her dress to reveal her bum; and once inside, she pulls her legs up under her chin. She is a master of her art. As she drives out of the mews, she throws me a big grin through the rear window. What a breath of fresh air she is, she could rule the world.

George has sent his secretary to wait for her at the Abingdon Street entrance of the iconic building. He hoped the side door would be free of photographers, but this isn't the case. The entrance is infested with 40 or more paparazzi, all clustered around the gate, even before the limousine has stopped, cameras are thrust into the car. As she exits, there is an explosion of flashing light bulbs, followed by a second burst when she trips on the kerb, sending her skirt flapping into the air. Tomorrow's papers have their front-page picture, one lucky photographer will sell the most naturally contrived picture of the day and make a fortune. George's secretary holds out her hand to welcome her.

"Good morning, Angela. The Rt Hon. George Baldwin is waiting for you in his chambers, please come with me."

The paparazzi scribble the details into their notebooks, 'Angela, 12:30, The Rt Hon. George Baldwin, secretary of state for works and pensions.' Some give her a three-star rating, which indicates 'worthy of further investigation'. One enterprising photographer is already emailing her picture to his editor with the question… 'Who is this?'

George's dull day is suddenly invigorated as she breezes into his office; he shakes her hand; and immediately, his depression has gone. He introduces himself totally failing to recognise his own stepdaughter, he was expecting a back-street girl, but it is obvious to him that Angela is anything but. As they chat, her charm overwhelms him. He is impressed with her intelligence, her awareness of politics and her understanding of world events.

"I have taken the liberty of booking the small dining room for lunch and inviting several close friends, is that alright with you? Between us, we hope to forge an objection against Lesley's arrest and possibly discover what happened.

Angela nods her head; the possibility of meeting influential people is more important to her than saving Lesley.

"Who are these other people?"

"Come, I believe they are waiting for us, I will introduce you."

Lunch with George

"Good afternoon, gentlemen… and lady," suddenly realising that Janet Cynthia Clynbourne is one of his guests. "I apologise for our late arrival. May I introduce Angela… err; goodness, I don't even know your surname. I am so sorry."

Angela has to think fast, eager to avoid the fact that she shares his name. "Err… people call me Angela Bee, but please just call me Angela."

"May I introduce you to Angela B," he repeats, not pronouncing it quite correctly, all five of them step forward to shake her hand.

"Any friend of Lesley's is a friend of ours," utters Janet to disguise the fact that she is embarrassed at meeting Lesley's latest lay.

"Thank you, I found him to be a nice guy. We must help him if we can."

Angela tries hard to remember their names. Remembering names has never been a problem for her, but these guys are not the norm. Their names are complex, hyphenated and accompanied with titles. As they flirt with her and ply themselves with wine, she focuses on each in turn and tries to associate their name with their title and then the constituency that they represent. Keith Mitchinson is a 50-year-old Yorkshire man, with an accent so broad that understanding his stories is difficult. He is MP for East Yorkshire.

"I am familiar with West Yorkshire but not East Yorkshire," she tells him. "That's on t'other side o'cuntry." They laugh at her, mimicking his accent.

Barry Cornwell must be the joker of the group, every remark he makes is a funny. At first, Angela laughs and thinks he is fun, but as the lunch progresses, he becomes wearisome. He is MP for Devon and Cornwall, anyway, that makes it easier to link his name with his constituency; Cornwell, Cornwall.

Then, there is Reginald Rolland Swordsmith: an immaculately dressed 40-year-old man, with a clear, precise English diction, although he could have a slight East European lilt. *He could be a BBC newsreader,* Angela thinks to herself. His vocabulary is vast, using words she is not familiar with; apparently he is secretary of state for health, Angela puts an asterisk against his name: Reginald Rolland Swordsmith, *could be useful.

The fourth man is Colin Brown: tall, young, handsome, attractive and entertaining, a 30-year-old guy, with deep green eyes. Berwick-on-Tweed should be congratulated for electing him as their MP. He also receives an asterisk. *Like him a lot.

Then last but not least… there is Janet Cynthia Clynbourne, MP for Barrow and Furness. She is a tall, stiff, upright woman and rather fearsome. She is wearing her identity signature, which is a tweed skirt and knitted cardigan. She is known for speaking out for equality and gay rights, but let's excuse her boring wardrobe; it is rather chilly up on the Furness peninsula.

As lunch progresses, Angela describes her first meeting with Lesley and explains how they became friends. She has to gain their trust, she needs these guys to believe her. It isn't long before they are laughing at the right times and smiling in the right places, she is slowly winning them over. Instead of sitting upright, they are leaning towards her. Their body language telling her they are involved and interested in what she is saying. This is confirmed when they ask questions: some simple and some stupid, she can sense their initial distrust of her relaxing. Luckily, the question of why Lesley gave her the key to Stephanie's apartment has not arisen. She knows her explanation is innocent, but she is pleased not to have to use it. They listen intently to the details of her conversation with Lesley during their trip to the escarpment and agree unanimously he needs their help.

Their interest moves onto the life and times of Angela. She makes it up as she goes but tells it so convincingly they are enchanted, even Janet is enthralled and hangs on her every word.

Lunch is a great success; Reginald invites her to accompany him to a council dinner in his constituency of Birmingham East. Colin Brown suggested she should visit China with him on a 'Buy British' promotional tour of Asia, next week; and Janet is determined they meet for dinner tonight. Only Janet Cynthia Clynbourne is a cause for concern, Angela is convinced she is gay.

George takes her arm and walks her back to his office along the dimly lit corridors of the Palace of Westminster. He is infatuated and rejuvenated by her; he is reminded of his valiant years when he was young, tall, slim and sharp. He drove an E-type Jaguar in those days and was a hit with all the girls at his university. Those days are long gone, but Angela has awakened a new passion for life within him. He remembers his daughter, they were wonderful days… just watching TV with his little girl sat on his lap made him proud. He loved it when she called him daddy, it made him tingle. He wonders where she is now and hopes she is happy and successful. No… he corrects himself… he hopes she is happy and content, what the hell has success got to do with it?

This is the first time that Angela has spoken to her stepfather in 15 years. He contributed nothing to her teenage years except to finance her, yet a part of her feels sorry for him. She can still see a sparkle in his eye, he must have been quite a catch in his day. She can understand what her mother saw in him, and why she still stands by him.

"So what are you going to do next, Angela?" he asks her.

"Well, I am dining with Janet this evening; and in a couple of days, I am attending a council dinner in Birmingham with Reginald. Next week, I am visiting China with Colin." She laughs, "A pretty full diary, hey what!"

"You must be careful, my dear. These people are vicious, they work hard and play hard, they are show offs, publicity is the name of their game, and they are always in the public eye," he pauses. "And they always have an ulterior motive for everything they do."

"I hope so, so do I."

"And what of you, are you always in the public eye?"

"I try to stay out of the public eye. I am happier just doing my job and keeping my head down, but I am always careful what I say, you never know when a camera and a microphone is watching and listening."

She links into his arm as they walk down the stone steps at the rear of the building to his limousine. The chauffer opens the car door for her. She jumps up and gives George a kiss on his cheek, which catches him unaware.

"Please, can I come and see you again?"

George is delighted. "Anytime, just call and I will send a car for you, did I tell you I have a daughter your age?"

"No, I didn't know that. I would love to meet her."

"Do you have my number?" he asks.

"Yes, you are already in my mobile." She clambers into the car and gives him a cheeky wave as she speeds out of Parliament Square. George stands and watches her disappear with mixed emotion, his daughter is forefront in his mind; he wonders where she is, and what she is doing. On the other hand, this girl needs his help and possibly his protection; his fatherly instincts are resurfacing.

The evening papers are full of Westminster's new sweetheart. One lucky photographer snapped Angela giving George a kiss in the courtyard, and another caught a very cheeky, up-skirt picture as she climbed out of the limousine. Today, she has definitely brightened a dull day in London Town.

"Wow, you have been busy." I flash the front page of the evening paper at her as she enters the apartment.

"Did I do good? George is lovely. I thought he deserved a treat, so I gave him a kiss."

"How is he going to explain that?"

"Easily, he is my stepfather, remember?"

"Yes, but he doesn't know that."

"And I don't want him to know, not yet."

"Now, I am having dinner with Janet Cynthia Clynbourne tonight. What do you know about her?"

"Not a lot, they say she is gay. Can you cope with that?" Angela nods, not as an answer to 'can she cope' but in agreement with her being gay.

"I think she is gay as well, I have never made love to a woman. I don't know how I feel about it, it could depend on how much she is prepared to pay."

"I hope you are joking?"

"Absolutely not, I need the money. Don't worry, my darling, you can have me any time you like, just keep lending me your credit card." She laughs at her joke, but I am hurt.

"You're jealous; aren't you? I do believe you are jealous."

"I am not jealous, I don't care a damn." I never was a good liar. "Just remember we are working for a bigger payout than some loose change for a bit of nooky."

I believe I have met my match with this girl. I am usually the one calling the shots, the one in control, it's the Leo in me, but this girl has me beat. I must be getting soft, letting her get through to me like this. Oh goodness! Am I falling in love with her?

As she walks into the lounge, dressed like a 16-year-old schoolgirl, the answer to 'am I jealous' is a big yes. She looks hot.

"You are asking for trouble dressed like that."

"I'm going to have some fun. If she is gay, I'm going to tease her, use her and rob her. How much do you think I should charge her for a grope?"

"I am not in favour of you groping with anyone."

"Just because you don't want me, doesn't mean others don't."

"I never said I don't want you, in fact…" She cuts me dead.

"Make up your mind, sweetie, time is running out. Didn't you just say that the pie is bigger than a bit of the crust?"

Beaten again. I am definitely losing it. "By the way, when is your birthday?"

"10 August, are you going to buy me a sports car?" With that, she laughs and slams the door shut, heading for a blind date without a guide dog. I collapse onto the sofa and sip an iced pineapple juice. I should have known, she is another bloody Leo. I drain the last remnants of my juice after pouring half a bottle of vodka into it.

First Time

Janet Cynthia Clynbourne is fussing over her apartment, trying to tidy it up and make it look respectable; it's at times like this, when she wishes her general standards of cleanliness were much higher. She just drops her clothes where she takes them off, she leaves her dirty crockery on the drainer for days and changes her bed sheets only when she is… entertaining; that was five weeks ago, when her cousin Elaine stopped over. She holds the pillowcase up to her nose, and Elaine's perfume is still evident, reminding her of a fulfilled night. *If I wore perfume, then this would be the one*, she thinks to herself. She has never had the desire to ponce herself up, but tonight might be an exception if that is what it takes to make it with Angela. After pointlessly moving her furnishings around for another hour, plumping up cushions and rinsing wine glasses, she looks at her work and gives a sigh of exasperation.

Janet's habits are not for the pure and innocent. Empty Gin bottles still litter the floor, one is hiding under the table, and she can see a second between the cushions of the sofa which she stuffed there only last night. Oh dear, and there is yet a third under the bed. A broken syringe lays abandoned in the bathroom basin and cigarette ash is scattered all along the edge of the bath. She tries to rinse the bath clean, but for some reason, the water will not drain away, a rotting cigarette butt is blocking the drain, and this is far too technical for her to resolve the problem. Every evening, she lays in the bath, smoking and abusing herself and listening to weird, psychedelic music performed by an underground German band called Drachen, which she thinks means dragon. She met them during a government incentive to Amsterdam last year and discovered she had a lot in common with them.

She has given up on her apartment; she needs help to give it that feminine touch which she is desperately seeking. *Now where is my mobile?* She eventually finds it down the back of the sofa, next to the gin bottle; it must have been there for days, as she can't remember when she last needed it.

"Jasmine, my love, I need your help. Send up a couple of your best cleaners, my place is a tip, and I have a guest for dinner. Oh yes, and the bed sheets need changing; white feminine sheets, patterned with flowers, will be ideal. Oh yes, and a bouquet of flowers for the table will look nice. You know the colours I like, and they must be real, not those pretend things you brought last time. I want sweet smelling flowers, my guest is class."

Jasmine has cleaned Janet's flat many times and knows exactly what she wants. For an illegal Estonian girl, Janet is an important client. She never asks any questions, and price is never an issue.

"My girls will be with you in ten minutes. Just relax and leave everything to me."

"Oh, thank you, Jasmine. I don't know what I would do without you." She gives a sigh of relief and turns her attention to ordering dinner.

Knowing that Angela likes salmon, she calls Fortnum and Mason and orders a full salmon salad hamper, with three bottles of champagne, then, she suddenly remembers she smashed her own dinner service three weeks ago, when she had a row with Joanna.

"And I need a set of crockery and glasses for two."

"Of course, Miss Clynbourne, would you like a personal waiter?" The store's events planner is quite aware of Janet's lack of presentation skills.

"Mm, is Claudette available, she is my favourite?"

"I'm sorry, Miss Clynbourne, Claudette is on vacation. I know you would prefer a girl, but on such a late order, Sebastian is my only available waiter." Janet is not impressed, this is to be a girlie night, and she doesn't want Angela distracted by a male waiter.

"Give it a miss, we will serve ourselves tonight."

"As you wish, Miss Clynbourne. The hamper will be with you at 7:30, but I do advise you to allow Sebastian to present the food and ice the champagne for you. It will only take him 30 minutes, and he will be very discrete." Janet agrees. Now all she has to do is decide what to wear, should she play masculine, feminine, dominant or gentle?

What's Going On?

The enormous leather settee in the VIP lounge of the Conservative Club is slowly devouring Colin Brown; he is slipping lower and lower until he is almost horizontal. Yes! Even within the membership of the Conservative Party status counts, you are either a very important conservative or a common conservative. Colin Brown has recently been promoted into the higher echelon; but tonight, there is doubt of his acceptability. He sips his vodka, enjoying his new, over-elevated social status. He used to drink Smirnoff until he attended a dinner at the Chateau de Versailles, in celebration of the French Republican Party winning the country's election. It was there he was introduced to Grey Goose: said to be the finest French Vodka. Since then, he only drinks Grey Goose; but to be honest, he can't taste the difference, it's all for show. Reginald Rolland Swordsmith sitting with him is stressing and giving him a hard time; tempers are rising.

"Reggie, I need two million in five days. I can't postpone my visit to China. What don't you understand about that?"

Reginald Rolland Swordsmith is totally frustrated. "How many times do I have to tell you, I can't get £2,000,000 in such a short period of time. Only Lesley can do that, and he is in police custody. Maybe, just maybe I could persuade his accountants to release £1,000,000."

"Look man! The consignment is already on the ship, and it sails on Saturday. We are dealing with the Chinese Mafia; and if I don't deliver the money, god knows what they will do. They might even kill me, you are scaring me, Reggie."

"Give them £1,000,000, and tell them they will have the other million before the ship reaches the English Channel, that will give us an extra two days to get it."

"No way, these guys don't play games. Look, British Chemicals is a massive company, they have many bank accounts within the group. Tell them to withdraw £5, 00,000 from four different accounts, they can easily lose it that way. Reggie, I am not joking. I have to take the full amount with me on Wednesday."

Reginald Rolland Swordsmith throws back his double whiskey and shakes his head.

"I will do my best, that is all I can promise."

"Look Reggie, we are about to make £50,000,000 out of this one shipment, make it happen; and another thing, Reggie! I want it in a flowery, female shopping bag because Angela, you know the hooker we had lunch with yesterday with George, she is going to act as our courier."

"Have you told her what she is going to do?"

"Don't be stupid, she knows nothing. She won't even know what is in the bag. She will be so excited at being in Beijing, she will be dizzy with excitement, so when you take her to the council meeting, tomorrow evening, sow the seed that shopping in Beijing is mind blowing and going with me is an opportunity she must not miss."

"Oh my God!" Reginald suddenly remembers. "I haven't booked a hotel room for her. I was going to book her into a back-street hotel, ply her with drink, screw her and dump her, now you want me to treat her like royalty, it will cost me a fortune."

"You better treat her good, we need her. Now get on the phone, you have a lot to do. Call her now so I can hear what you say." Reginald takes out his mobile and scans down his list of hookers. Angela B is at the top of his alphabetically arranged list.

This Must Be Love?

Thomas, relaxed and content, spoons up tighter into Louise; last night, he surpassed his own enigmatic expectations. Five years of wanting her exploded in a 60-minute expression of passion. Her response had definitely taken him by surprise. He thought she would be a typical untouchable rose and just lay there absorbing his attention, complaining if he went too far too fast, like most spoilt women of her status, but Louise was nothing of the sort. She was hot and willing. Not only did she submit to his demands, but she made demands of her own, some unknown to him. She enjoyed every minute of her night of love; she had never experienced anything like it before. She was at ease with him, and her body responded automatically to his touch. Her enthusiasm, passion and energy had come from within her. She knew she was pleasing him, but more than that, it was natural.

She gently pulls over the bedsheet to reveal his chest, wanting to look again at this powerful, tanned and muscular man; his flat stomach and ripped chest is to be admired, but what is this? She raises herself onto her elbows, so she can see clearer. Around his right nipple, there is a tattoo, she didn't see that last night and reaches for her glasses.

"Louise, what are you doing?" He opens one eye and grins at her.

She pulls her head back in surprise, abandoning her investigation.

"What is written on your chest?"

She runs her fingers around his nipple and over the tattoo, stretching his flesh until the word is revealed. She sits up, shocked at what she reads.

"Why do you have 'Louise' tattooed on your chest?"

"It's not on my chest, it's on my heart," he whispers.

"But it is my name, why is my name on your chest."

"Because that is the right place for it. I fell in love with you the first day we met. That day, I stood before you whilst you asked me all those stupid questions: how old was I; am I married; do I live alone? You even asked me if I had a girlfriend."

"I did not, why should I want to know if you had a girl friend?"

"Exactly my point! You asked if I lived alone, and would I be prepared to move into the house with you."

"That is what the job demanded. I had to ask you those questions."

"You knew exactly what you were doing, perched cross-legged on the edge of your desk, with your breasts sticking out. Goodness, your nipples were practically through your blouse: and not only that, your bony knees were swinging open, like a barn door. You knew what you were doing, alright, you knew I could see all you had in that sexy pleated skirt. I don't know how I managed to control myself."

Louise can't believe what she is hearing. She can remember thinking he was rather dishy, but she had no idea she was being so blatant.

"Well, I must admit I was slightly intrigued, but that is all. Goodness, all the times I have driven around the countryside with you, telling you my problems and secrets; and all the times I have accepted your hand, thinking you were being polite and helping me out of the car, I had no idea you felt this way towards me."

"It has been my secret. I was afraid you would reject me, maybe sack me… why should you want me. I am only a houseboy, a chauffeur, a gofer."

She reaches up and runs her finger across his mouth. His morning stubble excites her, it is rough and sensuous. She has to put her lips to his. He flips her onto her back, kneels up inside her open thighs and lifts her ankles high into the air. She screams in delight at his power and the control he has over her. Surely this must be rape; she has never been taken like this before, she has never been forced into total submission. No, she is not being raped, she loves every thrust of his body. His surge is stimulating; every nerve cell in her body. Her thoughts are of hot, sandy beaches, fleecy white clouds, and… and having this man's baby. She digs her nails into his back, determined not to let him pull out of her.

"Oh God! You are amazing."

He releases his grip on her ankles and drops breathless on top of her. She loves the smell of his sweating body and wraps her legs around him, this man is not going anywhere. She has given herself to him, and she has accepted all he has to offer. Sex has never been so good, she is invigorated, and when it comes gift-wrapped like this, there are no words to explain it.

The First Time

"Angela, hi! It's Reginald Rolland Swordsmith, you remember we met for lunch?"

"Of course, I remember you, are we still on for dinner in Birmingham, tomorrow evening?"

She stops herself, ringing the bell push adjacent to Janet Cynthia Clynbourne's name a second time. It is the top button of four, and Angela presumes that Janet must live on the fourth floor. She doubts this antiquated, Georgian building will have an elevator and is anxious at the thought of trekking up three flights of steps in her high heels. The bright blue door of 14 Riverside Mews remains shut, so she returns her attention to her mobile.

"That is why I am calling." Continues Reggie, "Text me your address, and I will collect you at 2:00 tomorrow afternoon. We have to be at the hotel no later than 6:00, as we are due at the town hall at 7:30."

"That's great, what do you think I should wear?"

"It's a civic reception, I suggest a long dress, we might do a bit of dancing later if we haven't eaten too much."

"A long dress, I can't afford a long dress." He senses the panic in her voice.

"Whoa, it's not a problem. Slip along to Shirlee Antonio, she is a dress-designer friend of mine, 110 Kings Road, Chelsea. Buy something on my account, keep the price sensible, don't waste money on pants, you won't need pants under a long white dress." Reginald passes the remark off as a joke, but he is deadly serious.

"Where will I dress, at the town hall?"

"Don't be silly, Joshua will take us straight to the hotel. We are booked into the Radisson Blu. I always stay at the Radisson Blu in the centre of town. I am staying until Friday, if you have a few days free, you can stay and sample the shops. Let me know."

"Okay, two o'clock. I will text you my address." She is pleased with herself, *a full-length dress and three days in Birmingham at the Radisson Blu, free, on the expense of a complete stranger. Not bad! Men are such simple animals.* She looks up to see Janet Cynthia Clynbourne standing in the doorway.

"Is that Reggie? A stupid man, you must be careful with him; he thinks he is god's gift to women. Anyway darling, you look amazing. Come on up, dinner will arrive in one hour."

Angela looks her up and down and is relatively impressed. Janet has definitely made an effort; she is wearing a tight, beige, woollen, knitted jersey without a bra, revealing an ample bosom, with nipples clearly defined through the threads. A tweed skirt hangs respectfully below her knees, and her shoes have a small heel, just a little too heavy for Angela's taste. Her hair is well groomed; and since this morning, she has trimmed her eyebrows, which has softened her features somewhat. Still no perfume that Angela can detect and no makeup, not even lipstick. She is a strange woman indeed.

Her apartment is colossal, the lounge alone is the size of most modern apartments, and the bedroom the same. Janet's enthusiasm to show Angela the bedroom is rather too obvious. The wardrobes and cabinets are made from old English oak, and the four-poster bed is a throwback to King John's days. The drapes are equally vintage, an intricate woven jacquard design in gold and red. Over the bed hangs a wall tapestry of a foxhunt, possibly a copy of one of the old masters, but Angela has no idea which.

"Here, let us drink to a new friendship." Janet pops a champagne cork and pours Angela a glass full.

"Down in one, my lovely. The first swig has to go down in one, we have plenty to get through." Angela splutters as the wine bubbles up into her nose.

"I can never get used to the fizz." She giggles, and Janet laughs at her.

"Don't you drink champagne?"

"Only on very special occasions, like when someone else is paying for it."

"Then enjoy because I am treating you. Would you like to share a line or two with me?"

"I don't understand."

"Goodness girl, where have you been?" Angela watches as Janet spreads some white powder onto her glass-topped coffee table and arranges it into a column, then, she gets down on her hands and knees and sniffs it into her nose.

"I don't do drugs, I have never done drugs," Janet is obviously surprised, "I get drunk now and again," she refills her champagne glass and takes another gulp to hide her innocence, this time without choking.

"Well, you are a goody-goody, are you always so good?"

"Not always," she laughs as the champagne is already making its presence felt and attempts to change the conversation to more innocent banter. "Janet, I love your apartment, but I can't help but notice you don't have a kitchen."

"I don't do cooking, Angela. I am far too busy, anyway, I burn everything."

"What about a tea or coffee?"

"I order from Starbucks, they are just around the corner. It takes them a minute to deliver. There are many things I don't do: I don't cook, I don't clean, I don't shop, I don't use makeup, and I won't visit hairdressers. I hate having people fondling my hair."

"You are strange, Janet. I thought every woman loved visiting the hairdressers."

"Not strange, my pretty, just too busy. As a child, I was spoilt something rotten. I got everything I wanted and did nothing to get it. I don't intend changing now."

"And what do you want now?"

"At the moment, I want you…" she pauses just for a second and then continues, "…I want you to have a relaxing evening and for us to get to know each other. What did Reggie want?"

"He was giving me instructions for tomorrow. He is picking me up at 2:00; we are attending a civic reception in Birmingham." Janet utters a deep sigh.

"Excuse me, darling. I must make a phone call," and with that, she disappears into the bedroom and grabs her phone.

"Reggie, I am telling you now, leave Angela alone; she is mine. I got her first, go screw one of your other tramps but leave Angela alone, or I will expose you for the sleaze bag you are, do you hear me."

Reginald Rolland Swordsmith is not intimidated by her; as far as he is concerned, Janet is a stupid, over-active lesbian. He would have nothing to do with her if it wasn't for her contacts: her street people who distribute the drugs.

"Janet, if you think I am letting a pretty little girl like Angela slip through my sheets, you have another think coming. We will let Angela decide if she prefers a dowdy lesbo like you, or someone exciting like me, so stuff off, darling. Go prepare your people, the shipment will be here in two weeks," and with that, he leaves Janet, listening to a dead phone.

She never liked Reginald, he is an untouchable lout. He never lets anything worry him and always manages to avoid the blame when things go wrong. Only the sight of Angela, sitting on the sofa, sipping her bubbly and pulling at her school blouse, helps her to forget him. Angela

85

is uncomfortable; she is in desperate need of a new blouse: a bigger one. She bought this one when she was 16 and has broadened out a little since then. She wants to stand and pull it straight, but the champagne is kicking in, she fears she might topple over.

"Sorry for that, my lovely. Dinner is on its way, it will be here in ten minutes. I have requested a waiter to prepare it for us, his name is Sebastian. He is a very sexy Spaniard and my favourite waiter; he serves for me regularly. Now let's finish this bottle of champers, we don't want it to lose its sparkle now; do we?"

The psychological battle continues throughout the meal. Janet's intention is to talk Angela into bed; and at the moment, Angela seems to be enjoying her attention. The food and the quirky entertainment are second to none. Angela is also besotted with Sebastian. He is just one hulk of a man, with sex appeal and charm, shame he is gay. Well, that is what Janet has told her.

By midnight, Angela is swimming under the influence of three bottles of champagne, or is it four? The touch of a woman is something she has never experienced before, and she likes it. Men just go for her sexy parts, but Janet is touching her where she hasn't been touched before, she knows when to stop and when to go, teasing her, then retreating, holding her in suspense before moving on. She thought she only had three erogenous zones, but wherever Janet touches her, she tingles. Her body lights up and wants more of the same. Janet knows she has Angela very close to submission; her arched body begging for a stronger caress is a giveaway.

"Let's go to bed?" Janet's suggestion is timed to perfection. She has practiced it many times on unsuspecting girls. She is confident of success, which is why she is taken back by the response.

"It's going to cost you." Angela whimpers as sexily as she can. She feels guilty at the brutality of the statement and senses Janet retract, "But I will go to bed with you, I would like that a lot," quickly realising a positive reaction to the suggestion is required.

"You little bitch! You dare to charge me, how much do you want?"

Angela has to think fast which isn't easy through the champagne vapour whirling around in her head. She lets the guys on the quay have a grope for £50, but this is different, this is the big time. Oh why did she sniff that stuff up her nose, and it hurts like hell, she has no idea how much to ask. Janet has done an amazing job on her, winding her up, exciting her body; and at the same time, deadening her mind. She splutters out the first figure that comes into her head.

"A thousand pounds for the night."

Janet pulls away and releases the delicate girl already in her grasp. She too is worked up into a state of intense passion, she is desperate to sample the fruits of this beautiful creature.

"Okay, but you will have to work very hard for me."

Angela holds out her hand and grasps the cheque that Janet is dangling in front of her.

"Is it going to cost me £1,000 every time we make love?" Angela giggles.

"We can negotiate a discount for a package deal if you are gentle with me."

Tough Dealing

"Who is that, go away?" I try to bring my bedside clock into focus; it's 6:00 a.m.

"Stop joking, it's me, let me in." Angela looks pale and tired but in good spirits. I get a friendly slap for my joke as she pushes passed me.

"Make me a coffee, darling. I am in need of an energy boost." Her request is my command; I stir two spoonful of sugar into a frothy instant coffee and wait for her to relax. Of course, I desperately want to know what happened last night, but I resist the temptation of bombarding her with questions. She will tell me in her own good time, and I don't have to wait very long.

"Well, do you want to know what happened or not?"

"Of course I do."

"Well," she takes a deep breath and folds her legs up under her. "The evening started just fine. Janet was sweet and the perfect hostess. She told me about her career and her ambitions, for the first two hours, she was interesting and entertaining. I must admit I liked her touching me, but as we emptied the second bottle of champagne, she got her smokes out; and her persona changed almost instantly. She became more dictatorial, more forceful and more sadistic. I was on the point of coming home when she collapsed and fell asleep. I too must have fallen asleep."

I listen to her story—jealous and fearful—the last thing I want is for her to tell me she enjoyed the experience. As for the details of her first time with another woman, I don't want to know, that will remain her secret. All I can be is thankful she is home; and apparently, none the worse for her all-girl affair.

"What are you holding in your hand?" Angela waves a piece of paper in the air.

"It's a cheque, a cheque for a thousand pounds."

"You charged her a thousand pounds?"

"I am worth every penny." She laughs. "Why are you looking so amazed?"

"I hope you still prefer making love with a man?"

"Of course, sweetie, especially you. But a girl has to do what a girl has to do, it could be my last lesbian affair if you promise to keep me in the manner to which I am accustomed." Oh no, I am not ready to go there.

"Not yet, sweetie."

"What did you say?" she jumps on my outspoken thoughts.

"I said," changing the subject as subtly as I can. "Don't you have a meeting with Vogue at 10:00?"

"Bloody hell, I had forgotten, what time is it now?"

"Seven o'clock!"

"Oh thank goodness, I still have time to shower."

"Is there anything else I need to know?"

"Not that I can think of, except I am leaving for Birmingham at 2 o'clock, and oh yes! The police have finished with Stephanie's apartment, so I am moving in."

"That is pretty important, Angela. I need to know things like that, how long are you staying in Birmingham?"

"Two or three days."

"Give me the keys to Stephanie's apartment. I want to take a look inside. I don't know what I am looking for, but I am convinced the police are missing something. I have researched Stephanie, she was handling three important accounts at the agency. There is a possibility she was bedding all of them, in which case, there could be several jealous guys with a motive to kill her."

It's 8:10 before she appears back in the lounge, dressed in what I can only describe as 'hiking wear'.

"I thought you were going for an interview with Vogue magazine, not a walk over Ilkley Moor."

"I take it you don't approve of my dress?"

"You are correct, I don't approve. You are visiting the icon of sophisticated fashion, what sort of image do you think that is going to achieve?"

She gives me a twirl and nearly trips over herself.

"See, you can't even stand up in those boots, they will laugh at you."

The hiking boots are only a part of my disapproval. They are mid-brown in colour with red laces. Her legs are bare and rather pale, which makes her short, red pants look even brighter than they are. A thick black belt separates them from a cream, buttoned shirt, under a loose-fitting, camouflage-patterned jacket. A bright green silk scarf around her neck completes the look.

"And I can see your tits, when the jacket swings open, shouldn't you be wearing a bra?"

"Look, clever dick. I am not going to stand out in a crowd of beautiful women, looking like a model. I can't compete with six-foot tall lollipops of sex appeal, get used to the idea that I am an ordinary Yorkshire girl."

"Yorkshire girl you are, ordinary you are not. If they don't let you into the building, don't blame me."

I shouldn't be criticising her. I should be telling her she is beautiful to boost her confidence, possibly go with her to offer her support, but I don't. I hope I don't live to regret it, you see I am falling in love with her. I tingle when I see her. I want her every time I touch her, she is getting through to me.

She perches on the arm of the large sumptuous settee in Sarah Thompson's office. Her hiking boots swinging in the air, hiding the fact that her legs are unable to reach the floor. The office is what you might expect; spacious opulence, with a touch of feminine delicacy. The view through the window must be one of the most impressive in London, it looks out over the River Thames towards the Palace of Westminster. The sound of the river and the city beyond can just be heard. What Angela didn't expect is the clutter of papers, magazines, photographs, cameras and computers scattered everywhere. This is definitely a creative working environment and must be taken seriously. When she stepped into the room, Sarah Thompson was standing at the window, looking through a transparency she was holding up to the light. She is not the glamour queen Angela was expecting, but an attractive, middle-aged, slightly overweight woman dressed in the simplest of Marks and Spencer's dresses. Angela recognised a sense of familiarity with her. They could have a common awareness, an inability to compete with the city's top models.

"Good morning Angela. My name is Sarah Thompson, and I am the editor of Vogue." She doesn't even turn to look at Angela, but keeps holding the transparencies up to the sky. "I spoke with you yesterday. I have an offer which I think will interest you. Please, make yourself comfortable."

As there is nowhere else to sit, Angela smiles and swings her legs even more vivaciously.

"Two coffees please, Miriam." Sarah's frilly little assistant, who Angela had not even seen sitting in the far corner of the office, dashes out of the room as if she is on a life-saving mission. So far, Angela is not impressed; she expected more attention and wanted to be treated with more respect.

"This is the deal, Angela. To be honest, we are taking a risk with you. We don't know you, or anything about you, yet you seem to be making waves in the press, so we are prepared to help you. We will follow you for two weeks, reporting on what you wear: what you wear when you go shopping, when you go clubbing, what you wear when out jogging or cycling, or whatever it is you do. Our readers are interested in a girl who can go on a blind date and come home with the keys to a luxurious apartment; you are the fastest rags-to-riches story in town. Now Angela, what might you be doing during the next two weeks?"

The thought of being followed by a photographer all day does not appeal, and Sarah's cocky attitude is starting to offend, so she sits in silence, hoping Sarah will put down the transparency and give her the attention she demands.

"How much are you paying?" Sarah puts down the picture, mission accomplished.

"It depends on what we can make of your story, the more interest your story generates, the more we can offer you. So for starters, we will pay all your expenses. Pay for the clothes you buy and throw in, err... let's say, £200 a week for the two weeks."

Angela jumps to the floor and heads towards the door, giving a look of total disbelief.

"You are joking, aren't you, you have dragged me here for this? Look honey, if you want to follow me around, I want £10,000 a week and a contract for a minimum of six months. I am not excited at having a photographer recording everything I do, nor am I excited at the world knowing everywhere I go." Angela is bluffing, of course, for £200 a week, she will do anything, but there is a game to be played here, and Angela enjoys playing games.

There is an uncomfortable silence as Angela stares straight into the eyes of Sarah.

"Sarah sweetie, let me tell you a little about myself, then you will feel better about your investment. This afternoon, I am going to Birmingham to attend a civic dinner with Reginald Rolland Swordsmith MP. On Friday, I am going to China with Colin Brown MP, with a Support Britain trade delegation. I am screwing Janet Cynthia Clynbourne MP; and to top it all, I am under surveillance by the police on suspicion of murder. If you want to record my days, the price is £10,000 a week."

"Goodness, you are a busy girl and a bossy one. I need to think about it."

"You have ten minutes. I am leaving for Birmingham in two hours, you are either on board, or you miss the boat... Nine minutes."

"Wait, I am interested, we need a story like yours. Let me contact our accountants."

Publicity

The minute Angela walks in through the door, I can tell she has enjoyed her morning.

"Boy! Did I do good or what, I had her eating out of my hand? They are writing a feature on me for the next six months. She has employed a photographer to film my every move, and they will describe the clothes I wear; and I will explain why I chose them, and what I hope to achieve by wearing them. Pretty good, hey what? Oh yes, and they are paying me £10,000 a week."

"Wow, you don't hang about, do you?"

"You said we needed publicity."

"Yes, but to hit 50% of the electorate in one week is amazing."

"How do you work that out?"

"English women do not relate the clothes they wear to what they want to achieve, they will be totally intrigued. You will educate, entertain and give them a reason for changing their wardrobe. They will adore you… and women are 50% of the population."

"So you honestly think I can become prime minister?"

"More than ever."

"I never thought leading the country would be so much fun."

"And that is the magic word… FUN, the people of England need some fun."

"What else can I offer them?"

"They need love, but you can give them that later."

"Okay, I'm off to visit Shirlee Antonio down the Kings Road. Your credit card can have another day off today; my trip to Birmingham is at the expense of Reginald Rolland Swordsmith MP. Don't wait in." I watch as she hails a street taxi, a white Vauxhall Astra pulls out from the curb and follows her down the avenue. I would have expected a more prestigious car from Vogue but not to worry, they are paying her well.

I too am on the case; I have been studying the government's policies, their campaign pledges, and their successes and failures. Their achievement rating is very low; to be honest, it is zero. Immigration control is a joke. The National Health Service is on the verge of collapse. 80% of the population are obese, 60% of the population where born outside the UK. Plans to improve the railway network has stalled, and new housing has only reached 50% of its target, oh dear... it reads like a death wish.

I am also engrossed in the research of the five MPs Angela met yesterday. Not one of them is ringing true; I am concerned. Colin Brown visits China three times a year and has done for the past three years; always in March, July and October. There is no apparent explanation or political reason for his visit. Reginald Rolland Swordsmith, on the other hand, is regularly seen down the back streets of Birmingham. The most likely explanation is a liking for degenerate women, but this does not ring true. He is a smart guy and very rich, and his relationship with models, actresses and even the occasional film star has been well documented. As for Janet Cynthia Clynbourne... well, she is an outspoken woman's liber, equal rights, equal pay, equal everything; a lot of people don't like her, mostly men. Her list of lovers reads like a Women's Institute register.

Keith Mitchinson is a director of British Chemicals, so he has a financial link with Lesley, which is worth investigating, and Barry Cornwell, the last, but I am sure, not the least of our favourite five, was born in Cornwall. After his marriage to a local school teacher, he bought a large Victorian house in Devon and now owns three restaurants in the area, a marina and a fleet of boats, which he hires out for fishing trips, river cruises and shopping trips to France. He is known in the town as the Pirate of Penzance.

Birmingham

"Angela, wake up, we have arrived at the Radisson."

Joshua steers the big black Jaguar up the main drive and stops in front of the over-designed entrance of the Birmingham Radisson Blu. The journey from London was slow and tedious, and Reginald Rolland Swordsmith wasn't the most entertaining of travel companions. He spent most of the journey on his tablet. Had he been playing games; then Angela could have joined in, but he was working on boring government business. He was polite, even charming towards her, but she certainly felt like an attachment to be dealt with later, so she curled her legs up tight into her tummy and fell asleep.

It is true that Reginald had work to do and rather waste this time in the car. He wanted to reduce his backlog of constitutional enquiries, but he found it difficult with Angela kicking him every time the car lurched left and right as it sped up the M1, overtaking car after car. Anyway, he survived the journey with only a few bruises.

Joshua is too old to be humping heavy cases about; this is the main reason he quit his job as a chauffeur on the airport run. His passengers now carry small overnight bags and brief cases, nothing like the two oversized designer cases that Angela has packed. He does eventually lift them clear off the boot, and when his huffing and puffing has subdued, he opens the car door for her, he finds her fast asleep. *Oh dear, this isn't the way a girl accompanying Reginald Rolland Swordsmith should arrive at the Radisson Blu.* Joshua passes the cases to the concierge and steps into the car and gives her a gentle shake.

"Wake up, madam, we have arrived." He shakes her more vigorously.

Too vigorously, she rolls off the seat onto the floor of the limousine. A camera flashes; a photographer has captured the incident. Joshua tries to shield her from further embarrassment but fails miserably; this is an opportunity the paparazzi are not going to miss.

"What is the problem?" Reginald Rolland Swordsmith pushes his way through the excited camera-wielding mob to find Angela staggering to her feet. In an attempt to steady herself, she grabs his arm. "Smarten yourself up, girl. Your picture will be all over the newspapers in the morning."

"Shall I kiss you?" Angela can't resist teasing him.

"Definitely not." But that is like a red rag to a bull; she stretches up and kisses him squarely on the mouth.

"Explain that picture in the morning, darling." Reginald Rolland Swordsmith doesn't know whether to be angry, embarrassed or simply to laugh it off. He will decide when the pictures appear, as for Angela, he has to admit she is beautiful. The chaos around the car increases as she pulls her black, rimmed hat over her face and sticks out her chest to tighten her black, long-sleeved jersey, a quick pull on her pink leather belt throws out her white, flowery, knee-length skirt, which flares out to reveal white knee-length socks. She is a picture of elegance, even Reginald Rolland Swordsmith is impressed. He walks her into the hotel, proud to have her on his arm.

"Who is she?" One of the photographers ask.

"I have no idea, but, wow! She must be a film star."

She stumbles again as she steps into the hotel, creating yet another photo opportunity. No one will ever know if she tripped on purpose or whether it was an accident, whichever, the pictures in tomorrow's papers will be full of her arrival; and hopefully, Vogue will have a winning story. Tweets are pouring into their publicity department from avid watchers on the magazine's live stream website: some are impressed, some puzzled, some sympathetic; but they are all massively entertained... she has the country totally hooked.

Reginald Rolland Swordsmith is angry; he doesn't take kindly to his girlfriends receiving more attention than he is. He usually ushers his girls into his room without anyone noticing them, but this little girl has an appeal all of her own, and a fan club he didn't account for. She is definitely not a brainless girl overcome by the big occasion. She draws back the curtains of her suite and looks down onto the hotel's arrival area; limousines are queuing at the front door, delivering council and government dignitaries attending tonight's banquet.

"Has my dress arrived?" Reginald Rolland Swordsmith points at a large white box, wrapped in ribbon, on the foot of her bed. "Good, how long do I have to dress?"

"Two hours, Joshua will be back at 7:00, we have to be at the town hall at 7:30."

"Have you made an appointment for me with the hotel hairdresser?" He looks at her in bewilderment.

"Have I hell, why should I make you a hair appointment?"

"Because that is what a gentleman does. As time is tight, you better call now and make me an appointment, or…"

"Or what?" he asks, trying to maintain his pride which is seriously under threat.

She thinks for a minute.

"Or I'll take your willy out whilst you are giving your speech."

He can't laugh at her joke; no girl has ever spoken to him like this before.

"Look darling," she whispers whilst palming the front of his trousers. "If you want a good time tonight, just do as you are told. You won't be disappointed, but it will cost you, now run along, I have to dress."

He does as he is told and takes refuge in the hotel bar, downing three vodka and tonics, one after the other.

My mobile rings with the soothing sound of a harp. I have allotted this gentle call sign to Angela; I think it very appropriate.

"I am at the Radisson Blu and having so much fun. This Reginald Rolland Swordsmith, or whatever his name is, is a poodle. I will call you later, got to go, got a photo shoot in the lobby with Vogue in 30 minutes."

"Angela, wait, I have something important to tell you… drat!" Her phone disconnects. I wanted to tell her about her five new friends, and I believe they are not to be trusted. Maybe I shouldn't worry about her, she can take care of herself; that is what Angela does.

From Rags to Riches

"What do you think of my little white dress?" Reginald stares at her; his mouth gaping. His opinion will have no consequence, she doesn't care whether he likes it or not. He tries to splutter out an opinion, but his two hours of drinking has taken its toll.

"That's a party dress. I think a full-length dinner dress would have been more appropriate."

"What, don't you like my legs?" She lifts the hem of the dress and swirls around.

"I love your legs, you are beautiful." He leans towards her and tries to kiss her.

"Not now, Reggie, you will smudge my make-up. Now! As I have your undivided attention, let's go and rock around the town hall clock." As they march through the hotel lobby, she is asked to pose for a couple of photographers who have been waiting patiently for her, she gives them a cheeky grin and stands on one leg. They are delighted, the pose is an instant success. This is the easiest job she has ever done.

Sarah Thompson downloads the photographs onto her office computer and has to admit Angela looks amazing. What a coup, she is fast becoming the talk of the town, and Sarah knows the sales of Vogue will rocket.

She scribbles the title of next week's feature on her pad: *From rags to riches,* then introduces the story: 'A girl on a mission needs to think fast and adapt even faster…' It only takes her five minutes to outline the flavour of the story she wants. Her copywriters can fill in the details and pull the story into shape. Choosing the picture with which to illustrate the feature is her job, and she is not finding it easy. She especially loves the shot of Angela in her big black hat and tight jersey, which she wore on her arrival at the Radisson Blu; and the little white party dress for the civic dinner is so cheeky, only Angela would dare to wear a sexy party dress at a civic dinner. Maybe it's the pale green crocheted shoulder wrap that gives it respectability; the silver-mirrored shoulder bag is a masterstroke. She looks tall and elegant, much taller than she actually is, maybe it's the way her hair is tucked behind her ears before flowing over her shoulders and down her chest. Only when she stands next to Reginald Rolland Swordsmith, it is obvious she is a mere 5ft 4in.

The Birmingham Post wins the picture of the day, the shot of her toppling over on her high heels outside the hotel and falling into Reginald's arms. His reaction to save her from injury was natural. The kiss she planted on his cheek was not but what fun, it turned a simple incident into a massive story of passion.

Prove It

Lesley Buchanan is told to stand; he grabs the rail of the dock to steady himself and faces the judge.

"How do you plead?"

"Not guilty, sir. I left her packing her bags." His nervousness and frustration far exceeds his ability to answer the question with a simple yes or no, which is all that is required from him. He continues to declare his innocence until the judge loses patience and has to silence him.

"That's enough, Mr Buchanan. All we want to know at this moment in time is how you are going to plea, so we can schedule a date for your case to be heard. The prosecution has requested four months to collate evidence; therefore, the case of the country versus Lesley Buchanan will be heard in four months' time on 19 December."

Lesley's brief rises to his feet.

"Your Honour, may I request that my client is granted bail during this time. Neither the prosecution or the police have found one piece of evidence that links my client with the murder of Stephanie Stirling." The judge scratches his head.

"Might I remind you that Miss Stirling was shot in Mr Buchanan's apartment, and Mr Buchanan has admitted being with her minutes before the estimated time of death."

"That is true, Your Honour, but I will prove that Mr Buchanan is an innocent man; and with no matching DNA samples, no murder weapon and a skin tight alibi, I ask you again to grant my client bail."

The judge pauses and taps his pencil on his bench.

"I will grant Mr Buchanan bail until this date. He must understand that he has to report to his local police station every day at a time of their choosing and not leave the country."

Lesley's brief looks down at him. "You are a free man, Mr Buchanan. Might I inform you the best evidence to prove your innocence is for us to find the murderer, so we hope you will tell us everything you know about Stephanie Stirling, who she is working for, with whom she could be having other relationships, who knew where she was living; and most important, who had a key to her apartment. The police believes she knew her killer."

Lesley shakes his head and grabs the hand of his brief. "Thank you, we will talk in the morning."

It's only when he steps inside his home, the true despair of his situation is apparent to him. Louise has left, the house is in lockdown, the windows are sealed; and the curtains drawn together, stopping all but a slither of light from entering. Louise must have left shortly after his arrest, turning off the heating and leaving the rooms cold and desolate. She has at least covered his valuable antique furniture with white dustsheets; but as he walks from one room to the next, it becomes obvious she has no intention of coming back. His beautiful house is a home no longer, the fridge is silent and empty, the beds naked of sheets, and his grandfather's antique family clock stands motionless on the landing, its heartbeat silent. He pulls the sheet off the sofa in his sumptuous drawing room, buries his head in the cushions and cries.

Council Chaos

Angela is suffering the third after-dinner speech. Each one more boring than the previous, for a breath of relief, she is arranging peas around her plate, making words with them. Her greatest success is 'shit', except she is one pea short for the dot on the 'i'. She has come to the conclusion that council dinners are not for her. She tried to engage the two gross, overweight councillors sitting on either side of her in conversation, but she gave up when their remarks became rude. They too are bored and rapidly draining the brandy decanter in front of them. She has done all she can to save the evening, but failure is staring her in the face. The man on her right is Tom Greenwood, a burly man who owns a construction company. He is a 'big noise' on the town planning and development committee, and his company wins all the council's housing and renovation contracts. On her right is Geoffrey Fitzgibbon; he is the council's senior architect and responsible for the approval or refusal of building projects. Geoffrey and Tom hate each other, they are in conflict every day. To make matters worse, Tom keeps touching Angela's knee, and Geoffrey consistently warns him to take his hands off.

"It's alright, Geoffrey." Angela smiles at him in an attempt to calm the situation. "He isn't aware of what he is doing."

"Of course he knows what he is doing, he is touching you up, he is a dirty old man." Angela has come to the same conclusion, but she can cope with dirty old men. If he comes on any stronger, she will slap him and show him up for what he is.

The treasurer concludes his report and returns to his seat to half-hearted applause. The chairman, Mr Rowland Watkins, roly-poly to his friends, dashes onto the stage to make yet another introduction.

"And now I call on Reginald Rolland Swordsmith MP, to enlighten us as to the plans of parliament." The lack of enthusiasm from the floor is only too obvious as Reginald takes out several crumpled sheets of paper from his pocket and tries to straighten them.

"Have you reduced that bloody deficit yet, Reggie?" Tom shouts before squeezing Angela's knee again. "Bloody, stuck-up bastard, the only person making money under this government is Reginald Rolland Swordsmith MP."

"Shut up, Tom, for God's sake, Angela is his girlfriend."

"Girlfriend my arse, she has more sense than to go out with a tit like him. He has hired her for the evening to make himself look respectable. I hope you are charging him a fortune, the bastard deserves to be ripped off."

Angela has had enough of his rude remarks; she excuses herself and retreats into the ladies washroom. It is her intention to relax in the quiet of the hotel lounge and enjoy a coffee, hopefully with a mint chocolate. She fails to make it; Tom is waiting outside the ladies loo for her.

"Look here, pretty!" He stutters, grabbing the wall to steady himself and blocking her escape. "I know you are on the game. I'll give you £100 for a shag, you will be back before old Reggie has finished his blagging." He grabs her arm and thrusts his hand up her dress. "Come on, let's do the business and have some fun."

Angela's well-aimed slap catches him square across his face. His spectacles fly down the corridor, and he loses his balance, falling heavily against the wall. She seizes the opportunity to escape back into the lady's room.

She is furious. These guys are supposed to be the echelons of high society. *Oh my God! The stupid man is following me.* There is nowhere for her to go. He grabs her by the throat and pins her against the hand basins; his hands are all over her as he tries to get inside her blouse. She screams and kicks him on the shin; but weighing in at over 20 stone, he easily holds her at arm's length as he pulls a bundle of 20 pound notes out of his pocket and stuffs them into her mouth. "Maybe this will shut you up, you little bitch." She spits them out and drags her fingernails down his face; screaming for help as loud as she can. The conference hall clears as everyone rushes to see what is happening.

Reginald pushes his way through the crowd.

"Get him off me, he should be locked up, he just tried to rape me," Angela's screams ricochet down the corridor.

Reggie wraps his arms around her. "You are safe now, the police are on their way, they will lock him up."

"They won't do anything of the sort," splutters Tom, wiping blood off his face. "I know what you are up to in Birmingham; it is you they will be arresting." Tom is silenced as a police officer cuffs his wrists together. "Hey, what the hell are you doing?" he foolishly lashes out at the officer. The two of them bounce off the washbasins, sending hair dryers and jars of deodorant flying.

The Birmingham Post is the winner of the day, their own reporter filmed the entire incident. His best picture is Angela scratching Tom's face, surely a picture worthy of high acclaim.

Tom is still protesting violently as he is dragged away to a police car, his days on the council are over. Angela will see to that, nobody gets away with insulting her. On the other hand, her feelings for Reginald Rolland Swordsmith have greatly increased. He is her hero, a true gentleman who rushed to her aid. As far as Angela is concerned, tonight he can do no wrong.

It is 3 o'clock when Angela calls me from the Radisson Blu.

"Are you OK, I have been worried sick, what happened to you in Birmingham is all over the news?"

"Tim, I have never had so much fun, making the headlines is so easy, what do you want me to do next?" She bursts out laughing, and I must admit I can see the funny side of her story. What a girl, did she really set these guys up? If she did, then this is one of the best stories I have heard in a long time.

"So, when are you coming back to London?" Then, I suddenly remember. "Hey! Aren't you going to China on Friday?"

"Yes, but why don't I come back now, why do I have to wait until morning?"

"I thought you might want to stay with Reginald tonight."

"Don't be silly, Tim, you know it's you I love." I wish I believed her.

Baby! What Baby?

Parker Street Police Station is like a war zone. Reginald, Tom and Geoffrey are sat next to one another along the back wall of the waiting area; and after several shouting matches, with punches being thrown, they have been ordered to behave. Each will write an account of the evening, and no doubt there will be a discrepancy as to what happened. They do have one thing in common, they are all crazy about Angela. Geoffrey wants to father her; Reginald wants to court her, and Tom... well! Apparently, he just wants to have sex with her. They resemble the three wise monkeys sitting in a row, Geoffrey has his head in his hands, Tom is scratching his head, and Reginald is impatiently tapping his knees. Only Reginald is sober enough to understand what is going on and is trying to play the incident down. He realises the damage he could suffer if the media delve deeper into his personal life. It takes three hours for the police to get a satisfactory statement from Tom.

Reginald is exhausted by the time he arrives back at the hotel. He is angry, disgusted and frustrated, yet still has hopes of making it with Angela and has been thinking about her all night. She could save the day, but as he enters the hotel room, his chances look remote. Angela is fast asleep.

"Are you asleep?" he asks, hoping to wake her. "I have been sat in that damn police station for three hours, waiting for them to get a coherent statement from Tom. What a rude guy, he was violent and totally non-cooperative. The police have locked him up for the night until he calms down. His moaning has done the trick; Angela sits up in bed and tries to focus.

"So what happens now?"

"It depends. If you are bringing charges against him, you will spend tomorrow at the police station, filling in a charge sheet. If you are going to forgive him, then you can go back to London."

"Forgive him! I want to teach him a lesson, he is a disgusting man. He put his hand up my skirt and offered me £100 for a shag."

"Do you want to bring charges or go back to London?" Angela has a think.

"I don't want to stay here. I have to get back to London. I'm going to China with Colin on Friday."

"So you will not be bringing charges against him?"

"I might, I haven't decided yet, is he holding something against you? What did he mean when he said he would expose you and have you arrested?"

"He was talking nonsense; I have some business interests in Birmingham which he does not approve of, or should I say does not have an investment in, it is nothing for you to be concerned about." He changes the subject. "Are you going to 'charge me' for this evening?"

"It depends on what you are going to do with me now."

"Well, darling, I am not in the mood to do very much. I need to sleep. I have had a terrible evening, and I have a very busy day ahead."

"Okay; in that case, I'll just keep the dress."

"That's okay. By the way, it's too small for you." He crawls into bed beside her; grateful the end of this day has finally arrived.

I wake early. The morning news is going to be a hoot, and the first thing I do is click the TV remote. I have to bear the bad news first, immigration up, employment down, trains cancelled, and yet, another series of bus strikes looks inevitable. Then, to brighten my day, there is Angela scratching Tom's face, with people rushing to her aid; and Reginald fighting his way through the crowd of onlookers. The report cuts back to the two of them arriving at the town hall and shows them arm in arm.

The reporter describes the story. 'There was uproar at the mayor's annual dinner in Birmingham last night, when Angela Bee, the latest partner of the secretary of state for health, was attacked by Councillor Tom Greenwood: leader of Birmingham's town planning and development department. Reginald Rolland Swordsmith had to abandon his after-dinner speech and dash to her aid. He alone saved Miss Bee from further violation. Councillor Tom Greenwood has been detained at Parker Street Police Station for further questioning.'

Angela Bee, partner of the secretary of state for health? I repeat the words over to myself. *This girl is incredible, how did she get that title?* All we need now is film of her crying, and the hearts of the people will go out to her. *Oh goodness, here come the tears, and doesn't she look amazing.*

Angela has to fight her way through the hotel lobby to get out, which is packed with camera-wielding reporters, all wanting her story; if she is delayed further, she will miss her train.

"Are you going to bring charges against Tom Greenwood, Miss Bee?"

"Is he going to be charged with rape?"

"What is your relationship with the secretary of state for health, is it true you are expecting his baby?"

Where did that come from?

"Yes, no, yes, yes no." The questions are coming at her so fast, she doesn't know which question she is answering. The hotel security officer rushes to her aid and clears a way through for her. Only when she is safely in the car, on her way to the station does she relax. She turns on the car's TV monitor and watches the report of her evening in Birmingham.

'Miss Bee, who is expecting the baby of Reginald Rolland Swordsmith, the secretary of state for health, announced this morning that she is bringing charges against Tom Greenwood for attempted rape during last night's mayoral dinner. This is a breaking story and remember you heard it here first on Sky News."

"I didn't say that, and I am not going to bring charges," Angela mutters to her chauffeur.

"You are now, mi lady. Don't worry about it, let the press make of it what they will. It's a good story, mi lady. We need a fun story; the news from Westminster is so boring."

"You are right, it's good that I can offer the country some fun." She laughs out loud.

"It's a crazy world, mi lady, and by the way, congratulations."

Laughter is exactly what she needs.

Get Tough

"Lesley, you have two days to deliver two million pounds before Colin leaves for Beijing on Friday." There is desperation in Reginald's voice. He is aware that Lesley needs time to get the money, but he should have organised it days ago. If the money fails to materialise, the consequences do not bear thinking about.

"Reginald, please give me some slack. Only yesterday was I released by the police after spending a week in a police cell, my wife has run off with the bloody house boy, I don't know where my kids are, and it's Stephanie's funeral today, how am I going to get two million pounds?"

"Lesley, our back is against the wall. The stuff is already on the ship. If Colin doesn't deliver the money, God knows what the Chinese will do to him."

"I'll get back to you, when do you need the money?"

"Thursday evening, Colin flies out on Friday morning."

"I will do what I can, I am not very confident; my accountants have to release it without a trace. Have you any idea how difficult that is?"

Reginald slams down the phone, more in fear than frustration, and calls Colin to pass on the latest update, but Colin is more concerned about Angela and requires reassurance that she is on her way back to London.

"Are you sure she caught the train? Did you see her get on it? What the hell happened in Birmingham, the last thing we need is the press watching our every move?"

"I'm sure she is on the train. I suggest you call her and meet her at Euston."

"She won't answer her phone on a train. What time does it arrive?"

"I don't know, just do your job; and for Christ's sake, organise your own sex life. Do I have to do everything?"

Reginald drops the phone and gives a big sigh. He has enough stress of his own to worry about, he has to meet a gang of street kids at the Tiger Club at ten. These are the guys who distribute the drugs to the thousands of users on the streets of London, Birmingham, Manchester and Newcastle. They are a scary bunch of hyperactive kids and have to be treated with the utmost respect. The Tiger Club is Janet Cynthia

Clynbourne's favourite hangout. She claims to have shares in it, but he believes she is the owner. It's a popular gay nightclub behind New Street Station; he hates the place. The area is the home of thieves, druggies and marauding gangs; and if he is seen, it will ruin his career.

He practically tiptoes down the street and quietly inserts the key into the heavy wooden door at the back of the club. He is hoping to collect this week's take, which should be £300,000 and get out as quickly as possible. If Colin didn't need the money so desperately, he would have postponed the meeting and taken the same train as Angela back to London.

The inside of the club is in darkness, except for the glow from a single light bulb in the back office. He gropes his way around the bar to find Janet arranging bank notes on a large oak table.

"I didn't expect to see you here, Janet. I thought you were in London."

"After that shambles at the town hall last night, I thought I better meet with the boys myself. I can't trust you to do anything, what was it all about? I told you to leave Angela alone, she is mine; I don't want your dirty hands all over her."

"Shut the fuck up, Janet. She's straight. You will never have her. How much have we got?"

"Two hundred and sixty five thousand, four hundred and thirty three pounds. The boys are still out collecting, they are owed another £100,000. I have told them to get tough and apply pressure."

"You bet they have. I have been speaking with Lesley, he doubts he can get the two million by tomorrow."

"How is he?"

"Fucked up, he is in a dreadful state."

"Is Angela still going to China with Colin?"

"As far as I know."

"Bastard, why can't you guys leave her alone. I have already spent a thousand pounds on her."

"You are an idiot, Janet, you are wasting your time and your money."

"I want her, and I will have her. Now get out of here, get this money to Colin and stay on Lesley's back." Reginald, for once, is delighted to do as Janet asks.

Euston station concourse is packed. When the Birmingham train spews out its load of passengers, it is practically impossible to move. Somewhere in this swarm of bodies is a pretty little girl, who if aggravated will bite your head off. I think I can see her; no, she has disappeared again. My only chance of meeting up with her is to attract her attention as she walks through the barrier. She will not be looking for me, as she has no idea I am waiting for her. There she is, I wave but get no response. A man steps out in front of her and kisses her, *who is he?* They talk for a few seconds before he picks up her case and leads her towards the taxi rank. I should know this guy, he looks familiar, but I can't place him: he is obviously a friend. I follow some 20 paces behind them, unable to hear what they are saying. A man with a camera rushes past me and points his lens at them. They are taken by surprise and shield their eyes from the flash.

"Hey, what's going on?" I call to the guy with the camera.

"Don't you know who she is?" he shouts back. "She is the girlfriend of the secretary of state for health. She has just got out of his bed in Birmingham, and now she is in the arms of Colin Brown, MP for Berwick-on-Tweed. It is said she is sleeping her way through the government. She is the hottest story in the country, a picture of her is worth thousands." He rushes after them towards the taxi rank. "Are you in the government?"

"No."

"Forget her then, you have no chance."

Shortfall

Lesley squeezes into the window seat at Starbucks coffee shop and stares down the high street. He is desperate, scanning every shopper and office worker, hoping to see Michael Sumner—his senior accountant—who should have arrived half an hour ago, but he is looking like a no show. Something must be wrong; Michael is a precise, detailed and punctual man. *Where the hell is he?* Lesley taps the table nervously. He checks his watch again; he only has two hours before he has to be at Stephanie's funeral. Could Michael be ill or even worse, has he been involved in an accident, neither bear thinking about. His heart quickens as he sees him running through the crowds. He eventually staggers into the café, gasping for breath.

"Where the hell have you been?"

"I have run all the way from the railway station, there wasn't a taxi."

"Taxis don't service the station at this time. Nobody arrives mid-morning, except you? Man, you look terrible."

"You don't look too good yourself, Lesley, get me a coffee, for God's sake."

Lesley calls to the girl behind the counter; he befriended her several months ago and usually shares a joke with her but not today.

"So have you got the money?" Michael takes a deep breath and shakes his head.

"Lesley, I need more time. It takes at least four days to transfer two million pounds. My team have been at the office all night, going through the accounts. They are doing all they can, this is why I am so late."

"Have they managed to transfer anything?"

"You can have one million in cash, by this evening. They need another three days to get the rest."

"Michael, I don't understand. We have borrowed money from the company many times and always given it back within five days. All they have to do is lose it for five bloody day; what is their problem?" He is angry, frustrated and scared. "Goodness! The amount of money each one of them has made out of us is life-changing. They have bought holiday villas, cars and goodness knows what else. You have to apply pressure, they have to get the money." Lesley turns from demanding to pleading. He knows it is his fault, but surely, they can do something to help him.

"Lesley, they appreciate what you give them; but this time, it is more difficult. We have a general election in eight months, business is losing confidence, and the company shares are plummeting. The future is unpredictable, and the accounts are low. Two million pounds will be spotted if it isn't dripped out slowly."

Lesley sits in silence, his head in his hands.

"Your coffee, Mr Buchanan. Can I get you anything else, maybe a cup cake? I know you are partial to a blueberry muffin in the morning."

Lesley looks kindly at the girl.

"No, thank you. That will be all for now." He hands her a £20 note. "Keep the change, darling. I know this place doesn't pay you very much."

"Thank you, Mr Buchanan. You are so kind."

"Michael! Colin is flying to China tomorrow. The shipment is already on-board the container ship; it sails early on Saturday morning. If he doesn't deliver the money on Friday, god knows what they will do to him."

"I have done all I can. Tell them they will get the money before the ship reaches the English Channel. They know they will get their money."

"Michael, we are dealing with the Chinese Mafia, nobody messes with the Chinese Mafia. Have another go at the bankers, please do all you can."

"Lesley, it is not my fault, you should have requested it two weeks ago. Colin will have to bluff, he is good at bluffing, he will have one million pounds. It's a miracle that I have got him that much."

"I was in police custody, how the hell could I action it?"

"You shouldn't have killed your mistress, whatever were you doing to her."

Lesley stops short at throwing a punch at him.

"Don't ever say that again. I didn't kill her. I left her packing her bags, but I am determined to find out who did shoot her." He looks at his watch. "Shit, is that the time, I have to go. It's Stephanie's funeral this morning. Keep me updated, Michael. Please, make it happen."

Fame

Vogue sales are breaking all records; Sarah Thompson has definitely hit the jackpot. Her idea to do a series of features on Angela has become the hottest read in the country; this is the boost to her career that she has been waiting for. Angela's pictures are captivating, and the stories accompanying them are changing the reasons why women wear what they do. Until now, they have chosen clothes for comfort and practicality: to go shopping in, to go walking in, to go out with girlfriends in. Now they are choosing clothes to fulfil a purpose: to get a new job, to create a new image, to make an impact; and of course, to attract that special man. It is causing a revolution in the retail fashion industry. No longer are women asking, "What should I wear to do something or go somewhere." Now they are asking, "What should I wear to achieve… Whatever?"

Vogue is capitalising on this revolution; Angela's modelling pictures are unique, and their descriptions original:

'What to wear if you want to become chairman of the company.'

'What to wear if you want to stop the traffic?'

'What to wear if you want to put your husband's mistress down?'

'What to wear if you want your man to buy you a new sports car?' The list is endless. The features are all about women achieving. The headline to the series is… 'Go, get it girls.' Angela is already known as 'the go-get-it girl', and the Vogue readers love her. Sales have increased by over one point five million, and all these women are striving to break free from their humdrum lives. They never had the courage to do it alone, but now they have a heroine to follow.

Angela's phone never stops ringing. The Sunday papers can't get enough of her, and the popular women's magazines are desperate to get in on the act. TV companies want her on their afternoon chat shows, she has been invited to dance on *Strictly Come Dancing*, be a judge on *The X factor*, be a guest on *Lose Women,* and be a judge on a sewing competition, even though she can't thread a needle.

Angela eventually comes home.

"Hey! Welcome back, how was Birmingham?"

"It started bad with boring speeches, spoken by boring people, accompanied with boring food, but it brightened up later. Have you heard all about it?"

"I think the entire country has read about your night out. Are you alright?"

"That Tom Greenwood is a disgusting man, how dare he offer me £100 for a shag. It's a £1,000 for the minimum service." She falls over laughing at her own joke.

"What have you been up to?" I tell her about all the phone calls and the research I have accomplished. She thinks the whole thing is just an outrageous laugh. "Anyway, Colin is collecting me tomorrow at 6:30. Our plane for China departs at 10:00; now what shall I wear?"

Whilst she is in the bathroom, I grab my laptop and book a seat on the same fight. I'm guessing she will be flying first-class. I can't afford that, but maybe, it is better if she doesn't see me.

"At which hotel are you staying?" I'm shouting to make myself heard over the spray of her shower.

"The Crowne Plaza. Do you know it?"

I quickly feed the name into my search engine and scan down the room prices.

Goodness! That's an expensive hotel. "Of course I have heard of it." Lying is coming easier to me these days.

"Don't worry, I am a guest of the British government. They are paying for me."

I wish I could stop worrying.

Fizz Is Fun

From the inside of the airport transfer bus, I can see Angela mounting the steps into the massive body of the 747 airliner. I can only assume the guy with his hand on her butt is Colin Brown, and the other six guys with similar black briefcases are members of the government trade delegation; the three women, tottering behind them on ridiculously high heels will be secretaries or girlfriends. Only after they have been shown to their seats are we released from the sweaty interior of the overcrowded airport bus and directed to the rear door of the aircraft and into the economy seats. My seat is 89F, as far from being a VIP as it is possible to be.

One by one, we are hurriedly welcomed onto the aircraft and directed to our seats until the cabin is packed with fraught passengers. I recognise the photographer employed by Vogue, I also know one, two, yes… three freelance reporters; they regularly accompany government visits. One formidable-looking woman, dressed in a tweed suit, is more stressed than the rest of us. She is shouting at an airline steward; she claims her seat is in club class, and they have mistakenly directed her into economy. The steward is politely trying to point to the seat number printed on her ticket.

"See, your seat is 70A, just three rows down on the right. I am very sorry, but there is no mistake." I feel sorry for him; he is only doing his job, but she is relentless and is having none of it. She turns and angrily gestures towards the front of the aircraft. *Goodness, it's Janet Cynthia Clynbourne, what is she doing here?* If it's a seat upgrade she is hoping for, then a little charm would not go amiss; but as she is totally devoid of charm, she is sitting in 70A. *I wonder what the chances are of her getting off in Dubai.* We have a three-hour stopover in Dubai before continuing to Beijing, to suffer a further seven hours of her complaining will be intolerable.

Angela, on the other hand, is enjoying her VIP experience. She has been served the most impressive lobster dinner, accompanied by a continual flow of champagne. The men sitting around her are infatuated by her infectious giggling. She is teasing them, of course; and they are loving her attention. Their usual business flights are suffered in silence but not this one; they are responding to her squeals of delight with jokes and innuendoes. Colin is totally embarrassed and finding it impossible to participate in her frivolity. He stares out of the window at the deep, blue Mediterranean. He thought Angela would be overwhelmed by the trip and subservient to his demands, but now realises she will not be as easy as the other girls he has taken on similar trips, and as for her innocently delivering the money, well that no longer bears thinking about.

His thoughts are of concern, how is he going to explain a short fall of one million pounds? How will he convince them the rest of the money will be delivered in three days? He drops his head into his hands in despair as his heart rate increases and feels the blood racing across his scalp. His lobster dinner sits untouched on the tray in front of him, his stomach unable to digest it. They might take the shipment off the freighter, and that would bring their supply to a halt. Janet will blame him, she blames him for everything. He doesn't try to conceal his hatred of her any more, he calls her an ugly, intimidating bully to her face. She puts unbelievable demands on him, continuously hassling him over price and delivery dates and complaining all the time about the quality and quantity; and now on top of this, she is obsessed with Angela. Last night, she actually threatened to kill him if he didn't keep his hands off her. How dare she?

He wipes the sweat from his brow and glances over at Angela, he has to admire her. She is pretty, sexy and fun, he had such high hopes of an exciting three days with her. She jumps to her feet and tries to reach the overhead locker. She can't reach it, so she steps up onto her seat; which isn't what a young woman in a short dress and high heels does on a swaying plane; unless your name is Angela Bee, that is. To the delight of her new admirers, she topples over and is saved by the arms of the steward who came rushing up the aisle to assist her. The passengers applaud as her legs shoot into the air, and she puts on a display worthy of the *Moulin Rouge*. Even Colin has to release a smile.

Janet's annoyance is maintained throughout the flight, and her impatience maxes out when the plane finally comes to a standstill at Beijing Capital International Airport. We have been held back until the first-class passengers have alighted, and all Janet can do is watch Colin and Angela walk across the airport apron. She tries to push her way towards the blocked exit but fails to make any progress, she has to wait with the rest of us.

Why is she so frantic? Is it Angela she is watching, or is it Colin? Why is she on the plane in the first place; she is not a member of the delegation? As she reaches the taxi stand, I am only a few feet behind her.

"To the Crowne Plaza Hotel," she screams at the driver of the cab.

"May I share your cab, I am also staying at the Crowne Plaza Hotel?" She slams the cab door shut, trapping my arm; it was pretty stupid of me to grab it, but a little sympathy for my pain would not go amiss.

"Get in young man, I am in a hurry." Then, she turns her attention to the driver. "To the Crowne Plaza Hotel, driver, and quickly." He does not respond. "Do you understand where I want to go?" She pokes the driver's shoulder due to his failure to acknowledge her. "Can you speak English, you stupid man, how dare you ignore me?"

He pulls the car into the kerb and stops with a jerk. "The Crowne Plaza, ma'am, that will be ten yuan, have a nice day."

Janet fails to show any embarrassment at not knowing the hotel is part of the airport complex, she continues her verbal attack on him. "Ten! You must be joking. You have only taken us one hundred yards."

In an attempt to salvage an embarrassing moment, I dig into my jacket pocket and hand him a £5 note. "I'm sorry, I only have English sterling. Is that okay?"

"Thank you, sir, you are very generous." I didn't intend to be generous. I calculated this ride to cost £12 in London; and knowing ten Yuan equals one pound, I actually thought I was being tight.

Janet's bad temper continues, even when she is signing in at the front desk, she is still shouting and complaining.

"Why do I have to fill in all these details when you have my booking confirmation, you have all my details?" The poor girl has the patience of job; she deserves a medal.

"Your room card, Miss Clynbourne, welcome to The Crowne Plaza."

I have had enough of her rudeness and wish her a pleasant stay; but unfortunately, luck is not on my side. I have been allocated the room next to her and have to suffer her complaining right to her room door.

"Why won't this damn lock turn green, they have given me the wrong key?"

"Can I be of assistance?"

"I doubt it, they have given me the wrong key."

I turn the card over and pass it through the slot. The door clicks open; and with a sigh of relief, watch her disappear inside, without a word of thanks or appreciation. *Goodness, Angela deserved not one but £2,000 for sleeping with this woman.*

Angela's arrival at the hotel is far more civilised. Two hotel porters rush to her aid, when they see her tottering on her heels and struggling with her oversized suitcase. The free champagne on the flight was fun, but right now, the fizz has gone out of it, she is regretting her lack of restraint.

"Oh, thank you, guys. You have saved my life." Her remark is aimed solely at Colin, who failed miserably in her eyes for not carrying her case, but his hands are full. He is grasping his black leather briefcase in one hand and trying to steer his own travel bag, which obviously has a damaged wheel. He struggles behind her as closely as he can, watching enviously as she flirts with the porters, enjoying every second of their full-on attention. He is angry, he invited Angela for some fun and relief, and so far, she hasn't even acknowledged him, she will pay for this privilege. She innocently collapses onto the bed and throws her arms above her head, still slightly giddy, but glad the journey is over. Colin locks the door behind him and sits beside her.

"Hey, what do you think you are doing, what kind of girl do you think I am?" Her negative response to him running his hands all over her body is only angering him more. He stiffens and pins her to the bed.

She wonders what is it that makes one man appealing and not another; Colin just does not do it for her. The sex books call it chemistry; she has a much simpler name for it, 'appeal'. Colin does not appeal to her. She would have slept with Reginald, he has charisma, charm, and he amuses her even when he is not trying to be funny. It was a shame he was exhausted the other night in Birmingham. As for screwing Lesley on the escarpment, she felt sorry for him. He was in need of love and understanding, and she wanted to mother him. He was only a victim of consequence, after all, and in need of her; and she gladly gave herself to him. He was gentle and sensuous, slow and deliberate, he is a nice guy. She hopes he is innocent of Stephanie's murder; in fact, she is sure he is. Sleeping with Janet was simply an adventure, something she had to try, and it was good after she had downed the champagne to dampen her inhibitions. Now she knows she is straight and determined to make the most of her sexuality.

As for sleeping with me, I don't know why we get on so well. We tease each other and laugh, just to hold each other is a delight, we are both aware of the spark between us, a respect and an understanding. Maybe it is chemistry, I call it magic; maybe you call it love.

As for Colin, she thinks nothing of him. Even the way he walks, talks, puts his drink to his mouth, she finds repulsive. There is nothing about him that appeals to her, and there is no way he is getting any closer. She can work with him, have fun with him, but that is as far as her natural instinct will allow her to go. She tries to fight off his advance by screaming and scratching him. This time, the champagne on the plane isn't helping her to focus her strength, but she is putting up a hell of a struggle. She had a boyfriend a year back who used to force himself on

117

her. Sometimes, she surrendered to him but not with Colin. There is no way this man is going to take her against her will.

There is a knock on the door. "Room service, Mr Brown; you have an urgent message from England. It needs an immediate response." The door rattles as the knocking intensifies.

"Stop, stop, stop, for Christ's sake, give me a minute." Colin jumps off the bed. "What is it, I am not expecting a message from London?" He throws a sheet over Angela and arranges his clothes. "I'm coming."

The knocking does not stop. "Sorry to interrupt you, sir, but it is very important." Colin reaches for the door, angry and stressed.

"Who has sent me a message?" He opens the door to find Janet standing there. "What are you doing here?" She pushes passed him and enters the room. "Hey, you can't come in, this is not your room, where are your manners?"

"This is not your room either." Janet circles him and pushes him out of her way.

"Janet, what are you doing? Oh my God, don't trash the room."

"Where is she, what are you doing to her?"

"Doing to who; who are you talking about?"

"I'm looking for Angela, if you have hurt her, you are a dead man."

Colin tries to stop Janet from entering the bedroom but to no avail. She pushes him aside to find Angela sitting on the edge of the bed, struggling to regain some dignity.

"You idiot, I told you to leave her alone, get me some ice cubes from the fridge. How the hell can she be seen with these bruises on her face?" Colin, like a chastised child, empties the ice tray whilst Janet bathes Angela's swollen face. "You will be alright, my darling. I am going to take care of you now."

The bedside phone bursts into life. Colin picks it up.

"What do you want?" he shouts angrily into it.

"Incoming call for you, Mr Brown."

"Who is it?" There is no response; the receptionist has already put the call through.

"Mr Brown?"

"Yes, who is this?"

"Be at the club tonight at 11:30." The phone goes dead.

"You look like death," Janet jokes. "Was it your mother?"

"I'm fine, everything is just fine."

"Then hand me the ice cubes and leave us alone."

Colin obediently does as he is told.

Intelligence?

Where the hell is that stupid girl?

George is impatiently shuffling files across his desk. His morning coffee has gone cold, and he has already drained his brandy glass. He is waiting for his secretary to return with the morning papers. She usually just slips down to the kiosk in the lobby, but this morning, she has to go to the newsagents in Horse Guards Parade. The latest edition of Vogue is out today, and they don't sell fashion magazines in house. He gave her strict instructions to hide it inside *The Times* when she walks in through the lobby, not wanting people to think him a dirty old man, but it is too late to save his reputation now.

Angela has definitely captured his imagination; it's not a sexual desire he has for her, or even a business interest, it's the... well it's the kind of love a man has for his new car, or for his perfectly manicured garden. George's job fails to fulfil him anymore; he needs an interest in which he can be passionate and for some reason, Angela ticks all the boxes. Hearing his secretary tripping down the corridor, he hides his brandy glass in the bottom drawer of his desk and picks up the coffee cup, pretending to sip it just as she enters the office.

"Thank you, Doreen."

"It's Dorothy."

"What's Dorothy?"

"My name, sir, my name is Dorothy."

"Yes, I know it's Dorothy. What are you blabbing about, now, I don't want to be disturbed for one hour. I have to catch up on the news." Dorothy knows better than to question the real reason for his privacy and closes the door behind her.

He goes straight for the magazine and searches the pages for pictures of Angela. They are easy to find, pictures of her are spread all over the four central pages, each page has a different headline:

'What to wear at the council dinner party?'

'What to wear on a free holiday to Beijing?'

'What to wear when you want a new apartment?' and across the top of the fourth page, 'What to wear to make the headlines?' *That's a bit unfair,* he thinks to himself, *anyway, she looks amazing.* Not all her dresses are what you would expect to see in Vogue, some of them she bought down Portabella Road, others she found in the Oxfam shop, but her style is exactly vogue, and her innocence and her sexuality is awe-inspiring. George sits and admires her for several minutes, reading the descriptions and trying to understand her reasons for wearing them. He is enthralled and finds it difficult to focus on the real reason for his interest; he wants to cross-reference her locations with the reports in the morning papers.

On page two of the *Daily Mail,* there is a full report of the council dinner fiasco in Birmingham, with the headline, 'Secretary of state for health risks his life to defend girlfriend's honour.' There is a second story on page three, this headline reads, 'Girlfriend, whose girlfriend?' with a picture of Angela kissing Barry Cornwell, MP for Devon and Cornwall, on Euston Station. He bursts out laughing; what a breath of fresh air she is. She is working her way through the entire government. He hasn't laughed so much in years. Then, as if to leave the story hanging in the air, and the reader wanting more, there is an up-skirt picture of her boarding the plane to Beijing on page five.

George smiles in admiration, *why did he not have the nerve to be so natural and carefree when he was 23.* She is beautiful, refreshing and intelligent, yes, intelligent, he believes Angela to be intelligent. To control all these hormonal men who are running around after her is a gift. It's going to be a very interesting summer.

He pushes his reading glasses up his nose and picks up his Nokia mobile phone. His wife bought it for him 20 years ago for his 50th birthday. She wants to buy him a new all-singing-and-dancing smart phone, but he doesn't see the point, he only uses it to call and text.

"Hi Angela, I hope you are having fun. Come see me when you get back from Beijing." He signs off with, "Your good friend George."

George isn't the only person trying to contact her. I have been trying to call her for over an hour and got no response. Without revealing my identity, I also leave her a text, "Call me back ASAP."

Janet hears the ding of the incoming texts and searches Angela's bag for her mobile. She laughs at George's message, *You are a dirty old bugger, George, but I love you.* She has no idea who I am, but as my London phone number is clearly displayed at the top of the screen, she can easily find out by calling me back. She taps my number into her own mobile; she will call me later. Damn! I should have been more patient and waited a little longer, but my concern for Angela has maxed out; I haven't seen or heard from her since we arrived.

Janet is furious.

"Look Colin, when Angela wakes up, we will move her into my room. You are a brutal sexual deviant, unable to control yourself."

"That makes two of us, Janet," Colin mocks her. "But I have to take her to 'The Club' with me tonight. I am delivering the money, and I need her on my arm. She will be a useful distraction."

"If anything happens to her, I warn you now, I will kill you."

"Get off my back, Janet, focus on the money you are making."

"I will be here waiting for you!" She shakes her finger at him. "Anyway, she might not want to go with you. You have just tried to rape her?"

"She was drunk from the champagne on the plane. She won't remember a thing."

"She will see the bruises on her face."

"I'll tell her she slipped on the staircase, and I saved her from falling down the stairs, now get those ice cubes on her face and make yourself useful."

"If you think she will believe that, you are an idiot, Colin."

"I have had enough of you. I have a meeting with the other members of the delegation, and they are waiting for me in the bar. Get real, Janet."

Colin is totally stressed. Apart from him delivering the money, he has six appointments tomorrow with China's most influential business magnates, and the PM is watching his every move. The government is expecting great things form him.

Angela utters a squeaky groan and tries to focus, surprised to see Janet sitting on the bed beside her.

"What are you doing here?" It takes her several seconds to remember where she is! "What happened? Why are you here? Why is my face hurting; hey, my dress is torn?"

"Shh, just relax, darling. You drank too much champagne on the plane and fell down the hotel steps. Colin caught you and asked me to sit with you, you will be okay."

"Why are you in Beijing, you told me you were going to your constituency in Barrow."

"I had to change my plans at the last minute. The prime minister added me to the delegation." Lying comes easy to Janet.

Angela slumps back onto her pillow and submits to Janet's caress.

"Be gentle, my face hurts." She can't remember falling down the stairs; in fact, she is convinced she took the elevator. She tries to sit up, but her body aches, and her arms are covered in bruises; if only she could remember what happened.

"You have to get up and dress, my darling. You are going clubbing tonight, and all England will be watching you."

"That sounds fun, ouch! Are you coming?"

"I can't dance, I am far too old. Colin will take care of you and introduce you to some very important people, but first, we have to get you cleaned up. I will call for the hotel masseur, you deserve a bit of pampering."

"Which club is it, is it the nightclub in the hotel?"

"No it's across the city, it's called 'The Club'. It's where the rich and famous go, you will love it." Angela likes what she is being told, and her mind as usual focuses on what she will wear.

"I believe the hotel masseur is quite a dishy guy. Behave yourself and do as he tells you."

"I always do, don't I?"

It takes ten minutes for the masseur to arrive. Janet opens the door to a dream of a man standing behind a trolley piled high with thick white towels. Clipped to the front of the trolley is a glass cabinet containing an impressive range of oils, soaps, creams and potions. Dressed all in white, Mr Dream could be straight out of a washing powder commercial. His trousers are immaculately pressed; and his tee shirt is so tight, it looks as if it was pre-shrunk onto him. Angela's eyes light up, and suddenly, she feels a whole lot better. *Mm, I am sure I am going to enjoy being pampered.* Her muscles flex, and her nerves tingle as he presses his thumbs into her neck, she can't wait for Janet to leave and for him to get down to the more serious business of easing her stress.

Janet scribbles down her room number and stuffs it into Angela's handbag. "Come and see me when you get back tonight, whatever time it is. I will be waiting up for you." Angela has no intention of calling on Janet at any time, day or night. Sleeping with her was a business agreement and not a habit she intends getting into.

"I will," she lies. "Now don't worry about me."

Angela is already submitting to the pressure being applied to her spine, her neck and into her shoulders. She never realised her arms were so sensitive. *This is worth falling down the stairs for,* a smile crosses her face at her thoughts, but she is rapidly brought back to reality when her phone vibes. She reads my message… "Call me back ASAP."

"I have to make a call, is that all right?" Mr Dream releases his grip on her. "Hey! Don't stop, just move down a bit, so I can use my arms." He runs his fingers down her spine and squeezes the fleshy part of her butt. His palm rotates her flesh, making concentration rather difficult.

"Hi, it's me, what's happening in London?"

"Apart from the papers reporting everything you are doing and wearing, not a lot." It is obvious she didn't see me on the plane; she thinks I am in London. "What have you been doing?"

122

"I had too much to drink on the plane and fell down the steps in the hotel. Apart from a few bruises, I am okay, now I have this wonderful Chinese guy running his fingers all over me."

"I am so sorry to interrupt, shall I ring you back?"

"No, no, he isn't fucking me. He is the hotel masseur. I am going clubbing tonight, and he is easing a few bruised limbs before I go."

"Is Colin taking you?"

"I haven't seen him since we arrived, Janet is here, it was her idea I had a massage."

"So which club are you going to this evening?"

"It's a club called 'The Club'. It's where all the rich people go, we will arrive there about 11:30 and dance all night, so don't expect a call." I can hear her laughing, she knows comments like that upset me.

"Okay, enjoy yourself, come home soon. London is missing you."

She puts down the phone and mutters instructions to her masseur into the pillow.

"Sorry, ma'am, I missed what you said, you will have to speak up."

"I said you can move down a bit lower."

"Yes, ma'am, I will, all in good time."

Something is not ringing true. Everything Angela has done since she arrived in Beijing has been filmed and recorded, but I have not seen a picture of her stumbling on the staircase, that would have been a real coup for any photographer, and then, there is Janet. She wasted no time in getting in on the act, she isn't a member of the delegation. I still can't work out what her interest is?

The Club

The hands of the large antiquated clock hanging over the hotel bar clearly show it to be nine o'clock. I fail to understand why the 'Crowne Plaza Hotel', the very latest in a series of modern hi-tech hotels in Beijing has, as its feature, such an icon of the past, but it does the job. It is accurate and clearly seen from every seat in the lounge. From my table in the back corner, I can also see the guests arriving and leaving through the street door. A pretty, Chinese waitress delivers my usual tipple, a Laphroaig 1977 single malt scotch whisky. It crossed my mind to change it for a lime and soda and stay sober, but what the heck, I dip my fingers into the bowl of salted peanuts and try to relax. I do love it here. The lounge is bustling with activity, the guests must be from all over the world. I can distinguish at least six different languages from the tables around me. The waitresses must be multi-lingual as well as beautiful; they have no difficulty understanding their clients' orders and always respond politely to their comments. Their femininity and grace is hypnotising; they glide from one table to the next, smiling, bowing, serving and being admired by all.

I feel safe and secure sitting at this corner table, no one knows me; I only have to avoid Janet, and that is easier said than done.

"Good evening, Mr Collinwood, may I join you?"

"Please do, and call me Tim." Ugh!

"How is your room?" *Oh goodness, I don't need small talk.*

"Fine, just fine, the lady in the next room is very noisy but…" I am joking, of course, but Janet takes it as a personal complaint.

"Oh dear, I am so sorry, I didn't realise I was making so much noise."

"Hey, I am only joking, I can't hear a thing. What have you been doing since your arrival?"

"I have had a terrible afternoon, my girlfriend had a row with her sponsor and got herself slapped about a bit. She is so lucky I am here. I arrived just in time to save her from a severe beating."

"Is she okay?"

"I had to ask the hotel masseur to work his magic on her. She will be fine, she is just a little bruised."

"I'm sorry to hear that. I didn't know this sort of thing happened in exotic hotels, such as the Crowne Plaza."

"The women do as they are told in China, Mr Collinwood. I mean, Tim, it doesn't matter where they are."

"Does that include you, Janet?"

"Absolutely not; nobody bosses me around."

I thought at first Janet was referring to Angela, but surely Angela would have told me if she had been roughed up. Janet must have a Chinese girlfriend which would explain why she is here in Beijing.

"Are you going out this evening, Janet?" She jumps to her feet.

"Sorry Tim, I have to go. My girlfriend is just leaving, and I must speak with her before she goes." She rushes off towards the street door. I search the 20 or 30 people massing around in the lobby, sure enough Angela and Colin are amongst them. I nearly missed her. Colin opens the taxi door and helps her into the cab, *what a fake example of British gallantry*, she looks happy, even excited to be with him. Janet fails to reach her and commandeers the next cab, following her out onto the highway. I join in the chase and throw a bundle of yuan notes at the driver of my cab.

"Follow that cab." The driver looks at me and then at the money. "Go, go, go," I shout to him.

"Yes, sir, hang on tight." He slams the cab into drive, and we race out of the hotel grounds. He is enjoying every minute and eager to show me how clever he is. We swing first right and then second left into Tiananmen Square, already we can see Janet in front and follow her passed the Mao Zedong's Mausoleum and the National Museum of China. These buildings are so majestic and look splendid, illuminated against the clear night sky, but I don't have time for sightseeing. Janet's cab is weaving in and out of the traffic and eventually stops suddenly outside the main door of a building that more resembles a temple rather than a nightclub, we pull up behind her.

"The Club, sir; no good, no go there." My driver's English is basic, but I get the impression he does not approve of my choice of venue. We watch Janet step out of her cab and race towards the entrance. "No good sir, not go, one woman not go." I eventually understand what he is telling me. A woman on her own will not be allow inside. The doorman confirms my understanding by escorting Janet back to her taxi.

"Can I go?" I ask, pointing at the door, then at myself.

"One man okay, not one woman." I thank him and acknowledge his assistance as he puts the stick shift into drive and leaves me to face the doorman alone.

Angela is excited as she enters the club. She clings tightly to Colin's arm as she receives a welcome fit for a film star. Her fame must have preceded her; the manager presents her with a bouquet of flowers and introduces five dinner-jacketed waiters, designated to serve her this evening. Each in turn shake her hand and one actually dares to lift it to his lips and kiss it. She likes being treated like a film star.

With all the attention, she has failed to realise Colin is no longer with her. Only when two waiters—one on each side—have safely helped her through the mass of energetic dancers and seated her at a table on the fringe of the dance floor, does she realise he is missing.

"Where is Colin?" she asks the waiter, who is holding up a bottle of champagne. She screams with delight as he releases the cork, and it shoots high into the air, the bubbles burst all over her.

"Mr Colin Brown will be with you shortly, ma'am. Is there anything else we can get you?"

"Please tell him to hurry, I want to dance." She giggles as a man sitting at the next table catches her gaze and gives her a suggestive wink.

Come on, Colin, this place is amazing. She sips her champagne, watching the main door, willing him to come for her.

Colin is standing in front of the meanest-looking, biggest Chinese guy he has ever seen. He inserts the key into the wristlock and releases the briefcase from his arm, placing it carefully on the table between them.

"Please open the case, Mr Brown. I hope everything is in order." The warm welcome he received at the front door has now turned into a chilly, intimidating confrontation. His legs start to shake, his hands are ice cold, his body language alone shouts insecurity and fear; he knows he must stand firm, be confident and occupy the high ground, but he is human after all. His voice is breaking up and beads of sweat run off his forehead. He has to think fast, he didn't plan on opening the case in front of them.

He scribbled a note, acknowledging that one million pounds is missing and placed it on top of the rows of neatly stacked £20 notes. He wanted to be far away by the time his explanation and the promise to deliver the rest in three days was read. He now realises that is not going to be possible, nor will they agree to wait. His shirt is sticking to his back, sweat is running down his neck, his nervous system is about to crash out.

"Could I possibly leave you gentlemen whilst you count the money?" he stutters. "My partner is all alone, she will be wondering where I am?"

"Angela is in good company, Mr Brown. You have no need to worry about her," growls the leader.

"This is not the way we treat our women in Britain." He somehow has to gain control of himself. "We would never leave a young girl alone in a strange club in a strange city. I am not going anywhere, no doubt you will have cameras on us all evening. I insist you let me join her."

The man looks at the two ogres standing either side of him and reluctantly nods his head.

"You may go to her, but you will not be allowed to leave the club until we have counted the money." Colin sighs in relief, he needs time to think and to get out of there.

"Thank you, gentlemen. I will look forward to your approval."

"Enjoy your evening, Mr Brown. Your drinks and meal are on the house, this evening, order anything you desire." A petite, hip-swinging waitress is instructed to take him to where Angela is waiting.

Angela can sense his stress.

"Cheer up, Colin, don't you like night clubs? Let's drain this bottle of champagne, then hit the dance floor." She fills a glass and places it into his shaking hand. "Come on, John Travolta, show me what you can do." Her frivolity is annoying, he tries to lighten up; surely everything will be all right? They will have their money in three days, but he won't feel safe until he is back at the hotel.

Back at the hotel, Janet is waiting for their return, fuming at being refused admission to the club. *How dare they turn me away? What a sexist country this is.* In frustration and in need of company, she rings my room, hoping I will speed away her evening, but her call rings out; she summons reception.

"Hello, I am trying to contact Mr Tim Collinwood in room 2482, can you page him please." The girl on reception knows the whereabouts of every visitor in the hotel; this is China after all. It is her job to know where each guest is, what they are doing, and most important, how much they are spending. She doesn't have to page me.

"Mr Collinwood is not in the hotel, Miss Clynbourne. He is at The Club, this evening." This news takes her by surprise, she collapses on the lounge sofa, desperately trying to piece together the parts of the jigsaw. Wherever she places them, they refuse to fit. Who is Tim Collinwood? Does he know Angela? Is it a coincidence that he too is at 'The Club'? Why is Colin stressing so much? Her mind is in turmoil.

A Dropped Petal

The man on the door asks to see my passport and for an entry fee, I pay with my credit card, having no idea how much it is and sign where he indicates on a membership certificate.

"Welcome to The Club, Mister Collinwood. Would you please read this list of services and tick the ones you require. The list starts with do I require a taxi home and at what time and ends with my choice of dinner 'a', 'b' or 'c', each with a full menu to read through. The other requirements I tick are a table for two, a sea and steer dinner, champagne and girl, where it indicates host/hostess (girl or boy).

"Can I choose the girl?" I ask.

"Sorry sir, not on this occasion, next time you can upgrade to a VIP, twelve month membership; and then, you can name the girl of your choice." *Goodness, what better incentive is there to pay the annual subscription?*

"That is fine, I will be pleased to be accompanied by any girl."

"They are all very beautiful, sir, and if she doesn't satisfy you, then discreetly refer to the *maître d'*."

"I am sure that will not be necessary." Then as an afterthought, "Will she speak English?" The look he gives me could sink a battleship.

"Of course, sir."

The club is vast, circular in construction with the bar running around the back wall. It's the longest bar I have ever seen. The room is polo-mint-shaped, with the dance floor in the centre; tables occupying the mint area. Above the dance floor, a DJ is standing in a suspended glass saucer, joking in English to the dancers gyrating beneath him. The music is not to my taste, but neither is European disco. I feel a tug on my coat.

"Hello sir, you requested my company?" Wow, European in colour, Asian in appearance, small in stature, with a smile bright enough to open an Englishman's heart and his wallet. A gold-shimmering pencil dress clings to her body, with a side-split up to her thigh. "My name is Petal." She adopts the traditional Chinese welcome and curtsies with her hands placed together, her face exhibiting a look of innocent obedience. "I hope you are pleased with me, sir. It is my desire to please you."

"You please me very much, Petal, what drink can I get you."

"Champagne, sir, what else?"

I turn to catch the attention of the waiter standing behind me, he is already pouring two glasses of bubbling champagne.

"I will keep the bottle chilled for you, sir. I will inform you when it needs replenishing."

"Thank you, how much is that?"

"You have already paid for it, sir. When you signed in, you gave us access to your bank account."

"I didn't know that."

"Enjoy your evening, sir. Petal will take care of you."

She invites me to sit on a high stool at the bar and then climbs on to a second. I offer my assistance to steady her, but she doesn't need it. She looks amazing perched on the edge, with her feet suspended in the air. She definitely knows how to use these stools to best effect.

"You must visit the gym, you keep yourself in beautiful condition?" What a stupid thing to say; only an Englishman would be so short of a decent intro line. She leans towards me, putting her hands on my knees to steady herself. For a moment, I think she is going to kiss me, but with her cheek next to mine, she confesses to not having heard me.

"I am sorry, sir, I cannot hear you because of the music. What did you say?" Thank goodness for that, I can start again.

"You are very beautiful, but you are not Chinese, where are you from?" That's a better line.

"Thank you, sir. My mother is Chinese from Hangzhou, in the province of Zhejiang. My mother is very beautiful and very artistic. She loves writing, and I treasure a book of poems she has written. My father is from Switzerland, a businessman from Geneva. Which part of England are you from?"

"Oh! Is it so obvious that I am English, oh dear?"

"I like Englishmen, you are funny and so naïve."

"I wish you had said we were handsome and great lovers."

"You are handsome, as for being a great lover, how am I to know?"

She laughs and her face lights up. We both reach for our champagne glass at the same time and touch them together; a splash hits her cheek and runs down her face. I reach over and stop it dripping onto her dress.

"Thank you, sir. You have a very gentle touch." I am totally impassioned by her; she could be 18. I hope she is 18; doubting her age with a feeling of guilt, I tell her how beautiful she is.

I must tear myself away to search for Angela; I know she is in the room, probably dancing amongst the 200 people gyrating to the latest European hit. I can see Colin, he stands head and shoulders above the rest. I can only hope the girl dancing with him is Angela. Why won't he turn around so I can see her.

There is a pause in the music as the DJ introduces the latest Asian rock band. For just a minute, there is order as the dancers cheer the group onto the stage. Through the crowd I see Colin being dragged off the dance floor by two security officers, leaving Angela standing alone and confused. Petal senses my concern.

"What is it, sir, are you alright?"

"Sorry, Petal, I have just seen someone I know. I must go and say hello. I will be back very soon."

"I am here to please you, sir, whatever you want."

"Petal, do you see those two guys leaving the dance floor with the tall Englishman?"

"Yes, do you know that man?"

"He is a member of the English government, who are the other two?"

"They are, what would you call them, bouncers, is that the right word, you call them bouncers?"

"A bouncer throws people out of the club if they are drunk or fighting."

"Those two guys work for Mr Cho Wang, they are members of his security force. Mr Cho Wang must have taken a dislike to your friend."

"He's not my friend, but I do know the girl he is with. I believe Cho Wang owns the club, is that right?"

"Not only the club, he owns half of Beijing, nobody crosses Mr Cho Wang. His girlfriend is returning to her table, she is very cute. You say cute?"

"Yes, we say cute."

"Mr Collinwood, I do believe you are in love with this woman. I can see it in your eyes." I blush and try to hide my feelings.

"Let us say I am her mentor."

"You are her manager, yes?"

"No, I am her… oh shit, manager is near enough. Yes, I am her manager."

"Do you want to go to her?"

"She should not be alone, I will be back in two minutes, don't go away." I call the waiter over and ask him to fill Petal's glass, but before I can cross the floor to her table, two security guards sit with her.

"Mr Brown has met with an accident." I hear one of them tell her. "We need you to come immediately, will you follow us please?"

"What sort of an accident, is he alright?" She is stunned; and in her confusion, agrees to go with them.

"Come with us, please, it is an emergency." They politely help Angela to her feet and guide her through the dancers. It is difficult to follow, they rush her to the back of the club, towards a door marked PRIVATE. They knock, wait, and when the red 'no entry' light turns green, they are gone. I force my way through a group of revellers and manage to insert my foot into the closing door, stopping it from locking shut. I count ten before easing the door open and peer inside only to see a dimly lit staircase. The steps ascend four or possibly five floors; I can hear Angela repeatedly asking where they are taking her. Her voice is getting fainter, she must be on the fourth floor by now. The thick pile carpet, and the long velvet drapes on the landings are deadening her voice. I hear a door open, and a shaft of light cascades down the stairwell then, there is darkness again. I can only feel my way up the steps, taking only one step at a time. At the top, I place my ear to the solid wood door.

"Where... is... Col... in... Brown?" The voice I can hear is threatening, deliberately pronouncing every syllable; I can denote a slight lisp, the only clue to his identity.

"I don't know. When your men took him away, he said he would be back in a couple of minutes." Angela sounds scared and rightly so.

"Do... you... know... what... is... in... this... brief...case?" I can only presume he is referring to the briefcase that Colin has had strapped to his wrist since he left England.

"He told me it contained government papers, and he had to deliver them to someone at the club. That is all I know."

"What... is... your... relationship... with... Mr Brown?"

"I met him a week ago, and he invited me to accompany him on this trip. A girl cannot refuse an offer like that, I don't really know him at all."

"So... you... are... his... mistress?"

"No. I am his friend."

"You... are... his... bitch?"

"No, I am his friend. Why are you being so horrible to me, what have you done with him?" The man sniggers.

"Whatever... you... are, you should take more care when choosing your friends. You are in the wrong place at the wrong time, now I have to decide what... to... do... with... you."

There is silence, *whatever does he mean?* I hear Angela give a high-pitched scream as a chair falls over.

"Take... her... to... the... boat and hurry, it sails in two hours. We do not have time to take the shipment back. She... sails... with... the... ship."

The door swings open, knocking me off balance. I need to hide, but there is nowhere to go. I freeze in fear for my life. Luckily, the door swings into me, pinning me against the wall, hiding me from anyone who is leaving the room. There are four men, two of them are holding Angela by her arms, practically dragging her down the stairs; the other two are following close behind: both are carrying guns.

"N a s s e r!" the voice bellows from inside the room. One of the gunmen rushes back into the room; how he fails to see me I do not know. "Nasser, stay with her on the ship. If we haven't received the million pounds by the time you sail into the Suez Canal, throw her overboard."

"And if the money does arrive in time?" Asks Nasser nervously.

"Do what you want with her." He takes a deep breath. "No, hand her over with the cartons, she doesn't deserve to die?"

"Yes, sir. Please, sir, if she is to be thrown into the canal, do we kill her first?"

"It doesn't make any difference, does it stupid, now get out of here."

Nasser catches up with the others just as they are forcing Angela into a large streetcar.

"Will somebody... close... that... bloody... door?"

A hand appears on the handle, and the door slams shut. I stand in disbelief of not being seen, what do I do now? I have no alternative but to chase after her. *Whatever have I got her into?*

Colin is laid on his bed; his head aches. His entire body is shaking; his nervous system on the point of breakdown. He knows he was wrong to leave Angela at the club, but what else could he do. As he was being marched through the foyer of the club, they walked into a group of arriving guests blocking their exit. The guests must have been very important, as the clubs welcoming committee were in full action: hands were being shaken, coats removed, and glasses of champagne handed to every guest. The ladies were complimented on their dresses, and the men congratulated on the beauty of their partner. As the party divided, the women heading for the rest room and the men to their tables, there was a split second for Colin to make a dash for the street door. He was out of the club before his guards realised what was happening. On the busy street, he dived into a taxi returning to the city and screamed at the driver to go. Through the rear window, he could see the guards pushing their way through the arriving guests, but there was no way they could catch him now. They stood and watch as his cab swung onto the expressway and sped off towards the city centre.

He is distraught, gasping for air. His chest is heaving in nervous spasms. His body gives one more surge, and he throws up. He lays there panting and sweating, his body is slowly calming, but his head is still in turmoil. He has abandoned Angela, she will be sitting at the club waiting for him, what will she do? Can she get herself back to the hotel? Does she have any money? How long will she sit there before she realises he isn't coming back to her? He had such hopes of an exciting night; and now, it has turned into a nightmare.

"A call for you, Mr Brown." Colin holds the phone to his ear.

"Is that you Angela? Angela, I am so sorry."

"Mr Brown?"

"Yes."

"You have three days to complete the payment. If the money has not materialised by midnight-Wednesday, you will not see your girlfriend again." The message is short and to the point. Colin places the receiver slowly into its holder and holds his head in his hands. The last thing he wanted was to put Angela at risk; now getting the money to them in time has taken on a whole new meaning. What if he fails? Surely, they won't kill her; he dwells on the thought, acknowledging the fact that they would! Anyway, even if they did, no one will miss her. No one knows her, she is a simple London street girl.

There is a knock on the door.

"Colin, it's Janet. I saw you arrive, let me in. Where is Angela? I did not see her come back with you?"

Oh God! Colin buries his head into the duvet. Janet is the last person he wants to see right now.

"Angela met an ex-boyfriend in the club, so I came back alone. I guess she is still with him at the club, or she has probably gone back to his place." He has no idea where this explanation came from. He is just making it up but encouraged as Janet seems to be accepting it.

"Who is this guy? Have you ever seen him before?"

"No, I don't know him."

"Is he English?"

"Yes, he is English," Colin stutters, thinking this to be the most logical answer.

Janet desperately wants to believe him. Her thoughts race back to her meeting with me and wonders who I am. If I was Angela's friend, then Colin could be telling the truth. If he is lying, then Angela is in danger. Knowing Colin as well as she does, she fears he is lying.

"I don't believe a word you are telling me, I have to find her. I will be back soon, so don't even think about going to bed."

"You are a shit, Janet. Go find your own slut and leave mine alone."

Janet is hysterical and picks up a gin bottle from the bedside table and throws it as hard as she can at him. She screams in frustration as she slams the door behind her.

"Has Tim Collingwood returned yet," she asks the girl on reception.

"No, he is still at The Club. Shall I tell him to call you when he gets back?"

"That is a good idea, please ask him to call me." She takes refuge in the hotel lounge, waiting for Angela to return, hopefully with me; as she slowly drains her bottle of red Beaujolais, she slumps down into her chair and sleep takes over.

I am no more a gentleman than Colin. I have left Petal sitting alone in the club. She will report my absence to her boss and tell him I have walked out on her. He will demand a check on who I am, what I do, and why I am in Beijing, my anonymity will be dashed. I have no option. I have to follow Angela and get her back.

"Taxi! Follow that streetcar." An instruction I seem to be giving quite regularly. My mind is trying to piece together what I understand of the situation. A 'power house' in Beijing is holding Angela hostage in exchange for one million pounds, a payment for a shipment, which is already on-board a ship sailing in two hours. Colin has the task of finding this money, and he has disappeared unless he is back at the hotel. I don't like Colin nor do I trust him. I trust the Chinese even less, will they release her if the money is paid? I doubt it, I have to get her back.

"Where do you think they are going?" I ask my driver.

He grunts in disapproval, obviously not a happy guy. Apparently, we have driven out of his allocated zone, and he will be heavily fined if he gets caught by the authorities. Neither does he want to drive any farther out of the city at this time of night. He was on his way home when I gatecrashed his cab. Angela must be a mile ahead; luckily, her car is the only vehicle on what appears to be a very desolate road. I can see the taillights of her car flickering on and off as it turns left then right. Then, they disappear, leaving the horizon in complete darkness.

"Where have they gone, driver?"

He shrugs his shoulders; all he wants to do is turn around and go back to the city.

"What is over there?" I point to the place where I last saw the lights. "Out there, what is over there?" I keep pointing and repeating myself.

"Nothing there, an old airport, nothing there now, sir."

"An airport, big enough for large planes?"

"No for…" He twirls his finger in the air, "choppers."

"For helicopters, an airport for helicopters?"

"Yes, but now no more, finish."

He has hardly stopped waving his fingers in the air when there is an enormous throbbing of air. The trees along the road shake violently as if a storm has suddenly struck them. Their branches crack and snap falling all around us, a helicopter rises from behind them.

"Well, it is definitely being used tonight." My heart sinks; Angela must be on-board, where are they taking her?

We pull over and watch it climb higher into the night sky. It veers left and heads towards the horizon, its flashing beacon gets fainter and fainter until it too fades into obscurity. I point in the direction of the plane. "Where they go?"

He shrugs his shoulders again. "Maybe go Tianjin. Big city, big port."

I stare into the darkness; desperate to see a glimmer of its beacon. There is nothing.

A port! Yes, they are heading for a port, I recall a ship was mentioned. They are going to meet up with a ship, but they also said the ship was sailing in two hours; it will have sailed by now. I am so tired, my brain is not making sense of this. Of course, a helicopter can land on a boat wherever it is, as long as it has a flat deck; it doesn't matter if the ship is tied to the quay or on the ocean.

"Take me back to Beijing." I have to find Colin Brown and tear him limb from limb.

Lost

"What do you mean you have lost her?" Back in her office in London, Sarah Thompson is on the phone, interrogating her photographer who is begging his innocence.

"Sarah, please listen to me, nobody knows where she is. We followed her to The Club last night, and she has not been seen since. She never came back to the hotel."

"How could you let her out of your sight, go and find her. I need pictures of her meeting Chinese dignitaries. God! The headline and the page layouts are finished, we just want pictures. Angela is the greatest story we have ever written. We can't risk losing her for one minute." Sarah is working herself up into a rage. "Goodness, every woman in the world is wanting to know where she is. If we miss her meeting with the general secretary of the Chinese central committee or screwing the paramount leader, your head will roll. Call me back in one hour, and for your sake, I hope you have found her."

Every London newspaper is searching for her, so desperate are they, a reward of one million pounds has been offered for the first photograph of her to arrive on an editor's desk. The cry is out, and everybody, including policemen, bus drivers, cab drivers, have their mobile cameras at the ready.

Someone else is also making the news headlines. 'Colin Brown, MP for Berwick-on-Tweed, leader of the UK trade delegation to Beijing, has been found dead in his hotel room with his throat cut.' His body was found at 9 o'clock this morning, when room service delivered his breakfast. The poor room girl is in shock, she is 16 and only started working at the hotel three weeks ago. The pressure from the police, press and TV reporters demanding details from her have reduced her to tears.

"He was laid on his back," she sobs, "I didn't know what to do. He was stretched out on a bloodstained bed. I shook him, his face was scary. He looked as if he had seen a ghost."

"Was there any sign of a murder weapon?" the police officer asks her.

"You mean a knife or a gun?"

"Anything, anything at all?"

"All I could see was a broken gin bottle laid next to his body."

Within the hour, Colin's murder will be breaking news all around the world; this is a terrible British government story to be coming out of China.

Janet Cynthia Clynbourne is rushing her breakfast in the VIP breakfast hall. She is steaming with rage, agitated and tired after waiting for Angela all night in the hotel lounge, but if that is her excuse for her rudeness, it has not pacified my opinion of her. Even when I sit with her, she doesn't even acknowledge my presence.

"There seems to be quite a commotion in the hotel, this morning, what is going on?" She continues to ignore me and shovels another spoonful of breakfast cereal into her mouth. I repeat the question again much louder, demanding her attention. She eventually drains her coffee cup and looks at me.

"Some guy has been found dead; they think he has been murdered."

"Do you know who he is, is he British?" I ask her.

"I don't know who he is, these things happen in China. He is a member of the British trade delegation, Colin something or other."

This woman deserves an acting Oscar, she knows Angela is missing. She knows Angela was with Colin last night, and I know she is a close friend of Colin. This woman is up to her neck in it, but what is worrying me, if it is Colin who has been murdered, who is getting the money to secure Angela's release? Apart from myself, nobody knows that Angela is being held for ransom, with an instruction to kill her if a million pounds is not paid.

I try to think the problem through. I know of three people who are involved. Lesley Buchanan was responsible for getting the money in the first place, he knows the payment is a million pounds short. Michael Sumner—his accountant—will know, it is his job to drip the money out of the company accounts, and then there is Reginald Rolland Swordsmith. He will know and must be devastated to learn Angela is missing, especially now, her escort is dead.

Janet Is a Joke

I am appalled at the lies Janet is telling; she is in total denial, yet this is not my concern. I am the only person who knows of Angela's whereabouts, and apparently, the only person admitting concern. I listen intently to Janet's account of last night's events and wonder if she can be Colin's killer. I can picture her in a moment of lover's jealousy, slashing out at him, maybe it was an accident; maybe it was deliberate. Whatever happened, one thing is for sure. Colin is dead, and the Beijing Police will never link Janet to him, but the British Police would if I can get the story to them, but not yet. I have to get Angela back; and to do that, I need Janet to admit involvement then her assistance.

"I have done my fair share of travelling," I tell her, "Especially around Europe and the Americas, but this is my first visit to China."

"What do you do Mr Collinwood, and what brings you to Beijing?" I have to think fast.

"Err, I work in advertising on major international brands, hence my travelling; and I am in Beijing, promoting the launch of M&Z. They are opening 50 new stores here in the next three years." *Hey! I am really proud of myself; my lying is almost as good as Janet's.*

"So, why are you interested in Angela?" Her direct question takes me by surprise.

"What makes you think I am interested in Angela?"

"You never take your eyes off her; and last night, you followed her to the night club."

"How do you know that?"

"I saw you."

"You are right. Apart from her being pretty, I thought she would be the ideal girl to promote the store, so I wanted to discuss a modelling contract with her."

"And did you?"

"And did I what?"

"Did you discuss a modelling contract with her?"

"No, I lost her inside the club."

Janet stares at me in silence, then after a pause.

"I will come clean, Mr Collinwood. Angela and I are lovers. I was concerned when she told me she was coming to Beijing with Colin Brown, so I decided to come with her. I followed her to the club last night, but they wouldn't let me in."

"Do you know Colin Brown?" I ask her.

"I know he has a reputation with young girls, all Westminster knows that."

"So you do know him?"

"What happened inside the club, Mr Collinwood?" she asks, completely changing the subject. I describe the events that lead up to Angela, leaving the dance floor accompanied by the two Chinese bodyguards. Her face drains of blood.

"Oh my God, I knew she would be in danger. Has she arrived back at the hotel?"

"No, she has disappeared. Everyone is looking for her, and now Colin Brown, who escorted her last night, has been found dead. I know you are involved, Janet, so what do you know?"

"Nothing, I have told you everything."

"You are lying, Janet." I watch as beads of sweat burst out on her forehead and run down her face, she jumps to her feet.

"You must, excuse me. I have an important phone call to make." She pushes her chair away from the table to leave, but a man stands in her way and holds a silver badge out towards her.

"Janet Cynthia Clynbourne, are you Janet Cynthia Clynbourne?"

"Yes, why?"

"Beijing Police, there has been an incident in the hotel, and we are questioning all British nationals. Do you mind if we ask you a few questions?"

"Now?"

"Yes, now if you don't mind; we have erected an office in the corner of the lounge. Would you come with me, please?" His instruction is more a command than a request. He is very confident for an over-weight, balding, five-foot Chinese police officer.

She obediently follows him across the lounge, without looking at me.

A sense of panic runs through my body. Janet is my only hope of raising a million pounds, unless... unless George Baldwin can help me, I have to call George immediately.

"A call from Beijing for you, Mr Baldwin. Can you take it straight away?"

The Rt Hon. George Baldwin, in his role of government minister and secretary of state for works and pensions, puts down his morning gin and splutters his name into his phone. He is hoping Angela is calling; he has

139

been thinking about her all night and can't get her out of his head. He is totally infatuated with her.

"Mr Baldwin, sir! My name is Tim Collinwood, and I am calling on behalf of Angela. She is in serious trouble, and you are the only person I can turn to for help."

"Goodness, Mr Collinwood. I thought it might be her calling me, in trouble you say. Of course I will help, who are you, and what can I do?"

"Mr Baldwin; before I explain, can you assure me that your phone is not being tapped?"

There is silence.

"No, I can't." He eventually admits, "What do you suggest?"

"You must buy a new mobile phone. Go somewhere remote, somewhere like Trafalgar Square, and I will call you in two hours. It doesn't sound very hi-tech, but it is all I can think of."

George rises to his feet and calls his secretary. He needs her help. He knows nothing about mobile phones, he doesn't even know where he can buy one.

"Get your coat, we are going out and put your running shoes on."

"What now? I have to type your speech for the trade association."

"Sod that, we are leaving, and we are walking."

"Walking?"

"Yes, walking; and bring your credit card." George has been suddenly activated. All I can do is wait, and hope he is doing as I requested; this is going to be a long two hours.

Please Help Me

The news of Colin's murder is announced on the 10:30, British news bulletin. Reginald Rolland Swordsmith is immediately on the phone to Lesley. Colin's murder has put the fear of death into him. He can only think the Chinese mafia have killed him, but shouting at Lesley isn't going to ease his concern.

"Have you any idea what happened last night in Beijing?" he screams at him.

"None, whatsoever, Reggie. Colin called me last night and said he was leaving for The Club to deliver the money."

"Was Angela going with him?"

"Yes."

"Are you aware she is missing?"

"I have just heard about it on the BBC news."

"Do you think they have killed her?"

"I don't know, Reggie. I dare not think."

"Bloody hell, doesn't anyone know anything?"

"The Beijing Police thinks Angela is Collin's killer."

"That is ridiculous, it's the Chinese mafia."

"You know that, I know that, but the Chinese police don't know that. They have instigated a massive search for her."

"Have they any evidence, have they found anything that points to Angela?"

"Not that I know of."

"Have you got the rest of the money?"

"Reggie, I told you before, I need time, there is no panic. The ship left Tianjin Port, last night, and the money will be delivered before it reaches the English Channel."

"It's a mess, Lesley, a bloody big mess. I can't relax until we deliver the money. I don't understand why we haven't heard from the mafia, why are they taking it so calmly?"

"We have heard from them, they have killed Colin and possibly Angela."

"You are scaring me, why should they kill her?"

"To make sure we give them the money."

"You are right, Lesley. You are so bloody right."

Janet is sitting opposite the police officer, shaking. She only threw the gin bottle to scare him, she aimed it at the wall but can't recall hearing a crash. Could it have hit Colin instead, could it have cut his throat, did she kill Colin? One thing is for sure; her fingerprints are all over the broken bottle and on the handle of his door. Under police interrogation, her account of last night is coming out all wrong. She loves Angela, but she loves herself a lot more. She knows she is doing wrong, but it's what she doesn't tell him that cast the blame onto Angela. She doesn't tell him about the argument she had with him in his hotel room. She doesn't tell him that Colin and Angela split up at The Club, and that he came back alone.

Where, Why and When

I sit, sweating over my laptop computer, I have no alternative. I have to find the name of the ship Angela might be on, and where it is bound. I am into my third hour of investigation when I stumble on the ship register of vessels departing Tianjin Port, last night; there were 14 sailings, but none were destined for Britain; but the two, which departed between midnight and one o'clock are worthy of further investigation. The 'Sea Lion', a Chinese registered container vessel heading for Murmansk; and the 'Ocean Wanderer', an oil tanker destined for Bahrain.

Where the hell is Murmansk? I bring up a map of the world's sea routes. Bingo! I suppose a destination of Felixstowe or London Gateway would have been too easy, but a shaft of light appears. The 'Sea Lion' calls at Singapore, then sails up the Red Sea, crosses the Mediterranean, up the English Channel, arriving at Murmansk, in Russia, at the bottom of the Barents Sea. Does that bring the ship close enough to an English port, could they drop a shipment onto the English coast? I conclude it does, Angela must be on-board the 'Sea Lion'.

"Mr. Baldwin, is that you, are you using a new untraceable mobile phone?"

"Yes, I am in Trafalgar Square as you requested. Tell me who you are, your story better be convincing. I am frozen stiff, sitting out here. The temperature is practically zero."

"I am Angela's fiancé, and as I didn't approve of her going to China with Colin Brown, I followed her." George is silent; I hope he accepts my explanation. I tell him that his parliament friends are in business with Mr Cho Wang, the owner of a nightclub in Beijing and a very powerful man.

"They are not my friends, they are just people I use." He sneers. "That is what we do in government, we use people."

"Sir, I believe Colin is involved in a deal with the Chinese underworld, and he is one million pounds short on a payment." I recount the events of the evening, describing in detail the conversation I overheard, and my encounter with the helicopter. "I believe Angela is being held hostage on-board the 'Sea Lion'; and if Colin fails to deliver

143

the money before the container ship reaches the Suez Canal, she will be thrown into the sea."

"Will Colin get the money to them in time?" I can tell he believes me. He is concerned, his voice is trembling.

"I doubt it, he was found dead in his hotel room this morning; and the police have named Angela as their number one suspect."

"Oh my God! We must get her back to London."

"The container ship is heading for Murmansk. It navigates the Suez Canal and then sails up the English Channel. Its route fits the description I overheard." George is furious.

"I knew they were up to no good, but it had nothing to do with me, so I didn't probe. Why should I create waves when I am retiring in two years, what can I do to help?"

"Because we doubt these friends of yours will raise the money in time, can you borrow a million pounds from the treasury?"

"Ugh, is that all you want?"

"No, you have to help me get on-board the ship. I have to be there for her, in case the money doesn't arrive."

"Bloody hell, how are you going to do that?"

"All I can think of… is…" I pause, I need a plan, *oh please God, give me a plan.*

"All you can think of is what? Come on, Tim; what is your plan?"

"I need to be in a boat, floating in the path of the 'Sea Lion'? If they think I am in distress, maybe they will stop and take me on board." *Goodness where did that come from?*

George is trembling with excitement; he hasn't been so aroused since Mary agreed to marry him 50 years ago. His mind flashes back to that hot evening on the Florida coast at Key West, when she said, 'I will'.

"To make that happen, I have to involve the secret service and that will take days."

"George, we do not have days. Is there any other way? Angela's life is at stake."

"You don't want much, do you?"

"Surely you want the same?"

"Of course I do."

"Can you come up with a better plan?"

"No, I can't. Listen, Tim, get to Beijing airport. I will arrange for a private jet to take you to Colombo. I have a friend there with an ocean-going yacht. He will know how to get you into the path of the Sea Lion. In the meantime, I will try and raise a million pounds."

"George, you are a marvel. When do I go?"

"You go now, get gone, call me when you are at the airport. I will contact the British Embassy in Beijing to meet you and escort you through the diplomatic lane. They will take you through immigration as a government official.

"Do you understand?" he hollows down the phone.

"Yes, I understand."

"Go."

I am totally overawed with George's action plan; he must have been dynamic when he was a young man. My phone goes dead, now it is my turn to panic. I have to get out of the hotel before the police call me for an interview; they have already spoken with most of the English visitors. I grab a clean pair of briefs, a pair of socks, my mobile and passport and throw them into a brief case. How minimal is that? I walk through the lobby and out onto the street, like a day tourist. Nobody takes any notice except the concierge who calls me a cab; I am out of there.

George is ranting instructions to his secretary, even before he closes his office door. "Get me, Tom Ramsey at MI5, he still works for the secret service; doesn't he."

"I don't know, sir. I am a temp, your permanent secretary is on holiday."

"Sorry, I forgot, fetch me the morning papers and put the damn TV on. I can never get it to work."

"Yes, sir, what shall I do first?"

"All of them, damn you. This is a matter of life and death."

Sky News is still reporting the death of Colin Brown, but now, they have added a sub-feature. The Chinese Police are looking for Angela, who they believe can help with their enquires. The mid-morning headlines have also picked up on the story. 'British Glamour Girl Angela Bee is wanted by Chinese Police for government minister's murder. George utters a sigh of desperation; he is in no doubt that what I told him is true.

"Tom, thank goodness, you are still working for MI5; do you know about the story breaking in China?"

"Good morning, George. We are working on it, the prime minister has given it a triple X rating. You don't happen to know where this girl is?" He is joking of course.

"I do actually, I have the whole inside story, and I need your help. Shall I come to you or you to me?"

"You to me."

"I am on my way."

"As soon as you can, George, this is a big embarrassment for the government."

George's secretary enters the room, waving his speech for tonight's dinner in her hand.

"What is that?"

"Your speech to the Guild Hall tonight, Sir George." He grabs it off her and scans through it.

"File it, I don't have time to read it in detail right now. No! On second thoughts, tell them I have come down with the plague and cancel the entire thing. I can't make it."

Scared

What do I do now? I didn't used to talk to myself, but it seems to be a habit I have developed recently. The arrival terminal at the airport is a vast space. There must be 2,000 people bustling around in here, and they all appear to have the same problem as myself. They haven't a clue where to go. I pause in the centre of the milieu and search for inspiration, there is nothing I can focus on. There are so many lights, so many signs and advertising hoardings. I can't even ask for help, I don't know what to ask for. I don't know which plane or airline I am taking, nor will I recognise anyone from the embassy. We haven't thought this through, there is no way George could organise this in only two hours. He is probably sitting at his desk, sipping his morning gin and being rude to his secretary. As for me, I am probably way down his list of priorities.

"Ping pong, call for Mr Tim Collinwood. Would Mr Tim Collinwood please go to the diplomatic lounge."

George you are a wiz, where is the diplomatic lounge?

I ride two escalators and cross the food hall, not once but three times; and now after a 20-minute search, I believe the blue glass door in front of me is the entrance to the diplomatic lounge. As I rush towards them, a sexy blue sign above the door clearly states DIPLOMATIC LOUNGE; and below it, in smaller lettering, DIPLOMATIC PERSONNEL ONLY. Now what?

Standing on either side of the doorway are two airport security guards, both with machine guns hanging from their shoulders. The guns are worn as part of their uniform rather than a weapon of destruction, but still, they look threatening. They are in conversation with several men requesting permission to enter but refusal looks imminent. Goodness, what chance have I got? These guys are smart, dressed in immaculate dark suites and obviously important businessmen. I am wearing a T-shirt over a pair of stained, shabby jeans, which are only just suitable for purpose. It never entered my head that I would be in the company of such dignitary.

A small, pretty Chinese girl pushes her way between the two soldiers and walks towards me.

"Mr Collinwood, I presume."

I nod like the stupid dog sitting on the rear parcel self of my uncle's old Humber Sceptre.

"My name is Liling Liang. I am from the British consulate in Beijing; and I am to accompany you to Colombo."

"I am so pleased to meet you. I didn't believe George could make this journey happen so quickly," she laughs.

"We can operate quickly if we want to, now come with me, we don't have a lot of time." She takes my arm and walks me away from the two guards. "First we have to dress you properly. Well, at least respectably, there is a tailor in the departure lounge. You don't have to wear a suit but not jeans, and choose a smart pair of leather shoes, shoes say a lot about a man, and…"

"And what?" I look at her all embarrassed.

"And get a shave, there are many shave shops in the lounge."

I run my hand over my face. Oh dear, just one other thing I forgot to do this morning.

"I will give you your new passport later; the police are already looking for Tim Collinwood." She pulls on my arm as we approach a gent's tailors. I will wait for you here.

I try to imagine what an embassy official would wear; and after trying on many shirts and jackets, I present myself for approval with relative confidence: grey flannels, black shoes, a short-sleeved white shirt, with a black cardigan draped around my neck. She bursts out laughing.

"What's the idea of wearing a pull-on as a scarf?"

"I thought this is how diplomats wear them?"

"You English are bonkers."

"Better than being boring, hey what!"

"Here is your new passport. You are now *M'sieur* Jacques Giger, a Swiss banker."

"Where did you get that name from?"

"It was your alias when you were working in Morocco. It suited you then, and it suites you now. We hope you will be more natural with it as you have used it before."

"Actually I prefer it to Tim Collinwood, what do you think?"

"Your name is not important to me."

I see myself in a shop window and can't resist a comment, *Good morning, M'sieur Giger. You are looking rather dapper, this morning.*

"You are completely bonkers. Stop admiring yourself, we have to hurry."

Liling Liang is the ideal travel companion. She is intelligent, interesting and a polite young woman. During the four-hour flight, we chat and swap stories and become the best of friends.

"I feel like James Bond," I tell her. "I am not even questioning the reason for my actions, nor am I considering the danger. I must be stupid."

"I don't think you are stupid, Mr Collinwood."

I correct her, "*M'sieur* Jacques Giger, my name is Jacques Giger." She laughs. I explain the reason for my mission and try to describe my feelings for Angela. Liling Liang listens intently to my story. Her big, beautiful brown eyes stare through me. Her lips are dry, and I realise my story is having an effect on her. She turns towards me and grips my arm. I can feel her warmth and her perfume is so sensuous, she is stunning. Maybe consulate people are not as boring as I thought.

"Are you frightened, *M'sieur* Giger?"

"I haven't had time to be frightened." She reaches up and gives me a kiss.

"I think you are amazing, please be careful."

Sitting in the middle of the Indian Ocean, sending out mayday messages from a beguiled catamaran, is giving me a lot of time in which to think about fear. The sun set two hours ago, and the darkness is over-powering. The only sound I can hear is the pounding of the waves on the hull of Martin Priestley's catamaran. Oh yes; and the thumping of the blood pounding through my veins. I cut the engine, so I can hear any approaching ship. The 'Sea Lion' should be passing within 20 miles of me any time now. Martin checked on its progress before leaving Colombo. Continually focusing on the horizon, my eyes are stinging in the sea-salted air.

I have to fire a distress flare the minute I see the ship. Martin has taught me how to do this without setting myself alight. Maybe I should practise the technique again, but I can't even remember where the flares are stored, my brain is a mush. Goodness, I wish I could swop the beating of this incessant sea for the beating of Liling Liang's chest. *Liling Liang, you are so right, I am scared to death.*

The Magic Word

"Get me Reginald Rolland Swordsmith."

"Now, what's the magic word Mr Baldwin?"

"The magic word is NOW."

"Now! You know that is not correct, the word is please." George despairs as it takes her over a minute to connect him.

"Reginald Rolland Swordsmith is in conference with the PM. Mr Baldwin, shall I leave a message for him to call you back."

George hates it when his permanent secretary is on holiday; his patience with temporary secretaries is zero. The staff agency always send him a young, sexy girl who spends all day playing with her make-up and texting her girlfriends. He has explained to them time and time again that the most professional secretaries are in their late 30s, single and overweight, and that's the only type of woman he wants. He looks Julia up and down; *I suppose she is in her mid-30s, overweight and single.* So far, so good, you might think, except she spends all her time chatting to her girlfriends on the phone. She is a complete and utter waste of time and space as far as George is concerned.

"Is he hell in a conference, he's in McDonald's, eating breakfast. He is always stuffing a McBreakfast into himself at 9:30 in the morning, call him on his mobile." She obeys.

"Good morning, George. What can I do for you this morning?" he answers, with a mouth full of egg muffin.

"You can tell me what the devil is going on in Beijing, what happened to Colin Brown?"

"I'm just reading about it now, George. It appears he has died on the job."

"He's been murdered, you idiot, and he wasn't on the kind of job you are referring to. He's been killed in his hotel room. Where is Janet Clynbourne?"

"I don't know, probably visiting her constituency."

"Reginald, do you take me for an ass. She is also in Beijing, why is she in Beijing? And where is Angela?"

"I don't know, George. If she isn't in the hotel, then she is probably doing a trick with someone who pays more than Colin. Anyway, why do you want to know?"

"Angela is the hottest news in the country, and she has gone missing. She could be dead, she could have been kidnapped." He pauses for a second, "She could be held ransom for whatever Colin Brown was up to."

"George, the leading story in this morning's paper reports that she is the number one suspect for Colin's death. I can't believe that. Even if he was forcing her to do what she didn't want, it's not a reason to kill him."

"Don't be so disgusting, this story could break the government and only eight months before a general election as well. Put your head on, can you remember the Profumo affair when Christine Keeler and Mandy Rice Davies brought down the government? It has been reported that Angela is having your baby, sleeping with Colin Brown, and if I am not mistaken Janet bloody Cynthia Clynbourne as well. For your sake, Reginald bloody Rolland Swordsmith, find Angela, and find her soon. She is only 24, for God's sake, where is your sense of responsibility."

George slams down the phone. It is obvious to him that Reginald has no idea where Angela is, and it is also clear that he doesn't care. Is nobody trying to raise the million pounds to release her? George automatically reaches for his gin bottle, as he does when he is angry, but with the bottle practically touching his lips, he thinks better of it.

Maybe Lesley Buchanan can help; he is a member of this group of idiots.

"Get me, Lesley Buchanan." Julia has given up trying to teach George his manners.

"Right away, Mr Baldwin."

"Lesley, George Baldwin, how are you?"

"Fine, George, under the circumstances, and yourself?"

"Lesley, where are you right now? I need to meet up with you?"

"I'm staying at the Hilton in Park Lane. I am just taking breakfast."

"Stay there, I will be with you in 30 minutes."

George puts down the phone before Lesley has time to reply. As he grabs his coat, he prays that Lesley doesn't call back to change his plan.

"Julia, a cab, now." She despairs.

Barry Cornwell

Barry Cornwell, MP for Devon and Cornwall, was expected at his surgery in Davenport High Street, half an hour ago. There are several people waiting to see him; his secretary is concerned.

Barry is the owner of a boat hire company. He has six boats, which he rents out to groups of fishermen, usually at night. The most successful fishing is at night, so he charges double for night hire. He says if they are stupid enough to go fishing at night, then they are stupid enough to pay inflated prices, and they do. He also owns two larger vessels, each capable of seating a 100 passengers. These he hires to coach companies who have included a sail up the river in their itinerary. But his pride and joy is a classic, sea-going, 59-foot luxury cabin cruiser named 'Marianne', after his wife. It has four berths, bedrooms to you and me, a 16-seat dining room, and a fully fitted kitchen, or should I say galley. He designed the boat himself and launched it ten years ago. He uses it for family holidays and shopping trips to France. Sometimes, he invites his friends to accompany him on a long weekend away, when the stress of Westminster is getting him down. His favourite holiday port is San Tropez; he sails there single-handed and rents a berth in the marina for the summer. His wife will then fly down to join him and stay as long as she can. His three children, now in their early 20s, join him if they can. They have done this every year, for the last eight years. The 'Marianne' is at the heart of his family.

The boat is in a dry dock across the river, undergoing its three-year sea-worthiness inspection. It should have been back in the water a week ago, but a fault in the engine management system is causing the delay. Barry is panicking; he needs the 'Marianne' for a trip to Brittany in two days' time. He has told his wife he is taking Keith Mitchinson to Roscoff, a picturesque harbour in Brittany, renowned for its architecture. He says the trip is to replenish their wine collection, which is true, but unknown to her, they will meet up with the 'Sea Lion' in the channel on its way to Murmansk.

Barry is harassing the boat yard daily to complete the repair. He is an important customer, and they are so apologetic. "The part should be here in the morning, and we will install it immediately," they tell him, but they have told him that before.

Angela's Life Depends on It

George searches the lounge of the Hilton. He spots Lesley engrossed in the morning newspaper.

"Hi George, I'm over here."

"Lesley; thanks for meeting me, mi! You have been through the mill since I last saw you, you look terrible."

"You can say that again, George. I had nothing to do with the murder of Stephanie Stirling, but the police are convinced I did."

"I'm so sorry about that, but it isn't Stephanie Stirling I want to discuss with you. It's Angela, the girl you met at the advertising agency presentation, do you know where she is?"

"I am reading about her right now. Apparently, she went to Beijing with Colin Brown, and the Chinese Police think she is his killer."

"Is that all you know? Be honest with me Lesley, it is very important."

"I swear that is all I know."

"Lesley, I am going to be honest with you; and as you have also been wrongly accused of a murder, you will sympathise with Angela's predicament. I know that you, Colin, Janet, possibly Reginald and Barry, are in business with the Chinese. I don't want to know what it is, but I know you are one million pounds short on a payment; and I have been informed that the mafia are holding Angela ransom until the sum is paid. I have also been told that if the money isn't paid by tomorrow, they will kill her. Does what I am saying make any sense to you?"

Lesley is shocked at what George is telling him. He rubs his chin and wipes his brow.

"It could make sense, George. I know nothing of Angela's involvement, but the payment will be made on Friday. I can guarantee that."

"Lesley, that will be too late. It must be paid tomorrow."

"I can't get the money that quickly, George, the bankers cannot release that much money so quickly. I have been in police custody for a week. I should have got the money earlier, but I couldn't. We are four days late with the payment, but they will get it."

"Angela's life depends on it, is there anything you can do?" Lesley shakes his head.

"I will call the bankers again and do all I can." George decides it is time to get tough.

"You must get this money tomorrow, Lesley, or the press will have a field day. I will tell them everything I know."

"George, calm down. Can you borrow that amount from the Treasury? We will pay you back, surely you can pull rank. I promise I will pay you back on Friday."

"At this moment in time, the answer is no. Keep me informed of any progress. Tom Ramsey is waiting for me at MI5. Call me every hour on the hour, do you hear me Lesley?"

"I hear you."

"Lesley! Make it happen."

Tom Ramsey is pacing up and down in his office at 'Thames House'.

"Bloody hell, George, what you are telling me can bring the government down. Why have you waited so long before telling me?"

"I only found out myself three hours ago and met Angela a week ago. What these five guys are up to has only surfaced because they chose to use her. She is an innocent and very pretty girl. Tom, we have to help her, we have to get on-board that ship. Please, Tom, help her. If not for her, for the country." Tom can see that George is upset.

"Legally, we can't board a ship outside British waters; and even then, it will involve the Admiralty—the special boat service—and HM Coast Guard; oh yes, and the Drug Enforcement Bureau."

George is frantic. "Stop right there, Tom. We have only hours to save Angela's life and the government from embarrassment. If you can't board the ship, help me to get this guy called Tim on-board the Sea Lion."

"Who is he?"

"He's her fiancé." Tom shakes his head.

"I'm afraid, all I can do is have the ship followed. We have a frigate in the Indian Ocean, *H.M.S. Offensive*. I will order her to make contact with the *Sea Lion* and sail with her up the Red Sea as far as the canal. In the meantime, I will order *HMS Enforcer* to sail down from Cyprus and follow her across the Mediterranean and into home waters."

"Can we offer Tim a means of escape? He isn't a member of the SAS, he is just an ordinary guy. I believe he works in advertising."

"Once he's on board that ship, he is on his own. Put a transmitter on him; and if he has to jump overboard, we can locate it and pick him up."

"How long will it take the frigate to reach him?" Tom stops to think.

"Twenty minutes."

"Bloody hell, Tom, 20 minutes is a long time to be floating on your back in the Indian Ocean."

"That's the best we can offer him at this moment in time." Tom Ramsey sinks into his chair and taps his fingers on his desk; after several thoughtful seconds, he eventually looks up at George.

"I don't suppose there is any chance of you raising the million pounds?" George shakes his head.

"You are not the first to ask me that. Do you REALLY think the Treasury will lend me a million pounds, with no guarantee of getting it back?"

"It was just a suggestion, forget I asked. Best of luck, George. We will arrest these bastards but saving your girl." He shakes his head. "I can't promise you that."

Sarah Thompson is in her studio, thumbing through the latest pictures of Angela. Her favourite pictures show her leaving the hotel last night on Colin's arm; she looks amazing, happy and excited. She was hoping to receive pictures of her dancing in the nightclub; but reports of the latest events in Beijing explain the reason why none have arrived. Why is she getting her information from the TV, when she is paying a photographer to watch her every move? She angrily taps his number into her mobile but only gets a recording of a woman saying, 'This phone is not active at this time. Please try again later.' Sarah hates computer-generated phone messages. *You can't shout at them,* she keeps insisting, *what is the point of getting angry with someone if you can't scream your head off at them.*

The *Vogue* website is receiving a thousand enquiries every hour asking after Angela. The majority of readers want to know where she is, others want to know why the magazine has dropped her story with no explanation, and a few, just a few, are concerned for her safety and begging the magazine to request help from the prime minister to find her.

Angela's whereabouts is causing concern right across the country. The newspaper offices are being inundated with phone calls, and the million-pound incentive for a recent picture of her has not born any results. She is the hottest posting on Facebook; and *The Sun* and the *Daily Mirror*, sensing a political scandal in the making, are running headlines which are straight to the point: 'Chinese trade mission sent packing after sex murder', 'Government disgraced over Chinese sex scandal'.

The Telegraph simply asks, 'Where is Angela?' and the *London Standard* begs, 'Come home, Angela; all is forgiven.'

The Sea Lion

You must have seen films where people are marooned in the middle of the ocean. Maybe a cruise ship sank or a battleship suffered a torpedo attack, but you will never see a film where their predicament was self-inflicted, and that's because it verges on utter stupidity.

Sitting here in Martin Priestley's catamaran, I realise how stupid I was to volunteer to do this. My shirt is drenched in water, and the salt-sea spray is ripping my face apart. This is a job for the most experienced SAS team, not an Ad Man. I have never been so miserable in my life. I search the horizon in the hope of seeing a ship or, better still, seeing land; even the sight of a seagull would raise my spirit, but there is nothing, just a black expanse of water bleeding into the night sky. The sun set two hours ago; and since then, the horizon has completely disappeared into the sea, and the temperature dropped to near freezing. At the risk of throwing up, I glance skyward where minute specks of light from the nearest stars give me something to focus on. The top of the mast is raking across them, pointing first to one and then stabbing at another; it only emphasises the rocking of the boat and exaggerates my dire situation. The only sounds are from the mast cables clattering into each other. I mean the rigging, of course. Martin has spent hours teaching me all the nautical terms, anyway, the ringing noise they make is as tuneful as a funeral bell, and I believe they toll for me.

I try to laugh at my own joke, but my depression is too deep, feeling as I do, nothing is funny. *How black is the Black Sea when the Indian Ocean is as black as this.* I expected it to be warm and blue, not a lake of lifeless black tar.

The sail suddenly billows out; a breeze blows across my face. *Oh God! Not a storm, please, not a storm. I can't cope with a storm.* The weather forecast was calm for the next 36 hours, but I never did trust weathermen. I glance at my wristwatch; it is 1:30 in the morning. I try to cheer myself up by remembering summer days on hot sandy beaches, where we had skinny-dipping parties and barbeques, with whole pigs roasting on a campfire. Maybe thinking of the girls I knew might help, there was Joan Riley, Samantha Braithwaite and Helena. Helena... goodness! I can't remember her surname; maybe I never knew it.

I think of Liling Liang. Now she IS a pretty girl, she will brighten my mood, except for a sense of guilt I have for sleeping with her. I didn't lead her on; she participated willingly. In fact, I would go as far as to say she encouraged me, but I definitely should not have screwed her on the plane, that was definitely wrong of me, goodness, we had only known each other for two hours. To be honest, it just happened, yes, that's what it did, it just happened. I visited the loo, and when I stepped out, she was waiting to come in. She pushed me back inside, what was I supposed to do? She said she wanted to talk to me in private, and the loo was the only place she would not be overheard.

She put her arms around my neck, I thought to whisper in my ear; but when I felt her legs wrapping around me, I realised she had an ulterior motive. I couldn't let her fall, so I pulled her onto me. She was hot, but her story was hotter.

"Tim, take me to England. I need a sponsor. I need somewhere to stay, and I need someone to take care of me until I get a job?" She took me by surprise.

"Why do you want to live in England?" I asked her, trying to regain my breath. "You have a good job in Beijing?"

She completely ignored my question. "I can take care of you, Mr Tim, you will be very pleased with me," and with that, she stretched up and locked her lips onto mine. Well, there is sensual kissing, and then there is Liling Liang's way of kissing; and all I could do was surrender and enjoy her. I could feel her arms and legs gripping my body, like the tentacles of an octopus, and her mouth started to explore my face, throat, ears and nose. In the confines of our mini love lounge, we joined the mile high club.

Our passion was brought to an abrupt end, with the announcement of our arrival in Colombo. Liling Liang never did complete her reasons for wanting to live in England.

At Bandaranaike International Airport, 22 miles north of Colombo, Liling Liang walked me straight through immigration by waving our diplomat stickers high in the air. I got the impression that she was known by the officials and well liked. She received several 'good mornings' and one guy kissed her hand. *You should have been on the plane, matey,* the thought actually brought a smile to my face.

"Over here." Liling Liang pulled me towards a chubby, overweight guy waving at her. He was wearing a flowered shirt, loosely hanging over a pair of cropped jeans; his flimsy sand shoes were struggling for survival under his excessive weight. At first, I thought he was sloppy and untidy; but after comparing him with the other people waiting in the arrival hall, he appeared to be wearing the ultimate in Srilankan fashion.

"This is Martin Priestley." Liling Liang announced and introduced me as *M'sieur* Jacques Giger. His response was friendly and polite, but his Yorkshire accent was impossible to mistake. Surely a fellow Yorkshireman would know that Jacques Giger wasn't my real name. He would have expected my name to be Ernest Feather or Walter Weaver, I bet he was laughing his head off. My first impression of him was very favourable; overweight due to drinking too much beer and heavily tanned with living a life out in the sun, yet his smile was as broad as he was tall, and he had a happy-go-lucky persona.

"Now young lad, I believe we have two hours to teach you how to sail my boat across the ocean." I remember laughing, but as he grasps my hand and crushed it into a deformed paw, the fun went out of our meeting; my hand still hurts.

"I believe that is true, sir, can you do it? I asked him.

Then, he cracked his first joke, "If you can make a cup of tea and shit over the side of a boat, I can make a sailor out of you." Well, I thought he was joking.

"Oh dear, I don't think I can do that; I might fall overboard?"

I like Martin, and I am very envious of his life. He lives on the marina, and it is idyllic. He is a long-time friend of George's. They met at university and hit it off immediately. Both being Yorkshire lads, since then they have kept in touch. Martin tells me George is a stuck-up bastard, but he still has a lot of respect for him. As for Martin, well, he is a joy to be with, he is friendly, bubbly and full of fun. He shares a joke with everyone who walks his boardwalk and flirts with every woman between the ages of 17 and 70. He was married once, but she ran away with a BOAC pilot on their sixth wedding anniversary, he now believes a women is a gift for Christmas and not for life.

Liling Liang is also a joy to be around; and during the last two days, I have grown very fond of her. We spent two pleasant nights wrapped around each other, during which time I promised to take her to England. Well, I wouldn't, but George would. He would find her a sponsor and a comfortable home: maybe she could live with Angela and in Lesley's apartment. I wonder if they would be up for a threesome. Now, now Tim, time to think of the task at hand, where is that damn 'Sea Lion'?

"She should be here by now, Martin. Do you think we have missed her?"

Martin stumbles out of the cabin, rubbing his eyes; he has been asleep for almost three hours, ever since I cut the engine. The bottle of rum he downed on the way out here has possibly had something to do with his relaxed attitude.

"Martin, we must have missed it. The 'Sea Lion' should be here by now."

"Stop stressing, Tim, you are making enough noise to waken Poseidon. Look, if I am to sail this boat back to Colombo on my own, I needed some sleep. Anyway, what is that over there?" He points directly east where lights can be seen flickering in the dawning light. "I thought you were on watch. I wouldn't like to think my life depended on you spotting an iceberg."

"Do you think it is the 'Sea Lion'? It is a container ship, that is for sure, I can see the crates piled high on its deck."

"It has to be, there is no other ship scheduled out here at this time. In one hour, she will be close enough to recognise. We can't hear her engines because the wind is blowing away from us; so I will excuse you for not hearing her."

"Oh thanks, that makes me feel a whole lot better."

"Fire off a flare, they must have picked up our distress call; so when they see a flare, they will know who we are." Martin stands back, watching me make a complete hash of sending up a flare. "You are bloody useless, Jacques, or whatever you name is, remind me not to sail with you again."

I eventually fire the flare, and it shoots high into the sky, three minutes later, I fire a second.

"Now all we can do is watch what she does."

"How will they pick me up, Martin? I don't fancy climbing up the hull of a ship that big."

Martin cracks out laughing.

"What are you going to do? Hold your hand out like you do for a bus and expect it to stop for you?"

"OK clever dick, how will I get on board?"

"They might come for you in a small life boat and haul you up the side, or if they have a helicopter, and you say they have, they will hover over you. Throw you a rope, and you hang on for dear life as they winch you up."

"Martin, I don't fancy that either, I think I prefer a boat."

"Well, I hope it's a helicopter because I don't want them to see me."

"Sorry Martin, I forgot about you, will you hide in the cabin?"

"That's all I can do, I am not getting into the water, not even for you... Look, they have seen us, they are flashing at us, listen... they are calling us on the radio as well, go answer the radio." The radio crackles into life.

"Sea Lion calling. This is the Sea Lion calling. Are you Catamaran X4968 from Colombo, do you need assistance?"

"This is X4968, yes, I need assistance. Engine failure, I repeat, engine failure, can you help me?"

"This is the container ship 'Sea Lion', prepare to be boarded, prepare to be boarded."

"Job done, Martin, wow! You made that look easy. If ever you need a favour, just ask. I am deeply in your debt."

"Your luck has just run out. They are launching a helicopter off the stern of the ship, looks like you have a bit of rope climbing to do. Whatever happens, don't let anyone come on the boat, they must not see me."

We watch for 20 minutes as the helicopter flies closer and closer. Eventually its throbbing engine and swirling blades are directly overhead, boiling the sea around us with its propeller updraught. A man leans out and waves as he throws down a rope; its end is tied in a loop. I assume I have to tie it around my waist.

"No! No, you silly idiot. Shouts Martin hiding inside the cabin. "Just step into it and sit on it." I can see him shaking his head in disbelief at my ignorance.

"Thanks Martin, see you again soon, I hope." And with an increase thrust of the rotor blades, I am whisked off my feet and lifted high into the air.

"Pray for me, Martin," I scream at him as my feet are dangling in space.

"May God go with you, my friend."

As I swing around and around on the rope, I manage to see his big beaming face through the cabin window. He is a big man, in a very small boat on a very big ocean; and as I am hoisting higher and higher, his sail home looks like a mammoth task. I reach into the copter and attempt to pull myself into it. A man is standing over me, holding a rifle, not an ordinary rifle but more a bazooka-type rifle… the sort of thing you fire at tanks. He lifts it to his shoulder. I suddenly realise what he is going to do.

"No!!!! Not the boat, don't sink the boat."

Sorry Martin

Bullets riddle around the deck of the catamaran, and then it explodes into hundreds of flaming fragments; some shooting high into the sky. I watch as the mast floats away, and the hull disappears beneath the surface.

The gunman is screaming at me over the hiss of the copter's rotor blades, but I can't make out a single word he is saying, the explosion is still ringing in my ears. He gestures that I grab his hand, there is no way I am going to refuse. The copter lurches into the dawn sky and accelerates back to the 'Sea Lion'.

I am speechless and in shock; in total disbelief of what has just occurred, all I can do is look back on the last remaining embers of the catamaran. How I want to see Martin bobbing about on the surface, but that is not to be. Martin is dead.

"We had to sink the boat," he tells me. "We cannot leave it floating in the shipping lane, now I must inform the coast guard of your safety." I am aware that the gunman was only doing his job, we should have foreseen that possibility? *Oh my God!*

Liling Liang is in the coast guard station at Matara Beach, glued to the station's radar scanner; she was watching the 'Sea Lion' bear down on us and witnessed the entire rescue. She was relieved at my rescue, but when the report of Martin's death was received, she became hysterical. The sinking of the catamaran and the murder of Martin has been too much for her. She was very fond of Martin, they were close friends and met every time she visited Colombo. She thought him charming, and he made her laugh, even his rugged appearance and flowery shirts she found appealing. He was her ideal man: mature, polite with a gentle nature; she classed him as a perfect gentleman. She will never forget him or forgive his unfortunate death.

The Matara Beach coast guard station patrols the northern straits, east of the Maldives. They are in close communication with the US naval base at Diego Garcia, which watches over the southern approaches. Nothing happens in these waters without one of them knowing. The usual incidents are pirate attacks, they are frequent and fast and practically impossible to prevent. Immediately, a distress call is received; a US motor torpedo boat races to the stricken boat, but by the time it arrives, the pirates have long gone; and usually their victims have also disappeared. Families on sailing holidays are easy-pickings; sometimes they are kidnapped, sometimes slaughtered. If they are lucky enough to survive, they are hysterical, battered, sometimes shot and raped. More often than not, the boat will be empty, drifting like the Marie Celeste, its occupants never to be heard of again, presumed drowned. There is no point towing the stricken boats back to Diego Garcia. After photographs have recorded the remains of the crime scene, the boat is sunk.

For the US navy teams at Diego Garcia, the sinking of the catamaran is nothing out of the ordinary, for the Captain of HMS Offensive heading south out of the Bay of Bengal with instructions to track the Sea Lion, his task has suddenly taken on a more serious objective.

George is sitting with Tom Ramsey at MI6 HQ when the news of the sinking of the catamaran comes through. Words are insufficient, they both knew Martin, and they do not have to be told he didn't survive the boat being shot up. There is nothing they can do.

"Bloody hell, Tom, that wasn't supposed to happen, can we arrest the bastards for killing him?"

"Unfortunately not, Tom, we should have known that was a possibility and avoided it. I have been speaking to Admiral Sir Kenneth Gargrave KSB DSC ADC DL, and he tells me we have to keep this out of the press at all cost."

"Goodness, who is Kenneth Gargrave when he's at home?"

"He is the first sea lord, now listen to me. We didn't think this thing through. With so many pirate attacks in the Indian Ocean, sinking deserted boats is common practise. If they didn't, the ocean would be littered with them."

"Just the same, Tom, Martin was a good friend of mine, and I want some revenge for his death."

"I feel the same, Tom. I will pull HMS Offensive up closer to the Sea Lion. I think your man on-board is going to need some help, let's try and keep the death toll to one."

"Thanks, Tom. Tim will appreciate that."

The Countdown Begins

I should hate this guy for killing Martin, yet he was only doing his job. I have to find Angela and get her safely off the ship. The helicopter is hovering over the rows of containers piled high on the deck; the difficulty of my task is clear to see, this ship is enormous; I try to assess the number of containers and count 16 across its deck. The ship must be three football pitches long; it is impossible for me to count the number of containers along its back. I hope and pray Angela is not trussed up in one of them, it will take me a month to search them all. The copter drops its nose and lines up with the ship, landing on a moving vessel always looks easy, but it isn't.

The captain is waiting for me and holds out his hand, in it is a welcoming tot of rum.

"You lo...ok as if yo...u could us...e this," he says in clumsy English, I guess he is Russian or East European. My first impressions are very favourable. He is polite, educated, smart, and so he should be with the responsibility of such a large vessel under his command. We talk for nearly an hour as I make up a story as to why I was in difficulty, and how thankful I am he saved my life. He seems to be at ease with my explanation. After a second tot of rum, or is it the third? I eventually find the courage to ask if he is carrying any passengers.

"No, I am not allowed to carry passengers, we cannot insure them. There was a time when we allowed the crew to bring their wives, but it caused chaos. Hearts were broken, marriages were ruined, and the crew were always fighting. We have to work as a team on a ship this size, and women get in the way."

"I can believe that," I joke. He suggests I take some rest in a cabin that he has prepared for me.

"I will have to put you ashore in Port Said," he tells me. "We will be there in 20 hours, can you get home from Egypt?"

"I will manage, thanks for your help."

"Do you say, glad I can help."

"You do, thanks again."

I follow a member of his crew down two flights of metal steps, then along a corridor with doors numbering C1-C8, alternating on either side.

I presume 'C' stands for the third of similar corridors, 'A' being the first. I try to remember the way and estimate my location in the ship to be on the port side, below and slightly behind the bridge. My guide unlocks cabin C8—the last door on the corridor—and indicates this is where I am to rest. If these are the crew's quarters, then 20, possibly 24, crew members are on-board.

"How many crewmen on the ship?" I ask him, in as few words as possible. He holds up ten fingers, then another five.

"Any women?" I indicate a pair of bosoms, which is all I can think of doing.

He laughs, "No women, women big problem." He is still laughing at my mime as he closes my cabin door.

The cabin bears no resemblance to those on the cruise ships I have recently enjoyed. It is sparse and cold and painted grey; it is so very grey. Pieces of sticky tape, which once secured pictures of wives, girlfriends and children, hang from the greasy metallic walls. These would have been the only comfort on-board this enormous lump of vibrating metal. The bunk bed indicates that two crewmen occupied this claustrophobic space; I shudder at their life style. I have the choice of up or down; as there is no indication of me sharing the room, I chose the lower; to be honest, I don't have the strength to climb onto the top.

I wake with a jolt; for several seconds, I try to remember where I am, and it takes me even longer to remember why. I have been asleep for four hours.

Did the captain tell me I would be in Port Said in 20 hours? I do believe he did, this means we will enter the Suez Canal in less than ten, leaving me only six hours to find Angela. I cannot delay. There are voices in the corridor; an argument is in progress. It doesn't occur to me at first, but suddenly I realise one of the voices is a woman, but it isn't Angela.

Tom Ramsey hands George his vibrating mobile.

"It's for you, George. It's Lesley Buchanan, why is he calling you on my phone? Don't you have a mobile of your own?"

"I hate mobiles. Anyway, I can never remember to charge 'em up." He reads the name displayed on the screen and places it to his ear. "Yes, Lesley. It's George. Speak up, will you. I can't hear you," Tom interrupts.

"George, you idiot, you are holding the phone back to front," he snatches it out of George's hand and positions it correctly to his ear.

"Sorry, Lesley, I had the phone back to front, now how are you getting on, have you raised the money?"

"Yes, I thought I would give you the good news straight away. The bankers will release the money tomorrow morning."

"Tomorrow! That's no bloody good, it's required tonight. They have to have it by 8:30, or Angela is dead."

"Can't you tell them the money is on its way, George? They will listen to you?"

"I am not personally in contact with them, nor do I want to be."

"I don't know what I can do, George, you have to help us. Please try to borrow it from the treasury."

"Lesley, get that money to Beijing as fast as you can. Keep me informed. If Angela dies, you and this government will be history."

"Yes, George." George slams the mobile down on Tom's desk.

"He can't get the bloody money in time. This guy Tim is on his own. He has six hours to get her off the ship. Is there any way we can get a message to him? Bloody hell, Tom; the reputation of the government depends on a guy we don't even know. Can you believe that?" Tom rubs his head and tries to think of something they might do.

"All I can think of is to put an SAS team on-board, and as we don't have any authority to do that, they will think they are under attack and start shooting at us. There is nothing I can do, your man is on his own."

"Can we move HMS Offensive closer, so they have sight of her, that might stop them killing her."

"I have already sent that instruction to the captain, but once they near the canal, she will pull back. HMS Offensive is not allowed through the canal, we do not send warships through canals; they are sitting targets.

Six Hours and Counting

"This is HMS Offensive calling Sea Lion."

"Sea Lion responding, what can we do for you, Offensive?"

"There are pirates operating in the area. We have been instructed to accompany you to the canal." Even the captain of HMS Offensive is blushing at his lies. He would rather go in with all guns blazing rather than playing a cat and mouse game like this, but he has to obey orders, and he is rather good at that. "We will stay on your port side, three degree to stern."

"Thank you HMS Offensive, glad to have your protection," the captain of the Sea Lion turns to his first mate.

"Whaat the hell is thees, pirates, my arsse. Do the British Navy think we are stupid?"

"Captain, we have to do what they say. We can't mess about with a British battleship."

"Let me know if they make a change of direction or come closer."

"Yes sir, immediately."

Five Hours Remain

The cabin door won't open, have they locked me in? But on closer investigation, it's only the old mechanism that has jammed. I force the handle over the rusty gear mechanism, and it eventually releases. At every door along the corridor, I stop and press my ear to it; all the rooms are silent except for C3, in which I can hear a guy snoring. At the end of the corridor, a flight of metal steps takes me up to a corridor marked P. *I thought B came before C.* Anyway, I continue with my stop and listen search until I am convinced all these cabins are deserted also. Yet a third flight of steps takes me to O corridor, there are only four doors on this corridor, and each bears a name. I commit each name to memory as I pass, Boris Yakov (Captain), Abhi Patel (First Officer), Nathanael Musson (First Engineer). *Maybe 'O' stands for 'Officer'?* The fourth door is blank, yet through it, I can hear a woman talking inside, she has an East European accent. Her tone is deep and menacing. A second woman responds, and my heart quickens. It's Angela, thank God I have found her.

I must hide and wait. I want to get Angela on her own. The door eventually opens, and Angela is pushed out into the corridor by an old woman, dressed in an Arabic abeyer.

"Yella! Yella! The captain is waiting for you," she shouts, bullying Angela to speed up.

Luckily, Angela doesn't see me. I watch them pass from beneath the steps, and when they have disappeared onto the bridge, I make a dash for the swinging cabin door in time to stop it slamming shut. The room is clean, comfortable and spacious. The furnishings are soft and attractive, brightly coloured, and she has a full-size bed. If Angela is being held against her will, they have at least given her first-class accommodation. The room is devoid of personal artefacts, except for her coat and heeled shoes laying on the bed. A broken lipstick sits abandoned on the bedside table, and next to it, a nail file and a pair of scissors.

Four Hours

Maybe I can wait for her in here, that is if they bring her back. I sit on the bed for over an hour, time is running out. I check my watch and decide another 20 minutes is all I can give her. Then, I will have to go and look for her. I haven't a clue why I have chosen 20 minutes, I just have.

I can hear voices in the corridor; one is definitely Angela and the other I think is the captain. I must hide, the wardrobe is empty, so I squeeze in, clattering several wire hangers. Through the narrow slit in the door, I can see into the room. Angela enters, with the captain behind her. She sits on the bed; and from a selection of liquor bottles in the mini fridge, he pours himself a gin and tonic. She appears to be quite at ease when he sits next to her on the bed. He is obviously excited and not only holds her hand but tries to kiss her; she laughs and puts her finger to his mouth. His advance is further interrupted by his mobile beeping. There is an exchange in Russian, with HMS Offensive being the only words I recognise.

"I am wanted on the bridge, please excuse me. I will come back to you very shortly. Don't spill my drink; I will fineesh it when I return."

She throws him a kiss, and he returns it like an excited schoolboy. As he closes the door, she gives a big sigh and collapses across the bed. I don't know what to do. If I just walk out of the wardrobe, she is going to scream, so I creep up on her, put my hand over her mouth and hold her tightly to the bed. It takes her forever to calm down.

"What the fuck are you doing here?" she sits up and throws her arms around my neck and burst out crying. All I can do is hold her close and wait for her to stop sobbing. Her tears are running down her cheeks, so I kiss her nose. This apparently isn't good enough; she wraps her mouth over mine as more tears flood down her face; all I can say is,

"You are in terrible danger." I want to tell her everything I know, but there isn't time, I try to explain my presence. "I didn't like you going to Beijing with Colin Brown, so I followed you. I even followed you to the nightclub, but there was nothing I could do to help you. Anyway, enough of this later, you are in danger, and I have to get you out of here."

"Tim, I am sure they want to kill me. I don't know why, and I don't know when, but I think I am being held hostage for something or other."

"How do you know this?"

"The captain told me. He fancies me, so I am leading him on hoping he will help me."

"You clever little bitch, talk about using what you've got."

Three Hours to Go

I try to tell her what I know about the deadline, without scaring her, which isn't easy. Even harder is admitting there is a possibility the money will not arrive, but the good news is, George is helping her.

"You know George is my stepfather, don't you?"

"Yes, you told me, but he doesn't know you are his stepdaughter. Is that right?"

"Yes, and I don't want him to know. I had little if no contact with him during my schooling, yet I do love him."

"I believe he loves you too. He is doing all he can to help you."

There are footsteps in the corridor.

"The captain is coming back. I must hide in the wardrobe, don't let him anywhere near the wardrobe."

"Sorree for leeving you, we have a British warship escorting us up the Red Sea. There is a danger of pirates in these waters." He takes a gulp of his diluted gin and runs his fingers through her hair. She doesn't flinch and lets him kiss her. He is quite a handsome guy: rugged and strong, it is a shame about the smell of oil she can detect on his shirt. His hands are rough and dry as he strokes her cheek and tries to force her lips apart. She lifts her chin as his finger follows the curve of her mouth and traces her throat down to her chest.

Oh goodness, do I have to watch this? I never realised how much Angela meant to me. I want to rush out and plunge a knife into him, but Angela is the star of this show. I hope she will control his advances, she will not thank me for interrupting him at this time. Boy, she is good, she doesn't resist him; but at the same time, she keeps him at arm's length, she strokes his face and runs her hand through his hair. Full of confidence, he slips his hand into her dress.

"I am on my period." I hear her whisper to him, "You can have me tomorrow. Tomorrow will be good."

I can sense his disappointment; this is disastrous news for a man whose desire is running high. She waits for his need of her to wain and lays next to him.

"I have to attend to business on the bridge," he sighs, "Is there anything you need?"

"Just for you to come back to me tomorrow."

His face lights up, with a big grin, he obviously isn't thinking this through. She might be dead tomorrow, unless he knows something we don't… but I don't think he does.

Two Hours

"You are indeed a skilled lover," I remark, emerging from the wardrobe.

"What a waste, he is a nice guy. He is not going to kill me, he wants me too much."

"I agree, but someone else might, who else should we be wary of? What about the helicopter pilot who brought you here? Is he part of the Chinese mafia?"

"I doubt it. I think he works for the shipping line, he just shuttles people between the ship and the shore. One guy got sick an hour ago, so he took him to a hospital in Singapore."

"Who else has been in contact with you?"

"Nobody, only the woman who works in the kitchen, she brings me my food."

"What do you know about her?"

"Not a lot, she is a close friend of the captain, and I get the impression she joined the ship when he did. She could be his mother."

"She's pretty strong for her age. She can climb those steps faster than I can. I'm going up to the bridge, maybe I can find out what is happening. Will you be okay, I will be back in an hour."

She nods as I turn to leave.

"Tim! Take care of yourself." She rushes over and gives me a kiss.

"It's you they want dead, they don't know who I am."

Finding the bridge is harder than I thought; the ship is a maze of corridors and metal steps, only by trial and error do I stumble on it. The captain is leaning over a table, discussing a chart with a member of the crew who must be his first officer. The old woman is clearing away the remains of a meal; the captain turns as I enter.

"Mr Giger, I trust you have recovered from your ordeal."

"I have, thank you. We must be nearing the canal?"

"We are, but we have a Royal Navy frigate to port; and if it doesn't pull astern soon, we will be delayed. We can't both enter the canal at the same time, it isn't wide enough."

"What are they doing?"

"They say pirates are active in these waters, and we need an escort. We don't believe them, pirates have been operating in these waters for years, and we have never had an escort protection vessel before." He laughs. "Excuse me for a moment, our helicopter is arriving back. An important member of OMEC, our biggest client, wants to check one of his containers."

"Do you know him?"

"I have not met him before, but I have heard of him. His name is Junjie Jhong, I don't know what he wants."

"Chinese eh!"

"I guess so, he has a reputation of being an angry, aggressive man. The sooner he has checked his container and is happy with it, the happier I will be. I don't like clients on-board my ship."

"How long will it take him to check his container?"

"Two hours."

"Hey! I thought you said you didn't have any women on-board."

I point at the old woman.

"That's not a woman, that's Mohammed Nasser. He has been with the ship since year one. He is a man but prefers to be a woman, I must admit he talks like a woman and likes cooking, but that is where the similarity ends. Now please excuse me, Mr Giger, have you eaten?"

"No."

"Mohammed, take Mr Giger to the kitchen and prepare something hot and nourishing for him."

He beckons me to follow him. "Please come with me, Mr Giger."

He places an enormous cheese and tomato omelette in front of me. It smells great and tastes delicious. I eat it with haste, much to Mohammed's annoyance. He complains that I am rushing it, obviously believing his cooking talent should be treated with more respect, but I want to get back to the bridge and check out Junjie Jhong, whoever he is.

One Hour and Counting

Lewis Gordon Bainbridge, the captain of HMS Offensive watches as the Sea Lion's helicopter returns and flies over his warship. He has been listening to the messages between the Sea Lion and the copter since it left Jeddah Port, but he is unaware of the reason for the flight. He reports its arrival to the Admiralty, Tom and George receive it simultaneously. The British embassy in Jeddah City has already confirmed the helicopter's departure from Jeddah port, it reads: Chinese businessman + Junjie Jhong + depart heliport Jeddah + destination Sea Lion.

"I don't like the sound of this, Tom. What do you make of it."

"The same as you, George. This guy could be a hitman, what do we know of him?"

"Absolutely nothing, we have no record whatsoever of a Chinese guy named Junjie Jhong. It could mean the name is made up."

"Shit! Can we take him out?"

"What! Shoot down the helicopter as it flies over HMS Offensive?"

"Yes."

"Well, we could if you want to start a war with China."

"Not a good idea?"

"I agree, not a good idea, George."

Exactly the same thoughts are going through my head. "How do you know this guy is who he says he is?" I ask the captain back on the bridge, trying to disguise the seriousness of my question.

"I doon't care who he iz, in fact, it is better if I don't know who he iz. I just do as I am told." He orders Mohammed to the helicopter pad to meet the visitor, "Bring him straight back to me here on the bridge." Mohammed grunts in acknowledgement of the instruction.

I need to check this guy out, but if he has been sent to kill Angela, he will be suspicious of an Englishman being on-board, maybe he already knows I am on the ship.

"I will go back to my cabin, Captain. I need to prepare for Port Said, about two hours you say?"

"Possibly three, there is no hurry." I slowly feel my way down the steps; and at the end of corridor 'O', I spot an empty life-jacket crate, an ideal place to hide. From inside, I can see the whole length of the corridor, all the way down to Angela's door. If anyone goes in or out, they will pass directly in front of me.

Time Out

"This is HMS Offensive calling Sea Lion."

"This is Sea Lion, what can we do for you?"

"We have to leave you now, we will fall back to your stern, take care."

"Thank you for your concern." Captain Boris Yakov looks across at his first mate. "What is that all about, Abhi?"

"I don't know, but I do know they can't follow us through the canal. A battleship is a seeting duck to terrorist attack in the canal, and they won't risk that. So we have seen the last of them."

"Thank goodness for that."

The captain has to forget the battleship; his client has arrived on the bridge.

"Welcome aboard, sir. I hope you had a comfortable flight."

Junjie Jhong ignores the question. "What time is it, Captain?"

"It's just gone 20:30, sir. Can I get you anything?"

"Yes, you have an English girl on-board, bring her to me. I will be in my cabin."

Mohammed Nasser jumps to his feet to get her.

In the dark, I have difficulty focusing on the dial of my wristwatch. I believe it to be 8:35. If this is true, then Angela's deadline has passed. Maybe the money has been paid, maybe her death sentence has been lifted, hope floods through my body, but only for a matter of seconds. Mohammed Nasser clatters down the steps and storms straight into Angela's cabin.

"Come on, come on, hurry up, the director wants to see you."

As he marches her down the corridor towards me, he pushes and prods her to hurry.

"Where are we going... who is the director?"

"He is the big boss. He wants to see you in his cabin. Hurry, or else, he will be angry."

My brain is racing, this does not look good. I have to work on the premise she is still in danger. Nasser is acting nervously, he is agitated. His body is visibly shaking, and his face is that of a frightened man. I don't have time to think; as he pushes Angela passed me, I grab an axe off the wall and smash it down on his skull. Angela screams in fright.

"What are you doing, are you crazy?"

"We have to get off this ship, we cannot risk your safety. I am convinced a member of the Chinese mafia has arrived; if the money for your ransom has been paid, he didn't have to come; I can only assume his job is to oversee your death."

"But why did you have to kill the maid?"

"That is no maid, that is Mohammed Nasser. He was one of the soldiers who brought you here from the nightclub. I am trying to save your life; and now with my cover blown, they will come looking for me. We are in this together, come on, run."

"Where are we running to?"

"I haven't a clue, just run."

My Cover Is Blown

"Do you know your way around the ship?" she screams.

"No, but we must go up. I want to be on the deck, at least, we can jump overboard if we have to."

"You're mad, I'm not jumping into the sea."

"Let's hope we don't have to, come on, we need somewhere to hide."

Boris is taken by surprise when Junjie Jhong storms onto the bridge, shouting obscenities in Chinese; he is at a loss as to why Mohammed has not taken Angela to him.

"Where is the girl? I asked for her half an hour ago. How dare you ignore my command? I will have you flogged for this."

Boris looks around, hoping Nasser can give him an explanation, but he is nowhere to be seen.

"I'll go myself and see where she is, sir. I sent Nasser to get her."

It takes Boris only a minute to stumble over Nasser's crumpled body. His first thought is Mohammed has fallen down the steps, but when he sees Angela's cabin door swinging open, he knows this isn't the case. He checks inside, but knows she will be gone.

"You idiot, you sent this dope to get her." Junjie Jhong stands at the top of the steps, looking down on the smashed skull of Mohammed Nasser. "Where is she, search the ship, I want her found immediately. My god, you are going to pay for this."

"She is not in her room, sir."

"Of course she's not there. Do you think she is going to sit in her room and wait for me?"

"What is going on, sir? I don't know what is happening here, tell me what is going on?"

"It has nothing to do with you, all you have to do is what you are told. How long will it take us to reach the canal?"

"One hour, sir, maybe less."

"Then you have 40 minutes to find her. Do you understand?"

"Yes, sir."

Boris bends over Nasser's body and squeezes his wrist in the hope of finding a pulse; there isn't one; Nasser died the instant his skull split open. He picks up the axe laid next to his body. Boris is aware that

Angela does not have the strength to lift it, he turns to Abhi who has come running to see what all the shouting is about.

"Angela has help, it has to be the Englishman. He told me he was going to rest, but I doubt he will be in his cabin. We are in the middle of something pretty nasty, and I don't know what it is. We have an English girl on-board, and we pull an Englishman out of the water. I should have realised that was too much of a coincidence."

"And we have an English battleship to port," Abhi reminds him.

"Bloody hell, it's all making sense, what is going on?"

"I'll instruct the crew to search the ship. One thing is for sure, they are still on the ship."

"Abhi." Boris grabs his arm to hold him back. "I don't want her hurt, be gentle with her."

"You're too soft, Boris. A pretty face, and you go all meek and mild."

"Don't hurt her."

Abhi has no intention of disobeying his captain. He respects and admires this man more than anyone else; they have worked together for many years.

Good News

"George, it's Lesley Buchanan, sorry for calling so late, were you asleep?"

George is struggling to regain consciousness.

"I wanted you to know that Reggie is on a flight to Beijing with the money. They will have it before lunch tomorrow. Have you any news of Angela?"

"No, nothing, we are not in contact with them. All we can do is pray she is still alive. I will call you if I hear anything."

"Thanks George, do you think they will kill her?"

"I have no idea! Get the money paid and let's hope we can save her life."

George swears out loud as he stretches out his hand and gropes for his glasses, he can't find them. He swings his legs out of bed in frustration and finds them on the floor. There is a sickening crack as his weight splits them into two pieces. He tries to piece them together, but the best he can do is balance them on his nose. With difficulty, he focuses on his phone and calls Tom.

"Good morning, Tom. Any news from HMS Offensive?" Without waiting for an answer, he gabbles into the reason for his call. "Lesley Buchanan has just been on. He tells me the money is on its way to Beijing."

"Well, that's good news, but we have heard nothing from the Sea Lion. This unknown Chinese guy arrived on-board about three hours ago, and HMS Offensive has now pulled back from the container ship."

"How far back, Tom? We need her close enough to despatch a search and rescue if Tim triggers his alarm beacon."

"The frigate is anchored off the coast of Jeddah. It's the best we can do. She isn't allowed through the canal, her air sea rescue crews are on permanent alert."

"Stay close, Tom. Nothing must happen to this girl. The government is trashed if she comes to any harm, anyway, she means a lot to me."

"You big, softy George, you are far too old for her."

Angela

I have never experienced cold like this before; I think of Egypt as a desert; and therefore, hot and dry. It always looks warm in the holiday brochures, so why is the Suez Canal so cold? I wrap Angela in a blanket; and even with my arms around her, she is still shaking violently. We huddle together in the corner of the container deck, hiding beneath the steps leading to the bow. Apart from the cold, the container deck is the most inhospitable place; with walls of creaking, groaning rusting steel, as high as we can see. Several containers are painted red, but most are grey, a few still bear the logo or brand name of the company to which they belong, but even this paint is peeling off and will soon disappear. The word 'scary' describes this deck, we have to find another place to hide.

"What are we going to do, Tim, we can't stay here. I'm so cold and frightened."

"I could trigger the alarm and call up the navy, but we will have to throw ourselves into the sea."

"I wouldn't last five minutes in the water, I can't swim."

"Now you tell me, I could find you a life vest, or better still an inflatable boat, and we could jump with that."

She looks into my eyes.

"No, read my lips, no, no, no way."

"Stay here, I am going to find another blanket for you."

"No, Tim, don't leave me. I am coming with you. Please, don't leave me."

"Okay, let's check out those boxes over there." I point to where three wooden crates are lined up against the bulkhead, but I don't even get to my feet before a gun is pressed into my back and two massive tattooed arms are wrapped around Angela. Unable to speak and finding it impossible to move, she watches in horror as a gun is smashed into my head. I lose consciousness immediately, I don't even hear Angela scream.

My sight and hearing is a haze. I can hear a man shouting, but I can't understand what he is saying. He isn't English; he could be Chinese. A second man is responding to him in a submissive tone, answering only with yes and no. Through the blur, I can see Angela standing between two men: the first engineer, Nathanael Musson, and another crew member I don't recognise. They are each holding her firmly by the wrists. She is crying, a short, skinny man is wielding a pistol as he paces up and down the bridge. Boris is standing in the centre of the room, leaning on the chart table. I am slumped in the corner of the bridge, with Abhi Patel standing over me. The China-man is relentless, screaming first at Boris and then at Patel, sometimes in English, sometimes in Mandarin. Who is this guy?

"When you are told to do something, you do it. Look at the mess you have got us into for not carrying out the simplest of instructions." Boris tries to speak in defence but is shouted down. "I have been given a job to do, I don't know why. I don't know what this girl has done, and it is not for me to question it. My boss says she goes over the side; and if I value my career and even my life, she goes over the side. My job is to kill this girl and throw her to the sea, and that is exactly what I am going to do; and if anyone here tries to stop me, they will go with her."

He paces around the bridge; and as he passes Boris, he wipes the barrel across his face. He stands in front of Angela; and with no hesitation, raises his gun to her head and pulls the trigger. The noise is deafening, one, two, three shots ricochet around the metal room. Angela groans and drops to the floor. Nathanael, unable to believe what he has just witnessed, is still holding her arm. An eerie silence fills the room, no one speaks, no one moves. The sound of the sea has been obliterated by the exploding gun. Junjie Jhong turns and stares at Boris, then at Abhi, before he too collapses to the floor, twitching as he blows the last breath of air from his lungs. Nathanael Musson prods his body with his foot.

"He's dead," he announces.

Boris and Abhi stand rigid, both pointing pistols at the body of Junjie Jhong. Their reactions were simultaneous, their aim perfect. Did they fire in time to save Angela?

Musson gently lowers Angela to the floor; her body twists around his leg as he relaxes his grip. He gently cradles her head in his big powerful arms and looks up at the captain. "She is alive, Captain. I think she has just fainted. You must have dropped him before he pulled the trigger. Can someone fetch her a glass of water?"

What Now?

"Mr Giger, pleaze explain and tell me what iz going on. I have two dead people, plus a pretty English girl and a marooned Englishman on-board my ship. Oh yes… and a British frigate off my port bow?"

"To be honest, Boris, if you don't know why Angela is here, it would be better that you don't know. But thank you, thank you, thank you for saving her life. She is an innocent girl who, like you, has been caught up in something bigger than all of us. What was Junjie Jhong's intentions after he had killed Angela, where were you to take him?"

"I have not yet received any instructions. I can only presume he was to sail with us to Murmansk."

"So you take the ship directly to Murmansk?"

"Yes." Then he remembers. "I do have to rendezvous with a boat in the English Channel, the exact position will be despatched to me nearer the time."

"Is this usual?"

"It has occurred before. That time we didn't even slow down. A small boat came alongside, and we threw several small crates over the side for them to pick out of the water."

"Did you not question what was in those crates?"

"I was told they were presents for the owner's children. He lives in England, somewhere in Surrey. You have a Surrey, yes?"

"We do, it is a nice place. Did it never occur to you that what you were doing might be illegal?"

"Of course it is illegal. Everything we do is illegal."

"You could be gun-running, delivering drugs, even people trafficking."

"I told you, they were presents for the boss' kidz. That's what I was told, so that's what they were."

I understand what he is saying; no questions are to be asked.

"Do you have a shipment on-board to deliver this trip?"

"We do. Mohammed was to take care of it."

"Can I see it?"

"You could if I knew where it waz. I told you Mohammed waz dealing with it."

"Can we assume this shipment might be in Mohammed's cabin?"

"We can take a look, but first, what am I going to do about Junjie Jhong?" He points at his crumpled body on the floor.

"Throw him over the side. He will not be missed until you arrive in Murmansk; it will give us time to think. Are you okay with throwing him over the side?"

"We do it all the time. You won't believe how many people disappear over the side of ships. They get minced up in the propellers and become food for the fish. Shall I take Angela to her cabin?"

"Yes, but come straight back," he scowls at me.

Secure Communication? Ha

"Can we send a ship-to-ship message to the British frigate to let them know Angela is safe?" Boris looks at me as if I am stupid.

"The entire world will hear it. There iz no such thing as secure communication. I doubt you want the Chinese to know Angela is alive and well, and that Junjie Jhong is dead, so we will keep it a secret."

"I want to tell her father, he is worried sick about her. What about those flashing lamp things I have seen in WWII American films, can we flash a message to the frigate?" Boris pats me on the head and bursts out laughing.

"Don't give up your job in advertising, Mr Giger. You have to be in visible contact with the other ship to do that, and HMS Offensive is one hundred miles away."

"Then, we really are on our own?" Boris thinks for a minute.

"We could broadcast our estimated time of arrival in the English channel. The Chinese mafia will think everything is progressing as planned, and the British Navy might realise we are telling them to be there."

"Good thinking, Boris, you're not just a pretty face."

"Pretty face!" He looks at me all confused.

"Just a silly English phrase, please do it."

Mohammed's cabin is littered with incriminating articles. On his table is a short-wave radio, there are three mobile phones, a 'Browning', hi-power, semi-automatic pistol; and under his mattress, a British passport in the name of a George Browning, but the picture is of Mohammed without a beard. Three wooden crates are clearly marked 'Secret and Confidential' and stamped with a British government seal, and to eliminate all doubt as to his intention, on his table is a map of the British Channel, with two lines intersecting 13 miles south of Dartmouth. Boris pulls a diving suite connected to a small oxygen cylinder from his wardrobe, he turns the valve and air gushes out. "It's full and ready to go, Mr Giger."

"Goodness, he was prepared for every eventuality; and you knew nothing of this, Boris?"

"I knew we were to rendezvous with a little ship, but that is all. Mohammed just throws the crates overboard, and the guys in the little boat pick them out of the water. There is nothing else for me to know."

I run my hands around the edges of the boxes. "There must be a floatation device inside, or else they would sink."

"I guess so, maybe that is why he has the air cylinders!"

Reginald Rolland Swordsmith arrives in Beijing with one million pounds in his bag and meets up with Janet Clynbourne in the lobby of the Crowne Plaza Hotel. She is not happy, she has been waiting for him for over an hour.

"You could have called to tell me you were going to be late."

"Oh shut up, Janet. Have you arranged a meeting so we can hand over the money?" Janet ignores the question.

"Where is Angela, is she back in London yet? I have not seen or heard from her since she left with that stupid Colin Brown. If she has come to any harm?"

"I told you to shut up, Janet. Let's go, or else we will all be dead if we don't deliver this money before twelve o'clock.

"Dead! Is she dead?" Janet jumps on his ambiguous phrasing.

"I don't know where she is, the English Police are looking for her."

"And the Beijing Police are looking for her as well. We have to find her before they do."

"Get a grip, Janet. We need a taxi, now." He grabs her shoulders and gives her a shaking.

"Stop it, the taxi is waiting at the front door. It has been there for half an hour. I hope you have enough money to pay the fare, we have 20 minutes to get to the club. Let's go."

Inside the club, four men are waiting for them. Reginald Rolland Swordsmith places the briefcase on the table in the centre of the office and springs open the release catch. The case is full of neatly bound bundles of £50 notes.

"We have been instructed to count it before we let you go," one of the men growls at them. "Sit over there and don't interrupt us, or we will have to start all over again." He points to two metal chairs in the corner of the room; and with a little encouragement from a second member of the gang, Janet and Reginald are persuaded to sit. It takes them three hours to wrap the notes up into £5,000 bundles. Without a word, they open the door and throw Janet and Reginald out into the street.

Janet is furious at being insulted and treated so roughly. She picks herself up off the pavement and brushes the dust off her jacket.

"I have never been treated with such disrespect in my entire life. We must find another supplier. I have no intention of working with these men ever again. Look, they have bruised my arm. I was so close to slapping that guy's face."

"Just be grateful you are still alive. Goodness, Janet, you are a complete pain in the arse at times."

"And I am desperate for a pee. I have sat there with my legs crossed for over an hour. As fast as you can, driver, to the hotel, before I make a mess of your cab."

The cab driver presses his foot hard to the pedal in a desperate bid to save his car from being soiled, but more important, to save his sanity from Janet's incessant complaining.

The Drop

Barry Cornwell, MP for Devon and Cornwall, is also pressing the accelerator pedal to the floor; he is taking a big risk, racing his family cruiser at top speed. The boat yard failed to get the original parts they needed to repair the stricken engine in time, a temporary fix was initiated in order to gain a new sea-worthiness certificate. They expressed confidence in the repair for his river cruises, as for it, getting him across the channel and back; that is a risk he has been forced to take. He is already two hours behind schedule, and this is one rendezvous he must not miss. His radar scanner is displaying a host of vessels in front of him, ploughing their way up and down the channel. It is at a time like this he wishes he had invested an additional £5,000 in a scanner that included a recognition device. This would have named each vessel, but he never thought he would need to know the names of the ships around him.

He knows that one of those blips on the screen is the Sea Lion, what he doesn't know is one of the other blips on the screen is the Royal Navy destroyer HMS Enforcer. Whilst the guided missile destroyer was patrolling the waters between Cyprus and the Turkish coast, it was given instructions to meet the Sea Lion when it left the Suez Canal and to shadow the container ship along the Mediterranean and into the English Channel. Her orders are to maintain a 24-hour alert and be ready to launch an air sea rescue at any time, but now her orders have been changed to observe, with the possibility of arresting a smuggling gang. Captain Marcus O'Brian was excited at the thought of showing off his crew in action. Most of his time is spent on mundane patrol duties, so the possibility of an air sea rescue was creating quite a stir amongst his crew. He has made the decision not to stand down his helicopter crews and inflatable rescue teams, it will be good training for them to remain at action stations.

Barry Cornwell is anxious, he should make contact with the Sea Lion in three hours; and on that premise, he points to one of the blips on the screen.

"That must be the ship. It is heading in the right direction and will be at the drop point in three hours."

Keith Mitchinson, MP for East Yorkshire, hauls himself out of the cabin and stares at the revolving scope.

"After our last trip, I said I wouldn't come with you again. I hate the sea. I just have to look at it, and I am sick." He wipes the perspiration from his sickly white face and tries to focus on the flashing blips, but the sway of the boat beats him, and he throws up all over the screen.

"Bloody hell, Keith. You better clean that up."

Keith looks around for a damp cloth.

"Not now, idiot, when we have the crates on board, you don't have time right now. Get on the radio and raise that bloody ship, we don't want them running into us."

Angela is exhausted. She is stretched out on her bunk, and Boris is standing over her, wanting desperately to run his hands over her body and take her here and now. Had she been a Russian girl, he would not have hesitated, but this girl is different, she excites him like no other. Maybe it's because she is English, educated and cuter than the Russian girls he is used to, or maybe it's just because she is absolutely beautiful, a pearl in the ocean to be treated with the gentlest of care and with the greatest of respect.

"I will take care of her now, Boris." Boris spins around as I walk into the cabin.

"Who iz she, iz she your wife? How can you let her get into so much danger? If she was a Russian girl, she would have every man wanting her, not trying to kill her."

"That is also the case in England, she is a very special girl."

Boris regretfully leaves to take control of his ship. In three hours, he has to meet up with Barry Cornwell and throw the crates over the side.

Who Can You Trust?

Angela opens her eyes and smiles up at me.

"What is happening, where are we now?" I bend down and kiss her, and she doesn't object.

"I'm so glad you are here," she whispers.

"We have found the shipment. We believe it to be heroin. It was in Mohammed's cabin in three wooden crates. The plan is to throw the crates over the side in the centre of the English Channel, and a small craft will come alongside and pick them out of the water and smuggle them into the UK."

"Can we go with them? I feel safer with English drug-runners than I do with Russian seamen?"

"I don't see why not. I will ask Boris."

Barry and Keith already have visual contact with the Sea Lion, but crossing the sea-lanes of the busiest channel in the world is a very dangerous manoeuver. There are hundreds of ships, tankers, container ships, grain ships, cruise ships sailing in both directions, with ferries weaving between them. Barry has to stay alert.

"Have you made contact with the Sea Lion. I need to talk with the captain?" Barry needs assurance that he is meeting the right ship.

"I am trying, but they are not responding. Everything is working perfectly, but they don't respond."

"Let me try."

"This is Marianne calling Sea Lion. Are you receiving me?"

"What is wrong with this idiot, why doesn't he answer?"

Marianne calling Sea Lion; Marianne calling Sea Lion.

"What did you have to do last time?" Keith asks watching the enormous hull of the container ship come bearing down on them.

"The captain told us to sail along his starboard bow; and as we drew parallel to the bridge, he threw the crates over the side. We stopped to pick them up, by which time he was three or four miles north of us."

"Then let's do that again?"

Barry swings the Marianne around and sails her 500 yards away from the container ship.

"Can you see, up there on the bridge, there are several crewmen watching us."

They appear to be waving, but as minutes pass, Barry and Keith realise they are being told to go away.

"The money was delivered. Reginald did deliver it yesterday, didn't he?" Barry asks.

"I spoke with him three hours ago. He confirmed he had delivered the money personally. It was counted and approved; and both he and Janet are now on their way back to London.

Marianne calling Sea Lion; Marianne calling Sea Lion. Still there is no response.

"The bastards, they are not going to deliver, they are keeping the stuff for themselves."

"What can we do, Barry, what do we do now?"

Keith gets an unexpected answer to his question as the engine splutters and coughs and finally gives up altogether. They sit helpless and speechless, watching the big black hull pass them by. The surge off water created by the enormous propellers threatens to turn them over. Barry freezes with fear; to be powerless in the English Channel, with the biggest ships in the world bearing down on him, is a terrifying place to be.

"Keith, go and radio for help. Call SOS we are in danger of being smashed to pieces by these other ships."

Keith picks up the radio microphone but doesn't get the opportunity to use it.

"This is Her Majesty's War Ship HMS Enforcer, prepare to be boarded."

The big black inflatable rescue boat swoops around them, throwing spray high into the air to fall across their bow. Within seconds, the little yacht is full of navy seals; and Barry and Keith are arrested on suspicion of drug-running. The boat is searched, but the only drugs they find are on the cabin table, the remains of a joint Keith was smoking earlier.

"It took away my sea-sickness," he tries to explain to Barry.

"You stupid, stupid idiot."

The seals report back to Captain Marcus O'Brian on-board HMS Enforcer.

"What! Nothing at all?"

"Only the remains of a drag, Captain."

"Is there a girl with them?"

"No sir, just two guys who say they are members of parliament, on a trip to France. Their engine is caput."

"Leave two seals on board, bring those guys back to Enforcer. We will have to treat them with respect until we have something to charge them with, I will dispatch a mechanic. Once the engine is repaired, take the boat to Portsmouth."

"Yes, Captain."

"Well, Abhi, looks like we have just been given five million pounds worth of heroin." Boris gives Abhi Patel a big hug, and the two men burst out laughing. "We tell the Chinese we delivered the crates and could only watch as the Royal Navy arrested the yacht; there was nothing we could do. The Chinese have their money, so they are happy: a win-win situation, hey Boris?"

"What about the disappearance of Junjie Jhong?"

"Mm!" He thinks for a minute before jumping up and down with delight. "That's an easy one. Whilst he was trying to throw Angela over the side, she put up a fight, and he went over with her."

"So she has to die?"

"I'm afraid so, and that Tim guy with her, but not before I have had some fun. Keep the ship on course for Murmansk. I am just stepping out, and I might be some time."

"You dirty bastard, Boris. Give her one for me."

Boris grabs two bottles of Vodka from his cabin before making his way to the cabin where Angela and I are imprisoned. He cracks open one of the bottles by smashing it on the iron handrail and pours half of it down his throat.

I have tried to pick the lock on this cabin door but to no avail. I check my watch; the crates would have been despatched 15 minutes ago. I can only assume we are heading for Murmansk.

"Shh! Someone is coming." Angela sits up on the bunk and swings her legs over the side.

"Who is it?" she whispers.

"I don't know."

We hear a key being placed into the lock and watch as the brass knob turns backwards and then forwards before totally rolling anti-clockwise and releasing the catch.

"Quick! Stand by the side of the bed and be prepared to make a run for it. Where are your shoes, put your shoes on?"

"It will be, Boris. He is on our side?"

"I hope so, but we can't trust him. I'm going to stand behind the door. If we are on opposite sides of the room, we will divert his attention."

Boris staggers into the room, making straight for Angela who is standing directly in front of him.

"Sorry, I had to lock you away, darling," he splutters. "I've come to make it up to you and to make you happy." He is well under the influence of the vodka.

He has completely forgotten about me. He is in a terrible state. I should crack him over the head and put him down, but instead, I give him the benefit of the doubt.

"What's going on, Boris, what do you want?" I yell at him.

He twists around towards me, swaying violently, and grabs hold of a chair to save himself from falling over.

"I had forgotten you were here, Mr. Giger. Never mind."

He pulls out a gun and points it directly at me. I don't have time to take evasive action; the gun explodes with an ear-shattering explosion, and I hear a bullet ricochet off the metal ceiling. I stand frozen in time as he turns to face Angela; a shoe is stuck in his neck, the heel embedded deep into an artery, spurting his blood in all directions. She grabs my hand.

"Wake up, sleepy head. He was going to rape me. What were you going to do, just stand and watch? Let's get out of here.

At MI6, Tom grabs the phone, and George Baldwin dashes to his side, intent on listening in on the conversation.

"Captain Marcus O'Brian from HMS. Enforcer for you, Mr Ramsey."

"We have Keith Mitchinson and Barry Cornwell on-board HMS Enforcer, sir. We picked them up from a stricken yacht in mid-channel. They say they are members of the British parliament on a trip to France. Are these the two men you were expecting?"

"Yes, but we were hoping there would be a girl and Mr Tim Collinwood with them."

"I'm afraid not, sir. We only picked up the two men." Tom gives George an anxious look.

"Ask him if we are still receiving a location signal from Tim's tracker."

"Yes, sir. Tim's beacon is still on-board the Sea Lion."

"Then, we must assume they are both on the ship, and god forbid, still alive. Tell the captain to go back to full alert and to put those two idiot MPs under arrest."

"What can we charge them with, their boat is clean?" Captain Marcus O'Brian tries to remain calm and polite.

"Goodness, dangerous driving, anti-social behaviour; anything at all, do I have to think of everything?" Tom is stressing.

"Captain, stay close to the Sea Lion. We believe our girl is still on-board and could need your help at any moment. If Tim activates his beeper, they will probably be in the water. Their life expectancy is 15 minutes, and that's if they are not mown down by another ship."

"We will be ready, sir. We will get them out."

When I Say Jump

"Tim, I can't jump over the side, I just can't do it?"

She grabs my arm and pulls me back under the steps. Two men run passed, revolvers held out at the ready in front of them. The steps are giving us little protection. This isn't the most original place to hide; and should they come back and make a more detail search, they will find us easily.

We need help. Our situation is impossible. I activate my rescue beacon, we can't just sit here. The navy will never find us here. I need to be at the top of these steps on the bow, from there, I can attract them to our position.

I have to risk being spotted by the crew, with my fingers paralysed with cold. I pull myself up the ice-covered, slippery steps until I can see over the side of the ship. To my right is the coast of France; and to my left, I can see rows of ships plodding up the channel: some faster than us, some slower. Most of them are container ships similar to the Sea Lion. Some are tankers, I guess, full of oil or grain. A brightly lit cross channel ferry is weaving across our bow, but there is no naval ship. I pull myself up one more step, which gives me a slightly wider view of the channel, but still there is no warship. I have to accept the fact that my beacon isn't working, then my heart misses a beat. From behind the ferry, heading straight towards us is the pointed bow of a frigate. Above it, a helicopter is hovering, and the sea around it is alive with speedboats and inflatable. Oh, thank God, they are coming to get us.

"They are coming, Angela, a frigate is racing towards us."

Angela bursts into tears and wraps her arms around my neck.

"Are we going to be saved?" she whimpers, "Are we going to be saved?"

Action Stations

The siren is screaming down the corridors of HMS Enforcer. The captain's calm, authoritative voice is directing his crew.

"Action stations, action station: helicopter crew airborne, inflatable teams to launch ports, light gun teams to turrets. He turns to his number one, "Hard to port and full speed ahead. Close the gap between us and the Sea Lion as quickly as possible." Adrenalin is pumping through his veins, he has been trained to cope with all emergencies but still the excitement of an incident at sea awakens his love for the job. He remains calm, cool and calculative. His first task is to find us, to do this, he has to steer the Royal Navy's prestigious warship between 20 other vessels in one of the busiest sea-lanes in the world. He also has to pinpoint our position and direct the boarding teams. He scans the radar screen, hoping to spot my beacon, but according to his calculations, we are still on-board the Sea Lion.

HMS Enforcer is not the only vessel responding to my beacon. Coastal command has dispatched two Sea King helicopters from Portsmouth, and the RNLI have launched lifeboats from Davenport and Falmouth, all are racing towards the Sea Lion. Their estimated time of arrival is 20 minutes. Captain Marcus O'Brian is totally aware that if we are in the freezing water, his team are the only people who can get to us in time.

Above us is the *Sky News* helicopter; its camera crew streaming the rescue live to the world's news network. Tom and George are listening to the chatter between the Admiralty and the task force; it is a mammoth operation. Commandos are on their way from Portsmouth in a landing craft; and HMS Mersey has been diverted from its fishing protection duty, off the coast of France. Its job is to escort the Sea Lion out of the busy sea-lane and stop and search it. To assist with this task, three patrol boats are speeding out of the Solent.

"You've definitely stirred up a hornets' nest now, Tom."

"This is for you, George, to save a pretty girl you have a fancy for."

"Nonsense, this is to save the reputation of the British government and probably the rule of democracy. It's good to demonstrate our control of the sea around us and to remind the rest of the world we are a power to be respected."

"Then let's hope Captain Marcus O'Brian is up to the job."

"I know him, he is a good man. Let's watch the show and be proud to be British."

Up, up and Away

"Listen, I can hear a helicopter, they are searching for us. They think we are in the water, we have to get on the top of the containers, so they can see us."

"How do we do that?" Angela is shaking with fear, so am I.

"We have to locate the hand and foot indents up the side of the containers."

I grab her hand and drag her between two containers, finding where to climb is not easy. I grope along the first container and then a second, turning left and then right, in fear of meeting a member of the crew at every turn. My hands are bleeding, torn with flaking rust. I must find the indents, I thought they were on a corner, but which corner.

"Here!" I cry out in excitement. "I have found them, can you see?" Angela looks up the side of the container. It isn't just one container we have to climb but four of them, in the moonlight, we can see the indents all the way to the top. Escape is suddenly a possibility. "You go first, I will be right behind you. Just keep going; don't stop for anything."

I watch as Angela pulls herself up, one foothold at a time; and when she reaches the second box, I start to climb. I can hear men shouting below me. A gun is fired, followed by a bullet ricocheting off the steel above my head. Angela screams.

"Keep going," I yell at her. "Keep going."

There is a second shot, then a third and a fourth; I feel a sharp pain on my heel, I am too scared to look back; my legs are still working, I must keep climbing. It seems to be taking forever. I keep telling myself, if Angela can do it, then so can I, but my strength is fading fast. I can't see her, has she made it to the top or has she fallen off? The mobs below me are shouting, there is another shot. I pull myself over the lip of the top container. A gale is raging, the wind at this height is vicious, making it impossible to stand up. Angela is several feet ahead of me, lying flat on her stomach, she made it! She is shaking and whining; exhausted and scared but more important, alive and unhurt.

"This is HMS Enforcer, you are under arrest for breaking the United Nations convention on the law of the sea. Put down your guns and prepare to be boarded."

The helicopter's searchlight flashes across the containers as it hovers above us. I can see the face of the pilot in the cockpit; and next to him, a second man is shouting into a microphone. His instructions can be clearly heard all along the deck. The Enforcer's copter is a mean-looking machine, several rockets are slung under its belly, and I count four machine guns sticking out from its nose cone. It is quite capable of subduing any resistance from the crew. A second helicopter appears from behind the bridge of the ship, a yellow Sea King helicopter. Its side door slides open, and as it hovers above us, a man lowers himself down on a winch. It only takes seconds for him to be standing in front of us.

"Mr Collinwood and Angela I presume?" He has a big smile on his face as he straps Angela into a sling around his waist. "Ladies first, is that okay with you, Mr Collinwood?"

"I wouldn't have it any other way," I stammer back.

He scoops Angela into his arms; and I roll onto my back, so I can watch him carry her into the belly of the helicopter. Thank God for the Royal Navy and Coastal Command. Never will I fail to give money to the RNLI when I next visit their station.

Only when we are both safely on-board and the crew are wrapping warm blankets around us, do I remember the burning sensation in my foot. My sock is soaked in blood, but luckily, the heel of my boot took the direct hit and a tight bandage soon stems the flow. Below us, I can see the Sea Lion. Navy Marines are swarming all over the deck, rounding up the crew.

George prises himself out of the big leather chair in Tom's office and turns down the volume on the TV monitor.

"We did okay, Tom: a job well done."

"We did indeed, George, but the job is not finished. In fact, it has only just begun. Everybody with a TV has been watching, there will be a lot of difficult questions to answer."

They both stare at the enormous TV screen hanging on the back wall of the office.

"Turn the volume back up, George. I want to hear what this announcer is saying?"

'*There is one question everyone is asking. Is the girl at the centre of this operation the political socialite and Vogue model Angela Bee who was last seen in Beijing with the government's trade delegation? Well, we have just received confirmation that the woman rescued from the Russian container ship is Angela Bee. For the past three days, she has been the subject of a worldwide search. She is reported to be the girlfriend of Reginald Rolland Swordsmith, the secretary of state for health; and is wanted by the Chinese Police for the murder of Colin*

Brown, MP for Berwick-on-Tweed, whose body was found in a Beijing hotel room three days ago. She recently became the talk of the town when Vogue Magazine released a series of features about her, which amassed millions of women admirers. Since then, her popularity has soared for her courage, her cheek and her sense of style. This is breaking news that you heard here first on Sky News, stay with us for further developments. This is a story that is going to keep running for many weeks.'

"He can say that again, hey George!"

"He can, indeed, Tom."

Media Mania

'And here is the six o'clock news read my Martin Leverick... The government is in turmoil as two leading conservative MPs have been arrested for smuggling drugs into the country, a third member of parliament, who has not yet been named, has been arrested on suspicion of the murder of Colin Brown, MP for Berwick-on-Tweed during a trade visit to Beijing. Reginald Rolland Swordsmith, the secretary of state for health, is also helping police with their enquiries, after a combined force of a Royal Navy frigate, an air sea rescue helicopter, and an attack force of 20 marines rescued his girlfriend, Angela Bee, from a Russian container ship. We believe she has been held against her will on-board the ship since she went missing three days ago... This daring rescue took place in the English Channel, in the heart of one of the busiest shipping lanes in the world and in front of thousands of seamen, all unable to believe what they were witnessing... The attack on the vessel was streamed live by satellite to TV companies around the world... The leader of the commando attack force told our reporter... This has been a fast and successful rescue, without loss of life, using a combination of the finest naval and commando teams in the world...

We have been told that the captain of the Sea Lion, a container ship bound for Murmansk, is Boris Yakov, a Russian national who has been placed under international arrest. As I speak, the ship is being escorted to an anchorage off the Yorkshire Coast, where it will be searched by NATO forces. The prime minister is scheduled to hold a press conference in one hour to explain the government's position. Stay with us for the very latest on this breaking action.

Now we are going live to Portsmouth, where Miss Bee has just arrived outside the Admiralty buildings. Over to Jon Winter in Portsmouth.'

'Here in Portsmouth, Miss Bee, who has been held captive on board the Russian container ship Sea Lion for three days, has just arrived aboard a Sea King air sea rescue helicopter. I will try to have a word her. Miss Bee, Miss Bee, BBC News...'

A gaggle of over 20 reporters are fighting to attract her attention. They are thrusting microphones into her face and swamping her with questions.

"Miss Bee, are you OK?" asks one of them.

"I am well." She splutters. "This has been a nightmare… I would like to thank all the people who have supported me and the authorities for rescuing me."

"Miss Bee, did you kill Colin Brown?" shouts a reporter from the back of the pack.

"I didn't know Colin Brown was dead."

"Miss Bee, are you going to continue your modelling career?"

"I didn't know I was a model."

"Miss Bee, are you Reginald Rolland Swordsmith girlfriend?"

"No."

The crowd is closing in, wrapping tighter around her; the police, in fear of her being crushed, try to push the press crews back. She looks tired, and her face is drawn and blank. She has a splitting headache and is shaking nervously. A police officer recognises that she is on the point of collapse. He supports her and ushers her into the naval building, to safety.

Yes Sir, No Sir

"Come on, wake up, we have a meeting with George at 11:30."

Angela gives a sexy sigh and snuggles into me. This is the third consecutive night we have slept together. I desperately want to demonstrate my love for her, but tenderness and warmth are the only things we have shared. We will make love when she has fully recovered from her ordeal. Even so, she is a joy to sleep with, she moans consistently, and her childish chattering is tantalisingly appealing. I try to make sense of what she is saying, to understand what is going through her head, but she is filing her thoughts under private and confidential. Thinking back over the last five days, I am not surprised. I comfort her, give her sanctuary, security and express my love for her, of course. Between you and me, I get the distinct impression that expressing love is something she has difficulty with.

She blames George, she says he wasn't there for her when she needed a father. He was so committed to his work, he spent most of his week in London, but for a young girl waiting and wanting her father to come home, she felt abandoned. I try to change her opinion of him, to help her think better of him, but she is having none of it. I explain the part he played in her rescue and tell her he loves her. Nonsense, she insists, he did it because he is a bored old man. He is infatuated by a young, sexy girl; she shrugs her shoulders and tells me he doesn't really care about her. At first, maybe that was the case but not anymore; please give him the benefit of the doubt, I beg her. Anyway, it is 9 o'clock; it is time to go meet him.

"What shall I wear?"

"You will be wearing your pyjamas if you don't hurry."

"That's a good idea. Do I look good in them?"

"Amazing." I call her bluff.

Her last two days have been hectic. She has attended a five-hour cross-examination at the Admiralty; spent a whole day at the police station, naming the people involved. She has given five press conferences, attended two fashion shoots and been inundated with mail, phone calls and texts. Her Facebook page is the most popular on the network, and she has received nearly four million tweets.

Sarah Thompson is struggling to keep up with Angela's hectic schedule. She is arranging and re-arranging the centre pages of the next edition. Her layout features the dramatic air sea rescue and is excited with the pictures. They show Angela dishevelled, vulnerable and frightened, the hearts of her readers will go out to her. She has now employed four photographers to cover Angela's every move, to ensure one of them is with her every minute of the day and night. She has also signed her top two writers to the case, to research Angela's life history. Angela is the biggest attraction the magazine has ever experienced, and her appeal is still growing. She reads out the headline she wrote yesterday and is still pleased with it, 'Bee the heroine'; just another inspired moment of creativity in the life of Sarah Thompson, and next to the pictures of Angela in distress, the feature is absolutely stunning. Her favourite picture is the one of her sitting in the lifeboat, surrounded by her rescuers. She knows Angela was never in a lifeboat, it was a posed shot, but the picture demonstrates not only her courage, but the affection the crew have for her. Of course, her immaculate sense of style and dress, even under such duress, shows through. *Vogue* has not only entered politics, but it is challenging the daily papers in news presentation. Suddenly, parliament and politics have become interesting; and that must be good for the nation. Sarah reads the editorial that has just spewed out of her fax printer. It is factual and informative and gives a clear insight into Angela's character, her beliefs, moods, feelings and values are all described and explained.

Other major papers and magazines are also singing her praises and creating Headlines, such as ''Britain's new heroine', 'Britain's next prime minister'. One headline in the *Daily Mail* is calling her 'the next iron lady', with the word iron crossed out and 'beautiful' inserted. It now reads, 'The next _beautiful_ iron lady.' The most popular headlines this morning are 'Welcome Home Angela, we love you', 'Angela catches drug gang single-handedly', and 'Angela cleans up parliament'. These are the headlines that lead the story about five members of parliament being arrested for importing drugs.

The Sunday papers are tendering for the rights to her story. The latest bid is a staggering £5,000,000, and the price is rising by the hour. There is no limit to what the papers will pay, Angela is about to become a very rich lady.

As we pull up to the houses of Westminster in the chauffeur driven Mercedes, George is waiting on the steps to greet us. He trips over himself in his haste to open the car door for her. The square is full of press reporters and photographers, hoping to report something newsworthy or interview someone interesting, today is their lucky day.

Hundreds of people who were simply passing are being held back by the perimeter wall, through the wrought iron fence, the police can be seen trying to maintain order. The crowd are calling her name and throwing her kisses, she is indeed a star. George reaches out to steady her as she steps out into the light; he utters a sigh of admiration when the slit in her black suede pencil skirt gapes to reveal her page-three legs. A frilly white blouse exaggerates her femininity; and as a touch of magic, she protects her modesty by hiding her face beneath a large-brimmed black hat. She raises her eyes and smiles at him.

"I believe I owe you a massive thank-you, sir," she says.

"For what, my dear?"

"For saving my life."

"I was lucky enough to be in the right place at the right time. You owe your life to Tim, not to me. Come inside before the crowd breaks through the police cordon."

I can't help but notice her arm linked into his as he proudly escorts her up the steps and through the iconic doorway. The paparazzi are falling over each other to take the best photograph; she stops at the door, turns, takes off her hat and waves it high in the air. The crowd erupts with appreciation. Only after she has completely disappeared inside the building, do they return to their mundane day. My presence goes without notice; I run across the grand hall and chase after them down the corridor into George's office. I arrive to see George giving her a big hug and telling her how happy he is that she is home safe, she seems to be enjoying her stepfather's affection.

"Sit down, you two, a coffee will arrive shortly unless you would prefer something stronger?" He suddenly bethinks himself.

"No, thank you, George," we both respond together. "It is far too early."

He is excited and proud, just as he was in the 60s when he had the world at his fingertips. Today, thanks to Angela, he is an important man again.

"At 2:00 p.m.," he announces, "we have been invited to attend an audience with the prime minister. Well, it's an order, not an invitation." We laugh at his reassessment of the instruction. "We have to be there precisely on time. I have explained the situation, and the involvement of our famous five MPs to him. The police will be dealing with them, but the prime minister is more concerned about the security of the country and the credibility of his government. As you know, we are about to enter into a general election, and he wants to retain the trust of the people."

"Ha! He has a problem." Angela snorts. "We were very gentle with him in his failure to sort out Europe, and also his failing to reduce the country's debt, which he promised to do. This guy can't even run his own house." George is taken aback by Angela's vicious attack.

"You seem to have an understanding of government, do you have connections with parliament?" Angela sidesteps his question.

"I only know what I read in the papers and see on the news bulletins."

George calms her down and continues with his briefing of how we should behave in front of the PM; we wait impatiently for him to reach the main point of his monologue.

"Democracy is the greatest and fairest way to run our country..." He is interrupted by the arrival of the coffee. "Leave it over there on the table. I will pour it later." His secretary, yet another new girl, smiles, looks at Angela up and down and leaves with a polite curtsey, closing the door gently behind her. "As I was saying, democracy is the greatest and fairest way to run a country, but unfortunately, several members of our parliament do not have the success of our country as their priority. They use their privileged position for their own gain; they have inside information about the stock market, they know every tax trick in the book, they claim for everything under the sun, for their kids' schooling and their exotic holidays, they make a lot of money. These MPs are destroying the credibility of our parliament, yet no one dares to speak out against them."

"Is the prime minister aware of this?"

"The prime minister is aware, but he doesn't know who these people are, and he does not have the time to deal with them."

"This is nonsense, George. He has no excuse; it should be his priority."

"I agree. The five MPs involved in this incident should be hung, drawn and quartered, and the others exposed for whatever they do. You see, I retire next year. There is nothing I can do in the time, but what this country needs is someone who can tell it as it is, until we find this person we are better off with the prime minister we have. He won't make much happen, but neither will he do much damage, so don't upset him. One lump or two?"

George pops two lumps into Angela's coffee and the rest into his own.

"See, I am also drinking coffee. No alcohol for me, well, not until 2:30."

Part Two

The Path to Power

The heavy, wooden panelled door to the prime minister's office swings open silently. A tall, regimented man, in a dark blue pin-stripe suite blocks our entry. I guess he must be the prime minister's secretary.

"The prime minister is expecting you," he announces, devoid of emotion. "Please step this way." He could be a robot, mentally he probably is, behaving exactly as programmed. We follow him into a heavy oak panelled office, with Dickensian-style furnishings straight out of Nicholas Nickleby. Silhouetted against a large stain-glass window, which is in desperate need of a clean, is David Cussack. He rises from behind his solid oak desk and beckons us to sit in the three chairs facing him. The first hint of life, in a very dreary environment, is a smile that creeps across his face.

David Cussack's second term as prime minister is coming to an end, and he knows it; his legacy for the eight years he has led our country will be 'respectful and uneventful'. He has upheld our nation's reputation throughout the world, maintained our position as a power in Europe and represented our country well at all the high-profile events and debates. He has introduced and fought for many long-term, futuristic projects which our country desperately needs, but none of which will see the light of day. It is said he is liked, but that's because there is nothing to dislike about him.

"Angela! Thank you for giving me your time today. I know you are a very busy lady. George has explained how you were innocently caught up in this dreadful and embarrassing incident. Please accept my sincere apologies, and I am so thankful you are safe and well."

Angela smiles at him.

"Now please recount, in your own words, the order of events, you see these people will be punished, so I need to be aware of all the facts, who was involved, the part they played, and with who they were dealing. My concern, of course, is for the security of our country."

Angela casts me a glance which says a thousand words, but to paraphrase her glance, if you can paraphrase a glance, she is saying who does this guy think he is fooling, he is looking after himself?

She attacks him without mercy, "First, Mr Prime Minister, let me remind you I have not been sworn to any act of secrecy, so I will tell it as it is; and if people in high places are dragged into the gutter or lose their jobs, it will be of their own making. I have been raped, kidnapped and several attempts have been made on my life. I am not feeling very sympathetic to you and your party."

The prime minister wipes his brow and jots down a few words on a pad in front of him. I have to give him credit for his patience; he sits and listens to Angela's story. It takes her over two hours to recall the details of her meetings with Janet and Colin and finally her trip to Beijing. Although I was with her, it is a shocking tale, what she has endured is definitely not for the faint of heart.

"We must take care of you, Angela. It hurts me to think that members of my government have brought this upon you." He leans forward and takes hold of both her hands, pauses and looks straight at her. "Have you ever considered a career in politics? Our party needs a person like you, someone who the people love and trust, someone who they can relate to and admire. We are choosing five new candidates to stand in the election, and you could be one of them. You have a choice of constituencies from Cornwall in the south to Barrow-in-Furness in the north. I can make it happen for you, just tell me which one."

Angela is seething with disgust; does he really think he can buy her off as easily as this. I can sense her anger increasing and fear she might insult him; I step in quickly before she totally blows what could be the opportunity we have been looking for.

"Thank you, prime minister. Angela needs time to think about your offer. George and I will explain what the position involves, and I am sure she will be delighted to help you sort out this mess... in the interest of the country, of course."

"I need to know your decision within the next couple of days, Angela. Politics never stands still." He rises from his chair, indicating he has heard enough, and it is time for us to leave.

"Come back to my office," whispers George, "we have a lot to talk about."

Angela still has not calmed down. "The man is a joke. He doesn't care about the country, all he cares about is his job. I bet he is on the biggest fiddle of them all."

"Now! Now Angela, calm down, we have an opportunity to put this country to rights." George adopts a stance of authority. He stands above her and pins her shoulders to the chair and waits for her to stop wriggling. "You, my girl, with my help, are going to put this country to rights. I think you should accept one of the constituencies, from inside

212

the party, you can do the most good. People will take you seriously, no longer will you be a sexy socialite. You will be a respected member of the government. You will quickly learn how government works, and then you can do something about it. The prime minister is not stupid, he knows that these five MPs can bring his party down, but if their exposure comes from inside his party, then maybe you can save the day for him. It will appear he is cleaning up his act."

"You want me to make him look good? No way."

George tightens his grip on her shoulders as she tries to stand.

"One thing at a time, Angela. Which constituency would you like?"

She shakes herself free and struts around his table.

"What are the areas again; I have forgotten?"

"East Yorkshire, an area you are familiar with, Devon and Cornwall which is absolutely beautiful, Berwick-on-Tweed, just south of the Scottish border, Barrow and Furness on the Lake District peninsula and Reginald Rolland Swordsmith's constituency of Oxford." He tries hard to make them all sound attractive and interesting if not beautiful. "For God's sake, Angela, sit down."

She stops and sits in his chair behind his desk.

"Will I have a desk as big as this one?"

"It will be much bigger than mine."

She smiles.

"East Yorkshire." Then, she laughs.

Poor Bastard

Louise Buchanan stares up at the ceiling; she slides her hands down her body and congratulates herself on the care she has bestowed upon herself. After 15 years of playing the good wife, taking her children to school and organising exorbitant business dinners to keep her husband's firm in favour, she is determined to use what she has, to get her life back and to enjoy every minute in its pursuit.

Not only has she been a slave to her husband's job, but now she knows she has been playing second fiddle to Stephanie Stirling, she pauses for thought... and been the support act for her younger sister Collette. Not any longer, she rolls over in bed and runs her hand down the curves of her sister's body.

"Did you enjoy last night?" she whispers.

Her sister puckers her lips and Louise locks her lips over them.

"Goodness sis, you are insatiable, have you not had enough?"

"I have tolerated 20 years of restraint, and I intend making up for it. Just lay back and enjoy it." She raises herself onto her knees and shuffles up Colette's outstretched body.

"Louise, I am still asleep, give me a break."

"Don't be silly, sweetie. We have to make the most of our time together before he wakes up."

Both girls glance across the crumpled sheets to where Thomas Jones is still sleeping—so masterful and oh, so impressive—he is a fine hulk of a man.

"He's in good shape, isn't he? Just look at him, so strong, so sexy. I love his smell, especially when he is all sweaty. I have never submitted to a man before. I always had to be in control, but this guy can do anything he wants with me."

"You got yourself a good one there, Louise. I'll give you that, and thanks for sharing him with me." Louise changes the subject, arching her back and pushing her boobs out in front of her.

"Come on, darling. You can do better than that, excite me before he wakes up." Louise enjoys making love with her sister. She has listened to her sexual exploits with envy, never believing they were real or as

214

good as she made out, but now, as she collapses on top of her, she believes everything her sister has ever told her.

"We must have worked him very hard last night, he hasn't moved yet."

They explore the rippled body of Louis's ex-chauffeur. He used to drive her everywhere, now he drives her wild, she would never have believed that the two men in her life could be so different. She stares at him in admiration and gives him a little stab with her finger, he doesn't move. She pokes him again a little harder before placing her hand on his chest. He is cold and still; she sits up and stares at him.

"Collette, the poor bastard is dead, he's bloody died on us."

The girls shake him but to no avail. It takes them several minutes before they eventually come to terms with the fact that Tom is dead.

"What happened, we weren't that rough with him. How can he do this to us?"

"He was putting quite a lot away last night. He was drinking whisky as if it was going out of fashion, and as for Viagra, he was popping one of those, every time I came up for air."

"And he smoked that joint you gave him," Louise reminded her. "We should have let him rest, expecting him to serve both of us was expecting a lot. Poor bastard, his heart must have given up the ghost."

"We've worked him hard before, it's not as if last night was the first time. Oh bloody hell, what are we going to do now?"

"Break in another chauffeur?" giggles Collette. Both girls crack out laughing.

"That's not going to be easy. Not one who drives as good as he does, I mean did," she corrects her tenses. The girls roll over each other, crying with laughter at the drive joke.

"Let's get dressed. You clean up the bedroom, and I'll call a doctor."

"What doctor? We don't know a doctor down here in Devon."

"There must be a doctor down in the village. Leave it with me; I'll find one."

"Choose a sexy one."

"Ha-ha, trust me… and Collette."

"What?"

"Put a coffee on."

"OK."

Any Publicity Is Good

Everything Angela does is news; everything she says is interesting; everything she wears is admired. She has been the main attraction in the *Sunday World* for three weeks now. This Sunday's edition has nine pictures of her, the largest taken outside 10 Downing Street. The others range from her dining out at Pierre Mattel's French restaurant in Knightsbridge to her shopping at her local Tesco supermarket. The editor has introduced a new feature on page six, a food advisory column written by Angela, 'Beat the Eat.' If you want to be beautiful and successful, cut down on the carbs and eat what Angela eats.

The centre pages are reporting her visit to Beijing; 'Angela's Beijing nightmare' is the lead headline; over the last few weeks, this has become the most sensational serial of the year. People are named; sexual activities described, and greed and corruption in the UK government exposed. The paper's circulation has doubled, and still the people are demanding more.

The paper is expecting yet another boost in sales. The drug gang is named, and the prime minister has admitted that five of his MPs are under arrest. The breaking news does not stop here, five constituencies are up for grabs, and Angela has announced her intention to stand as the Conservative candidate for East Yorkshire. The story breaks across the network, and the TV media are running full speed with it. David Cussack is being held to account. The people need the facts: Did he know about these rogue MPs? How many other government ministers are corrupt, and what are they up to; and the big question is, why did he not stop it?

Angela's phone rings and keeps ringing.

"Check that out, Tim. I have my hands full, I am pouring us an Australian Sauvignon."

"Where is it?"

"In my handbag."

"I mean my drink; not your phone."

"Ha! Ha!"

I rummage around in her handbag, which resembles a trashcan; it takes me so long to find it, the caller has rung off.

"Who was it?" I check out the name on the screen.

"It was George; he has rung off."

"I wonder what he wants."

Her phone rings again.

"You are about to find out. It's George again."

She puts down her wine, and her smile turns to a grimace. "Yes, okay, straight away." She looks up at me.

"We have to meet with George. The cabinet has been summoned to attend an emergency meeting at number 10, apparently, all hell has been let loose.

Great Sex

Collette and Louise sit in silence, waiting for the doctor to complete his autopsy.

"Were you in love with him?" Collette eventually asks.

"I thought I was, but now I realise it was just lust. His strength and dominance was totally appealing, even his smell excited me. Mind you, I hadn't had sex for over three years. Lesley was always away, so maybe I was easily appeased. He was a stallion though, rough on the edges, do you know what I mean? His touch was clumsy, even scary. I never knew what he was going to do next, he never hurt me, but I did have to tell him to stop on more than one occasion."

"Did he stop when you told him to?"

"For a second or two. He bit me once and drew blood. I screamed out in pain, well more in shock than in pain, me screaming seemed to excite him; he turned me over and took me, still shouting at him. I hated him after that and told him we were through."

"What did he do then, did he change?"

"Not one bit. I remember thinking about it in bed the next night and found myself getting excited, sex is a funny thing. Don't you think so, Collette?"

"Very funny, indeed, but nice." They both laugh.

"I am still in love with Lesley. Lesley is gentle and sensitive, and I love him for that, and he is the father of my children, of course. Lesley and I have come through a lot together, and we will come through this. Maybe it is my fault as much as his. I thought our lives were perfect, except for him working too hard. I wasn't aware our relationship was lacking in the bedroom, now I know I should have been more willing and enthusiastic. Yes, I should have welcomed him home instead of complaining at him; but bringing up three kids practically on my own was hard work. We will get through this; I know we will.

"But he was screwing a city hooker and telling you he was working late, that is outrageous."

"That is when I realised I had subdued my own sexual needs and controlled my passion for nothing." Louise wipes away a tear running down her cheek, she pauses and gulps. "When Tom stood over me, with a body out of a sex magazine, I just thought 'what the heck, I want some of that'. He wanted me as much as I wanted him, and it was wonderful to be wanted. Lesley never made me feel wanted, not sexually. Tom was forceful, full of passion, he had my hands tied to the bed before I realised what was happening and used me like a rag doll. At first, I was in shock and scared; but soon, I was impressed and respected his strength. I actually found myself encouraging him. I have never experienced feelings so intense before, my body was sending messages to my head that it couldn't process. I couldn't distinguish right from wrong. I just gave in and surrendered to him. He must have thought I was rubbish; just his touch made me scream. Even then, he didn't stop, he took me again and again. I remember him slapping my face and holding my throat, I thought I was going to die. We laid wrapped together for over an hour. It was the best hour of my life."

"So are you trying telling me you enjoyed it?" Collette asks, mockingly.

Louise tries to slap her sister who is laughing out loud.

"Welcome to the club, sis. At last, you are in touch with your sexuality."

"I am, thank you very much. Anyway, I am over it now. I have a family to care for, and I love Lesley, and he is being held by the police. I have to get him back... and to answer your initial question, no, I didn't love Tom."

Parliament in Shock

Angela is an instant hit with her constituents. The people of East Yorkshire love her, they listen intently to what she has to say, they recognise her sincerity, admire the way she speaks from the heart and respond to her initiatives for the area. Her passion and love for the people is obvious; and her intent to improve the quality of life, especially for the women of Yorkshire, is reflected by the support she receives. 'Women's rights for a righteous world' is her slogan, and she hammers it out at every opportunity. As for her appeal to Yorkshire men, well apart from her being pretty, bright, bubbly, with a magnetic personality; she adds colour and energy to their hard-earned day.

I have scheduled several public appearances for her, all in high-visual places. Last Saturday afternoon, her presence at the football game was simply awe-inspiring; she learnt the names of every player in the town team, knew the club's position in the league and remembered their recent score lines. Cameras followed her all day, and the sneaky sight of thigh as she kicked the ball off the centre spot scored her a winning goal on the front page of the *Bridlington News*. She has totally immersed herself in the everyday events of family life. She rides the trains at rush hour to experience first-hand frustration of the morning commute, she sits in the hospital waiting rooms with the old, the injured and the concerned, understanding their impatience at the failing NHS service. Yesterday, she walked to school with a group of young mothers and stood with them in the playground as they waited for their children. She refuses to call it canvassing and refers to it as bonding, and that is exactly what she is doing. She says men only supply answers, women supply sympathy, understanding and companionship; and when she feels totally in tune with the people, only then will she be confident to fight for their cause in parliament. She is the talk of East Yorkshire, and suddenly, East Yorkshire is back on the map. It is hip to live in East Yorkshire. The people are uplifted with their new-found leader.

"She is amazing," George tells me with pride. "There is no stopping this girl. She simply lifts the spirits of everyone she comes into contact with. You are doing a great job with her, Tim."

George pours out his first tipple of the day. It is 3:30 in the afternoon. He is a changed man, and with only one year before his retirement, I believe he is determined to change the world. It is time to share my dream with him, to explain my ambition for her as I am in need of his help; I wait as he comfortably relaxes in his large leather chair and balances his spectacles on the chair arm.

"George, let's take her all the way."

"What do you mean, Tim, where else can she go?"

"Let's take her to the top, the very top, let's put her name forward for leader of the party, she would make an incredible Prime Minister. What she is doing for East Yorkshire she can do for the country, she is exactly what we need. She will add life and energy to the corridors of this drab, dusty establishment and put the pride back into our country."

George cracks out laughing.

"I'm not joking, George. The prime minister will announce his resignation tomorrow. He has no option; the country and the party have lost all trust in him. There is no one else in the party fit to be a leader."

"She knows nothing about politics, Tim."

"But you do. Teach her, show her the way, introduce her to the important people, she will impress the party leaders and all the EU leaders just as she has the people of East Yorkshire. She is a natural. Come on, George; you have one year to retirement. Have some fun and make a mark on the future."

"It would be rather fun, I must admit. I would love to wipe the smile off the faces of the chancellor and that stupid internal affairs minister; they both have sights on becoming prime minister. Okay, I'm in."

"Brilliant, we will wait until all the other nominations have been received and heard their boring campaign plans. Then, we will drop her name into the hat at the last minute, she will blow the system wide open. I will handle her PR campaign; you take care of the internal matters."

"Our new Lady Britannia, I must admit, with Angela at the helm, we will never be slaves, neither to Brussels or to America. She will have them eating out of her hands. Do you know, Tim, it's time this place got shaken up; and there is nobody I would rather see shake it than a sexy young girl. Oh, I'm sorry, did I say sexy, I mean intelligent?"

"You mean sexy, George. You are forgiven for being so observant, so here's to our new, sexy prime minister."

"To our new prime minister." George lifts his coffee cup towards me.

"To our new prime minister."

Four nominations have been received for the leadership of the Conservative party. The chancellor of the exchequer: Gordon Armitage. The deputy leader: The Rt Hon. Frederick Brooksbank. The internal affairs minister: Marcus Leopole Uxbearing; and a young backbencher, the MP for Dover: Michael Day.

Angela is staying in London with me, this weekend; she says it's too cold in East Yorkshire at this time of year. We have ordered a curry; tired of being photographed and hampered by marauding reporters, we plan to stay home and watch a film tonight. We were looking forward to an intimate evening, but George has turned up. If that isn't bad enough, he doesn't like curry. Well, he says it's the curry that doesn't like him, but he is prepared to risk a very mild lamb Rogan josh. His intervention takes a turn for the better when he pulls a bottle of the finest house wine out from under his city coat. I thought he was being very humble when he referred to his gift as 'only house wine', it never occurred to me that the house he referred to was the houses of parliament, a bottle he just happened to slip into his pocket after yesterday's luncheon.

"Just a little perk of the job." He jibes as he prises out the cork and empties the full-bodied red liquid equally into three large wine glasses.

"George! Who is Michael Day? We didn't expect a young back-bencher to be competition."

"Michael Day is the MP for Dover. As you might expect he is a big European, he thinks his constituency has a lot to lose if we come out of Europe."

"What do we know about him?"

"His father is Sir Barnaby Battersby Codspike."

"Who? You must be joking, nobody has a name like that?"

"Tim, I never joke about such unfortunate things. The young Michael Codspike changed his name to Day for only one reason, and that was to avoid the butt of so many jokes. Sir Barnaby is a big techno mogul; he owns a company that installs hi-tech communication apparatus into our submarine fleet. He owns a stately home, with 50 acres in Kent, it's just on the outskirts of Canterbury. To put it in a nutshell, he is stinking rich."

"Is Day a threat to us?"

"We have to investigate his motives, obviously his father will benefit enormously if he was to become prime minister. His military contracts with the government would be secure, and they are worth billions."

"He seems to be causing quite a stir. He is the youngest nominee by 20 years and will appeal to the younger generation." George scratches his head. "I must admit I know very little about him."

"Let the media calm down for a couple of days, then we will announce Angela's nomination. She will be the only woman in the running, we will maximise on her appeal to the women of the country."

George gives me an anxious look.

"First, we have to maximise her appeal to the members of the Conservative party. How are you going to do that?"

"Leave that to me, George, we must think outside the box. I'm not going to push her through, I'm going to pull her through."

"Pushing and pulling, what are you talking about, Tim?"

"Watch and learn, George. My campaign will not focus on persuading the members of the party that she is the right person to lead them. I am going to increase her popularity on the streets to such an extent that she will easily win the election for them."

"You cunning bastard, Tim, why has nobody done that before?"

"Because politicians don't have creative brains."

"Hey, I take offence to that." George picks up a pencil and throws it at me.

"Except you, George, of course."

"That's better."

Pulling, Not Pushing

Angela peers at me from behind her wine glass. "Okay, clever dick, prime minister eh! How are you going to get me that job?

"I'm not going to get it for you, you are going to get it for yourself. You are already a popular model, and you have never done any modelling. You have exposed a drug ring, and you don't know the difference between cannabis and baking powder."

"I do, how dare you say that? One raises cakes and the other raises your spirits."

"Ha-ha."

"Don't drink that wine all at once, your curry will be here shortly."

"Go on, tell me more?"

"You have practically brought down a prime minister, and you know nothing about politics."

"I have, haven't I? I never thought about it like that, so what else am I going to do?"

"You are going to raise a lot of money for deprived children, and you are going to become an animal lover."

"I hate pets. They smell."

"Not only pets, sweetie, wild animals as well."

"What! Elephants and tigers and things?"

"Elephants, tigers, crocodiles and snakes, you are going to Africa."

"When?"

I hand her the two tickets I purchased yesterday.

"You're going to South Africa next Monday morning."

"I'm not going to South Africa."

"Why not?"

"I have nothing to wear?"

George cracks out laughing.

"You will find something, it has to be rugged, revealing and look sweaty. Am I right, Tim?" George is pleased with his input; a big smile crosses his face.

"Quite right, George, you got it in one." A knock on the door interrupts our joviality.

"Come on. Angela. As the woman of the house, it is your job to serve dinner." She jumps to her feet and wishes she hadn't downed that glass of wine quite so quickly.

"Whatever happened to sexual equality, you told me to promote sexual equality?"

"Sexual equality, you serving dinner has nothing to do with sexual equality. If George or I served the food you wouldn't want to eat it, so shut up and go get the curries."

George taps me on the hand. "It's not going to be easy to blag her all the way to top, Tim. These people are professional politicians, they will see through her." He looks concerned.

"They are all blaggers, George. They are all blagging their way through. Every time I listen to a party's political broadcast, all I hear are promises they can't keep and claims that are untrue. Nobody in this race is more sincere than Angela, but to lead the country, she must be aware of the world, she must be in touch with people and events. She is going to learn so much about life in the next few months, you will be amazed. Who wants a rich, spoilt, university-bound anorak leading the country? What this country needs is a caring, creative, exciting, forceful individual who people can love and respect."

"Who ordered the chicken biryani?" Angela walks in from the kitchen, with a tea towel over her arm. In her other hand, she is delicately balancing a plate of curry whilst clinging on to her glass of red wine. We are forced to smile in admiration.

"May I introduce the next prime minister of the United Kingdom?" announces George. "She can do it, Tim, she can bloody do it." George turns his attention to the food. "I believe the biryani is yours, Tim. I would rescue it quickly before she drops it if I were you."

"Good idea, George, here's to our next leader of the country."

"I'll drink to that."

I Hereby Nominate Angela Bee

Parliament receives the news of Angela's nomination for leader of the Conservative Party as a joke, but ten million women across the country are delighted. This is the best news they have heard in years. For one woman in particular; it is a dream come true. Sarah Thompson lets out a scream of delight at the announcement; with Angela under contract, to her, she could own the publicity rights to the next prime minister of Great Britain. Not only that, now that Angela is a political celebrity, she is international news, escalating world sales. Sarah fingers through the last two months of *Vogue's* circulation figures, they show an increase of 80%. Her career review in three weeks will be very interesting, she will sail through it and intends to demand a substantial salary increase. She had to fight hard to persuade the features department to approve her idea of filming a real woman instead of models posing on beaches and catwalks. Now her idea has proven to be truly inspirational, she will enjoy watching them grovel. Of course Angela is an interesting and beautiful woman, but she laid her career and reputation on the line, she deserves the credit.

She turns up the volume on her office monitor when Angela appears, standing on the Thames embankment; Big Ben is behind her, chiming eight o'clock. Sarah listens intently as she promotes the launch of her latest charity. 'Save the wild, the wonderful and the beautiful' has already caught the imagination of the country's eight million nature lovers. She announces her imminent visit to the Great Kruger National Park in South Africa to film the animals and emphasises the care they need. She will also spend one day at Victoria Falls, where she intends to record the first in a BBC series titled *Angela's wild and wonderful World*, filming the most spectacular places on the planet. Sarah cannot believe her luck; the opportunity to splash Angela's sense of fashion in places previously unheard of has taken her breath away. She picks up her phone and calls Bernard Van Blinburg, a Dutch photographer friend who is famous for his wildlife photography; no expense will be spared on this project.

"Bernard, listen to me, of course we want you to focus on the animals," she tells him. "Just have Angela in the picture somewhere.

When you meet her, you will love her and find her as interesting as the lions and tigers."

Blinburg is not convinced; the last thing he wants is to discredit his reputation as a leading wildlife photographer.

"Sarah, I am not a fashion photographer." His pleading is of no avail.

"I don't want a fashion photographer, I want Angela to look natural, dirty, sweaty and interesting. I want you to focus on the animals, Angela will take care of herself." She sits on the edge of her desk, the phone in her hand. "Name your price, Bernard. How much are you going to charge me?"

Blinburg thinks of a figure; then doubles it.

"$2,000,000."

"Done!" Van Blinburg is taken aback; now he can't refuse.

Yet Sarah is concerned, concerned that he will in fact focus only on the animals, so she has ordered Darren McCaulty to go with him. Darren is the photographer who filmed Angela's visit to Beijing. He didn't exactly excel on that trip, but at least he understands the type of pictures Sarah needs.

Michael Day is in the conservatory of his father's stately home, looking out over the rose garden, the one thing he is not is a nature-lover. He takes the view for granted, but its beauty is outstanding. Beyond the garden, the river flows across the bottom of the garden and meanders for a mile down the valley, before disappearing amongst the cottages of the village of Green. It eventually navigates around the back of the parish church to reappear in the fields to the north of the village and twists under the arches of the railway viaduct. On either side of the valley, farms are scattered, higgledy-piggledy, for as far as the eye can see, the shadows of the buildings and cottages are long and dramatic at this time of day, a mesmerising spectacle that would leave anyone speechless but not Michael Day. Michael and his father are only concerned about his campaign to become party leader. Sir Barnaby reaches for the port whilst puffing on his after-dinner cigar and lets the ash drop onto the carpet.

"Damn, blast, I hope your mother didn't see that." He rubs his foot over it. The roast beef dinner was... well let's just say it was too grand; his stomach is bloated to bursting; and even with his trouser belt undone, he is suffering discomfort.

"Michael, this hooker has got to be taken out, she is a threat. The other nominees are no problem; they are old school. The country is fed up with the establishment, politicians who waddle in and out of Downing Street, wearing badly pressed suits. But this girl is fresh and exciting, I am not going to lose the contract on those two submarines because of a bit of skirt."

"Stop worrying, Dad. She is a silly, stupid girl, she is just a passing fantasy. It will be easy to discredit her."

Sir Barnaby passes air as he sits back in his chair and attempts to raise his feet onto his pouffe.

"Do it, Michael, she has to be stopped."

All Stressed Out

Tonight, the five contenders in the leadership race are to appear head-to-head on the first of a series of TV programs titled, *The fight for the top*. Angela is nervous to say the least; she is way out of her comfort zone.

"I need to relax and focus. Could you take me to the apartment, Tim? I need to be alone."

"I had forgotten you still have the keys to Lesley Buchanan's apartment. He won't be using it for a year or two; that is for sure."

"Unfortunately, he will go down for more than two years for his part in the drug ring. He won't be able to talk his way out of that one."

"Come on, let's go, don't forget your bag."

It takes us nearly an hour to twist and turn our way through the London traffic; thank goodness, there is an underground car park to the apartment.

"What's the code to the car park, darling?"

"I don't know. Lesley never told me. I don't have a car, why should he give me the code to the car park."

"Is it on the key ring, just a thought?"

"No, it bloody isn't on the key ring. Tim, I am stressing out, get off my back. I have a question and answer session on TV, this evening. You are sending me to Africa, and I hate animals; and now you are having a go at me because I don't know a bloody car park code."

It never entered my head that she would not know the code. I try to find a park on the street, but it proves to be impossible. She opens the car door and jumps out, slamming it behind her.

"Angela, I am sorry, I wasn't thinking," I shout out to her.

"Just fuck off and pick me up at 6:00."

"I'll find a park around the corner and come up to the apartment."

"Don't bother, I want to be alone."

And without another word, she is gone. Maybe I should ease off, hopefully, she will be calm by six o'clock.

The apartment is in a mess. The police search was thorough, and they haven't bothered to tidy up after themselves. Drawers are open, and their contents scattered on the floor. Books from Stephanie Stirling's library have been pulled off the shelves and lie torn and broken. Her collection of vinyl records is scattered un-respectfully on the sofa. At least it is warm, the heating system is on, and the automatic temperature gauge has maintained the apartment at a pleasant 22 degrees. Angela checks the bathroom shower; and to her delight, hot water sprays out from the three-foot diameter sky spray head. She thrusts her hand into the flow and squeals in admiration as it cascades around her fingers. *Now this is what I call luxury,* she thinks to herself. *Poor Lesley, he gave all this away for sexual favours; and now he is being held in police custody for a murder he didn't commit. I bet he only got involved in the drug thing, so he could afford Stephanie. Poor bastard, he is a nice guy.*

She finds a large white towel in the bathroom chest, steps out of her dress and climbs into the droplets of the pre-perfumed spray. Well, that is a first, the selector points right for 'fresh' and left for 'perfumed'. Left it is, and the essence of lavender cascades down her body. She lets out another squeal of delight as it splashes against her face, and the enclosure fills with sweet smelling bubbles. Along the back wall, there are several dials, she wonders what they do and turns first one and then another. Water shoots out of jets positioned around the sides, first stinging her waist, then her shoulders, then her thighs. She activates each dial in turn and water sprays in sequence onto the sensitive parts of her body. She plays like a child, just as she did every Saturday morning at the municipal swimming pool, 20 years ago.

The final dial is red in colour; it has a posture of importance. *Should I or shouldn't I. Oh, go on, you silly girl, give it a twist.* The spraying water ceases and is replaced by jets of warm air. She spins in the enclosure, drying every part of her anatomy. First the obvious parts, and then as she gets more confident, the discreet bits, laughing and whimpering as she raises and lowers her limbs to accept the air.

Dry, perfumed and stimulated, she steps out of the shower and parades in front of the 180-degree full-length mirror, draping the towel around her. She gyrates to Bowie's *Space Oddity*, piped through the bathroom audio system, which she must have activated when she entered the shower. *Wow! Wow, wow, this is amazing,* running her hands through her hair, she presents herself to the mirror, like a disco pole dancer, throwing kisses to herself every time she comes in for a close up.

It's more a sense than a noise, but suddenly, she feels she is not alone. She ceases her frivolity and stands rigid, tightening the towel around her. A door in the lounge clicks open.

"Who is there? Is that you Tim? Come and see this bathroom, it is amazing."

Bowie is silenced as the bathroom door swings open, and a middle-aged woman storms in on her, screams abuse and knocks her to the floor. Angela trips over the towel wrapped around her legs and is totally unable to defend herself. The woman grabs her hair and practically pulls it out by the roots.

"Who are you, what do you want?" Angela tries to free her legs of the towel; at the same time, avoiding an onslaught of swinging arms and feet.

"Did Lesley give you a key? Are you another of his mistresses, or just a street hooker screwing him for what you can get?" The woman is ranting hysterically, "How many of you whores are living off him?" Kicking out relentlessly, Angela suffers hit after hit and only just avoids a hair-dryer smashing down on her head. It misses her by inches and crashes instead into the shower screen behind her, which shatters and splinters over the floor. She tries in vain to defend herself, but the woman is too strong, grabbing her throat and scratching her face hysterically. Angela screams out in pain, thrashing the air, hoping to fend off the attack. Her towel will not release, she is tied to the floor. All she can do is lay there helplessly, taking strike after strike with no way of escape.

"I have served Lesley and brought up his children all alone, and you come along, wag your tail for him without a thought for me, you deserve to die." Her screaming builds up into a hysterical crescendo, ranting on and on. "How dare you come between us, that stupid cow of a mistress he had, she got what was coming to her. How dare she call me sexless and blame me for him screwing around."

Angela freezes as she realises who this woman is. She is Lesley's wife, and she is admitting to killing Stephanie. Of course she would have a key to his apartment, she has just let herself into the apartment now. She must have arrived that evening after Lesley told Stephanie to pack, let herself in and come face-to-face with Stephanie, who probably insulted her; and during a fight, the gun went off.

Angela is fading in and out of consciousness; making sense of this abuse is impossible.

"The bitch deserved to die, and so do you." Louise Buchanan releases her grip on Angela's hair and empties the contents of her handbag onto the tiles, a small pistol drops out. Angela tries to grab it, but Louise gets to it first. Bang! The gun goes off, and Angela slumps to the floor, with blood oozing out of her body.

At 6:00 p.m., I arrive at the apartment as instructed. It has taken me 30 minutes just to find a parking space, and even now, I am parked several hundred yards down a side street. It's a good job I left in good time. I ring the bell expecting to hear Angela's cheery voice inviting me in, but I get no response. I press the bell a second and third time until frustration sets in. A taxi pulls up at the kerb behind me, and a woman dashes out through the apartment street door, slamming into me. She clambers into the cab, shouts instructions at the driver and is gone, leaving the apartment door gaping open. *How rude can some people be?* I can only conclude that Angela has already left and is probably on her way back to my place, but just to make sure, I run up the steps to check. Her door is open.

"Hello, Angela are you there, Angela, it's Tim." There is no response. The apartment is trashed. The bathroom door is slightly ajar, and Angela is trapped against it. She is lying across the bathroom floor, tied up in a white towel, with blood pumping out of her shoulder.

"Bloody hell, Angela; what has happened?" I reach for my mobile to call an ambulance. She is alive, her face is scratched, and her body badly bruised. She has been in a hell of a fight and come out the loser, which isn't like Angela. I stroke her face and press the towel to her shoulder in an attempt to stem the flow of blood. Her eyelids flicker as she manages to look up at me.

"What happened, who did this to you?"

I am not thinking clearly, asking her questions is the last thing I should be doing. Her lips quiver, her mouth falls open, she is swallowing heavily and panting, she is trying to tell me something, but nothing she says makes sense. Her sounds are only grunts and sighs, lo lo looo, se se and bew bew bew. I can't make a coherent message out of her gasps. Her eyes are open wide, full of fear. If she can read my face she will know that I don't understand what she is telling me. Her head flops onto her chest; and her arm drop limply from my grasp. She slips into unconsciousness.

Thank God she is still alive. I rip a blanket off the sofa and cover her, all I want to do is hold her tight and pull her close to me. Whatever have I got her into? Is this because of my ego, my ambition to demonstrate the power of advertising? Oh God! How can anybody do this to an innocent, pretty girl like Angela? The ambulance crew burst into the apartment, followed immediately by the police who drag me off her.

"Are you her husband, a relative, a friend?" I look at them, unable to think straight.

"A friend," I eventually stutter.

"Did you find her, sir?" snaps a police officer.

"Yes, I am a friend, and I found her." It is going to be a long night of awkward questions, demanding very difficult answers.

The news of Angela being shot interrupts the scripted, early-evening news bulletins. Allan Formby, anchorman for this evening's political debate, looks confused as his producer hands him a slip of paper just before his introduction. The candidates stand white-faced as he reads the scribbled note out loud.

"We have just been informed that Angela Bee, the fifth nominee for the party leadership has been found shot at the apartment of Lesley Buchanan. Mr Buchanan is being held in police custody for the murder of socialite Stephanie Stirling; she too was found shot at his apartment, ten days ago. Lesley Buchanan is also a member of the parliament drug gang, exposed by Angela Bee. She has been taken to Charing Cross Hospital, where we are told she is stable with a gunshot wound to her shoulder. We will keep you informed of her condition."

Sir Barnaby Battersby Codspike is in shock upon hearing the announcement. He knows he suggested that Angela should be taken out, but he never thought for one minute that his son would kill her.

What Have You Done?

The hospital spokesman reports that Angela is the luckiest girl in the world. The gun was fired less than five feet from her head, yet the bullet hit her left shoulder and went straight through. She is stable and comfortable, although still in shock. Hopefully, she will be allowed home within the next few days. A police officer has been seated in the corridor outside her hospital room, his instruction is to report in when she gains consciousness and capable of answering questions. There are a thousand questions needing answers, and the entire country is desperate to learn what happened. As for me, I need to know who Angela's attacker is.

I haven't slept for days. I find it impossible to relax; my brain is going over and over those terrible moments when I held Angela in my arms, believing she was dying. The panic I felt when she tried to tell me what had happened, and the frustration when I couldn't make out what she was saying? Her gurgling sounds made no sense at all, lo-se-bew; lo-se-bew. *Whatever was she trying to say, I am convinced she was telling me the name of her attacker, who could it be?* I repeat her words out loud; putting them securely into my head, hoping my brain will decipher them whilst I sleep, if I can get to sleep.

This is a trick I use many times. Try it if you have a question that demands an answer, put the problem into your head just as you are falling asleep, and your brain will work on it during the night. You must have a pen and paper handy when you wake because you only have a matter of seconds to write down the solution. Once your brain recognises the reality of the day, all thought is lost. Try it; you will be amazed.

Sir Barnaby Battersby Codspike summons his son and demands an explanation for his actions. Michael drops his tennis racket and rushes to the library, leaving his cousin batting balls into the tennis net, all on her own. When his father is in a foul mood, Michael knows better than to keep him waiting.

"What the fuck have you done now, Michael? Have you anything at all to do with the shooting of Angela Bee?"

"Father, this has nothing to do with me." Michael is upset that his father should even think him capable of such a dreadful deed, "but someone wants her dead, and they nearly succeeded."

"Well they didn't succeed, she is still alive, so if you have orchestrated her death, you messed up. I advise you to pack your bags and get the hell out of here before the police come sniffing around, might I suggest Syria."

"Dad, don't be so stupid, this is not a joking matter."

"I am not laughing. I hope for your sake you are telling the truth. God damn it, I hope for all our sakes you are telling the truth. Now get out of here and plan what you are going to say; and more important, how you can turn this to our advantage."

Michael Day knows that whatever he says in his defence will not restore his father's trust in him; he turns to leave.

"You have nothing to worry about father. Our campaign is solid; you will get your government contract." Sir Barnaby swings his leather chair around to face the window, resisting his urge to tell his son exactly what he thinks of him. He knows that shouting at him will only summon his mother wrath; and at this moment in time, he can't cope with her ranting and raving in defence of her beloved, spoilt baby.

Apart from the press and the paparazzi, there are several hundred anxious fans on the street outside the hospital's main door. The impressive Greek colonnade is a famous icon in the area and a sign of better times; it must be protected at all cost. The police have instructed the council to construct a barrier to keep the crowd away from the giant pillars and to protect the more enthusiastic of them from the stream of ambulances rushing in and out. A death involving an ambulance would not make good reading in tomorrow's press.

The prime minister has called an emergency party meeting to discuss the shooting. He is distraught at the thought of his party members shooting each other. George receives the order to attend, never in a good mood, first thing in the morning, his reaction is to huff and puff, but on this occasion, he is the first to arrive at number 10.

Lo lo looo, se se se and bew bew bew. I wake covered in sweat. Angela's attacker could be linked to the party leadership race, yet they could easily be someone with a grudge against woman and women's rights; or even an ex-client with an identity to protect. There are lots of people who might want her dead, so why is the name Lesley Buchanan going around and around in my head. He was in police custody at the time, so he definitely could not be Angela's attacker. The Se se se, could be Stephanie Stirling, the woman they claim Lesley killed. To think it could be her is ridiculous, but my brain never lets me down. I must not let go of this thought. I must be missing something obvious. I close my eyes and try to capture the moment when Lesley stormed out of his apartment, leaving Stephanie packing her bags, who then let themselves in and shot her? Who had a key? Whoever it was still has a key because they came back and walked in on Angela. I sit up in bed with a start, of course, she was saying 'Lo…se', Louise, she was trying to say Louise Buchanan. Lo…se…bo, that would make sense. Louise Buchanan would have a key to the apartment, she also had a motive to kill Stephanie, she was the woman screwing her husband. I would never have thought of Louise Buchanan; the quiet, dedicated mother; the victim of her husband's infidelity.

Louise Buchanan is not in a good mood. She hardly slept a wink last night, she points the remote at the TV. The bedroom monitor bursts into life with an account of Angela's condition. The reporter outside the hospital is desperately trying to make the story into something bigger than it is. In fact, he is turning it into a quiz show by asking the people in the crowd who they think shot her. The answers range from the prime minister to a jealous woman. One woman even suggests that she shot herself because she doesn't want to go to Africa.

Louise storms out of bed in disgust, dresses and races out of the house, breakfast can wait.

A Full English Breakfast

I call at the hospital before racing off to Sussex in search of Louise. If Angela has regained consciousness, maybe she can save me the trip.

Angela is in one of the hospital's private suites, thanks to the generosity of Vogue; even the corridor is sumptuous, with a deep pile, yellow ochre carpet running its entire length. Hanging on the walls are enormous abstract paintings. A visitor would be excused for thinking they were in a five-star hotel.

"How is she this morning?" I ask the police officer sitting outside her room.

"Good morning, Mr Collinwood." The officer stands as I approach him.

"Has Angela regained consciousness, how is she this morning?"

"There has been no change throughout the night. I have to report to my station commander immediately, she is able to speak to us."

"Is it okay if I go in and sit with her?"

"The nurse is in with her at the moment, Mr Collinwood. She took some food in on a tray and said she also needed to change the bed. I suggest you sit with me for a couple of minutes and wait until she has finished."

I pull up a chair and sit next to him; we pass the time with man-talk: the weather, Chelsea's performance at last night's game, and what patients get for breakfast in a five-star wing of a London hospital."

He laughs. "Well! I was offered a coffee and a slice of toast, but the nurse has taken a full English breakfast into Angela. I offered to eat it if Angela refused it, she thought that was very funny." We sit in silence, with our thoughts.

"Why is she serving bacon and eggs to a patient in a coma?"

He looks at me in shock, as realisation of the ridiculous gesture hits him. "Who the hell was she, are you sure she was a nurse."

We both make a grab for the door handle and charge inside. The nurse is standing over Angela, holding a pillow over her face. She turns towards us and grabs a gun off the bedside table and fires it at us without a thought. The police officer drops to the ground, clutching his stomach. I am fully exposed to receive a second shot; the bed shakes as Angela

237

lashes out at her, and she is momentarily thrown off balance. I have a split second to react and knock the gun from her grasp; she fights me like a demon. It takes all my strength to pin her to the carpet.

"Louise Buchanan, I presume?" She continues to thrash about furiously. I have never met Louise Buchanan before. She is an attractive petit woman, but at this moment, demonstrating the ferocity of a tiger. The police officer is writhing on the floor, holding his stomach. Blood can be seen oozing through his fingers. A nurse is tending to him, trying to stop him from losing more blood. She begs him to lay still, but her advice is having little effect. Angela has collapsed back onto the bed, with a big smile on her face. She lifts her left arm, the one wrapped in heavy bandages and held in a sling; the one she whacked Louise across the back with. She stares up at me, her eyes sparkling as they always did.

"Welcome back, I'm so glad you are feeling better." I bend down to kiss her; she closes her eyes and submits her lips to my searching mouth. "Is there anything you need," I whisper to her, "can I get you anything?"

She looks up at me, "A plate of bacon and eggs, with toast and coffee, would be nice."

Is that the police officer I hear laughing?

It is late afternoon before Angela is dismissed from the hospital. She looks pleased with herself as she appears at the hospital door to face the cameras. The last time such a large crowd waited on this street was for the arrival of the royal baby. She looks amazing, beautiful and elegant; and with her arm in a sling, she is a picture of injured innocence. The crowd erupts with cheers of 'welcome back'; their love for her is obvious. She is their hero, as well as being a leading politician and a charity worker, she is now a killer catcher.

"Are you still going to Africa?" shouts one of the cameramen.

"Saving the wild life of our planet is not something you can put off because of a broken arm," she shouts back, the crowd erupts into a second bout of applause.

"Angela, Angela," they chant.

"I will be back in five days," she shouts at them. "We have an election campaign to win, and we will win it if we stick together."

The crowd erupts a third time.

"We love, Angela. We love Angela." Their chanting can be heard until we are out of earshot. I reach over to her and give her knee a reassuring pat. She smiles back at me.

"Thanks for being there for me," she whispers.

Our taxi crawls painfully through the busy streets of Mayfair, but we are not in a hurry. It is nice to have her back and to savour her smell, to hear her chatter and be able to kiss her.

"You are getting rather good at this political game."

"I am not playing politics, Tim, I mean it. I mean every word I say. It's at times like this we have to take care of people and of our world."

I relax into the back of the car seat. I am full of admiration for her and wonder what the true potential is of this amazing little girl.

Be Prepared

Bernard Van Blinburg has excelled himself. Sarah is in raptures with his pictures. Angela is spectacular in her torn safari suit; and in every picture, she is interacting with the animals, pointing at them, standing next to them or hiding from them. In one, she is standing only meters away from an elephant; and in another, she is watching a pride of lions stalking a herd of grazing gazelle. Yet, her favourite is the one of Angela holding a baby gibbon in her sling. Her sling is now the symbol of her tour, illustrating her strength and dedication to the cause. Vogue, the leader of high fashion and the ultimate in style on the catwalk is now encouraging better dress sense in the political arena and even promoting good taste in the jungle.

This morning, the press and the TV news bulletins are focused on the race for the party leadership. Each nominee during their interviews are stupidly trying to discredit the others instead of promoting their own positive innovations, resulting in the usual lacklustre, boring, backbiting campaign that British politics is renowned for. Only Michael Day has energy in his campaign, his appeal is also aided by his vigour and good looks, which is making him very popular with teenage girls. Even so, he is taking Angela's challenge very seriously.

He is spending a fortune researching Angela's history. He is desperate to identify her parents and to know where she was educated, and what qualifications she has. He is also interested in the rumour that she is a street girl. Proof of this could be his master card in removing her from the race, and the first reports from his private detectives are making very interesting reading. Michael and his father are thumbing through the evidence they have just received.

"She was a hooker. We have statements here from people who have seen her hanging around the street." Sir Barnaby Codspike bursts out laughing. "My God! And she thinks this qualifies her for the post of prime minister?"

Michael delves deeper into the pile of documents, pulls out a certificate and waves it in the air.

"This certificate states that at the age of two, foster parents were found for her, taking her out of the orphanage, but it doesn't state who they are."

"They must be very rich. They invested a lot of money in her education, they sent her to a finishing school in Switzerland."

"Well! If the only thing she did with her posh education was to become a hooker, she blew it. Anyway, we have enough evidence to discredit her, but I would still like to know who adopted her?"

"We need copies of her adoption papers; keep your guys working on it, Michael."

Chit-Chat

"What are you doing during the next four weeks, George?"

"Whatever you want me to do, Tim."

"Excellent, I want you to accompany Angela on a four-week tour, in which she will meet the most powerful and influential women in the world. We need to position her amongst the elite, famous and respected."

"So who have you in mind?"

"The European chancellor, a Scandinavian princess, a film star, TV chat-show hosts, women promoting world charities, members of our own royal family, American first ladies, do I need to go on?"

"No, I understand. So what do I do, call them and ask if she can call around for a cup of tea?" George laughs at his own joke.

"Do you know, George, that is not a bad idea. Women love to natter over a cup of tea, but they must have something important to natter about."

"Like what?"

Now, have you ever put yourself in a situation where your mouth is working faster than your brain because that is what I have just done? I have asked myself a question to which I don't have the answer.

"You have gone quiet, Tim, that is not like you."

"I'm thinking… What's getting press coverage in parliament at the moment, George? We need something, like women rights, air pollution, child care, child nourishment, family health, you know the sort of thing."

"These are all heavy subjects. Can't you think of anything lighter and more fun?"

"I must admit something a bit lighter would be better… George, I've got it. It's just come to me."

"What is it, Tim? You have got me excited, tell me what it is."

"It's 'chit-chat'. Angela is going to promote the art of chit-chatting."

"Chit-chatting, what is chit-chatting?"

"It's the art of light-hearted conversation, usually about nothing. Women are very good at it, and do it all the time, whilst they are chit-chatting with each other, they feel so much better about the problems of the world. They bond together, they share secrets and problems, they make friends much easier than men. Men are problem-solvers, but women don't have the need to solve problems. They are happy if they can share their concerns, they are happy if they are understood; and in so doing, their problems dissolve, and that can't be a bad thing for the world, can it."

"So who do they chit-chat with?"

"Angela is going to promote the concept of chit-chatting with other women across the world. Women of different cultures, women of different religions, of differing ages and with different traditions; and in so doing, they will pull the world together."

"I like it, I will make a list of influential women."

"And I will approach American TV chat shows and programs, like *Loose Women*, *A girls' night out* and *the Graham Norton show*. Let's make it happen, George. I will write the press releases, and you organise the chit-chats. Try to arrange out of hour chats as well, casual meetings, fun meetings."

I can tell George is excited at the idea, and the thought of escorting Angela around the world is a job beyond his wildest dream.

Hate Mail

Angela is reading through her day's e-mails. She used to receive 20 in one day, now it's more like 200. "How did all these people find my email address, it's a full-time job, answering them all."

"You don't have to answer them. In fact, you don't have to read them. Most will be trash, filter them into your trash folder." She suddenly looks up in horror. "Tim, have you seen this, this is horrible."

"Let me see." She holds up her tablet, so I can read it. "Goodness, how can people write such terrible things about you?" Angela reads out yet another disgusting mail.

"This guy claims to have slept with me and is threatening to tell the newspapers if I don't pull out of the leadership campaign. Goodness, here is another, this guy is asking for a date and wants me to send him a price list for services. He has even given me the list, this man is sick, see what he wants me to do."

"Oh Tim, how can we stop this; it is awful, shall I call the police?"

"Wait, we must stay calm. Telling the police will only attract attention, the chances are the press will pick it up. We must not overreact, ignore them for today, and let's hope they stop."

Angela puts down her tablet and picks up the Sunday paper. Her face turns white. "I don't believe this, the *Sunday Sun* is running a feature about 'The Street Girls of London', and there is a picture of me outside a nightclub. I haven't been to The Palace Night Club for years. Tim, do something."

Michael Day is very pleased with himself. He turns the pages of his *Sunday Sun* with a big smile on his face. His campaign to discredit Angela is turning out to be an even greater success than he had hoped.

"Your government contract is assured, Father. Angela is history." He folds the paper open on page three and passes it to his father for approval. "All I did was leak an old picture of Angela talking to a police officer outside The Palace Night Club, and the *Sun* has inserted it into the 'Street Girls of London' feature. It was a no brainer, they are desperate for a filthy story, so I gave them one."

Sir Barnaby, for the first time in years, is pleased with his son. Maybe he has been too hard on him in the past, maybe he should spend more time with him, guiding him and advising him, he has potential. Maybe he should play the part of being a considerate father, instead of a dictator. It would be good if he could give him a place on the board of the company, and that would please his mother; and she, in return, would give him some peace.

Angela is in shock, so am I; I have experienced some dirty tricks in my time, but nothing as disgusting as this. The paper hasn't named her. It just implies that the police officer is arresting the girl, and the girl is clearly Angela. The caption reads: 'Police clearing the streets of London.' The look on her face this morning says it all, she has lost her spirit and her sparkle, and her clothes are drab and colourless. This is the first time I have seen her in a pair of trousers, she knows I dislike women wearing trousers, and Sarah Thompson will not be impressed either.

"What would you like for breakfast, Angie, we could even go out for breakfast if you like?"

"I don't want any breakfast, Tim, and don't call me Angie."

Ups, it's time to back off, the one thing I have learnt is to know when to back off. At the moment, whatever I say is wrong, so I will say nothing, but my brain is spinning. I am convinced the feature and the hate mail are not a coincidence, this is a planned attack, and in my mind, the person at the top of my list, the person with the biggest motive to discredit Angela, is Michael Day. He wasn't expecting a challenge of any kind to his leadership bid, I should have expected something like this. The question is how to silence him, and time is not on our side. It's time to consult with George.

Angela appears from the bedroom for my approval of her appearance. "I know you don't like trousers, and you are probably thinking I have lost the plot." A smile spreads across her face.

"Is this the latest Vogue fashion?" I ask, "I don't think it will catch on with the Chelsea set."

"I take it you do not approve."

"Oh… I approve alright. It's just that if I saw you on the other side of the street, I would not rush across to make mad, passionate love to you."

"Is sex all you men think about?" *I suppose it is really, but I'm not going to admit to it right now.*

"Absolutely not, I quite often think about the weather, the latest sports cars, and even the possibility of me taking up golf." She reaches up and gives me a kiss on the cheek.

"You don't have to go to those lengths. I like you as you are, obsessed or not, now get this Michael Day off my back. Do I have to do everything myself?"

"So you think Michael Day is behind these obscene emails as well, do you?"

"Of course he is, and regarding my 'dull' dress today, I am attending a rally in support of single mothers, so I don't want to project an image of glamour. Come on, Tim, if anyone understands the importance of image, it's you."

What a smart girl, I should never have doubted her.

Angela thumbs through her diary.

"Goodness! The second of those TV debates with Michael and the other three is tomorrow night?"

"Yes, you missed the first one, remember. We all thought you were dead."

"I nearly was."

"Well, you have to be at the television studio at 6:00. I will be there waiting for you, and George is coming as well. Do you want me to write you some answers to the more obvious questions?" She glares at me, with a look of disgust. "I take that to be a no."

"You understand right. I am not reciting a script, I will play it by ear."

In an attempt to lighten the subject, I ask her what she will be wearing.

She leaves without saying a word and slams the door shut behind her. Oh dear, I seem to have upset her. Then, the door opens, and she pops her head around the frame.

"Trousers, dark brown baggy trousers." Then she is gone.

I watch her climb into an equally dull brown Ford Mondeo, hired especially for the protest, she glances back through the window and gives a cheery wave. *Back on track!* I do say the wrong things sometimes, like all men do, but I have survived, and we are still friends. Now, how do I sort out Michael Day?

Good Old George

"Hi Tim, it's George, I have invited 23 women to take tea with Angela. When I explained what she was doing, their support was unbelievable. They all knew of Angela, and when I told them she could possibility become the leader of the Conservative Party and our prime minister, they were excited to say the least. Madam Jacqueline Ellen Rousseau asked if Angela is as beautiful in real life as she is in Vogue or were the pictures of her heavily retouched."

"Who is Madam Jacqueline Ellen Rousseau?" I ask.

"Tim! She is the French president's wife. When she is not at the side of her husband, she is known by her own name. Come on, Tim, you must keep up with these socialites."

"I saw her last night, she was on TV, a very attractive woman; surely, she will not play second fiddle to our English rose."

"To the contrary, she was very positive. Have you written the press releases yet? Angela and I leave on the tour in three days." Having completely forgotten about the tour, I have to make up an excuse.

"George, I have an appointment, can we meet for lunch, and I will run the press release passed you then? And George! Angela is receiving obscene e-mails. Any idea who might be sending them? I would appreciate your thoughts."

"That's an easy one, Tim. Michael Day is your man, or if not him, it will be his father. They have a lot to lose if Michael doesn't win the leadership race."

"He is at the top of my list also, how do we stop him?" George thinks for a minute.

"We will discuss over lunch; see you at Claridges around 2:00."

"I was thinking nearer one o'clock if we are to have lunch."

"Tim, you will be late, you are always late. Forget lunch, I will book a table for two o'clock, and we will take afternoon tea."

George is right, of course. I still have to write the press releases and create a title for the tour. It is essential that the title along with a catchy slogan appeals to the media. I need every minute I can get.

I scribble my first ideas onto my pad. 'Talking links the world together', but I trash that immediately. It isn't slick enough and doesn't have the mass appeal that I want it to have. 'Talking is easy', 'Talk together'; one after another, I write down what is in my head, only to screw them up and dump them in the bin. I need a headline that refers to women talking, with the idea of binding the world together. 'Girls talking together'. Now that has a nice ring to it, I will test it on George.

It is 2:30 before I pull up outside Claridges. I can see George through the window. He is sitting in the corner of the tearoom and already munching on a fruit scone.

"You are late. I couldn't look at these beautiful cakes any longer."

"It's me who should apologies, George." I scan the cakes on the top tier of the solid silver stand. "Which cake do you recommend?" I pass him the press release for him to read and watch his face as his eyes scan down the explanation; I don't get the enthusiastic reaction I was hoping for.

"Do you have a problem with it, George?"

"The title is too long, it needs to be snappier. How about 'Girl Talk' or 'Girls Together'.

I sit back in amazement, "I love it, George. 'Angela's Girl Talk Tour.' You have nailed it, and the slogan will be 'Girl talk links the world together'." George's face lights up, he is very pleased with himself.

"Not that cake, Tim," as I reach for the one coated in marzipan.

"Why not; is it horrible?"

"No, I want it."

"You deserve it, George. You can have it."

We munch our way through two layers of delicate pasties, tarts and cakes, completely ignoring the salmon and cucumber finger sandwiches. George is relaxed, it is time to introduce the subject of Michael Day.

"So George, what are we going to do about these obscene mails?"

"We could have him arrested, but he will deny knowing anything about them and talk his way out."

"And it doesn't clear Angela of being a street girl," I remind him. "Can we discredit his father, revealing what they have to gain by Michael becoming leader?"

"They are not doing anything wrong, Tim, business is business." George is right again as he explains that the other candidates also have business reasons for being nominated.

We sit for three hours, discussing ways of stopping Michael Day. The ideas range from ignoring him to killing him, but by the end of the afternoon, we still do not have a satisfactory answer.

"Angela is on TV tomorrow in the *Big Debate*. Michael Day will make the most of these latest newspaper accusations."

"You are right, George. All we can do is hope the discussion doesn't degenerate to such depravity."

"Politics is a dirty game, Tim, and Michael Day knows every dirty trick in the book. I can guarantee, that depravity will be on the menu."

A Dirty Game

The five candidates are shown to their rostrums. You could cut the air with a knife, the tension is so great. The invited guests have been silenced as the cameras are positioned, and the final sound checks are taken. The mood is set for a battle, for the second in the series of head-to-head debates, hence the title, *The Big Debate.* The other four candidates have been here before. They took part in the first debate on the night that Angela was attacked. They appear to be relaxed and almost enjoying the occasion; Angela is not. The evening will commence with each speaker explaining why they should be the party leader in an allocated four minutes, then it will be an open debate, accepting questions from the audience. In addition to the party members, 15 million viewers are expected to be watching the program.

Gordon Armitage, the Rt Hon. Frederick Brooksbank and Marcus Leopole Uxbearing are received with an air of boredom, each recounting his career history and exaggerating his achievements, even so, they are not very impressive. Michael Day, on the other hand, is a breath of fresh air. He is positive about creating more jobs for the unemployed and giving support to entrepreneurs and small businesses. We have heard most of his rhetoric before, and we didn't believe it then, but at least he is positive and enthusiastic. Angela waits for her turn to speak, shuffling nervously from one foot to the other. She has listened intently to every word the others have spoken, hoping to pick up on something they have said. She looks down at her hand, it is bleeding. She has unknowingly been picking her fingers and grabs a tissue to wrap it around the nail. It is time, it is her time. Whilst Michael Day accepts his applause, she steps forward of her rostrum and smiles at the camera. Her angelic look immediately captures the affection of the people. The studio audience calms after their enigmatic applause for Michael Day and watches as she shifts her weight from one leg to the other. Her eyes say look at me, her body speaks words of confidence; but inside, her stomach is twitching, and her legs are shaking, like jellies.

"I know nothing of politics." She says loudly and clearly, "I know nothing of finance. I know nothing of big business, stocks and shares," she pauses and waits for the audience to stop murmuring agreement.

"But it is not my job to know about these things. I am surrounded and supported by a truly professional and dedicated party of people who the country has voted to represent them, and these men and women do know about these things. What I can bring to the table is an understanding that they possibly have not experienced. I know what it is to be rich, I also know what it is to have nothing, to be living on the street and sleeping under bridges and seaside piers. I know what it is to have hope and be unfairly put down. I know what it is like to have the answer and for nobody to listen to you, but even more important, I know how to overcome and to succeed. I know that every one of you in our party is dedicated to making life better and this country great again, because your needs and dreams are the same as mine. As your leader, we will work together, we will work as a team. I will support you and give you the opportunity to make a mark on history, and history will remember us for what we are and for what we achieve." She takes a breath as a light applause spreads across the audience.

Michael Day cannot understand why the audience is even giving her the time of day. Surely, she has no chance of being voted leader, yes, she is pretty, but that doesn't make you a great leader. He can't restrain his eagerness to embarrass her. He has heard enough, and his respect for the others is zero. It is time to expose them and to reveal what he has learnt and to put them down conclusively. He interrupts, breaking the rules of the program and talks out of turn. His first onslaught is on the three men, ridiculing them for failing to achieve anything of importance during their careers. He throws personal insults at them, announcing that the Rt Hon Frederick Brooksbank's son is in prison for money laundering, and Marcus Leopole Uxbearing's daughter is attending a drug rehabilitation clinic.

"How can these people lead a government when they can't even control their own children?" he shouts at the camera, but he is saving his best for last, he points at Angela. "And as for Angela B, C, D or whatever your name is, please tell us what attributes a street hooker can bring to the position of party leader and prime minister of our country?" He stamps his foot against his rostrum and throws down the crumpled remains of his typed speech in disgust.

Angela is shaken. She didn't expect an outburst of this magnitude. She releases her grip on her rostrum. Her face is expressionless, she has only contempt for this mad man. She wants to scratch his eyes out, but knows self-control is the answer. She must stand firm, think clearly and stay calm. She responds in a soft and delicate voice.

"Thank you for the opportunity to quell the stories which are being circulated about me, but first I would…"

251

Michael shouts her down a second time. "Oh, so you think you have an answer. We can't wait to hear it."

The program anchorman tries to silence the audience; they are fired up at Michael's boastings and rudeness, yet desperate to hear Angela's defence of the stories. The program director screams into his earpiece.

"For God's sake, control the debate, shut Michael up; the debate is turning into a laughing stock."

"Michael, please let Angela answer," he begs him. "You must give the others a chance to speak."

"They have nothing of importance to say," he jeers back at him. The audience erupts again at his rudeness, throwing programs and water bottles onto the stage.

Angela's quiet, gentle voice is all that is needed to silence the crowd. The audience is calm, eager to hear her speak.

"Michael!" She lets go of her rostrum and steps toward the excited studio audience. A microphone on a boom is hurriedly slung into place above her head, so she can be heard. She counts to ten before continuing her story. "Firstly, you have no evidence of what you are trying to discredit me with; and if you do not withdraw the accusations, you will be facing a very expensive law suit. I do admit that there was one time in my life I found myself homeless, but during that year, I gained the understanding of the 7,000,000 people in this country who are homeless today. It also strengthened my determination to help ease the burden for the four million families, who are living on the bread line. As for my name, a cause of concern for you, I was adopted at the age of two by two wonderful people, who have given me a home and all the love I need. I admit I do not know the identity of my real mother, but I do not understand why my parents should be brought into this discussion. Shall we discuss your father and his government business interests here this evening?" Michael shakes his head. "I guess not, but your claim that I make a living from prostitution is something I will strongly defend. I would like to recall an incident that happened one evening last January, the evening of Saturday, 20 January to be precise, which will illustrate exactly why the members of our party should vote for me and not for you."

"This is going to good," Michael jeers. "We are all ears." Angela walks slowly towards him as she recalls the events.

"It was a cold night, and my boyfriend and I were walking home across the marina when we were confronted by a gang of drunken yobs; they were singing, shouting, swearing and swinging, like monkeys, from the lamp-posts as they passed. They were so drunk that even standing was a problem. They tripped repeatedly over the ropes, coiled up along the quay. I recognised these guys from the previous evening when I was walking home alone; they made a pass at me. One was abusive and a bully and he tried to stuff a £50 note down my blouse. He pushed me into one of his mates and then another grabbed me and held me against a wall whilst the first guy started ripping at my blouse. I screamed for help as he slapped me, but no one heard my cries. I kicked out with my heels and luckily landed a hit on his shin. I broke free whilst he was rubbing his leg and ran, leaving him screaming like a hyena. As my boyfriend and I sat talking, one of the men recognised me and shouted, 'Hey, it's that whore from last night. She owes us £50, let's have our money's worth', and he immediately started to run towards us. But as luck would have it, he stumbled over an iron rope ring and rolled over on the quay. His mates dragged him to his feet, then they all chased after us. My boyfriend wanted to make a stand and to fight them, but there was no way he could confront all four, so I kicked off my shoes, grabbed his hand, and we ran for our lives.

We ran around the corner of the quay and lost sight of the yobs for a couple of seconds. This gave us time to hide in a boat anchored at the end of the pier, under a canvass tarpaulin that covered it, we were scared to death. We could hear the men staggering towards us, when they reached the boat, they stopped and shouted to each other, 'Where the hell as she gone?' I really fancied... I believe 'fuck' was the term their leader used; she must be here somewhere? She can't just disappear. One guy called him a randy pig. We could hear them snapping, open more beer cans as they searched up and down the quay. The noisy-one noticed the boat in which we were hiding and jumped down onto the creaking walkway and fell head first into the water. His friends were not very sympathetic. What an idiot, his mate shouted, and the rest burst out laughing and turned to leave him. We were peering out from under the tarpaulin, watching them. He was thrashing about in the water, screaming that he couldn't swim. I don't know why; the water was only three feet deep, anyway; one of the guys came back and pulled him onto the walkway.

With their interest in me totally forgotten, they squeezed into a small car and drove off. I should have called the police and reported them as they were way over the drink limit, but I was so relieved they had gone, all I could do was cry. Now Michael, does this story sound familiar, because it should."

Angela closes the gap and walks right up to him; she stops, short of raising her finger to his face.

"That drunken yob, Michael, was you, and I doubt there is anyone in this country who wants a yob for their prime minister."

The studio falls silent. You could hear a pin drop. The camera pans across the horrified faces of the other contenders, finally focusing on the face of Michael Day.

"This is an outrage. Who is going to believe a whore? I can't believe the BBC is taking this woman seriously." The program director orders the lights to be turned off, and the discussion to be brought to a close.

Sir Barnaby Battersby Codspike wraps his face in his hands. He is ashamed and embarrassed, shaking his head in disbelief. He was looking forward to the debate, confident that Michael would make the others look stupid. He had seated himself in front of his 60-inch TV monitor, lit himself a cigar and positioned his favourite brandy within arm's length. Now the golden liquor is soaking rapidly into the carpet, his cigar is a crumpled mass in his hand, and the monitor screen is blank due to his brandy bottle smashing into it.

Disbelief

Last night's debate is the talk of the city. Angela awoke at five o'clock and right now is being driven from one TV studio to another. She has already been interviewed on a park bench in St James's Park, questioned on a red sofa overlooking the Thames and politely answered some very difficult questions about her personal life whilst strolling along the embankment. The media are relentless in their revelation of her own life and that of Michael Day.

Watching over her is her guardian angel George. He sits close to her in the plush limousine and squeezes her hand, he is so proud of her. *If this girl becomes prime minister, the country will be in good hands. This country needs somebody who can stand up for themselves, who isn't frightened of stating the truth; and most of all, a person who the people love.* Nobody can love her more than George. He wants to tell her how he feels but thinks better of it. Her eyes are twitching, and she keeps frowning. He can feel her fingers tightening, her head must be full of thought.

"What are you thinking about?"

"I am so angry. People like Michael Day should not be allowed on the streets, let alone be leading the country."

"You were amazing last night," George tries to reassure her. "Tim and I spent all afternoon wondering how we could expose him for the disgusting person he is, and we couldn't think what to do in time. You nailed him to the mast in five minutes. When did you know Michael was the idiot on the quay?" Angela's face lights up with that cheeky grin that makes her so appealing.

"I knew when he backed off and stopped attacking me. I sensed a look of recognition of that horrifying night on his face; so I just pursued him until I was sure."

"You mean to say you were bluffing?"

"George, I never bluff, I just tease the situation and in this case... Okay, I admit it, I bluffed, and my bluff paid off." George squeezes her hand.

"You are amazing. I really do have to take good care of you." They sit in silence, both thinking through the events of the past 24 hours.

George is feeling the strain, he prays he has the energy to keep up with her, to protect her and give her the support she deserves. Oh, why has he not taken more care of himself, the amount of alcohol he has poured down his throat during the last five years has been outrageous, and the food he has gorged on can only be described as abusive, but the habit he regrets the most has been the smoking of cigars which he has maintained morning, noon and night. He can feel his blood pumping across his temple. He hasn't slept for 40 hours, and the pain in his chest is sharper than usual. After all, he is 73 years old and five stone overweight. He has never had a reason to take care of himself before, but now he has Angela, and the idea of failing her is of major concern. He makes a promise to himself; from now on, he will only order porridge for breakfast, salad for lunch and completely cut out the after-dinner brandy.

The chauffeur drives the car into the entrance of the 'Good Morning' Studio and Angela jumps out and holds the door open for him; she can see him wilting under the strain.

"Wait in the car for me, George, and rest up for a while. I will be back in 20 minutes."

"No fear, I wouldn't miss this for the world." He hauls himself out.

The announcement of Michael Day pulling out of the leadership race on the 9 o'clock news has thrown the newspapers into panic mode. Headlines are being hurriedly changed, and Westminster is alive with the speculation of Angela becoming the next prime minister. As they head towards the studio reception, a news broadcast team outside intercepts her and bombards her with questions. She is taken by surprise and tries to push her way through. George rushes to her aid.

"Do you feel responsible for Michael Day pulling out of the leadership race?" The presenter shouts at her. Angela grabs the microphone he has thrust into her face.

"The decision was for Michael Day and him alone. If he has realised he is not fit to be party leader, then I respect him for his honesty. Now I have to go, I leave on a world tour tomorrow, in which I will talk with 20 of the most important and influential women of our time. Between us, we hope to bring love and understanding to this troubled planet of ours."

"Who are you meeting?" he asks. "Where are you going?" His list of questions is endless. George steps between them to stop his intimidating onslaught.

"You can read all you need to know in our press release," he shouts at him. "The tour will be on the web at www.angelasgirltalktour, all one word, she hopes you will support her during her campaign, to make this a better world for us all to live in."

Finally, they slump exhausted onto the rear seat of the limousine. The news teams are still hanging on to the car as it pulls out of the TV forecourt, but once on the open road, they leave them behind.

"Enough is enough, Angela, please no more interviews today, let's go home?" George is shaking; she can feel his body trembling as she wraps her arms around him.

"Thank you for rescuing me, George. I had no idea it was going to be as intense as this. Yes, we can go home; that was the last studio call. You must relax, but I have a wardrobe to sort out. Do you think I should wear a trouser suit in India?" George stares deep into her eyes and manages an exhaustive laugh.

"I am not going to tell you what to wear, my love. YOU are the fashion queen."

"You see, George, what I wore used to be the most important thing, but now that people want to hear what I have to say, what I look like doesn't seem to be important anymore."

"You are growing up so very fast, my dear, but at the moment, keep flashing those rags. We need a leader with style and good taste; and don't forget 'Vogue' is your sponsor."

"George, you are a wonder, I couldn't do this without you. If I didn't have you by my side, I just couldn't do it." She slides her hand inside his jacket and squeezes him even tighter before resting her head on his shoulder.

'Angela's Girl Talk Tour'

Out on the airport apron, under the nose of the latest Boeing 777X airliner, Angela steps up to the strategically positioned microphone. She looks up at the enormous Boeing plane towering above her. She hasn't a clue what plane it is, and she doesn't care. She understands that it is the latest thing in comfort and speed, and Boeing will add £50,000 to her campaign fund if she refers to its superior technology.

George is standing at her side to give her moral support as well as protecting her from the photographers, who are more than capable of knocking her over. I am standing to the left of her, out of shot of the cameras. No one knows who I am, and no one bothers to ask. This is the way it has to be; no one must think her campaign is being staged; her natural innocence and sincerity must come through. Anyway, I will not be going on the tour with her; there is too much work for me to do in London. The election is only three days after her return. I have to maintain the momentum of her campaign and make sure she is in the public eye at all times. Every day, the news machine will demand updates; my job is to edit the reports and release the best pictures that illustrate what she is doing, who she is talking to, what is she wearing, and what she is achieving.

I also have to counteract any bad publicity, respond to what the other candidates are saying and answer the many questions that will be asked. I don't expect to get much sleep during the next three weeks, but this is my job, this is what I do, and I am loving it.

"First, I would like to thank Boeing and British Airways for the use of their taxi." She turns and points at the gleaming aircraft towering over her. Everyone laughs at her joke. "My 'Girl Talk Tour' is an innovation that I hope you will all support. It is my intention to bring back the art of conversation. You can keep your texting and messaging, twittering and chattering from your bedrooms and bathrooms, talking to each other face-to-face is much more fun; and fun is desperately lacking from our fast, furious lives. Women have a natural ability to talk. Sometimes it is about nothing; sometimes it is about our children's latest cough or the rising cost of washing powder, but I promise you this, when women are talking to each other, something magical is happening. We create friendships, we develop an understanding, and we cement a bond that no one can pull apart. I believe women hold the secret to how the world can work as one. During my tour, I am going to meet the most influential women in the world, and I am going to meet them in coffee bars, in the back seat of taxis, during shopping expeditions and strolls on the beach. We are going to enjoy natural, honest chats, to explore our similarities and to overcome our differences. I hope this will encourage all women to meet up and talk, to talk with your neighbours; to talk with your new friends that you made on holiday and even to talk with strangers. I am convinced our ability to talk will make the world a better place. Follow me on www.angelasgirltalktour.com and join in the fun."

She steps off the rostrum and heads towards the aircraft, more than 50 cameras from newspapers and TV station are focused on her, recording every step as she climbs the stairs into the airliner. She looks amazing, at the entrance of the super-liner, she pauses, turns and raises her big, floppy-rimmed hat to wave at the millions of people wishing her *bon voyage* across the globe. In her right hand is a simple plastic shopping bag, the type you buy at Tesco or Asda; and she lifts it into the air, so all can read the message printed on it. It says, 'Girl talk is good.' She shouts, "Come on, girls. Let's start talking." Then she disappears inside the aircraft.

George is already at work inside the aircraft. His number one priority is Angela's safety, and this is the first opportunity he has had to brief the ten bodyguards employed for the tour. He has sat them in a semi-circle in the boardroom at the rear of the aircraft.

"The reason for this tour is for Angela to meet with the world's most influential women. Your task would be easy if she was meeting them in the confines of their homes or offices, but she isn't, Angela is meeting them in more natural places. She wants to talk with them whilst they are drinking coffee in a cafe or during a shopping expedition in a mall. She wants people to understand the importance of being friends whilst sharing the good times."

All ten security agents nod their head and say they understand, but George doubts if they do.

"That is impossible," shouts Samuel Ledger, the leader of the squad. "We can't protect her in such open, public places, we need twice as many guards." George waits for the murmurs to cease.

"Yes, you can, and this is how you are going to do it. The press will be given a fictitious location over one mile away from the actual meeting place. Several of you will accompany look-a-like actors to the fake locations, leading the paparazzi and media away. The rest of you will position yourselves discreetly around the real meeting place, drinking coffee or even walking around with a shopping bag if necessary. No one must know who you are, or why you are there. The importance of secrecy is essential which is why you have all been asked to sign the official secrets act."

"Will anyone be filming the meetings?" Samuel asks.

"Yes. Two photographers have been given official clearance to document the meetings. One man is Darren McCaulty, Vogue's leading fashion photographer. He has worked with Angela many times and is responsible for most of her pictures in the magazine. His task is to shoot character studies of her for the magazine. The second photographer is Jamie Coine, I have chosen him for his skill and artistic talent; he has won several awards for his reportage photography. His pictures will focus on the meetings and be released to the international media organisations, appearing in newspapers and on TV news bulletins; both men will be working independently of each other. If necessary, they will hide their cameras in brief cases, under hats and in shoes, so as not to draw attention to the two women.

"Will the meetings be recorded?" Samuel asks, demonstrating an unusual interest in the job.

"We are not going to record the conversations. This will free us from microphones and cables. Does anyone have any more questions?"

Samuel again raises his arm. "When will we have the opportunity to check out the area before the meetings? We need to look for bugs, bombs and snipers?"

"You won't. The security teams of Angela's hosts will be given that responsibility. In fact, you will only be told the actual location five minutes before the meeting takes place."

"I take it you don't trust us." More murmuring from the now uneasy guards.

"I don't see the point of taking unnecessary risks. The fewer people who know, the better. Some people are prepared to do anything to stop this tour and to discredit Angela, and that is only from our perspective. The women she will be meeting will also have many enemies."

The men grumble to each other, but George can't spare the time to listen any longer to them, nor does he have the patience to discuss the plans any further.

"Now enjoy the flight and the tour. It will be fast, furious and fun. George leaves them still moaning amongst themselves, he is exhausted. *This is not the job for a 70-year-old man, what am I doing?* He thinks to himself. His body aches, and the pains in his chest are only too evident. He pops a couple of aspirin into his mouth and rinses them down with a glass of water. He is a changed man; he used to wash them down with a large brandy.

The Secret Is Out

"You are a complete idiot, Michael. I can't believe a son of mine can be so stupid. Will you never grow up?" Michael Day tries to explain the reason for his behaviour that night, but his father is having none of it and continues to insult him.

"Every day, we read how the careers of talented and clever men are ruined because of a slight faux pas. Sometimes it was their failing to resist a bit of nooky, sometimes it was a lie that got out of control, but I never thought for one minute that I might be ruined for just that."

"Father, I am sorry, but it wasn't how you think; anyway, I have taken care of Angela Bee. She will never be leader of the party, she has no chance of becoming prime minister that I can guarantee."

"I don't care a damn about Angela Bloody Bee. All I care about is that submarine contract, and you have put that at risk. No, you have ruined my chances of winning the business, I have spent years working on this contract; I have hosted hundreds of expensive dinner parties, given away millions of pounds on bribes and sweeteners. You know how much I hate having to bow down to people, especially those I have no respect for. Oh! Just get out of my sight; I have had enough of you. Go play with your little girls; you disgust me."

Michael Day is humiliated and ashamed, and for the first time, he has to admit his father is right. He was expecting him to be angry. This isn't the first time he has taken his father's rage on the chin, but his ranting usually ends with him, putting his arm around his shoulder and telling him to do better in the future, but not this time. This time is different, he has never seen his father so angry. Maybe he should leave home and take control of his own career. Even so, there is one person Michael hates more than his father; he sees it as his duty to expose Angela for the hooker that she is. Yes, he was drunk that night on the marina. He admits that what he did was wrong, and he is sorry for that, but he wasn't so drunk as not to recognise a girl who is coming on to him. Angela was definitely touting for business. He might have roughed her up a bit, but isn't that what you do with a hooker? Have a bit of fun, release a few frustrations, fulfil a few dreams, act out a fantasy or two? Angela has ruined his political career, lost his father a multi-billion pound contract and made himself look stupid on TV in front of millions of viewers. Nobody makes Michael Day look stupid and gets away with it. Angela will pay dearly for this.

He picks up the phone.

"Samuel, are you free to talk?"

"Yes, sir, what can I do for you?"

"Have you devised a way of recording Angela's conversations yet? I need evidence that she is a street worker, and there is no stronger evidence than her admitting it; I need to expose her for the hooker that she is?"

"Sir, I am on the plane with the other members of the team right now, and we will arrive at Charles-de-Gaulle Airport in 30 minutes. I have just attended a tour briefing. Apparently, the locations of Angela's meetings will be disclosed only minutes before they happen. I will only know where Angela is going five minutes before her meeting takes place, this doesn't give me time to plant a microphone."

"You have to find a way, Samuel. I am paying you a fortune, make it happen." Samuel can sense Michael's frustration.

"Wait, sir. There is one piece of good news you should know. Angela will be filmed during her meetings, but they are not recording her conversations. This is to give the publicity team freedom to script what they think is appropriate for her campaign." Michael tries to understand the consequence of what Samuel is telling him.

"So, if I understand this correctly, the two women can be talking about shades of lipstick, and the public will be told they are saving the planet."

"Exactly sir, so if we just recorded the conversations, we can at least prove the tour is a fake." Michael suddenly feels a whole lot better.

"Samuel, you must attach a microphone to her somehow, you are right, just record her conversations."

Samuel's next question is how, but by the time he asks for money to purchase specialised recording equipment, he is talking to himself. Not to worry, he will add it to his expenses. Now with a stronger sense of directive, he can action his task in hand; he stretches out on the large leather sofa and positions his arms behind his head, his eyes slowly close. His sense of relief is overwhelming. He already knows how he can achieve this; and as he fades into a deep sleep, he dreams of what he will do with the £200,000 Michael has promised him should he be successful.

Michael's mobile vibes, the incoming call is from the research team he has employed to search Angela's history.

"Mr Day, we have some good news for you. We have the name of Angela's real mother and also the name of the couple who adopted her."

"Do you have proof? Do you have the certificates and signed documentation? I must have proof."

"Yes, sir, we do."

"Then I need to see them straight away."

"Yes, sir, I will be with you in 30 minutes."

Michael starts pacing up and down the lounge in excitement, wondering if he should tell his father the good news. He decides to keep the information to himself, until he is confident the evidence is correct, and even then, it might depend on who her parents are. He knows if he can use this information wisely, he can win back his father's favour.

He reads the certificates spread out on the table before him. He can't believe what he is seeing. Angela's stepfather is the Rt Hon. George Baldwin, now the government secretary of state for works and pensions, the biggest drunkard in the house, and the man accompanying her on the tour. Angela's full name on her adoption papers is Angela Grace Rebecca Louise Baldwin. Her birth mother is Oksana Malvina Smirnov, Michael looks at the researcher.

"What nationality is her mother?"

"Russian, sir, she is from Russia."

"Are you telling me the next prime minister of England could be of Russian descent?"

"Yes, sir, there is no father's name on the birth certificate."

"What do we know about her mother?"

"We have found her immigration papers. She came to Britain from Novosibirsk, a city in the south of the country in 1989. Her occupation reads 'secretary'.

"Nothing very special about that, have you got anything else on her?"

"Yes, sir, we have tracked her national insurance number. From 1990 to 1999, she worked as a temporary secretary in London."

"And?"

"We know the staff agency she was registered with, but we don't know the companies she was assigned to."

"So where is Oksana Malvina Smirnov now?"

"She was killed in a motoring accident on the Kings Road in 2001. She was knocked over by a delivery van which ran out of control and mounted the pavement. Oksana Malvina Smirnov was standing in a queue at a bus stop, she died instantly."

"Are you sure this was an accident? Did the police suspect anything suspicious, could she have been targeted, could she have been murdered?"

"Sir, there is no evidence of an investigation."

"Keep up the good work, see what else you can discover."

"You bet we will, sir."

The Campaign Comes Together

George is wishing he was 50 years younger; he refers to his 20s as 'his good times' years when he was energetic, enthusiastic, handsome and had an answer for everything. He was the political equivalent of a rock star. The media followed him everywhere, he even had a fan club of young women, and a sexual appetite to match. His peers respected him and were envious of his drive and the captivating way he converted people to his views. The city listened to him, and what's more, they believed in him. Common sense was at the core of his decisions, and to be honest, he was kind, thoughtful and generous. He was indeed a nice guy.

He married late. He used to say, "Why should I marry when I can have any woman when I want?" Maybe you agree with his thinking, or maybe you don't, but this was acceptable practice in the 1970s. He eventually married Lady Cordelia Eleanor Lockwood, the daughter of Kenneth Lockwood, one of the most successful entrepreneurs in the leisure industry. He bought a hotel in Scarborough, and after five years, owned a chain of motels called 'Stop Over', ideally located at every service station on the country's motorway network. After this success, he expanded into package holidays, car hire and fast-food restaurants.

Lady Cordelia was a prize amongst roses and totally infatuated by him. He ticked all her boxes, her only regret was having to change her name to Baldwin. Being a Lockwood meant a lot to her, and the thought of becoming a Baldwin did not have the required appeal. She surmounted this enormous obstacle by sticking Baldwin on the end of her original title, becoming Lady Cordelia Eleanor Lockwood Baldwin.

Her biggest disappointment in life was being told she would never bear children. She was devastated and refused to accept it for many years. They tried and tried but to no avail; and over time, this had a negative effect on their relationship. The stress on their physical relationship was immense, with George spending more and more nights in London, staying at first just two nights a week, but then, it increased to three and then to four.

The idea to adopt a baby was a desperate bid to save their marriage; it had always been their dream to have a family and to share the joy of

266

bringing up a child together, so they started the adoption process; but at the time of completion, when they came to signing the papers, George was totally committed to a life in politics, which kept him away from home weeks at a time.

Even to this day, he ponders over his failings, both to his wife and his daughter. Maybe he should have been honest and told Lady Cordelia that he was having an affair, but she would have left him, and that was the last thing he wanted. It was a very short affair and a stupid one come to think of it. At the time it made sense, he was young, virile and in need of gratification. All the MPs had mistresses, it was the thing to do. Anyway, that was many years ago. Lady Cordelia is still by his side, and he has a daughter, even if he has no idea where she is. Money leaves his bank account every month for her maintenance, maybe he should question what happens to it, and where it goes, but to be honest, he is frightened of what he might discover, so he just lets it go. Now Angela has reawakened his fatherly instincts; and by helping her make a success of her life, he feels he has been offered an opportunity to put things right, but really it is to ease his conscience. *And they are both called Angela, what a coincidence.* His mind reflects on what should have been, and his memories strengthen his resolve to protect her and to give her all the support she needs.

It is ten o'clock; he must send today's report of Angela's latest meeting. He collates the photographs of her taking coffee with Madam Jacqueline Ellen Rousseau at the pavement café along the Cour du Commerce-Saint-Andre. He laughs at the shoppers and tourist who are walking past, ignorant as to the identity of the two women taking coffee. Finally, he attaches the photographs to the email, along with a report from Angela, reporting on her conversation. He checks the address and presses 'send'; now he can relax.

I listen to the ten o'clock news headlines, then wait for George's incoming mail. He is five minutes late tonight; it is not like George to be late, but it's not a problem. Angela's report states that Madam Jacqueline Ellen Rousseau is concerned about the failing Euro, the lack of confidence in the currency, and the impact it is having on the French family's shopping basket. She is surprised at her honesty; the French don't usually publicise their concerns. News from France is always positive and projects confidence and success; such is the pride of the French nation. The second part of her report excites me; she goes on to say… "Madam Jacqueline Ellen Rousseau and myself are determined to bring the French and English women together; we believe we should share our problems. We discussed the possibility of promoting the old concept of 'Pen Pals' and to encourage women in both countries to mail each other. If the women of Europe link up and talk with one voice, then our governments will have to listen."

What a great story! I script it out and mail it to Sarah Thompson. She agrees and claims it will work perfectly with the fashion pictures she has received from Darren McCaulty, she sends me the picture she thinks will best illustrate the article. It is a picture of Angela linking arms with Madam Jacqueline Ellen Rousseau, standing on the pavement outside the coffee shop. "Isn't this picture great; the headline we have written is 'Linking together in style and mind'. Do you approve?" I can sense the excitement in her voice.

You bet I approve; I love it when a campaign comes together.

Every evening, George emails me his report of the day; it arrives exactly at 10:05 p.m., directly after the evening's news headlines. On the second day, she met with Celine Suter Von Bos. She is the eldest daughter of the Swedish royal family, and immigration was the subject of concern. Sweden cannot accommodate the thousands of refugees entering Europe. She desperately wants to help these unfortunate people and is convinced there must be other ways. Angela has offered to work with her.

On the third day, she met Fakhriya Aquila Al Sulaiman, a Saudi princess whose ambition is to link the world's religions. Every meeting is pure gold. George is working miracles, he never complains, never admits to being tired and never stops to rest. He praises his security team for a trouble-free tour and for protecting Angela and her guests with the minimal of intrusion. Every day, Angela appears on the front page of the British tabloids, demonstrating how women can work together to solve the problems of the world. If there was a Nobel Prize for promoting friendship, Angela would win it.

The tour has been exhausting. George is relieved this is the last day, the final meeting, the climax of a campaign that has caught the interest of the world. She is meeting Elaina Hicaddie; Elaina is a leading campaigner against human trafficking, especially from her own country in Eastern Europe. Her own younger sister went to work in Germany three years ago with dreams of a better life; she has not been seen or heard of since. She searches relentlessly for her, it is a powerful and compelling story that singularly illustrates the plight of these girls, and the importance of bringing this outrageous trade to a close. George has great hopes of a spectacular finale to the tour.

He picks up his phone to wish her well, but she does not respond. He counts to ten and calls again, still no answer. She should be in her room, waiting for her car, he is concerned and calls her driver.

"Where are you?" he snaps at him.

"Waiting for security clearance, sir."

"Is Angela with you?"

"No, sir, she is in her room."

George throws down the phone and goes running towards the elevator. He knows something is wrong. He feels it in his bones, the door to her hotel suite is open.

"Angela, are you ready?" He doesn't wait for an answer but bursts through the door and scans the lounge, there is no sign of her. Yes, she was here only minutes earlier. Her coat is on the coffee table, waiting to go, the coffee in the cup is still warm. Maybe she is in the bathroom. He knocks on the door; there is definitely someone in there. "Hi Angela, its George, are you ready?" Nothing, he gets no response; so in desperation, he smashes the door open to see Samuel, his chief security officer, standing in front of the washbasin mirror. In his hand is Angela's make-up case, which he appears to be going through. Taken by surprise by George's violent intrusion, he spills its contents onto the floor. The bathroom is a shambles, towels have been discarded onto the base of the shower enclosure, and paper tissues are scattered everywhere.

"What are you doing in here, Samuel, where is Angela?"

"Hello George." He immediately regains his composure. "She has just slipped down to the laundry, what is all the fuss about?"

"She should be in the car by now, why is she late?"

"She spilt on her dress and has taken it to the laundry. The hotel offered to remove the stain. She will be back in a minute."

"So what are you doing in her apartment, what are you doing in her bathroom, you don't have permission to access Angela's suite?" George's first thought is that he and Angela have spent the night together; he prays this is not the case.

"I'm just checking her room, sir, giving it the once over, it is on the general security schedule." George is puzzled, this is the first time he has heard of this.

Angela rushes in clutching her dress.

"Hi'y George, is it time to go?"

"I was worried about you. I called, and you didn't answer."

"I spilt on my dress, so I took it to the hotel laundry, see! They have cleaned it for me, can you zip me up?" She slips the dress over her head and lets it slide down her body. "Come on George, I won't bite you." George hesitantly fingers the fastener above her hips and eases the zip up her back. He watches as the dress tightens and grips her body. He has to admire the smoothness of her flesh, and her perfume is a treat.

"What do you think, George, do I look good or what?"

"Yes!" he admits, "You look good. What is Samuel doing here?"

"He came to check my room." She turns to him for confirmation, but he has gone.

"Where is he; where has he gone?"

"He left a minute ago, did you not see him go."

"No, I was concentrating on your zip. When I arrived, he was in your bathroom."

"My bathroom, what was he doing in there?"

"Would you believe he was going through your make up case?" Angela looks in at the trashed bathroom.

"Why is my make-up bag on the floor?"

"Why is your bathroom in such a mess?" Angela looks cheapish.

"Errr, that is my fault, I was in a hurry." She pauses. "But I wouldn't leave my make-up bag on the floor, that is far too important to me."

"He dropped it when I burst in on him."

"That's strange. If he wanted to borrow my lipstick, all he had to do was ask." She laughs at her own joke.

"This is not a laughing matter, Angela. Show me your make-up bag."

They both stare down at the brightly flowered bag, and its scattering of lipsticks and brushes, tweezers and girly things.

"What is this, George?" Angela picks up a small, black circular object, similar to a watch battery. "This does not belong to me." George knows immediately what it is.

"It's a bug, it's a bloody microphone, it will pick up everything you say, it is probably picking up what we are saying right now, but why is it in your make-up bag?"

"This bag goes with me everywhere. I might change my clothes, I might change my watch or my handbag, but I only have one make-up bag."

George comes out in a cold sweat.

"It looks as if we have a spy on the team. Samuel says he was doing a security search, he could have been checking for bugs, that is his job, or he could have been planting it?"

"Could Samuel be a spy?" Angela asks nervously.

"Go and enjoy your meeting with Elaina Hicaddie, she is an amazing woman, but watch what you say. There might be more of these things about, they could be clipped to your dress, hidden in your shoes, in the car or under the table. Don't talk about yourself, don't promise anything, and don't give anything away. I am going to find Samuel."

Worst Fears Realised

George is furious, angry with himself for not checking the sincerity of the people he has employed. He took it for granted they applied for the job because they wanted to help. He goes in search of Samuel. It is essential that he discovers the truth, but Samuel has left the hotel. He is already in position with his team around the Domino Café.

The security team is discreetly hidden in the Rynek Starego Miastaon (Market Square to you and me), and Samuel is amongst them somewhere. The Domino Café is located outside the Adam Mickiewicza Museum of Literature; a popular tourist square in the heart of the old town. The museum was chosen for the rendezvous because it represents education, history and culture. It is also a reminder that human slavery is part of our past and plays no part in the future. George's promise to protect Angela has suddenly taken on a new dimension, as from this morning, he trusts no one, especially the people who he has employed to care for her. As his car weaves in and out of Warsaw's rush hour traffic, he calls me.

"Tim, it's George, sorry to call you so early." The Wi-Fi connection in the speeding limousine is definitely deficient; he is barely audible.

"George, it is 4:30 in the morning, speak up, you are breaking up?"

"Tim, I caught Samuel, the head of the security team, planting a bug in Angela's make-up bag. We can only assume that everything she has ever said has been recorded. God knows why he is doing this, and who he is working for." It takes me some time to understand what George is telling me.

"We must find out who it is George. They will use the recordings against her. Are you sure Samuel is a spy?"

"Well, I didn't actually see him put the bug into her make-up bag, but if he didn't, he knew it was there, and he knows who did. What can I do, Tim?"

"Where is Samuel now?"

"Out with the team, in the market square."

"Are we confident that he is the only security agent involved in this deceit." George freezes; it never entered his head that Samuel will have accomplices.

"Tim, I can't guarantee that. He could be working with one, two or more of the team, goodness, they could all be in on it. Oh Tim, I am so tired, I am not thinking clearly. I have failed her; I am so sorry."

"Hey George, stop talking like that, you have done an amazing job. Have you told her about Samuel, does she know she has to be careful what she says?"

"Yes."

"Just keep her safe and get her back to England tomorrow morning. If Samuel comes back on the same plane, which I doubt, I will have him arrested at Heathrow for breaking the official secrets act. We will soon know who he is working for. Just get her home safely, George." The phone connection finally breaks down. George does not respond. *I should be there with George; he is too old to be chasing around after international criminals.*

Michael Day is sitting in his office, working at his computer. It is nine o'clock London time, and he is listening in on Angela's conversation, as he has done every morning this week. His phone vibes, there is a text from Samuel. 'Bug in bag found, mobile bug still active. I will need your help to get back into England.' Michael reads the text again to make sure he understands it correctly. The bug in her make-up bag was the inspiration of a truly professional spy and attaching a second bug to her mobile phone equally innovative. All women change their clothes regularly, their handbags, their shoes, but never their make-up bag and never ever their mobile phone. These two items will go with her wherever she goes. Michael laughs to himself, *Samuel is a true professional but apparently not as bright as I first thought. The idiot will have to get himself into England, I'm not getting involved with immigration and the police.* Anyway, he now understands why the sound quality this morning is not as clear as the previous times. He turns the volume up on his computer. He has high hopes of Angela admitting she was on the game and proving he was right in his assessment of her intention that night. He sits back in his office chair, adjusts his headphones and listens intently to Angela ordering a coffee 2,000 miles away. Elaina Hicaddie has not yet arrived.

Who Can You Trust

Elaina's late arrival is causing concern; George glances at his watch. From his position opposite the museum, he can see every corner of the square. He tries to identify the people standing around. Ten don't appear to have a purpose for being here at all, they could be members of Elaina's security team, they could be plain-clothed police, they are probably office workers who have taken time out to have a smoke or just to enjoy the morning air. All he can do is wait; he glances at his watch again. *The sooner this meeting is over, the sooner I can get her back to Britain, and the happier I will be. Come on, George, you old bugger; stay alert.* He knows his mind is wandering. He must stay focused, but he is tired and worried and doesn't know if he can trust Samuel or not. The tables of the Domino Café are arranged in a semi-circle around the front of the shop. He counts 24 tables in all, all elegantly prepared for breakfast; and the tablecloths are all embroidered around their edge, with the word DOMINO, both for branding purposes and to signify possession. Angela is sitting at a table in the centre of the arrangement. She is a bright kid, by sitting in the centre, she has given herself a clear view of anyone approaching her. Samuel is sitting three tables away from her; she keeps glancing at him, throwing him an occasion smile to disguise the fact that she no longer trusts him.

She recalls the moment she opened the door and he stepped into her room, knocking the vase of flowers on her table to the floor and spilling the green, slimy water down her dress. It appeared to be an accident, but then again, he could have done it deliberately to get her out of the apartment. No! It must have been an accident; he was so apologetic and even offered to take her dress to the laundry for her. Thinking about it now, she should have accepted his offer, but she wanted to make sure her dress was cleaned according to the instructions. It is a designer dress, and she is very fond of it, so she had good cause to take it herself. Maybe she shouldn't have left Samuel in her apartment, but if she were to trust anyone, it should be her chief security guard.

George said he found him in the bathroom, with his hand inside her make-up case; surely Samuel is not to be trusted. She too glances at her watch. It is 10:18, her meeting was scheduled for ten. She wonders if she is mistaken and reaches into her handbag, looking for her mobile, maybe she has received a message changing the time. There is no such message, so she pulls out a lipstick and runs it around her mouth. A girl must look beautiful at all times. *Why is Elaina so late?*

Samuel returns Angela's smile and lifts a cold mocha to his lips. George watches his every move and wonders why he keeps scratching his ear? Two members of his security team are within earshot; one is hiding in a doorway to the left of the café, and the other is leaning against the wall of the museum. Seated at a table on the periphery of Cafe Domino are Carol and Toni, the only two women members of the security team. Their job is to stay with Angela should she go where men are not permitted. George tries to assess the relationship each team member has with Samuel. Is he working alone, and if not, which one of them is working with him? It is difficult to tell, there is no visible communication between them, but why should there be. These guys are experienced undercover agents.

There is a flurry of activity in the far corner of the square, and from out of the shadow, a group of women wearing girlie dresses totter in high-heeled shoes. They are grouped around a tall, mature woman, with a stiff walk and dominant nature, yet for her age, which must be 50, she is quite attractive. She could be the head mistress of a girl's school or a town councillor. She marches up to the tables and instructs the waiter to clear path for her, through the chairs to Angela. He hurriedly pushes tables out of her way.

"Angela, I am pleased to meet you." The other girls with her occupy two of the other tables, sitting in pairs, two at each table.

"Good morning, Elaina, may I call you Elaina?" asks Angela slightly intimidated by her bold introduction.

"Of course, you must, this is a friendly natter between friends, isn't it, do you say 'natter' in London?"

"I believe it is more a term from the north of England rather than from London, but it is recognised as a friendly conversation."

"Perfect, let's natter." She giggles; Angela also laughs. Through Elaina's professional persona, Angela can spot a gentler woman. In there, somewhere, she believes is a caring, fun loving woman.

Darren McCaulty is lining up his first picture of the day. Elaina's immaculate dark suit and starched white blouse looks perfect amongst the regimental arrangement of white table clothes. His only concern when he peers into the lens is Elaina being considerably taller than Angela. There is a danger she will dominate the pose, and this must not happen. He repositions his camera, bringing Angela slightly forward of Elaina, making the two the same height in the composition. He is a true professional. Jamie Coine is also working wonders, silently and as discreetly as possible, he too is moving around the two of them. He wants to position the museum behind them, the museum is an important prop to the story he has to illustrate… the story of two women creating a better future and putting right the mistakes of the past. George watches his team at work, he is impressed. What a shame Samuel has thrown doubt on their commitment.

Angela has a list of questions she wants to ask Elaina. She wants to understand why Polish girls are so desperate to leave their homes, and why they choose Europe. She knows only too well how difficult life is in the west, and how dangerous it can be. The two of them get on famously. George can see them smiling at each other, their body gestures are relaxed, and they touch one another regularly. They are obviously enjoying the moment.

"So why do girls want to go to Western Europe? What is there in France, Berlin and London that they don't have here in Poland?" Elaina looks around the square.

"Our girls are attracted by promises of equal opportunity, respect and freedom, especially freedom. I estimate over a thousand girls every week are leaving for Western Europe." Angela is alarmed at the numbers involved.

"I am confused." Angela leans closer, so no one else can hear. "These girls listen to TV reports, they have internet access, they must read about the slave trade in newspapers and magazines and know what could happen to them, yet they still subject themselves to the risks?" Elaina laughs.

"I have to admit; it doesn't reflect well on the education of our girls. You see, Angela. All they have is hope, a dream of a career, a kind husband to have kids with, safety, security and money to have fun with."

"Who are the men, the girls are willing to go with?"

"Not always men and not always gangsters, this is a social problem. Some are popular business men, city councillors and even police officers, some are relatives, uncles and brothers; and sometimes, sometimes Angela, they are their own parents who need money and are willing to sell their daughters, yes, even the people they love and trust are responsible."

"That is so sad, what can we do to help these girls?"

"I am running an agency to protect them. We act as a clearing house and check out the men the girls are involved with. We check the promises they have been offered, and the legitimacy of their employment and destination."

"And if you find the girls to be in danger?"

"We tell them, but still they go, their need is so great."

Angela sits back and orders another coffee from the waiter, "Shall we have a chocolate croissant this time?" Elaina nods in agreement.

"Elaina, I believe you advertise safe routes and employment for girls in most of the capitals of Europe, you actually place the girls in jobs yourself."

"That is correct. We have contracts to supply several international hotels, health services and travel companies with girls. These are places we know the girls are safe, and they will get the opportunity to achieve their dream."

"Mm! I am not totally in favour of you flooding our cities with Polish girls. In the UK, we have a policy of immigration selectivity, but if what you are doing is keeping these girls out of the sex trade, then I wish you well."

Elaina turns and points towards the four girls who came with her.

"I have brought four girls with me. I was hoping you would speak with them. It might help you understand their plight."

"Can they speak English?"

"Well enough."

"OK, call them over."

George can see the four girls joining Elaina and Angela, but his attention is focused on Samuel. Why does he keep scratching his ear, is he adjusting a hearing aid, could he have planted more than one bug and still be recording their conversation?

This is exactly what Samuel is doing. He slipped a second listening device into the cover of Angela's mobile; and at this moment, he can't believe his luck; she has placed her handbag on the table in front of herself. It is so close, he can clearly hear everything they say. The microphone is working perfectly, and through a booster in his pocket, he is transmitting the conversation via satellite live to Michael Day in London.

Michael is scribbling instructions on a note pad as he listens: 'Check out Elaina Hicaddie's safe route agency – find which companies she is working with – trace the girls she has helped – discover what these girls are doing now?' In the devious mind of Michael Day, Elaina's business sounds like a scam. Elaina Hicaddie could be the biggest human trafficker of them all. He smiles to himself, *and Angela is helping her, this could be too good to be true.*

Elaina shifts the conversation back to Angela. "I believe you have spent some time living on the streets of London, Angela. You managed to sidestep the issue on the Grand Debate. I was watching the program on satellite, so you will be sympathetic to the danger my girls can find themselves in."

"I did a trick a two," she admits, "but only with respectable men. In fact, only with men I found attractive. I never classed myself as being on the game."

The waiter arrives with fresh coffee and two warm croissants. To place them on the table, Angela removes her handbag and places it between her feet on the floor.

"Damn!" Samuel sits up as his earpiece falls silent. He definitely thinks Angela's phrase 'a trick or two' is proof of her being on the game. He is desperate to restore contact; he mustn't miss this conversation. In panic mode, all he can think of doing is to call Angela on her mobile. Hopefully she will pick up her handbag to answer it and place her bag back on top of the table. He turns away from her, so she can't see him dialling. There is a delay as the call is diverted via the UK; he waits for what seems an eternity.

Elaina introduces the four girls; they are excited and giggly. "This is Nikola, Katarzyna, Dagmara, Justyna; and this is Angela from England. She would like to help you get into England."

"That isn't quite right," Angela, corrects her, "I am sympathetic to their problem, but I can't get them into my country."

"They will tell you more if they think you can help them, don't worry, darling." Elaina pats her on the knee, so Angela lets the statement drop. She is more concerned about a group of men who have occupied several tables nearby. She feels uneasy. She doesn't know why, but they are lurking, yes, lurking would be a good description of their presence. They have positioned themselves far too close. George is also concerned. Why isn't Samuel moving them away?

"Who are these men sitting around us, do you know them?" Angela whispers to Elaina.

"Which men?" Elaina turns and looks at each one in turn, "These men are the carers of the girls. They watch over the girls, day and night. They are part of the gang who will eventually ship the girls out to selected destinations."

Angela is seriously concerned but manages to smile at the girls.

"Are these men with you?" Dagmara answers.

"Yes, they stay close to us all the time. We are frightened of them, we are like prisoners."

"Why?"

"We signed a paper, agreeing they can take us to Germany. Now they say we belong to them as they have invested money in fares and accommodation. They promised to make us rich."

"Do you want to go to Germany?"

"Yes, but not with these men, we want to go with Elaina."

"Can you get the girls employment in Germany?" Elaina looks unsure.

"Yes, we have a choice of jobs in both tourism and health."

"So what is the problem?"

"These men will not release them. They will follow them every minute of the day, kidnap them and sell them to local gangs who will put them to work on the streets."

"Does this happen all the time?"

"Not every time, but we have lost three hundred girls, they just disappear. Their employers call and ask us why they have not turned in for work, and that is the last we hear of them."

Angela jumps to her feet as the table is suddenly engulfed in smoke. Within seconds, flames are bursting from her handbag between her feet. The hem of her dress catches fire, and her tights crinkle with the heat. The cafe erupts as people run in panic. Carol and Toni rush to her aid and pull her clear of the table and into her waiting car. Elaina runs down the colonnade outside the museum to escape from the square. The other four girls are nowhere to be seen; nor are the men who were sitting around them. After ten minutes of chaos, all that remains of the scare are three burnt tables, two charred chocolate croissants and a group of seated tourists still waiting for their breakfast and wondering what happened. Oh yes! And Samuel, he is sitting at his table, in shock, holding his mobile to his ear.

George walks over and sits next to him. "I'm arresting you for the attempted murder of Angela. Anything you say will be taken down and possibly used in evidence against you."

Samuel gives him a look of contempt. "You have no authority to arrest me in Poland. Anyway, I haven't done anything, I was just drinking coffee."

"Who are you working for Samuel?" Samuel turns towards the burning handbag and stares in disbelief at the wrecked cafe.

"I am working for you, you stupid old man. I found a bug in Angela's make-up bag this morning. I wanted to tell you, but you didn't give me time?"

"Old I might be, but I am not stupid. You placed the bug in Angela's make-up bag, and I am guessing you placed another in her handbag. Give me your mobile."

"Why?" George snatches the phone out of his hand.

"Because you phoned Angela just as her bag exploded, I was watching you. See, the call is in your phones memory." He holds up the phone to show Samuel the proof. You used your phone to explode a device in her handbag. When the boys in the laboratory have finished their investigation, they will tell us exactly what you did." George calls two of the security team over and orders them to escort Samuel back to the hotel and to hold him there. "Stay with him all day and night and make sure he is on the plane to London in the morning. Once in England, we will hand him over to the British Secret Service at Heathrow."

George is interrupted by the arrival of the local police in a siren-screeching police car. It's time for him to make a sharp exit. No one was hurt, so no one needs to know the truth as to what really happened. This is an English incident which he will solve.

Accidents Do Happen

Back in London, my time is spent promoting Angela's tour success, and I must confess I am enjoying every minute of it. I must have written 100 features and as many news bulletins. Selecting the photographs is great fun and responding to political and personal attacks an interesting challenge. Yet the most enjoyable part of the job is making life as difficult as possible for the other nominees by asking them questions and demanding answer to their more outrageous promises.

My greatest achievement is the massive success of Angela's new social media app, which I have called 'Girltalk'. It's an app, which connects women from all over the globe, enabling them to share problems and discuss solutions. The idea is not original; in the 1950s, school children were encouraged to write to their counterparts in other countries to increase their understanding of each other's lives to heal Europe after WWII. Thousands of schools in England and Europe linked their students with kids in other schools. It wasn't long before they were visiting each other and experiencing different cultures and traditions. 'Girltalk' already has over 50,000 subscribers, and it is only two days old.

My phone vibes, it's George and he sounds stressed. "First let me tell you everything is okay," he announces. "But the meeting with Elaina Hicaddie turned out to be a disaster."

I tremble as he recalls the events of the Adam Mickiewicza Museum meeting, when I hear how near to death Angela was; I wonder if we are doing the right thing.

"Have we any idea what exploded, did Samuel detonate a bomb in her bag?" George laughs for the first time this morning.

"Excuse my mirth, Tim! I have just been handed the laboratory findings of her handbag. You won't believe this. Apparently a second bug was attached to the back of Angela's mobile phone, which was in her handbag. Samuel was listening to her conversation, and I presume recording it, but when the waiter brought her breakfast she removed her handbag off the table and placed it between her feet. Now on the floor, the microphone in her bag could no longer pick up their conversation, so Samuel dialled her mobile, hoping she would pick it up and place the bag back on the table. As soon as his call connected and activated her phone, it short-circuited across to the bug and burst into flames. A scarf in her bag then ignited, causing the plume of smoke, the burning scarf made it appear much worse than it was. Samuel must have been more surprised than Angela, and that explains why he was in shock when I approached him.

"Stupid idiot, the man is a buffoon."

"So, it looks like an accident. I doubt you will get attempted murder to stick."

"We will arrest him for breaking the official secrets act. Try to keep the incident away from the world press George?"

"It is already in the local press, but hopefully, the world press will not see it as a major incident."

"Is Angela okay, are her legs badly burnt?"

"No, just reddened, they are still beautiful. Will you be at the airport to meet us tomorrow, Tim?"

"You bet."

The Game Is Up

Michael Day can't wait to put pen to paper; his report for the *Sunday Sun* is practically finished. Barry Tomlinson the editor and close friend of Michael is waiting for it with anticipation. They have been friends since junior school but more important, he was one of the guys on the marina that fateful evening. He didn't participate in the manhandling of Angela, but he did nothing to protect her either. He could have restrained Michael, but to be honest, he was enjoying it.

"This is a mind-blowing story, Barry." Michael exaggerates its importance, in an attempt to persuade his friend to give it headline status. "It will be a coup for you and your paper. To reveal the truth about Angela, you will be saving the country from making the biggest political mistake since Blair took us into a war with Iraq."

"That's big, Michael. Can you finish it before lunch?"

"I can, but I need big bucks for it. Dad has thrown me out again, I need every penny I can get?"

"I will tell you what I think it is worth when I have read it, but I can offer thousands if it lives up to expectation."

"It will."

"OK, I can hold page three until lunchtime, I'll look forward to reading it." Michael puts down the phone and continues to embellish the story; he can't believe how the evidence against Angela is structuring into such a compelling read. After a further two hours, with a flurry of exclamation marks, he sends the final draft to Barry. He also CCs it to his father and to put the final blade into Angela's back, he sends a copy to George with the subject title, 'The game is up.'

George receives it in disbelief. He struggles to open the top right hand drawer of his desk to find a packet of aspirin. The pain in his chest is severe, the worst he has experienced. Stress is his worst enemy, and he has never found a way to combat it. *How on earth has this story got out? I was so careful to keep the facts hidden; and now, only six months before my retirement, I have been exposed?* He grabs for the gin bottle on the mantelpiece and pours out his pacifier, filling the glass to the brim and swallows it in one gulp. If he were a young man, he would go around to Michael Day and beat the living daylights out of him, oh God!

If only he was a young man again. This story will kill him. It will destroy his wife and ruin Angela's chance of becoming prime minister.

"Tim, I have to see you immediately, we are in trouble." He puts the phone down and reaches again for the gin bottle. Something stops him, it could be his conscience, it could be his sense of guilt. He doesn't know what it is; it could be the remaining remnants of his determination never to give up, to keep fighting to the bitter end whatever the cost. In his prime, his vigour saw him through; he remembers the days when he was afraid of nothing or no one. If he had a problem, he didn't dwell on it, he sorted it out there and then. If someone spoke against him, he would retaliate and hit back at them. His chest tightens, and he has to steady himself against the fire surround. The pins and needles in his arms and legs are warning him to ease up, they are reminding him that he is no longer a young man, and this is too much for him: retire, go home, give in... he looks down at the dirty, grey fire-grate; he has never seen a fire flicker in it. Since he moved into this office years ago, it has always laid there; dark and cold and covered in soot. He prods the crumpled sheets of paper scattered in it; he remembers what they are, he once wrote his own speech and threw it away in disgust; admitting it was rubbish. The front rails of the enormous surround are covered in dust, an old cast iron poker is sticking through them. He kneels beside it and tears a couple of pages from his newspaper, rolls them up, loops them into a knot and arranges them around the grate. Inside the brass coal scuttle, used to carry coal from the porter's room at the end of the corridor he finds a box of matches. The matches must be over 40 years old. He picks up the box and pushes his finger into the side; and a drawer slides out from the other end, giving him access to five matches. A picture of Mr Punch doing the splits is still visible on the lid and it makes him smile. Punch matches, it says in big letters, 2d, contains 40 matches. He shakes a match out and rubs the pink phosphorous tip against the roughened strike plate along the side of the box; the match sparks into life. He stares at it for a second as it flickers in the draught coming down the chimney and watches it slowly burn down the stick. In a hypnotic trance, he watches it burn closer and closer to his fingers.

"Ouch, bloody hell!" he lets out a yell and lets it fall on top of the rolled up newspaper. The insignificant, delicate flame grows stronger; and within a minute, the grate is full of life and light, alive again after all these years, bringing life to the room, giving a friendly, comforting warmth. George raises his hands to the flames to feel the warmth, *how nice that is*.

"What the hell are you doing, George, remembering the good old days?" He laughs as I walk into his office.

"Come in, Tim, isn't that a beautiful thing. Feel the energy, feel the warmth, see how bright the room has become."

"Yes, it is a beautiful thing. I remember when my father lit the fire every morning before he went to work. By the time my brother and sister and I were dressed for school, the fire was always blazing brightly. It was the centre of our home. We ate our cornflakes around it, we did our homework in front of it; and in the evening, we watched TV and warmed our feet on it. They were happy days. Now what is this problem we have?"

George smiles. "We don't have a problem, Tim, we just have another challenge. I would like your thoughts on how we put this bastard Michael Day to bed."

"Those are attacking words, George. Are you ready for a fight?"

"You bet your life I am."

"Then, tell me all about it and let's make it happen." George relaxes, he can feel his blood pressure coming down and use of his legs returning. He watches the paper burn, curl and disappear up the chimney. He feels inspired, even invigorated by its energy.

"OK, Tim, it's like this, are you sitting comfortably?"

"Yes, I am."

"Then, I will begin."

Tomorrow, the Start of Another Day

George's story is unbelievable to say the least. I agree Michael Day's article must be silenced. The result of the leadership poll will be announced next Monday, six working days from now. The *Sunday Sun* will run Michael's article this Friday, that means we have to stop it going to press today. On Thursday evening at 7:30, Angela will make her final bid for the leadership. This will be the speech of her life, given in front of 329 Conservative MPs. TV companies will simultaneously broadcast her presentation to 65 million people, everyone in the UK will be listening. In the meantime, Angela has three TV interviews, 12 charity meetings, and a journey of 500 miles in order to visit ten areas of the WI the women's institute, these women are the foundation of her support. She is their patron and hero.

"Are you ready for a busy seven days, George?"

"You bet."

"Then let's kick start tomorrow now."

"I have been thinking about this feature by Michael Day." A smile crosses George's face as he speaks.

"Your face tells me you have a solution, are you going to drown him in the marina?"

George laughs, "I would like to. In fact, I am not going to do anything. I am going to let his father, Sir Barnaby Battersby Codspike do it." Now it is my turn to laugh.

"I'm sorry for my mirth, George, but that name always makes me smile."

"Sir Barnaby wants the government's nuclear submarine contract. He has placed a very competitive bid, and the government is under pressure to buy British. The chances are his tender will win, but I intend to put an element of doubt in his mind. I will warn him if Michael's article appears, he can say bye, bye to this and to future contracts. What do you think?"

"Brilliant, when can you action it?"

"I am meeting him for dinner, this evening, just the two of us."

"Wow! That is leaving it a bit late. Are you convinced you can pull it off?"

"Tim, there are three decision makers on the nation's defence committee, and I am one of them. I can pull it off."

George never fails to amaze me. "It's called politics, Tim. You stick to advertising, leave the politics to me."

"OK, I will work with Angela for the next five days. Keep in touch, stay close."

"Will do."

To say the least, the establishment is against Angela winning the vote. A pretty, glamorous woman standing outside number ten has never been heard of. It is unimaginable in their eyes. Does this stem from the 1950s when a blond with long legs was expected to be dumb? Or has the old sexist joke stuck: to impress a pretty girl, compliment her intelligence, if she is intelligent, then tell her she is beautiful. There is one fact that we cannot deny; there has never been a beautiful, smart, sexy woman in the British government. I cannot believe that all intelligent, caring women are incapable of expressing feminism and looking pretty. As Angela's marketing guru, do I encourage her to dress down and look plain? I look towards America for inspiration; in the middle of the presidential election, I notice that Hilary Clinton is wearing the most appalling trouser suits, straight out of a catalogue. Donald Trump surrounds himself with the most glamorous women on the planet. It does appear that beauty is being accepted into politics.

Angela is beautiful, she is also young, and she admits to knowing nothing about world affairs or even British political etiquette. On the positive side, she is in touch with the people, she has massive appeal and an enormous following. The opinion polls are stating that 15 million people openly support her, and that number is split 2 to 1 in favour of women. This isn't bad, in other words, five million men are also supporting her. My next consideration is the immediate poll. Angela has to persuade 329 straight-thinking, narrowly focussed politicians that she is the right person to lead them. The word 'help' springs to mind.

I have to discuss the dilemma with Angela, finding the right time is not easy.

"Are you awake?" I shake her and try to roll her over towards me.

"No!"

"I have to discuss something with you."

"I said no, I am fast asleep."

"It's about what you are going to wear in parliament." She opens one eye. "What am I going to wear in parliament?"

"That's what I am asking you."

"Something short, sharp and hot," she snaps at me.

"You don't fancy wearing something more subdued, something more politically polite?"

"No!"

"Oh."

"Why?"

"I just thought you should kill the glamour a bit, you know, take life a little bit more seriously."

"I am what I am; and they either love me or hate me, right."

"Right. Do you love me?"

She opens both eyes, and a big smile spreads across her face, she looks amazing. "Of course I do, you know I do."

"Do you fancy a...?"

"No." Finding the right time has always been difficult.

A Little Persuasion Will Do the Trick

Sir Barnaby Battersby Codspike feels at home in the Carlton Club. He can relax here and does so with a port and lemon. The waiter always mixes his favourite tipple as soon as he walks in. He collapses in his personal armchair and gives out a big sigh.

"Are you staying for dinner this evening, sir?" asks the Lord of the tables. The waiter was awarded this title some 20 years ago, when the members realised he was in fact a miracle worker. He would always find them a table, serve them a drink before they asked for it and fluff up the cushions in their favourite chairs. Now he runs the club, he is front of house, waiter, chef, caretaker and friend. The exclusivity of the men's club would cease to exist if it wasn't for him.

"Has old George arrived yet, we are dining together."

"Mr George has just this minute arrived, sir. Shall I show him over?"

"Yes, and have his tipple at the ready, the poor bastard has had a bad day." George and Sir Barnaby are old sparring partners. There is no love lost between them, but they have a lot of respect for each other.

"Come and put your weight down next to me, George. The lord is bringing your tipple. Are you losing weight, have you joined a gym or something?" George laughs.

"I have been running around the world after a 22-year-old girl, I am exhausted."

"I hope you caught her. Did you remember what to do with her when you caught her?"

"It wasn't like that. I have been mentoring Angela Bee. A bloody amazing girl, I'll introduce you sometime."

With the introductory pleasantries out of the way, George goes straight to the core of the meeting. "Now what are we going to do about this ridiculous article your boy has sent to the *Sunday Sun*?"

"Nothing to do with me, old boy, he is a man now. I have no influence over him, he has left home. He must stand on his own legs and make his own bed."

"He might be a man, Barnaby, but isn't it time he grew up. He is an embarrassment to you and a danger to your company."

"It appears he is a bigger danger to you, is that article correct? If so, the country has a right to know the truth."

"Of course it's not correct, but at this moment in time, I do not have the time or the inclination to deal with him, so I was hoping you could persuade him to withdraw it."

"I doubt it. It's going in Sunday's edition, it's Thursday today. It will be in print by now. Shall I order dinner, do you prefer chicken or salmon?"

"Beef for me. What is this poncey food you keep eating."

"One salmon and one roast beef and another round of drinks please, Lord."

"Yes, sir, with starters and sweet?"

"Of course."

"Your usual table is ready, gentlemen. Make yourself at home."

"Come on, George, let's eat." They grab their glasses and shuffle over to the table next to the bay window; Sir Barnaby likes watching the city girls as they walk past. "They just keep getting prettier, don't you agree, George."

"I can see where your Michael gets it from. Now Barnaby, about your tender for the submarine contract, I have some bad news for you. The French company UNMO has come in 60 million less, that is going to take some shaking off." Barnaby places his drink slowly back onto the table.

"George, I have to win that contract, you know you can trust my company to deliver on time and to deliver on quote."

"Like hell I can, the cost of the last job you did for us increased 20%."

"You changed the specification and held the job up for two years."

George gave him his famous look of disgust and wallowed in the silence. Barnaby started to shuffle on his chair; George knew he had him up against the wall.

"Can you get your quote down 60 million?"

"George, my old friend, what are you doing to me, 60 million, I can't do 60 million. I could possibly come down 20 million. George, you have to help me, we have worked together a long time." George shakes his head and watches Barnaby squirm.

"You bastard, George, I know what your game is. You want me to stop that article."

"You are a bright guy, Barnaby, you are not as stupid as you look. Twenty million, stop the article, and you can be sure I will do all I can. Are you having the pate or the soup?"

"The soup."

"So do we have a deal?"

"Getting Michael to pull that article is not going to be easy. I admit he is stupid and an embarrassment to me, but his mother, George, his mother loves him and protects him."

"Barnaby, kill the article or learn French, the contract is going to France."

"Enjoy your dinner, tell me about this girl, is she really as pretty as you say."

"So can I take it we have an agreement?"

"OK, OK, somehow I will pull the article. I will call Michael now. Put a hold on dinner, I hate cold salmon." George knows the problem hasn't gone away just yet. Michael is a difficult guy; and if he hates his father as much as Barnaby hates him, he might not play the game. George spoons his soup around his plate and prays.

"Michael, it's your father, where are you?"

"At the Carlton, playing snooker."

"I am upstairs in the dining room, I need to speak with you. I will be with you in five minutes."

Michael is already boozed to his limit. Barnaby watches him lose his game and another hundred pounds.

"I have to speak with you, put down that cue and come over here."

"What the fuck do you want?"

"I want you to grow up and to see sense.

I want you to stop this article in the Sunday Sun."

"No way, anyway it is too late, it is already being printed."

"Listen Michael, the winner of the defence contract is announced on Tuesday, winning it depends on your article not appearing." Michael slurps on his whiskey. "Michael, this contract is worth 15 billion pounds. If you stop the article, I will give you a directorship and a salary of £5,000 a week."

"I don't want your money, and I don't want anything to do with your company."

"Good grief, man, do it for your mother's sake. Have you no respect for her." Michael finally shows signs of thought; he sits staring at his father. Barnaby says nothing; he waits for him to come to his senses.

"The announcement will be made on Tuesday, you say, Angela will already be prime minister by then. Sorry Dad, the article must appear on Sunday."

"Michael, delay publication by one week, we will have the contract, and it will not be too late to destroy Angela. Just get us that contract."

"One week, just one week?"

"One week."

"OK, but you can stuff your job, I'm doing this for Mum."

"Call Barry Tomlinson now, get him to call it off."

"OK, OK, you will get your bloody contract."

Talk the Talk

It is 7:00 p.m. In 30 minutes, Angela will face the country and explain why she is the right person to lead the government of the United Kingdom. Last night and the evening before, the other candidates presented their case. They were very professional, they knew what they were talking about, and they all had many years of political experience to call on. Angela has no experience at all, but in her favour is the certainty that should she win, should her party embrace her and support her, the Conservatives will definitely win the next general election. The polls have reported her lead to be a staggering 78%.

"Twenty minutes, Miss Bee." The TV director is counting down the minutes. I am sitting with her in a makeshift changing room in the Queen Elizabeth Tower. As I take hold of her hand, I can feel her starting to shake.

"Why am I doing this, Tim? It started as a silly idea to prove the power of advertising and expose our political leaders as being out of touch with the people. I thought it was a joke, a game, and I admit I have enjoyed every minute of the past nine months. Nine months, Tim, goodness! If we had slept together that first night we met on the marina, I would be giving birth to our baby tonight. The truth is, I feel as if I am having a baby, I am scared to death."

"You are amazing. This is the biggest night of your life, and you can still joke."

This afternoon she was shown around the Grand Chamber. It was the first time she had ever been in it. She stood at the table where if she were to win, she would spend hours in discussion, defending polices and arguing right from wrong. Tonight, she will face the people who can make or break her. They are not her friends, she doesn't know their names, or what positions they occupy, or which constituencies they represent. Behind the camera, there will be a possible 16 million viewers, 20,000 of them members of the party with the authority to vote. These people, she will never see or meet, but the polls state 80% of them support her, possibly because the other nominees are uttering the same old rhetoric, we have heard for the past ten elections. Spouting polices and making promises we are fed up of hearing.

"Ten minutes, Miss Bee."

"Do you have your notes?"

"I'm not reading from notes, Tim. I will speak from the heart."

"Five minutes, Miss Bee."

Angela lets go of my hand and jumps to her feet.

"I don't like my dress. Why have I chosen a boring dark suit, why did I let you persuade me to dress down? It does not represent me; I have to change. I can't possibly face these people dressed like this.

"Angela, you have five minutes."

"I have to change, I can't do it dressed like this, delay them. Help me, Tim, go out there and tell a joke, dance, just delay them."

She throws open the wardrobe door and gathers a selection of dresses up into her arms.

"Two minutes, Miss Bee, let's go." The director stands in the doorway in shock. His mouth opens when he sees Angela stood in front of the mirror in her bra and pants. "What are you doing, you are on national TV in two minutes."

I put my arms around him and lead him out into the corridor.

"Everything will be all right, she will be there, she didn't like the dress she had on, she says it is too conservative." I grab his arm to stop him rushing back into her dressing room. "You will make matters worse, you will panic her. Go to your studio and start the program."

He walks ahead of me, and at the end of the corridor, he stops outside his studio. I smile at him, "Go on, you are needed behind your control desk, or whatever you call it." I pat him on his back and watch him slide through the half open door and wait for him to close it behind him.

Oh my God, whatever is she doing. I should rush back to her, but realise it will be to no avail. All I can do is take my seat and wait with the rest of the country; resigned to the fact that whatever happens will happen for the best. The recording studio is already playing the program's signature tune and running the intro captions, the credits are rolling, and the cameras are scanning the room. Gladivere Gochevnec, the director is cueing in the announcer. There is still no sign of Angela.

"Welcome to the fourth and final evening of this spectacular race for the leadership of the Conservative party, and the leader of the oldest parliament in the world. Should Angela Bee arouse you into voting for her, she will be the youngest prime minister this country has ever had. At the age of 22, she has come from being unknown, nine months ago, to one of the most famous and best-loved woman, not only in this country but throughout the world."

293

The director is waving his hands about like a lunatic, "Keep going, keep talking." The announcer understands the gestures, but what else can he say? Still there is no sign of Angela. I am coming to the conclusion that the occasion was too great for her. She has either fainted or gone home.

"So may I introduce, possibly your next leader and prime minister, Miss Angela Bee."

The camera swings towards the door through which she is to appear. The applause is starting to fade and still no Angela. The camera crews scan the ceiling, then the walls, and then the architecture of this iconic room. All that is left are the faces of the party members. Row by row, one by one, the camera picks out every single member. Unrest settles over everybody. Murmurs and grunts of disapproval can be heard. Frustration, anxiety and even signs of anger are setting in.

One, two minutes pass, an absolute age in the life of a TV programme, then just on breaking point, just as people are about to get to their feet, the door opens. Angela steps into the room and is a picture of elegance, youth and energy. The camera follows her as she steps daintily down the centre of the red carpet towards the table. Her dress is out of this world. Black with large white polka dots, a flurry of fabric engulfs her shoulders, then stops to reveal her long bare arms. The bodice is fitted, and it fits her perfectly. Her waist is tight, but the skirt billows out in one, two, possibly in three layers, the hem stops just below her knees. Natural-coloured tights and bright yellow high-heeled shoes complete the look.

What no hat, you might ask? Of course, she is wearing a hat, an enormous yellow-rimmed hat, with a white band around it, out of which are large white feathers. No jewellery, no gloves, no handbag, just a simple, beautiful woman straight out of the pages of the world's most famous international fashion magazine.

The people, who were on their feet protesting, hide their embarrassment by busting into applause. They are joined by the entire party membership, only a small group of media reporters sitting along the back row fail to applaud her, and they are busy scribbling notes and reporting her entrance. She is a picture of perfection, a breath of fresh air; she brings new life into the doldrums of political boredom. She reaches the table and waits for everyone to settle. Once silence is restored, she counts ten, looks up from under the rim of her hat, and like the Mona Lisa, she looks at everyone at the same time and clears her throat.

"I do not see why the lady representing the greatest country in the world should be boring." She turns and shows her dress. The room bursts into laughter and then into applause. "Against the general census of opinion, women can be beautiful and intelligent, and I am going to demonstrate this to you. I want you to see me as a symbol of A NEW ENGLAND: fresh, exciting, vibrant, enthusiastic, and above all, proud. Proud of what we have achieved in the past and proud of what we are going to achieve in the future. I want to introduce a new type of politics into the country, a politics in which everyone is interested, and in which everyone has a voice. During the past three months, I have been promoting one simple concept. It is something that we women are extremely good at. It is to talk." The room bursts into applause again. "Because talking links people, helps people to understand each other; and by talking, we can solve problems and mend misunderstandings. This works within families, within communities and across nations. We spend billions on defence and security, yet the best weapon in the world is free. It is to talk."

"Hear, hear, shouts one over enthusiastic supporter." Although those sitting around him agree, they persuade him to sit down and shut up.

I am mind-blown, all I can do is stare and admire her. She is beautiful to look at, enchanting to listen to, captivating and so inspiring. She is what she is. If the people of this country don't support her, then so be it. It is not to be, but I am convinced she will not disappoint. She is a joy, to be loved for what she is, and for what she believes.

"Do I have to know the ins and the outs of how parliament operates? Do I have to know the names of every world leader and statesman? No. I will be working with the best team I could wish for. You are the professionals; you are the people who know these things and understand them. You are the members of this party who will make good happen and achieve success for our country and for our people. I will set the scene, make your path easy, so you can go about your work with confidence and sureness.

I have discovered one talent that I do have, one gift that I have been given. People like me, people want to be my friend, and people find me honest and sincere. I hope the leaders of the world will appreciate my talent. I hope they will want to do business with the UK because of me. I hope they will visit us and welcome us to their countries. If I can do this, then Britain will continue to be known as Great Britain, because that is what we are."

The members erupt in respect. Several rush forward to shake her hand, she is clearly overwhelmed. I must get her out of here.

"When did you write that speech? It was amazing." She rolls over onto me and runs her finger down my face. Her body is hot and oh so soft. I feel her lips on my brow, then on my mouth; her love means so much to me.

"So was I good or what?" she whispers.

"You were good. You should have taken up a career in advertising; you would have done very well. So, when did you write that speech?"

"I didn't write that speech, it just came out as I thought it, thank you for holding up the start. I couldn't have done it in that boring suit. It was only when I became myself, found my freedom that I had the confidence to do my own thing. That is a lesson to be learned, don't you agree, Tim?"

"I agree. Are you tired?"

"No."

I wrap myself around her and smoother her in love. Boy, am I a lucky guy

The Result

Time: 9:45.
Day: Monday
Date: 18
Month: September.
Place: The Conservative Party Conference, Birmingham.
The hall seats 3,650 people, and every seat is taken. Some people have
been queuing since five o'clock; they have stood in the rain eager to buy
one of the 500 tickets that are available to buy on the door. Some are
concerned for the future of the party, some are confident of success; they
are all watching the massive clock above the stage tick around to the
magic hour of 10:00, when the party will know who its next leader is,
and the country will know its fate for the next four years.

The nominees are called to the stage. The master of ceremonies is
Tom Pollett; the party secretary; and he will announce the winner. He is
checking the hall's PA system. He claims to be a professional speaker,
but I think he spent his apprenticeship in a bingo hall. He taps the
microphone and shouts testing, testing, one two three into it. He is
surprised when his voice booms out to confirm all is well, you can tell
by the look on his face he didn't expect it to work. On Thursday nights,
at the con club, the microphone never works first time. The TV camera
crews are checking their positions, and the BBC commentator has
lowered his voice as he describes the excitement to two million viewers.
Angela squeezes my hand.

"I have been called to the stage, I have to go now. If I win, I have to
look surprised and thank everybody for voting for me. If I lose, I have to
smile and congratulate the winner. Tim, they are telling me what to do,
is this how it is going to be? If I am elected prime minister, surely I do
what I want."

"Do as they ask today, darling. It's so the camera crews know where
to position themselves, and who to focus on next."

The proceedings are chaotic. People are running around like crazy,
others are shouting instructions. I start to sweat when I see the
contenders standing in a line, the time has come. The hall falls silent. It
is 9:59; every single person is motionless. Life as we know it has ceased.

The red light on top of the camera turns green, and the country is about to learn its fate. Tom Pollett steps up to the microphone and explains who was allowed to vote and who wasn't. The number of votes received and lots more boring facts and figures. No one is taking the slightest bit of interest. Then he gets to the result.

"Gordon Armitage, 14,348. The Rt Hon. Frederick Brooksbank, 38,920. Marcus Leopole Uxbearing, 74,856. Angela Bee 107,049. I therefore declare that Angela Bee has been nominated the new leader of the Conservative party." The room erupts into applause but not everyone is happy. There was a massive vote from the establishment, for the old school, in fact, more people voted against her than for her. That is going to be a problem, especially as she is so young and inexperienced. Outside the country is frantic, her support on the street is massive, people are cheering and waving flags, shouting, "Angela, Angela, we want Angela." The country is in celebration mode.

The last 20 hours has been hectic; it's been a day of meetings and interviews. I left the hall first, and hope she can join me for a quite drink before the day is over. I put on a CD of her country favourites and wait for her to arrive home. It is late when she eventually staggers in. She looks me up and down, kicks off her shoes, kneels astride me and wraps herself over me.

"Are you okay?" I ask.

"Tired."

"Are you happy?" She thinks for a minute.

"Not exactly."

"I know you aren't, what are you thinking?"

"I don't want this job, Tim. Some people today were quite nasty, some called me horrible names. Others said I would never succeed, and that I should quit."

"The world is full of horrible, negative people. You have to either ignore them, sack them or beat them. This is the case in any job."

"I can't deal with them, Tim. I don't want this job." Then, she bursts out crying and cries herself to sleep, still sitting on top of me. I pick her up and carry her into the bedroom, unzip her dress and cover her with the duvet. Maybe she is just exhausted, maybe she will think differently in the morning.

But I doubt it.

****

The announcement that Angela has declined the leadership shocks the country. The reason she has given is understandable, she says she can achieve more by promoting her 'Talk Together' initiative and progressing her work with the other women of the world. The establishment is in shock, but she doesn't care. She has awakened politicians to the needs of the people and proven they are out of touch, that is enough for one little girl to do.

****

The Truth Is Known

One thing chauffeurs are not good at is driving fast. Joshua prides himself on driving with care and giving his passengers a relaxing and safe journey. Style and safety has always been his priority, not speed; and this has promoted him from being a London cabbie 20 years ago to chief chauffeur for the government. Every day, he drives the prime minister, visiting royals and world politicians carefully around the streets of London, but today he is driving Angela to the hospital. Time is of the essence; he swings the big stretched jaguar in and out of the city traffic, yet his progress is very slow.

"Where is that police car, it should have been here ten minutes ago."

Angela is sitting in silence; she is wringing her hands together and biting her lips. She looks straight at me, her big, beautiful eyes screaming 'desperation'; a hint of a tear is running down her cheek.

"Are we going to be in time, will he be conscious, will he recognise me? Oh Tim, I have something very important to tell him. I should have told him months ago. We have to get there quicker."

Eventually, we hear the siren of a police car as a large range Rover patrol car races passed, forcing the oncoming traffic to pull over. The driver instructs our chauffeur to follow him. Angela breathes a sigh of relief as we pull out into the traffic and actually get up to 30 miles an hour. Driving along the embankment is easier and faster now, from bus lane to outside lane, over box junctions and through red lights. We will be at the hospital in five minutes. It has been 18 minutes since we received news of George's heart attack. It's serious, the doctors thought he was dead on arrival at the hospital, but they have managed to restore a pulse, but it is only a matter of time; it could be hours, it could be a matter of minutes.

I have difficulty keeping up with Angela as she races up the steps to the third floor of the hospital. George is in intensive care, inside a luxury suite at the northern extremity of the new Margaret Thatcher wing. The entire extension overlooks the Thames and across the river towards St Paul's Cathedral. Its dome dominating the rooftops of the city, but there is no time to enjoy the splendour of this masterpiece. Angela rushes straight into the room where a nurse is sitting at the side of George's bed, she jumps to her feet. George is wired to every device you can image, he lays motionless on his back; there is no sign of life or recognition. Angela pulls up the chair at his bedside and holds his hand; it is warm. She can feel a pulse and runs her finger across the palm of his hand. His skin is rough, a tell-tale sign of his long, hard life in politics.

She leans over him to caress his face, a muscle in his cheek twitches. She bursts out crying, her tears flood down her face and drip off her chin onto his arm. She kisses him.

"Don't cry, my love, it is time for me to go. We have had fun and achieved so much." He gasps, "And by the way, congratulations on becoming leader of our country. I know you will be a great success and lead us to better and happier times." Angela has no intention of telling him she has turned down the job, he would be disappointed and would not understand. Anyway, now is not the time to explain, she has something far more important to tell him.

"George, I want to thank you for everything you have done for me. Without you, I would not be the woman I am today."

"What are you talking about? I just did my job, and I really enjoyed it. It was the best fun I have had in years."

"George, you don't understand. I am not thanking you for helping me win the leadership. I am thanking you for supporting me throughout my life, for paying for my schooling, for giving me the freedom that I needed and for not asking too many questions. I want to thank you for taking care of my mother. I know your relationship was not ideal, but you stayed with her and supported her." He opens his eyes and searches for her.

"I do not understand, darling. What are you saying?"

"I have not been totally honest with you, George. You once told me you had a stepdaughter my age, and that I reminded you of her. Well, that is not surprising because I am your stepdaughter. I am that little girl you used to play doll's house with, that girl you sent to Switzerland hoping she would become a woman you could be proud of. George, you are the only father I know, and I love you so much."

A tear appears in his eye, and she becomes a blur to him. He tries to raise himself but strength fails him. He wants to hold her, to say sorry for neglecting her, and to tell her she has been in his thoughts every day for the last 20 years. He has consistently wondered what she was doing, where she was, what she looked like, and what she had become. Now he knows, and he wants to tell her how proud he is of her. She lays her head on his chest, and he lifts his hand to stroke her hair, they are bound together by love. Five, ten, 15 minutes they lay together in silence, George utters a deep sigh as submission spreads around his body.

He beckons her to come closer; she lifts her head towards his trembling lips, straining to catch his every word.

"Don't talk, Daddy. Save your strength, let us lay here and hold each other." It must be 15 years since she called him daddy. She used to ask him if she could sit on his knee, he would lift her up, and they would listen to the radio together. He liked it when she called him daddy, and just now when she called him daddy again, it filled him with joy.

"Angela," he whispers, "I love you more than you can ever believe. You see, I have not been honest with you either. We adopted you as our daughter, mine and Lady Cordelia's beautiful little girl, but actually, you were not my adopted daughter." He gasps for breath. Angela looks up at him, wondering what he is about to say. "I am not your stepfather, Yes, Lady Cordelia is your stepmother and loves you as she would have loved her own child, but she can never love you as much as I do. You see she never knew, and she still doesn't know. Nobody knows, but I am your real father, your birth father, and your mother was my secretary, she was a wonderful woman. I hope you can forgive me."

Angela bursts into floods of tears; she wraps herself around him and refuses to let him go. I have to pull her from him. He has passed away in the arms of his baby girl. His dream has finally come true, Angela knows the truth.

****

302

Michael Day's Article

'Angela Bee is not the angel the country is led to believe. The sincerity of her 'GirlTalk' tour is under close scrutiny. The pictures we are shown of her meeting with some of the world's most famous women are real, but the conversations she has with them is not on record. In fact, we have no proof as to what she said, until now that is. Thanks to a conscientious undercover agent employed on her Girl Talk Tour, we have been given a recording of her conversation with Elaina Hicaddie, the high-profile Polish women's rights campaigner. Elaina is fighting human trafficking in her country and claims to be saving thousands of young girls from being exploited in the European sex industry, but this recording has exposed the truth. Elaina Hicaddie is actually shipping these girls to London, Paris and Berlin herself. Over 300 girls from Elaina's legitimate agency, which receives a grant from her government, have disappeared during the last year.

The recording also hears Angela Bee agreeing with and offering to help Elaina Hicaddie to get these girls into Western Europe. Angela met four of these girls whilst taking coffee with Elaina in front of the Adam Mickiewicza Museum of Literature in Warsaw Old Town Market Square, last Thursday. The meeting ended dramatically with a bomb scare, smoke filled the square where the women were seated. Under the smoke screen, the four girls were snatched by several unidentified men and have not been seen or heard of since. Angela Bee was rushed back to her hotel and came back to Heathrow on the first plane.

Angela Bee was accompanied on the tour by the Rt Hon. George Baldwin, government minister and secretary of state for works and pensions. It was stated that George Baldwin was her mentor, protector and promoter. We have proof that the Rt Hon. George Baldwin is Angela Bee's biological father from an illegitimate relationship he had with his Russian secretary Oksana Malvina Smirnov in 1997. Angela was born in St John's Hospital, Chelsea on 20 April 1998. Oksana Malvina Smirnov arrived in England from Novosibirsk; a city in southern Russia in 1989, her occupation was secretary. By tracing her national insurance number, we have discovered she worked as a temp in London from 1990 to 1999.

She signed up with 'Toptemp', a staff agency whose biggest client was and still is the British government. We believe she worked for George Baldwin on many occasions and became his mistress. Oksana Malvina Smirnov was killed in a motoring accident on the Kings Road in 2001. She was knocked over by a delivery van, which ran out of control and mounted the pavement, she was one of nine people standing in a queue at a bus stop, she died instantly. Although an enquiry was requested, the police had no evidence to suspect anything suspicious. Could she have been targeted, could she have been murdered to keep her quiet, we will never know?

After the death of Oksana, George Baldwin secretly persuaded the foster home to let him and his wife Lady Cordelia Eleanor Lockwood adopt Angela in a desperate bid to save their failing and childless marriage. Lady Cordelia Eleanor Lockwood has never known that the girl she lovingly brought up was her husband's illegitimate daughter. Angela Bee's real name is Angela Grace Rebecca Louise Baldwin.'

Closing Time

Michael Day is sitting in the corner of the Ship and Flag. He tries to make conversation with a group of drinkers who are out, revelling. They are doing a pub-crawl around the historic East End pubs. Michael counts five girls and three guys and thinks he will gatecrash the party and even up the score, but they aren't interested in a down and out city slicker. He closes in on one of the girls, not realising she is the girlfriend of one of the guys. He escapes being punched as the girl pours a glass of beer over him, much to the amusement of her boyfriend. His ego is in tatters, but at least, she has saved his boyish looks from a battering. The group leaves him wet, dejected and humiliated.

The landlord offers him some advice.

"Michael, go home," he begs him. "You have had enough to drink, you are going to get yourself into serious trouble."

"Just one more, Colin, then I will go," Michael pleads.

Colin feels sorry for him. He has known Michael for many years. They have been on many similar boozy nights out together, but those were happy days, and those days are long gone.

"OK, just one more, then, I will call you a taxi."

"No, I don't want a taxi. I will walk."

"Just as you like." Colin hands him a cheap double malt whisky. He doesn't see the point of pouring him one of the better ones. Michael is way beyond appreciating the difference. He picks up the stocky glass and is just about to throw it down his throat when he thinks better of it. If he drains the glass, he will have to leave; and as he has nowhere to go, that isn't a good idea.

It is difficult for him to accept what has happened to him. Three weeks ago, he was going to be prime minister of the country, and now he has nothing. Nowhere to live, no money, no friends, and no idea what he will do. He sits in the corner, his hair stuck down with beer, and his shirt drenched with stains. Only the hope of destroying Angela and clearing his name kept him going this long, and now she has taken that away from him. Angela has resigned the leadership, what he has to tell the country won't make the slightest bit of difference to her. No one will want to know.

"Time gentlemen, please," yells Colin, "It's time you all went home. The good news is, you can all come back tomorrow." Two girls standing next to the door giggle. Patrick, who has been balancing on a bar stool all evening, grunts before finding the courage to get to his feet and stagger out into the street. Doreen the barmaid approaches Michael to take away the remains of his dismal night. He catches her arm.

"Come on, Doreen, let's go back to your place," he splutters.

She pulls away from him, escaping his grasp. His thumbnail rips down her arm and blood slowly oozes out over the surface of her skin.

"You bloody idiot! Look what you have done now." She bursts into tears and rushes into the kitchen and tries to stem the flow.

The rain is beating down, the street is dark and dank, and the temperature has dropped to six degrees. He buttons up his jacket and turns up the collar. He could go home, his mother would take him back but his father? Well that would lead to his mother and father having yet another row over him. He walks across the street, staggers over the uneven surface of the cobbles and looks at his watch. It is ten past something, but he can't make it out, it doesn't matter anyway. What does matter is finding somewhere to sleep. Down on the marina, there are several seat shelters, maybe he should go there. Who knows he might be able to stow aboard a yacht or motor cruiser left by its owner until the weather picks up.

God! This rain is disgusting, why am I living in England, who in their right mind would want to live in this God forsaken country. His thoughts are deep and dark, being drunk and depressed is not a healthy state of mind to be in. *What is the point, can't a man have a bit of fun, exhibit his prowess without getting into trouble, without losing his job, his home and his future.* He stands proud on the side of the quay and looks down into the murky water. The boats beneath him are swaying violently, every gust of wind crashes one into the next, with a rattling of masts and a scream of creaking deck timbers. The tide is at its height, splashing his shoes and drowning his sanity. The water must be 20 foot deep, it is dirty, cold and ugly. A plastic drink bottle rises and falls as the waves scrape it down the side of the hull of a cruiser named 'Happy'. He laughs, *What is this, a joke, what is there to be happy about?* He has had enough: unwanted, unloved, even his best friends have abandoned him. He looks up and shields his eyes from the relentless rain. The ferocious clouds are racing across the sky, and the vicious gusts of wind unbalancing him. He takes a deep sigh; and in a moment of the darkest depression, he raises himself onto his toes and leans out over the water. A rustle behind him stops him. A girl is watching, her hair flattened to her head; her blouse stuck to her body, her skirt piping water down her calves, onto her toeless shoes…

"Hello sir, would you like a good time?"